Wild About Harry

Wild About Harry

Daisy Jordan

W F HOWES LTD

This large print edition published in 2006 by
W F Howes Ltd
Unit 4, Rearsby Business Park, Gaddesby Lane
Rearsby, Leicester LE7 4YH

1 3 5 7 9 10 8 6 4 2

First published in the United Kingdom in 2005
by Bantam Books

A CIP catalogue record for this book is available
from the British Library

ISBN 1 84505 902 6

Typeset by Palimpsest Book Production Limited,
Polmont, Stirlingshire
Printed and bound in Great Britain
by Antony Rowe Ltd, Chippenham, Wilts.

For Kim and Sherrill, with all my love
XXXXX

ACKNOWLEDGEMENTS

Imagination is a wonderful thing, but unless you've been everywhere, known everyone, felt everything, it's impossible to write novels without a little bit of help. My thanks then to all those who were kind enough (and brave enough) to share their knowledge and experiences during the writing of mine.

Special thanks to Liz Davies, for her wisdom and input. As well as being one of my very dearest friends, she's been the finest head teacher I've known.

Thanks to lovely Mark Wordley, of Wordley Productions, who generously gave me so much of his time and a particularly nice cup of coffee. The DVD you lent me is in the post now, Mark, honest.

Thanks also to Lord Alan for letting me loose on him in the first place, to my brilliant agent, Jane, for keeping me sane, to Lynn Allbutt, for passing on the unicorn joke, (to everyone who *understands* the unicorn joke . . .), and to all my dear, clever, supportive friends and fellow scribes in the Mewriters forum; you're the absolute best.

Finally, big thanks (and a unicorn) to Francesca and Nicky. And to everyone at Transworld. Big hugs to you all.

CHAPTER 1

My mother, God bless her, had two abiding mantras. That a smile is the first thing you should put on every morning and that a well-cut suit will take you anywhere.

I hate to sound picky because I loved my mum dearly, but she was absolutely wrong on both counts.

A smile, as any teacher will tell you, is the very last thing you should stick on your face, certainly not before first play on any weekday, and definitely never before Christmas. And though a well-cut suit will take you all sorts of places, it will not take you across a rain-infested playground, round the back of a climbing-frame, through an enthusiastically manured conservation area or, indeed, the bit of battered beech hedge that separates said area from the aged oak tree that resides in Mr Tinkler's back garden. Well, it will, but not half so efficiently as full fatigues, a gas mask and a pair of stout boots.

Which is a pity, because today I am in such a suit, and kitten heels too, worn for what at the time seemed the entirely reasonable purpose of persuading the advisers who are arriving at noon that I Am Fully In Charge of This School.

'He won't come down,' announces Glenda Heaven, with an air of complete confidence, having followed me through in her mac.

I don't have a mac. Just a well-cut suit. And a suspicion that a gauntlet's just been thrown at my feet. Testing times, these. Every day a challenge. It's late January now, but I'm not smiling yet. But I am, I am, I am, I am, I *am* in charge of this school.

'Of course he will,' I say crisply. 'Won't you, Harry? You know, you can't sit up there all day.'

There is a little light rustling overhead and a sprinkling of sappy water rains down. 'Leave me *alone*,' he growls.

His tone suggests he's been saying it for a while. I don't suppose he's smiling either. 'Now you *know* I can't do that, Harry,' I counter. 'What would your father think of me if I left you sitting up in a tree all day, eh? I don't think he'd be very impressed, do you?'

There is no response to this because, in the three weeks I have been back at Cefn Melin Primary, I have learned that Harry is the sort of boy who doesn't feel the need to concern himself with the largely uninteresting twitterings of the women who populate his life. He has much more important things to do. Like getting into trouble. Which he does very well. There's been barely a day since the beginning of term that he hasn't had an input in seizing.

2

Another child bursts through the luckless beech. A girl called Millie with a lisp.

'Mish! Mish! He's hurt himself, Mish! You know he's hurt himself, don't you? Mr Patterson just told me to come through and tell you, because we saw blood on the trim trail, didn't we, Owen?' Another child behind her mumbles assent. 'And he fell off ever such a long way, and there's, like, this *really* big splodge of it on the bark under the monkey bars—'

Glenda Heaven, who is the school secretary and, as such, always prides herself on being fully conversant with anything that happens, wherever it happens, however it happens, in this school, at all times, glares at Millie through narrowed eyes. 'Fell?' she barks accusingly. 'What do you mean, fell? I wasn't told that anybody fell.'

'He fell off the trim trail, Mish. He was doing an assault stunt thing – wasn't he, Owen? – we saw it. We told him he wasn't supposed to be on the trim trail because it was our class's turn today, but he did, and he—'

'Harry!' I shout up, with feeling. 'Are you hurt?'

'No.'

'Are you sure?'

'*Yes.*'

'Are you bleeding?'

A short pause. 'Er . . .' Then a longer one. 'Yes.'

'Then, Harry, you must come down at *once.*'

'You'll tell me off.'

'I won't tell you off, Harry.' I pause to consider

this. So, evidently, does he. One of his trainered feet stirs the green canopy. 'Well, I will tell you off, of course, but not nearly as loudly as you might expect, because I will be much more concerned about how badly you're hurt. Whereas if you refuse to come down and you bleed all over Mr Tinkler's tree, I cannot be held responsible for the consequences. There. Are you going to come down?'

Glenda Heaven looks at me as if I am quite, quite mad.

Another rustle. 'Are you going to tell my dad?'

'That depends on how badly you're hurt.'

'I'm okay.'

'I think that's for me to decide, don't you?'

'But I am.'

'So come down, then, Harry, and *prove* it.'

It's a tense thirty seconds. Reputations are at stake here. And it remains to be seen whose will win out. But today is my day to prevail, it seems, because, to my probably ill-concealed elation, he does.

My mother had another pearl of wisdom. The thing to do with blood, she always said, is to take quick action and make sure the water never goes above thirty-eight degrees. Otherwise the proteins denature and you can't get it off. I don't know if this is true (it sounds feasible enough) but as I help Harry slither down the last bit of tree-trunk it occurs to me that my suit and I may soon find out. He has two bloodied knees, a badly scraped palm, and a gash below his mouth you could slip a pound coin in. The legacy, I think, of a run-in with his teeth.

4

'Oh, my Lord!' says Glenda, and begins bustling around him. Glenda bustles most of the time. Into rooms, under desks, around vomiting children. The bustle is her weapon against all forms of anarchy and the currency with which she negotiates the day.

'Minging!' say the two year-sixers, in unison. Glenda bustles them back through the hedge.

It's raining steadily now, but nevertheless quite a crowd has gathered at the perimeter of the sensory garden (most children in this school being conversant with the rules regarding trespass on it outside the prescribed times), which John Patterson, my deputy, who has been on playground duty, is attempting to corral into orderly lines. Harry's gash, stimulated by the attention most probably, pours blood profusely and obligingly as we walk.

I almost say, 'show over,' because they're such a rapt audience, but instead I help him back across the playground, stern-faced, while Glenda click-clacks behind us.

I sit him down on a chair in the medical room and inspect him. He's been crying. There's a brown abstract study on his cheeks. But now he's chewing his top lip and being brave.

The expression 'medical room', as applied in a modern school, is a bit of an anachronism. Whereas in my youth it was somewhere with a bed, and where the school nurse would smear Anchor butter on burns after over-enthusiastic bunsen burner adventures, there are now all sorts of rules regarding the administration of first aid in school situations (most related to the application of plasters and their unthinkable consequences) that render it virtually useless. In Cefn Melin Primary, it's home to the photocopier. And flute lessons, Fridays at twelve. I pull some clean paper towel from the dispenser on the wall and apply it as gently as I can. 'This is going to need stitches, Harry.'

He looks up, his grubby face alight with sudden hope. I have a feeling any telling off will be as nothing compared to the heady delights of his impending notoriety. 'Wicked!' he says. 'D'you think I'll have a scar?'

'Don't speak, Harry,' I tell him, as I minister as best I can to his knees and his hand, 'or you'll bleed all the more. Here.' I take his other hand. 'Just hold that firmly against your chin, okay? Now. Your dad. We'd better get hold of him, hadn't we?' He nods. 'Come on. Let's take you into my office.'

Glenda, whose office is adjacent to mine, has already pulled out the card-index box.

'Got hold of Dad yet?' I enquire, sitting Harry in my chair.

'You'll be lucky,' she mutters, squinting at a dog-eared card.

There are five phone numbers for the Meadows family, the first four of which we draw blanks at without delay. The first is a home number (answer-phone on), the second a moble number (ex au pair, currently working in a bra shop in Bath), the third

6

a work number (irritating, *faux*-jaunty voicemail), and the fourth another mobile (present nanny, presumably) 'It's Liv. I'll get back to you, *Ciao*.' The fifth, on the face of it, looks like bearing fruit. For it is answered by a human. Glenda starts.

'Ah. Bingo! At last!' There's a pause and a bustle. 'No, no. I really need to speak to Mr Meadows himself,' she is saying. 'No, no, please don't. We've already done that. It's on voicemail . . . Well, if you would, please. It's urgent. It's—'

She rolls her eyes. 'Where *do* they get these girls? She's gone to find him.'

'She's gone to find him,' I tell Harry. He looks glum again. And rather pale now.

Except the girl doesn't find him. He is, apparently, out 'on a shoot' and she doesn't know how to get hold of him. She's going to ring back when she's tracked down someone called Dill, who will apparently know where he is.

In a field, perhaps, with a brace of pheasants in his pocket? I'm first at the phone when she rings back.

'He's in *Bristol*?'

'Yes, Bristol, I'm sorry. I've got a mobile number now, though. For the assistant producer. Do you want it?'

Ah. *That* sort of shoot. Harry, I notice, is even paler. But I can't give him a painkiller because that would be in direct contravention of rule 130, subsection 47A. Decided, I scribble down the number. 'But perhaps you could ring for me. Tell him his son has had an accident. It's not serious – do make that clear, won't you? – but I think he's going to need a few stitches in his chin. We're going to get him down to Accident and Emergency and perhaps Mr Meadows could meet me there. Okay? If he needs to get in touch he can ring the school, all right?'

'I'll call an ambulance, shall I?' Glenda asks, as I put the receiver down. 'And have a look see who we can find to go with him.'

I shake my head. 'No need. I'll take him. It'll be quicker.'

'*You*'re going to take him?'

'Why not?' I reply. 'Besides, everyone else is teaching, aren't they?'

And I can't send Glenda because she's busy with the dinner money. Plus . . . oh dear. I can't help it. I *want* to go with him. He looks so forlorn now, so utterly wretched, so in need of someone kind – namely *me* – to hold his hand. I grab my bag and car keys. 'Tell John he's at the helm.'

Harry pouts. 'Aren't we going in an ambulance, Miss?'

'Absolutely not,' I say crisply. 'You've got legs, haven't you? You can come down on the back of my bike.'

Once Harry's in the car with me he perks up considerably. 'Do you really have a bike?'

'No, I don't, as it happens. Not right now. I used to.'

'I've got a really beast bike,' he says. 'I got it for Christmas. It's a full-suspension one.'

'Really.'

'But this is a beast car as well.'

'Yes, it is, so try not to drip on it, okay?' I tell him. In fact it's not even my beast car, it's Max's beast car, which I suspect Harry will think is a whole lot more beast than mine. Max has taken mine to work today so he can get a new tyre for me on the way home. He's thoughtful like that. But he's precious about his upholstery. 'In fact, don't drip on it, full stop,' I add.

'I'm really sorry, miss,' he says suddenly. 'My dad's going to go ballistic. Am I, like, in *really* big trouble?'

It's not something children do, as a rule – try to quantify the awful ramifications of their trans-gressions with the person who'll be meting them out. But Harry is not like most children. But, then, perhaps he wouldn't be, having so recently lost his mum. I try for my stern face but his is all tear-stained. And he's soon to have stitches. So it comes out as a smile even so. 'No, Harry,' I tell him. 'Not really big trouble. Just medium-size trouble. Think you can handle that?'

When we get to the hospital I immediately curse my decision to bring Harry myself rather than wait for the paramedics, because there isn't a single park-ing space free except the ambulance ones, and a queue for the multi-storey. Why? Is it a special-offer day or something? Have a cataract done and they'll throw in a tonsillectomy? Confused by the mysteries of planning that result in a newly built hospital multi-storey-for-visitors having a queue at ten forty-five on a Monday morning, I do two circuits and return to A and E, where I park at the edge of the threateningly yellow-hatched ambulance bay and hope for peace and harmony on the roads.

The throbbing, Harry tells me, has abated some-what, and while the endorphin that is no-lessons-for-the-rest-of-the-day does its work, I take a moment to call Glenda and check the state of play. It has not escaped my memory that the advisers are due, and will have to be rejigged for later. Much later, in fact, and ideally at a point when another (and cleaner) well-cut suit is in play.

'Still no joy from the nanny,' Glenda tells me, 'but I've left messages at home and on her mobile.'

'And the dad?'

'Not a peep. I'll let you know when he calls.'

'Don't worry. I've got to switch my phone off now anyway. Just have one or the other of them head down here when they do.'

I slip my mobile back into my bag and try to recall when last it was that I visited a hospital Accident and Emergency department. But then decide I'd rather not. The sun's only just come out, after all. 'What's he do, your dad?' I ask Harry, as we head for the entrance.

He lowers the paper towel to inspect it. 'He's a director.'

I can hear the pride in his voice. 'Put that back, Harry, or it'll start bleeding again. So. What kind of director is he?'

'A film director. You know. Like Steven Spielberg.'

'Is that so?' Three weeks and I have the father pinned down already. I feel for the child. I shouldn't, I know. But I do. 'So. What film is he making at the moment, then?'

Harry thinks for a few seconds. 'He did tell me,' he says finally. 'Hmm . . . I know! It's the girl on a unicorn one.'

'The *which* one?'

The A and E door parts to admit us.

'For an advert. For, you know . . . those things.'

'What things would those be?'

'You *know*,' he says. 'He did the bike one as well. For those things ladies wear in their pants.'

Because most children are considerate enough to confine their more life-threatening activities to when they are safely out of school for the day, there is little in the way of a queue in the children's section of A and E. Nevertheless, we are still third in line, and the triage system means that Harry's minor blood loss (and failure to have passed out at any point – something to remember for next time) has us relegated to fourth by a fracture. But it is less than an hour and a half before we're ushered to a treatment room, much of which we spend in an amiable viewing of *This Morning* punctuated by Harry saying, 'My face *wrecks*,' at five-minute intervals and then scowling at my too public pats and there-theres. We're soon joined by a young female doctor, who is carrying a kidney bowl and a clipboard.

'Now, Harry,' she tells him, having finished the question-and-answer session that is designed to divert his attention away from the fearsome syringe she is busying herself with (and having established that Harry mainly likes Eminem, Pot Noodle Sizzlers and the *Fresh Prince of Bel Air*), 'let's get you fixed up, shall we? I'm going to put some painkiller in your chin so you won't feel it when we do the stitches. It will hurt just a little – like a bee sting, no more – but it'll be very, very quick. Okay?'

He looks grey all of a sudden and I reach for his hand. This time he doesn't shrug it off, but clutches it tightly. 'That's the way,' says the doctor. 'You hang on to Mum. We'll be quick as a flash, I promise.'

'She's not my mum,' Harry answers gravely. 'She's dead.'

'I'm sorry,' says the doctor.

'That's all right,' he says back.

'I'm his head teacher,' I explain. 'We're waiting for Dad, aren't we, Harry?' I squeeze his hand, which suddenly seems tiny in my own. It's hot and damp. I cover it with my other hand. Tears are glinting in his eyes. 'Look at that,' I tell him. 'See that cobweb on the ceiling? Keep your eye on it, okay? When I was your age I slept in the top bunk and, do you know, one night a spider came down on its silk and almost landed in my mouth? Can you imagine that?'

'Urgh, gross!' he tries to say. And the anaesthetic's in. But where the hell's his father when he needs him?

It is never a good thing to make assumptions about people you don't know that well, so after I have driven back to school, settled Harry – plus Twix, and now sporting impressive knee-bandaging – under a blanket in the staff room, got the low-down from John Patterson, cross-examined all the witnesses, inspected the scene, written up an accident report, double-checked Protocol 862, subsection 11B, gone back and added an explanatory addendum, eaten a banana and a *Be Good To Yourself* pasta florentina and made myself and Glenda a mug of tea each, I go straight to the files and pull out Harry's. Even given that I've spent the last two years as deputy head of the sort of primary school that most people appeal *not* to have their children sent to, it does not make for edifying afternoon reading. Harry's mother, Glenda tells me, died about eight months ago of breast cancer, having been ill for two years. Since then, she adds, it's been a bit of an uphill struggle, so I am less than impressed, but sadly unsurprised, that even when I've finished reading the father is still nowhere to be seen. I look at the time. At this rate 'Liv' will be here to collect Harry before he is.

'I wouldn't hold your breath,' Glenda comments dourly. 'She never shows up much before four.'

There's been a phone call, at least, an hour or so ago, and much rhetoric, apparently, about the intractable problems of Mr Meadows's childcare arrangements and the inexplicable disappearance of his nanny, but Glenda, who excels in parental chastisement, has cut through this monologue with a prioritizing slap, the upshot of which is that he is now apparently *en route*.

By the time he arrives in school it is almost three thirty and home time, and Harry is asleep across three chairs in the staff room. I'm just coming out from having checked on him when I see a tall man in jeans and what appears to be a fright wig battling with the security door. I press the button and he lurches into the vestibule. 'Will Meadows,' he pants. 'I've come for my son.'

He looks like he ran all the way here from Bristol, but I suspect he is breathing hard for dramatic effect. I note he has a little laminated ID card swinging from a pocket in his jeans and a heavy silver chain round his neck. He is, I conclude, a 'media' type. Which, of itself, is absolutely fine – it's not for me to decide the world can live without panty-liner commercials – but in tandem with everything that's happened today it irritates me beyond measure. As does his hair, an unruly, pre-Raphaelite, almost shoulder-length tumble, which, though grey-streaked among the coffee-coloured curls, is very like Harry's, and so, it would appear, is his own.

'Good,' I say merrily, with just a soupçon of tartness. 'We were beginning to think you'd got lost.'

I lead him into the staff room, where Harry, refreshed by his nap, is up and throwing off the blanket in moments. He is a very intelligent boy. He knows the stitch-and-bandage combo will act as garlic to a vampire. You don't get grief from grown-ups when you're hurt. So why shouldn't he make the most of it?

'Eight stitches,' he says proudly. 'Eight stitches, Dad!'

To which his father replies, 'Way to go, son!' which I feel is quite possibly the last thing he should be saying, given the fun and games we've had today. Which I think he realizes, because he then launches into a lengthy monologue about the unbearable unreliability of nannies and au pairs and much of his current one's mental, social, emotional and pharmaceutical history, in the manner of a long-suffering mother. Which I think he then realizes sounds even worse. If I didn't know his date of birth to be earlier, I would put him as hovering around his early thirties. But you never know. If he's cornered the panty-liner market, perhaps he has an 'in' with a Botox firm too.

'The point,' I tell him pointedly, 'is that it's really important that we can get hold of you. Or if not you, someone else. Someone reliable.

15

Someone who is generally contactable during the day. I do appreciate that it's not always possible, Mr Meadows, but—'

'It's Will, *please*,' he says. I don't nod. As if.

'But I understand this isn't the first time we've had difficulty getting hold of you. I do appreciate the problems you've had to face in the last year, but supposing it had been something more serious? Thankfully, it wasn't. But I'm sure you'd want to be there if . . . well . . .' Perhaps not. He's already *been* there, hasn't he? 'Well, anyway. The main thing is that he's okay. Aren't you, Harry? Though perhaps, Mr Meadows, it would be a good idea if we . . .' No, I think. Save it. I shall call him tomorrow.

'I know, I know, I know,' he says. 'And I'm really sorry. I'm *really* sorry, mate,' he says again, to Harry.

He is humble and contrite and, like Harry, even likeable, albeit in a dishevelled, rather flaky sort of way. It might just be an excess of Mother Earth genes on my part, but by the time I'm ushering them out, I'm almost feeling sorry for him. Most fathers don't have to concern themselves with the front-line logistics of weekday parenting. Most fathers have wives. Most wives have friends. Most families don't have to operate like this. It must be tough, I think, as he clunks his car key remote. A gleaming yellow sports car signals back from the road. Hmm. Almost. *Almost.* But no. Not quite.

'One thing—' I call, as they head for the gate.

Mr Meadows turns, eyebrows arched in enquiry. 'I'd be most grateful,' I say, 'if you wouldn't park on the zigzags.'

Harry grins. '*You* did, Miss. At the hospital,' he says.

CHAPTER 2

Harry Meadows is without a mother. Well, yes, fine. So are lots of children. Some children never had mothers in the first place. Some mothers should never have had *children* in the first place. Scratch the surface of any society and tragedy wells forth everywhere you look. Harry Meadows, therefore, is not exactly unique.

Or different, or special, or even noteworthy. Not really. I have 352 largely well-adjusted children in my school (*my* school!), but I've come across others in my time who would make Harry's circumstances seem positively congenial, and the antics he gets up to decidedly benign. So there was really no reason why it should have been Harry. It could have been anyone. Boy or girl. Five or fifteen. Who knows why one particular child should get under your skin over and above any other? But he has clearly aroused *something* in me. But, as is often the case, you sometimes don't know you've got a bee in your bonnet about something until someone points out to you that you have been talking about little else for the best part of an hour. Well, as much as is possible between lengths of a swimming-pool, which apparently is what I've just done.

'Oh, but you should have seen him, Toni. My heart just went out to him, poor little mite. I mean, can you imagine how upside-down his life must have been this last year? Before that, even. I mean, when she was ill. And he's a really bright kid too. It's such a shame.'

'Oh dear. Do I detect a certain dewy-eyed lack of detachment here? You seem very fired up about this kid, Holly. You want to watch that,' says Antonia, winking at me. 'After all, you know what you're like.'

Knowing what you're like is one of those things that conventional wisdom would have us believe means the difference between making informed and sensible life choices and being a complete twit who lurches from one unsatisfactory state of affairs to another and never learns from the experience. It doesn't matter whether it's an inability to avoid Danish pastries or a career path strewn with abandoned Open University courses in fifteenth-century Etruscan pottery and Cartesian dualism. The effect is pretty much the same. And though I don't generally align myself in the second camp (the only rogue decision I made in my life was once to embrace Sun In as part of my hair-care routine) there's no doubt that there could have been a moment during those early weeks in my new incarnation as a head when knowing what I'm like could have led me down an altogether different path. But knowing what you're like is only a useful tool if what you're like is something you're prepared to admit to. Which I'm not. So I snort at this.

To be fair, Toni's bound to think she knows what I'm like. She has every reason to. For starters, she's my best friend. And apart from a ten-year virtual absence caused by marriage, mileage, and the divergence of our different careers, she has been my best friend since we first shared a room at college, when what I was like (as with her, for that matter) was a concept still blessed with glorious potentiality. And she is also Max's younger sister, which means that in less than six months from now she will become my sister as well. Only in law, but then the law is an ass.

'Get your knickers on,' she adds. 'I need a drink.'

So do I. I've swum a full twenty lengths and my fingertips are raisins, but I'm still feeling wound up. Nothing major, just that uncomfortable sense that everything I've handled today hasn't gone quite as I intended. I suspect it's going to be a feature of the job spec. Along with the suits and the low-grade existential *angst*. The morning after my unscheduled visit to A and E (a day that, minus one Harry Meadows, *enfant terrible*, had at least some sort of prospect of happening mainly in sequence and without medical interventions), I had a thoroughly unsatisfactory conversation with John Patterson. John Patterson hates me. It's sad and unfortunate but It Cannot Be Helped. He has every reason to, of course. I'm sure *I* would hate me if I was deputy head of the primary school I had been teaching at for the past fourteen years and I was fully expecting the deputy tag to be expunged at any time soon. I have no idea why the governors chose me as head over John Patterson (and I have made it my business not to wonder) but, suffice to say, it does not make for a harmonious atmosphere in the staff room. The atmosphere of a staff room is a finely balanced mixture of chemicals, some pleasant and some odious, and any tinkering with its constituents can cause gales of bad air. The atmosphere in my office with John Patterson standing in it was – generally *is* – all too odious. He has, I know, applied for every headship this side of Narnia. He hates me. He simply can't help it.

I don't hate him – why should I? – but his feelings are so ill-concealed it's no surprise that I don't like him much either. 'Hi, John! Come in!' I gushed at him nevertheless.

'Harry Meadows,' he growled, throwing an open exercise book on my desk. I was, I assumed, supposed to pick it up and scrutinize it. Harry Meadows is in John Patterson's class this year, a circumstance I think both view with some dismay.

I flicked the exercise book closed and looked at the cover. It wasn't Harry's. It said 'Owen Rhys-Woodruff, 6JP, Topic Book' on it. I opened it again, not at all sure what I was supposed be looking at.

John Patterson tutted. 'You know I had the Rhys-Woodruffs on the phone after school last night, don't you?'

'No. I didn't.'

'They're talking about speaking to the governors again.'

He managed to convey every nuance of that circumstance's gravity. Governors, like stop lights, were disregarded at one's peril. I turned my attention to the page once again, specifically to the place where the words 'piss off' were written, double-underlined and with a handwriting pen, directly beneath the eaves of a carefully drawn Tudor house. I flipped it closed. 'Lovely,' I said. 'This is Harry's work, is it?'

'What do you think?'

'Are you sure?'

'Of course I'm sure!' he snapped. 'You don't think the child would lie about something like that, do you?'

I do, as it happens. It's been known, after all. But not in *this* school, apparently. Every child in *this* school is (in theory) a testament to the universal faith that the price of your property is directly proportional to the quality of education your child will receive and, by implication, the sort of person they'll become. So they say, anyhow. I taught just as well at St Hopeful in the Quagmire. Every bit as energetically at Thugs r Us C of E.

'And what did Harry have to say about it?'

'Nothing, as yet. He's not in today, is he? But *I*

22

shall have plenty to say about it. Oh, yes. Too bloody right I will.'

'Well, perhaps you could leave this with me, then, John. I'm getting Harry's father in some time this week, and I'd like to show him, if I may.'

'Much good that'll do.'

'Even so, that's what I'm doing.'

'Yeah,' he replied. 'Whatever.'

Yeah, whatever? What kind of a response was *that*? How old did he think he was – fifteen? But it figured. John Patterson, cuckolded-acting-head-teacher, did masterclass category pubescent sulks.

Later that morning, shortly after the thoroughly unsatisfactory conversation with John Patterson, I had a thoroughly unsatisfactory conversation with Mr Meadows as well.

'Ah, Mr Meadows,' I said. 'I'm glad I caught you. Are you able to speak?'

'I'm not sure. Hang on. Yep, as far as I can tell there's a noise coming out.'

I ignored this. 'It's Holly Connors, Mr Meadows. From the—'

'Holly, eh? Don't tell me, Christmas baby.'

Oh, ho ho bloody ho. 'It's Holly Connors from Cefn Melin Primary, Mr Meadows. I'm calling because I think you and I need to have a chat about Harry.'

'I wish you wouldn't do that.'

'Do what?'

'Insist on calling me Mr Meadows.'

'I'm sorry. What else am I—'

'Why can't you call me *Will*? Mr Meadows sounds so cold and unfriendly.'

'I'm sorry. *I* thought I was being polite.'

'I'm sure you are, but I'd much rather you called me Will. Where's the problem with calling me Will?'

'There's no *problem* with calling you Will, Mr Meadows. It's just not the way we do things. It's normal in school to address each other by surnames. It's so that the children learn resp—'

'So do *I* get to call you Holly, or should I stick with Mrs Connors? Or Miss Connors? Or should it be *Ms*? Is there a Mr Connors?'

'No,' I said, and I do believe I might have sounded snappy at this point. 'But Mrs Connors will be fine.'

'Or *ma'am*, if you prefer.'

I got cross then. I was sure I heard him snigger. 'Look, you can address me in any way that makes you happiest, Mr Meadows, but right now it doesn't feel right for me to call you Will, okay?'

'*Why?*'

'Because in the first place I hardly know you, and in the second place, you are the parent of one of the children in my school and when I am engaged in a professional relationship with some-one I try to observe the usual protocols in my deal-ings with them. Of course, I'd like to think that at some point in the future our relationship will be such that it feels comfortable for me to address you by your first name, but that time isn't now, that's all.'

'Phew. I shall consider my wrist slapped, Mrs

Connors. So,' he said, in a rather cooler voice, 'what can I do for you today?'

I pay for our drinks and Toni and I thread our way across to a booth at the back of the wine bar. 'Where do you *start* with someone like that?' I say. 'He just doesn't seem to have any sense of the seriousness of the situation. I mean we're talking about a child here who rarely does anything he's told to, goes AWOL when he feels like it, writes rude words in other children's exercise books – oh, all right, only one child's book, but it was written in ink and it wasn't the first time, apparently – and seems to make it his life's work to antagonize every teacher, child and parent he can. And that's aside from the stunts.'

'Stunts?'

'Eight stitches. I told you. When he fell off the trim trail.'

'What's a trim trail anyhow?'

'A kind of mini assault course. Parallel bars, rope nets, balancing beams and so on.'

Toni takes a sip from her glass, then snorts. 'Then more fool the school. Because he sounds like a pretty average ten-year-old boy to me.'

Toni would say that, of course, because Toni is in the early stages of pregnancy, and as it has taken her and Keiran eight and a half years to reach this happy state, she cannot see a child of *any* persuasion without thanking the good Lord for the miracle of life and wanting to hug them to her ever-expanding bosom. More specifically, she is hormonal. But I agree that she does have a point. Because actually it's precisely my own.

'Yes, I don't doubt he *would* be a pretty average ten-year-old boy, except that he's had the extremely *un*average experience of losing his mother, and because, as a consequence, he has been causing above average grief in my school, as far as I can see he's getting below average sympathy from pretty much everyone there.'

'Except you,' she observes. 'You sound like Jean Brodie.'

'Well, perhaps that's just as well,' I say huffily, 'because he isn't getting what he needs from anyone else, as far as I can see. The staff have had it up to here with him, and the father is completely bloody feckless.'

'So you're a woman on a mission.'

'Absolutely I am.'

Toni smiles indulgently and pats me on the forearm. 'You and your waifs and strays,' she says. 'Bless.'

I get this all the time. To be expected, I suppose. Everyone makes all the usual assumptions, and sometimes they're right and sometimes they're wrong. Oh, all *right* then. Okay. *Yes.* Waifs and strays, that's me.

But I do have a very special reason for collecting the waifs and strays off the kerb of life's highways. Back in the dark ages, so long ago that in some ways it feels like a life I only borrowed and had to return to the library with a fifty-pence fine, I looked upon my profession as a job. A nice job, for sure, a stimulating and worthwhile job, for certain, but essentially just a job. I finished university with little in the way of plans, a great deal of grant money tied up in a collection of LPs I no longer listened to, and not the least clue what I wanted to do with the rest of my life. I'd been rather enjoying the bit I'd *been* doing and was in no rush to start anything else. It was to the great relief of my parents, therefore, that I eventually decided to enrol on a post-graduate teaching course. But despite their joy and pride, my principal aim in training to become a primary-school teacher was not so I could forge a glittering career in public service, but so that once I'd finished it, I could spend my days doing cutting and sticking and reading stories and making things out of old cereal packets and putting on outrageously over-the-top end-of-year productions and playing rounders and singing carols at Christmas. A bit like college, in fact. And which, to the in-experienced person with no great skill at any one thing in particular and a fervent desire not to do something that involved sitting in an office being sensible, i.e. me (which I know is ironic from my current viewpoint), seemed just about the best kind of job imaginable. I didn't want a career. I wanted to have fun. Plus a side-order of all those deeply unfashionable things that women only whisper about furtively these days. A family, a nice house, bucket-and-spade holidays. To re-create my own idyllic childhood in its image, in fact. I cringe to admit it now, but in my defence I've decided I was probably a late developer, and as my brother – he of the early-O-level, four-A-level, first-at-Oxbridge persuasion – had enough of the family complement of stupefying brain power, it seemed reasonable that that was what I'd do.

Primary teaching is not like that at all, of course. For starters it involves being able to do maths. O-level-standard maths, at the very least, which sounds like nothing much at all until you realize that a significant majority of the population of Great Britain (most of which, we assume, went to school at some point) does not have that qualification.

But maths was only a part of the curriculum, and much of the rest of it *was* fun. So there I was, having fun, doing a job I liked in a school I liked, and not thinking terribly much about a career profile, and then I met the man who was to become my husband, got married, produced Emily, went back to work part-time, and settled in my cosy little having-it-all niche. And would have been settled there still, I suspect. No, I *know*. Except that it went so wrong.

But that was then and this is now. And though I still enjoy scraping the glue from the scrapers, these days, indisputably, I have a *career*. On the board that stands at the entrance to Cefn Melin Primary School it says 'Mrs Holly Connors, BA Hons, PGCE, Head Teacher'. Which is impressive, but not strictly true.

It should read Ms Holly Long. Or Miss, even, if it didn't sound so prim and pejorative at my age. I haven't been Mrs Holly Connors for four years now, but as I have been it for much of my professional career, and as, in a matter of months, I am going to become Mrs Holly Stapleforth, I've decided there's no point in complicating things, even if I don't like the name Stapleforth a whole lot. But then, who would? It sounds so, well, worthy. So not terribly fun. So – I'm sorry, Max – *dull*.

Which Max isn't. Not in the least. Max is anything but and is unquestionably lovely. But in some ways it's a shame I didn't ask them to change the board, because I know my dad would have been so proud to see his name up on something so grand. But at least I *am* it. So far so good.

CHAPTER 3

Harry Meadows, though skinny, is certainly not a waif. He has come to school today in a pair of Converse basketball boots, and a sweatshirt whose relationship with the Cefn Melin school uniform extends only in as far as it has two sleeves and a hole you put your head in. And he's not a stray either. He is altogether here. Had he taken to straying there are several in this building who'd be fighting each other to lock the front gate in his wake.

After a short sabbatical (some of which, by the look of the footwear, has been spent shopping), he has returned to school, the better (and earlier) to make his mark on the week. Looking at him now, it occurs to me that providing designer kit does not happiness bring, and that perhaps his father would be better employed in the energetic pursuit of providing some continuity of care. Humph!

'Now, Harry,' I tell him, 'you and I need to talk. Tell me, where do you think we ought to start?'

I allow him ten seconds but he elects to remain silent and scrutinize the rug, so the list of things

I might use in evidence against him is clearly about ready for a run-through.

'What are the rules regarding the trim trail, Harry?'

'That Six C are allowed on it on Fridays.'

'Yes, but?'

'But what?'

'But-what – *Miss*.'

'What?'

'What, *Miss*. It's "What, *Miss*", Harry.'

'Oh. Yes. Sorry, Miss.'

'What else, Harry?'

'But *I'm* only allowed on it when I get permission. Er. Miss.'

'Exactly.'

'But—'

'There are no buts, Harry. No buts and no exceptions. The trim trail is for exercise. Not daredevil stunts. So why were you up there?'

'Because Hywel Stevens dared me.'

'And that's supposed to be a reason, is it? If Hywel Stevens dared you to eat your own body weight in ear-wigs, you'd do that as well, would you?'

'No.'

'So why this? When you knew perfectly well how dangerous it was? And when you knew perfectly well you'd get into trouble to boot?'

'Because I had to.'

'You had to.'

'I *did*, Miss.'

'But why?'

'Because I *did.*'

'Okay. So what do you suppose might have happened if you'd said no to Hywel Stevens?'

'I dunno.'

'Well, think.'

He thinks. He shrugs. He doesn't attempt an answer.

I pull out Owen Rhys-Woodruff's topic book and flip it open. 'And I suppose Owen dared you to do this as well, did he?'

He bends to look. Cringes a little. 'No.'

'So why did you?'

'I dunno.'

'That's not an answer, Harry.'

'But I don't remember.'

'Well, I'd be grateful if you'd *try* to remember.' I study him and wait, keeping my expression stern. Which today, as on most days, I find difficult, as mine is one of those faces that, left to itself, generally wants to be smiling. I've had so much practice at not feeling like smiling it feels unfair that now I do I'm not allowed to. But I play by the rules because that's my new job. 'Did you have an argument?' I ask him.

'No.'

'Did he say something unkind to you?'

'No.'

'Did he write something in one of your books?'

'No.'

'So what, then?'

'Nothing. He was just, like, *bothering* me, Miss.'

'In what way?'

He shrugged. 'Just . . . You *know.*'

'So he *was* saying things.'

'No.'

'So I don't know, do I? Not unless you tell me.' He continues to invoke his constitutional right not to split on anyone else to a teacher. But there is clearly *something* going on. I will have to find out some other way. I close the book and sigh and this time it's genuine. 'We're not getting very far, are we, Harry?'

'No, Miss,' he agrees. Almost happily, in fact.

There's a light rap at the door, closely followed by Glenda's head. 'The educational psychologist's on the phone. Shall I put him through?'

I shake my head. 'No, no. I'll take it in there.'

When I return from Glenda's office, Harry has left his spot at the edge of the rug and is standing at the window, with something in his hand. He turns as I enter. 'Who's this, Miss?'

I follow his gaze. 'Hmm?'

'This girl. In the picture.'

He is clutching a photo frame. 'Ah,' I say. 'That's Emily.'

'Who's she?'

'My daughter.'

'Oh. I didn't know you had a daughter.'

'Well, you wouldn't, would you? I've been here less than a month, after all.'

'Yeah,' he says. 'I s'pose.'

I spend a moment or two in consideration of the fact that it's not strictly necessary for my pupils – indeed, anyone in school who doesn't know me already – to know anything about the life I led before they knew me. Not necessary, and not particularly useful, even. Quite apart from anything else, it is a chapter of my life that has long since closed. And a private place I visit only rarely. Keep Out. No Trespassers. Beware of the Dog.

Kind of. A realization hits me. Perhaps here, at least, is something constructive I can do for Harry. Perhaps here's the reason we have made a connection. No, I think. There's no 'perhaps' about it. I absolutely *know* how he feels.

I go and join him at the window and take the smallest of deep breaths. 'But Emily's not here any more anyway,' I tell him. 'She died, you see, Harry. Like your mum.'

He says nothing for a long, long moment. People do. Or else they reconfigure their expressions and leap in very, very quick. Harry doesn't. Harry stands. Then he sniffs. Then he frowns. Then he says, 'Skank, Miss. How did she die?'

'She was ill, Harry. She got ill and she didn't get better.'

He frowns some more. 'That's sad,' he says. 'When did she die?'

'Quite a long time ago now. Eight years. She'd have been a teenager now. Older than you.'

I find myself swallowing a familiar tickle at the back of my throat. There are only a handful of people here who know about Emily, and that's exactly how I like it.

Harry pores over the picture for some moments, his eyes flicking back towards me once or twice, as if to confirm the existence of a likeness. Now I smile, and he finds it. Seemingly satisfied, he puts the photograph back on the windowsill and turns to me. 'Do you write to her?' he says.

'Write to her? No. I try to visit her grave on her birthday, and I—'

'Only the lady – you know, that lady who comes to talk to you about stuff when your mum dies?'

I nod.

'Well, she told me I should write to my mum. I did, like, a *bit*. But I haven't done for ages. And I feel a bit bad. I mean, Dad and I go and chat to her – in the park and everything – almost every week, but that doesn't really count, does it? It's not the same as writing.'

'You shouldn't feel bad, Harry. If you feel like writing, then fine. If not, well, that's fine too. I couldn't write to Emily because when she died she was too young to be able to read very well. But I like to think that when someone we love dies they know what we're thinking anyway, don't you? I'm sure your mum won't mind you not writing.'

He looks doubtful. 'You think?'

'I don't think. I know.'

35

He grins. 'Shame Mr Patterson doesn't think like you do.'

Hmm, I think. Quite. I had originally intended to give Harry some lines to sit and do outside my office (his handwriting needs the practice, for sure, and John Patterson is always whining that he needs the break), but instead I tell him to go and do something constructive and stitch-friendly with the last few minutes of afternoon playtime, and then, perhaps, when he gets home, to sit down and write a letter to his mum. To tell *her* why he'd written a rude word in Owen's topic book, tell *her* why he'd skimmed along the top of the trim trail, tell *her* why he does all the things that he does that mean he's standing in my office four days out of five and wearing a hole in my rug.

He looks stunned at this unexpected shift in his fortunes. 'Do I have to show you?'

'Absolutely not,' I say firmly. 'This is strictly between you and your mum.'

'And that's it?'

'That's it. You might like to promise her you'll start behaving yourself at school, though. Your dad's coming in for a chat with me soon, and it would be nice if I didn't have anything else bad to tell him. Something good, even. Hmm?'

'Okay, Miss,' he says, grinning. 'I'll try.'

I stood a moment, watching him head off down the corridor, ten going on eleven, hands stuffed in pockets, head down, shoulders hunched, shirt hanging out. And then several moments more lost in thought about Emily, and what sort of ten-year-old *she* might have become. Which is something I don't do very often these days, because one thing I've learned in the last eight years is that the words 'what if', once slotted together, are two of the most useless in the dictionary. A little, come to think of it, like the words John and Patterson.

A lot like, in fact. Stupid man.

I had lots of words for John Patterson. An eclectic selection that I had, in the few short weeks of our re-acquaintance, honed and refined, and which, from the safe haven of being under my breath, could be chanted like a mantra when he got on my nerves. In much the same way, I fancied, that people like Toni dabbed Bach flower remedies on their temples in times of spiritual need. But none of them centred on his libido, for sure. John Patterson had dandruff. John Patterson wore corduroy. John Patterson, manifestly, wasn't a catch. Which it occurred to me was in direct contrast to the man who was staring at me now. Namely Henry VIII (no libido issues there), whose head, my moment of idleness caused me to notice, had become partly unattached and was listing to the left, making considerable headway towards Anne Boleyn's ruff. Not wishing Cefn Melin Primary to be responsible for subverting the noble cause of historical accuracy, I walked along the corridor to where I knew the box of display stuff still was, and began to rummage in it for the wall stapler. Which placed me just outside the slightly open stationery cupboard door, from which a great deal of whispered and somewhat furtive-sounding conversation was emitting. None of which would have been of concern to me – these were not children's voices and, as far as I could make out, nothing of a physical nature was occurring – except that one of the voices was that *of* John Patterson, and it didn't take much of a leap of faith to suppose that he might well be whispering about me. Well, so be it, I decided. He could bitch all he liked. But just as I was continuing in my quest to re-acquaint Henry's head with his body, the door of the stationery cupboard flew open and Clemency Bright, somewhat red-faced, emerged.

'Oh!' she said. 'Oh! Mrs Connors! Hello!'

Clemency Bright, in direct contravention of the rule that states that certain names are only suited to a career stomping about and warbling for Lloyd-Webber *et al*, was in her mid-thirties and had come late to teaching, via management consulting. Thus she still had a patina of corporate gloss about her, and had yet to find out all about PVA glue. The sort of cool and understated blonde who wafted through the corridors as if blown by a breeze, she was, I didn't doubt, the object of adoration of many a pre-pubescent boy. Though she wasn't looking cool and understated right now. She looked altogether rather fraught and somewhat pink about the cheeks. Almost the same colour, in fact, as the roll of pink paper she had clasped to her chest.

'Hello,' I said, waving the stapler towards the wall. 'Very nice display work, Clemency. Well done.'

'Oh,' she said. 'Thanks. Well . . . hmm. Sugar paper!' And then she wafted off, at some speed, with hers.

John Patterson emerged backwards a few seconds later, arms full of exercise books. He didn't speak to me and I didn't speak to him. Instead I turned and went back to my office, via Glenda's. She was sitting at her desk, typing. Well, well, I thought.

I pushed the door to. 'Glenda,' I said. 'You know Clemency?'

She glanced up, still typing. 'What about her?' she said.

'She's not married, is she?'

She shook her head. 'Not to my knowledge, no.'

'But John is, of course.'

'John?' She stopped typing and turned her head. 'What is this? Twenty questions?'

I reached behind me and clicked the door properly shut. 'It's just that . . . well . . . d'you think there might be, you know, something going *on* there?'

Glenda did a bustle with her mouse. 'Going on?'

'You know. *Between* them.'

Glenda bustled big-time now. She jiggled her mouse, she wiggled in her seat, she put her pen in its pen pot and her hands in her lap. I suspect I should have read something into the bustles, but I didn't connect. Not at first.

'Whatever gave you that idea?' she said finally, in the manner of an elderly cook in an Agatha Christie novel who's been caught with a ham up her pinny.

I folded my arms and nodded towards the door. 'Just now,' I said. 'I saw them. It seems odd, that's all. They're forever emerging from cupboards together. Looking shifty. Well, *she* does. John looks like that most of the time. But then he would,' I hurried on, now at last sensing her unexpected and undeniably stiff disapproval. 'I mean, I'm public enemy number one right now, aren't I? Anyway. Whatever. I just wondered, that was all. None of my business. Just thought you might know.'

'I don't know everything about everything,' she said tartly. 'And I don't make it my business to either.'

Well, well, well. Now, *here* was a thing.

'I'm disappointed, Glenda,' I said, smiling hard against the sub-zero blast of her gaze. 'I thought I'd be able to rely on you for all the gossip. Ha-ha. Look, it's something and nothing, I'm sure. Forget I even said it.'

She did another little bustle and went back to her typing. Ha, I thought. *Ha*. So it seemed I was right.

Though I am a little disappointed about Glenda.

Not because I would wish to spend any but the most cursory amount of time speculating about the extra-marital shenanigans that might or might not be going on between any of my staff. That sort of thing is rife. Universal. And not even interesting. And, yes, I do know. It's *obviously* not appropriate for me to be gossiping in any case. But I had thought, perhaps naïvely, that Glenda was an ally. Glenda started at Cefn Melin almost exactly when I did the first time round. My first job after college. Her first job since having her kids. And she'd been there ever since. It had been nice, coming back full circle to pilot a ship with a completely unknown crew, to know that Glenda was still there, a familiar and friendly face. But it wasn't the same now. *She* wasn't the same. Things change, I thought. People change.

A lot had changed with my return, that was for sure. My predecessor (and former boss) at Cefn Melin Primary was an esteemed and much-lauded practitioner of the old school. I'm not altogether sure what a teacher of the old school should be like, but my hunch is that the doughty Mrs Plum could have written the guide book. She had taught all her life, collected an impressive number of accolades and plaudits and, until she left, could still apparently be relied on to reduce any transgressor to a quivering heap. And that was just the staff. But she'd been felled by a stroke during the previous term, and though she was now recovering and would no doubt rise again to campaign for the reinstatement of the

41

slipper, her days of terrorizing North Cardiff's progeny were done. John Patterson, as deputy, had stepped in as acting head and the job had been advertised forthwith.

Which would doubtless have been his, had I not applied for it. I was a deputy head at that time, in a small inner-city primary where I had, I knew, little hope of progressing. The head, only recently appointed herself, was just a few years older than me. And as I'd taught at Cefn Melin a few years before, I thought I might as well try for the job. It would be great, I'd thought – if unlikely that I'd get it. I knew Glenda, I knew John, and I knew my way around. Worth a shot at least. And I'd be among friends.

'But there's only Barry, really,' I told Toni now.

'Barry?'

'Barry Huckley. He's the school caretaker. He's been there for ever. I suppose at least I should feel grateful that there's *someone* on my side.'

It was Monday evening and Toni and I were at one of her work beanos: the inaugural gathering of Mangleweed, Feinstein, Carruthers and Slake. As opposed to the marginally less catchy Feinstein, Carruthers and Picton, which was what they'd been *before* they became Mangleweed, Feinstein, Carruthers and Slake, which was when Mangleweed and Slake, whoever they were, had merged with them both, ejected the Picton and book-ended what remained of their names. This was the world of advertising. Toni's world. A world where company letterheads changed almost monthly and everyone wore linen every day of the week. (And presumably *de rigueur* on 'dress down' Fridays was to come in to work in your pants, if at all.) Max (who being a lawyer never wore linen and whose firm was called an altogether less flamboyant Perkins and Stapleforth) was out with clients, doing his regular corporate wheel-oiling stuff, and as all I had on offer in the leisure-pursuits line was the school budget, it didn't take much persuading to drag me along. I liked going out with Toni after work. It made me feel there was life beyond SATS.

'They'll *all* be on your side,' she told me, as we threaded our way through the crush at the bar. 'You just have to give it time. Get to know everyone. And get rid of Laughing Boy, of course. But that can't be too long, can it?'

'I'm not so sure. I can think of at least one job he didn't get. Mine.'

'But he'll get something else and then he'll clear off and the atmosphere will change. You'll see. Or perhaps he'll run off with that teacher. You never know.'

You never did. I could only hope, I supposed. That John would be gone and everyone would start to take me more seriously, and I would begin to feel like the head teacher I was supposed to be instead of the lamb in wolf's clothing I felt I'd resembled up to now. I might have a good line in power-dressing get-ups, but it was all on the surface, all part of the front.

Which was a pertinent thing to be thinking, as it turned out, because as we approached the bar I realized that a man I thought I recognized was standing beside me.

But it wasn't John Patterson. It was Will Meadows. I didn't know much about Toni's work, but I guess I really should have known that a party at the offices of Mouthful and Hiccup and Strepsil would be exactly the sort of place where the likes of Will Meadows would hang out. But as he was only in my thoughts when his son was in my office (which was admittedly more often than I would have liked), I hadn't. So I did a double-take when our eyes met. So did he. One that took in the whole picture and found itself temporarily unable to compute. Which galled me and pleased me in about equal measure. I'm a woman after all. These things matter.

'*Hola!*' he said cheerily.

He had the most unusual amber eyes. I wondered if he might be half Spanish. Or just plain old pretentious. 'Hello,' I said.

He edged over to make room for me beside him at the counter. 'What brings you here, then? Absolutely the last place I would have expected to find you.' I listened hard for any traces of sarcasm in his voice, but there were none. Which, when I thought about it, was worse. He obviously couldn't believe I ventured out after dark and interacted with normal people at all.

'Really?' I said. 'Where would the first place be, then?'

He laughed. 'I kind of imagined they might keep you locked up in a cupboard with the PE equipment and the blackboard rubbers.'

I felt altogether too short, too insubstantial, in my trainers. Too Will o'the Wispy in my stretchy lace top. Too trying-to-be-rock-chick and looking like an arse with my own impulsively twizzled head of temporary curls. 'We don't have black-boards any more,' I told him. 'We use interactive whiteboards in the classrooms these days.' Which he wouldn't know, of course, because I'd already checked. He was apparently as familiar a sight at Cefn Melin Primary as free school milk. I almost said so, but then I remembered where I was. And *who* I was, as opposed to what I was, as well.

I smiled politely at him instead and gestured along the counter, where Toni had touched base too and was collecting some drinks. 'No,' I continued. 'I'm here with my friend, actually. She's—'

'Right beside you. Here.' Toni handed me a bottle of something blue, called Coral Atoll. Which figured, because mainly it tasted like fish poo. 'Oh, wotcha, Will! How's it hanging?' she said. 'Haven't seen you in an age. What are you up to at the moment?'

Will Meadows accepted the obligatory brace of kisses and took another swig from his own bottle. Which seemed to be beer. Which was what I should have had.

'I'm knackered. Post-production. Spent all of last night in the edit suite,' he said. Which I presumed was media speak for whatever work it was he did. The panty-liner image came instantly to mind. And then the unicorn cantered up to put it through its paces. 'Busy,' he added. 'Which is good enough for me. But as I was just telling your friend here,' he nodded towards me, 'right now I'm mainly trying to keep my errant off-spring out of trouble. Actually, no. Trying to keep *myself* out of trouble, more specifically. With his school. They've got this new headmistress, you see.' He winked at me then. 'Bit fierce.'

I gaped at him, Coral Atoll arrested mid-tide. 'Is that right?' I managed finally.

He nodded and grimaced. 'Terrifying,' he added. 'Scares the pants off me.'

'Well, isn't that just *such* a coincidence!' exclaimed Toni. 'Holly's a headmistress too, Will.'

He winked again. He seemed to be enjoying this. 'Really?'

She nodded. 'I'm sorry, I didn't introduce you, did I? Holly Connors, Will Meadows. Will shot the ads for the Naked Truth campaign for us last year, Holly.'

Underwear again. Did he specialize or something?

'Well, hello, *Holly*,' he was saying, with elaborate emphasis. 'That's a very nice name. And you're a headmistress too? Well I *never*! I have to say, you don't look like one in the least.'

46

'That just goes to show,' I said, trying not to feel needled.

'Show what?'

'That you should never judge a book by its cover.'

'Ah,' he said, nodding at me. 'Ri-ight. Good point.' He tipped the neck of his bottle towards me and grinned. 'But then, perhaps neither should you.'

Now I felt needled. 'I don't,' I said back.

'Tell you what,' he said, smiling eyes fixed on mine. 'Bet you do.'

'Hang *on a minute*,' said Toni. 'Am I missing something? Do you guys already know each other, or what?'

And we all laughed and it was all terrifically funny and Will Meadows explained to Toni that he was one of the parents at my school and that he absolutely *hadn't* recognized me when he first clapped eyes on me and I said that was because I only made the effort to look scary when I was at work, the better to frighten the children, and we all laughed some more and it was all very jolly and then he told Toni he was just about to start shooting the new commercial for the Outrigger (some car or other) campaign he'd done that presentation for back in November and that he didn't have the first clue where they were going to lay their hands on thirty-four six-foot-two blondes and that it was a dirty job but someone had to do it and why, oh, why couldn't it be him and she laughed and I

47

laughed, and all the while I stood there nodding and smiling I thought dark thoughts and rather wished I had my heels on so that I could accidentally on purpose stamp super hard on his toe. Feckless. Feckless bloody wise-guy bloody git.

After he'd gone, Toni turned to me. 'What the hell was *that* all about?'

'He's the *dad*,' I hissed at her. 'You know. Of the boy I've been telling you about. The one whose wife died.' I felt all flustered now. God! The front of the man!

Toni's mouth dropped open. 'What? Will Meadows is? Good Lord. it was *his* wife who died? Oh, that's such a bitch. God, I even remember her. Stunning woman. She came to something here once. Oh, poor Will. And he's such a sweetheart, too. Oh, the poor guy. That's so *sad*.'

God, I thought, as he was probably all ears by now. God, me and my big mouth. I groaned. 'Though of course now I wish I hadn't told you.'

'Oh, don't be so twitchy. I'm not about to blurt your trade secrets all over Cardiff, am I? But – well I never! So he's the father of your *enfant terrible*, is he?'

'Yes, and he's coming in next week to see me about it and I wish, I really wish, I hadn't seen him right now.'

Sweetheart, my eye. I watched him standing chatting to someone a few feet away and then he turned round and I ended up catching his eye again. He raised his bottle and grinned and I looked away quickly. The temerity of it! And who was looking after his son precisely? And what did he think he was doing in the first place? He should be at home helping Harry with his homework or something, shouldn't he? Or at the very least *being* there. *There.* Not here. Not spending all nights in edit suites or whatever they were. And 'bet you do'. What was that all about? Bloody cheek.

'What is that a problem?' said Toni, who inhabited his world. Who clearly didn't have the first clue what I meant.

'Because,' I replied.

'Because what?'

'Because *because*. Because jeans. Because trainers. Because push-up bra and lash-lengthening mascara. Because turquoise bloody drink. Here. This. Now. It just doesn't feel right, that's all.'

'Oh, don't be such a *drear*, Hol. D'you intend spending the rest of your life not having any fun in case one of the parents clocks you? Come on, you don't honestly think he imagines you spend your free time embroidering samplers and making soup for starving refugees, do you?'

'I think he did, as it happens. But I don't think he does any more.'

'And that's a *bad* thing?'

'No. Not *bad*. Just, well. I don't know. It's just that under the circumstances . . . well, I wish he wouldn't speak to me like that.'

'Oh, come on.' She tutted. 'Listen to yourself! Like what? Like you're not the Queen?'

49

'No! Just all . . . well . . . like I'm not Harry's head teacher. It's difficult, okay? That's all.'

'Dear me, Hol. Don't you think you might be in danger of taking yourself a teeny bit too seriously here? Hey, it's only a job, you know. Not a lifestyle statement.'

I do know that. I don't *want* to take myself too seriously. I just want other people to, that's all. When it *matters*, I do. Wouldn't anyone? And I'm sure they *do*. Some of them, some of the time, at least. But sometimes I imagine John Patterson doing my job (not the happiest of pastimes, for sure, but shit happens) and I just know *no* one would come up to him and be all funny and jokey and flippant and familiar. They'd shake his hand and treat him with a bit of respect and generally behave with a bit more . . . well . . . God, *propriety*. Not make jokes about him being locked in a cupboard after school. Though, thinking about it, that's what they should do, perhaps.

As a consequence of having had yet another (deeply) unsatisfactory brush with Will Meadows, Harry is very much on my mind when I get home. Which is fine, because it reminds me that he has told me he's going to bring some pictures of his mum in to show me tomorrow, and that I promised him I'd bring some pictures of Emily in to show him.

Max arrives just as I'm slipping my favourite out of its frame.

'Oh,' he says, plopping his jacket over the back of the sofa and looking suddenly concerned and sympathetic. 'Are you having a bit of a moment?'

Max always seems uncomfortable when he catches me looking at pictures of Emily. I think it frightens him. No. I *know* it frightens him. Not because it makes me burst into uncontrollable tears, because I haven't done that sort of thing for a very long time. (And, besides, I wouldn't anyway. Max is understandably sensitive to overt displays of feminine hysteria because apparently his divorce involved lots and lots of that.) No, it's because I think it makes him worry that I'm suddenly going to rip out my coil, hurl it out across the balcony and demand the right to express what remains of my fertility and make him have fifteen more kids. It's so silly. Because I won't. I don't want any more children. I've got my memories, haven't I? And now I have my career, and my whole future ahead of me. And what with his ex-wife and his two teenage daughters, we have enough of a complement of difficult relationships to negotiate as it is. But I know where he's coming from. He has been there already. And now that he's post-Barbie (and post full-time parent, for that matter) he doesn't want to be dragged back to Babyville.

I put down the frame, close the album and gather up my little stash of pictures. I feel a bit irritable with him suddenly. I know it's probably because I feel so cross with Will Meadows, but even so.

51

Why *shouldn't* I look at pictures of my daughter? 'No, Max,' I tell him. 'I'm not having "a bit of a moment". I'm just getting a few snaps together to show Harry.'

He looks relieved. 'Harry?'

'You know. The boy in school I was telling you about the other day. The one who lost his mum last year. He said he wanted to bring in some pictures of her to show me, so I thought it might be nice if I took some in too. You know, I honestly think I can make some progress with him.' I gather up the various packets of photos, stray negatives and so on. (No shrine, this. Just a box full of old stuff.) 'He really began to open up with me today—'

'Hmm?'

'Well, as much as any ten-year-old boy would, which isn't much, as you can imagine. But I think he feels he has a friend in me, you know? Someone who he can—'

'Good Lord! What the hell does that guy think he's doing?'

I look up. Max is peering out across the bay.

'What? What guy?'

He laughs his big laugh. 'That guy! Would you look at him! Jesus. They'll rent boats to anyone. He nearly had the leg off the Bosphorus!'

'Max, you're not listening to me, are you?'

'What? Er . . . um. No. Sorry. What were you saying?'

'About Harry. The boy at school.'

'Oh, yes, sweets. Great stuff.' He's still looking out over the balcony and chuckling.

I pick up the box. 'So. A baby. How about it? What d'you think?'

He spins round. '*WHAT?*'

Bless him. 'You see?' I say. '*Now* you're listening.'

CHAPTER 4

I know I'll get the hang of it eventually. I've wanted this so much, haven't I? Yes, of course I have. This is the pinnacle of my career. An achievement. I am only thirty-nine and I have achieved. I have prevailed over John Patterson, the man with the extra toe (he told me) from Swansea, and the woman with the MA in droning (she didn't need to). In fact, everybody else who applied for the job, basically, which means I must be darn clever, or what? And now I am in charge of a whole school. Fourteen teachers, one caretaker, three cooks, six dinner ladies, three and a half hundred children, two rabbits and a fish tank (twenty-seven guppies and a snail at the last count). *All* this. Sometimes it overwhelms me to think of it. So mainly I try not to in case I turn tail and flee.

The very charming man who headed up 'effective leadership in the modern primary' (which was one of the lectures during a three-day course I went on six months back and that I remember principally for the interminable humming of a special-needs expert from Tring) said that one of the greatest weapons in the head-teacherly armoury was to cultivate an atmosphere of authority from the off.

Thus it is with some dismay that my eyes alight not on the triad of certificates that I have framed and carefully mounted on my office wall, but on the bag of shopping I dashed out to pick up at lunchtime. Most specifically the pack of seven-denier black stockings that is peeking provocatively, like a hooker, from the top.

'I am so sorry,' says Will Meadows, who has spotted it also. He is standing on my rug, looking very like Harry, and grinning disarmingly at me from under his hair. In lots of ways he looks like just another pupil. A tall one, certainly, and an indisputably masculine one, too. But even so, his whole demeanour is essentially boyish. Like he just bounded in here after playtime, perhaps. Perhaps he did, come to think of it. It certainly seems a very racy way to make a living. But though the hedonistic lifestyle may work well for *him*, it won't, as I shall aim to impress upon him, for his son. He's so flippant. It's like he doesn't even much *care*. I know I don't know that, and I know he is probably just putting on a brave face but, even so, he is a father and he must think of his son.

Yes, *that*. He fingers the chain round his neck, then spreads his hands in supplication. 'I hope I didn't offend you when I saw you the other evening. I thought about it afterwards and, well . . .

it seemed funny at the time, but now I'm standing in your office I have a powerful sense that my jocularity was both ill-advised and not altogether well received. Or even appropriate. I'm sorry.'

I have a powerful sense too. That he is taking the piss. 'That's okay, Mr Meadows,' I say politely. 'I don't much do offended.'

He frowns at me. Perhaps he's not. 'Or Christian names.'

'Not at work,' I say. 'No.'

Will Meadows, standing on my rug and refusing to refrain from being friendly and familiar. Refusing to observe all the silly rules that govern my life. Refusing not to be nice. Infuriating man.

'Point taken,' he says, grinning again. 'Anyway, like I said, I'm sorry. I didn't mean it. You're not scary really. Er . . . shall I sit here, Miss, or should I stay standing up?'

Oh, oh, oh, oh, *OH*! *Damn* the man. I'm trying to be professional here, okay?

The trouble is that there are all sorts of tedious protocols one must take heed of when one reaches the dizzy heights of head-dom and one of them is a proper observance of parent-teacher interactions. Thus it is not an option for me to open conversations with 'Wotcha, Will. How's it hanging?' or any variant thereof.

'So—' I begin.

'Yes, *so*,' he interrupts me. 'Forgive me, but I'm not altogether sure why I'm here.'

'Because I thought it was time we were properly

acquainted. Because I thought it would be good for us to have a little chat.' He raises one eyebrow. 'About Harry,' I add.

'Okay,' he says, arms opening expansively. 'Shoot.'

So I sit Will Meadows down and attempt to outline the theory behind the behaviour-modification programme I have decided to implement for his son. He laughs. He nods. He says it sounds like something that should be practised in a gulag. He looks, more than anything, just a little bemused. No. *Not* bemused. Bored. As if there is, after all, more than a nugget of new appointee's over-zealousness in my plans. But what the hell? It's his lucky day, if he'd only grasp the fact. It could have been so different. John could have been in charge. Poor Harry might have found himself spending much of the remainder of his primary-school life being barked at and made to sit in corners on his own. Which is how, I imagine, he has spent much of the last term. What with elderly Mrs Plum busy gasping her almost-last, with John fretting about his job and busy bonking Ms Bright. With no one like me to give him time and attention. So I sit and I explain and I like to think Will Meadows is at least mildly impressed with my commitment to the cause. Though I'm not at all sure that he is impressed with my ideas.

'We've already done charting,' he tells me. 'And had the bereavement counsellor in for a session and all that. And, yes, they've already given me all that special-needs crap. And, no, I'm really not

57

interested in hearing any more about pupil-support services or psychiatrists or psychologists or any other ologists for that matter. Harry doesn't *have* any special needs. There's nothing *wrong* with him.'

'Mr Meadows, I do appreciate what you're saying, but there is no stigma in accepting the various support services that are available to us in situations like these. That is what they're there for. And if we work together on this then I'm sure we can—'

'Can what?' He spreads his hands again. 'And more to the point, *why*? Just what does he do that's so bad?'

So I show him the exercise book and I remind him about the trim trail and I point out that two pages and a drawing of a tap does not a project on the water cycle make. I cover rubber bands, graffiti, balls of wet loo roll on toilet ceilings, using other pupils' Groovy Chick erasers as missiles, landing footballs in neighbouring back gardens (with special reference to Mr Tinkler, who is a war veteran and only had the one leg), the damming up of the fountain in the sensory garden (twice), spitting contests, calling dinner ladies 'old mingers' (he had the bad form to smirk at this item), and singing a very alternative version of 'We Are All Special In God's Eyes'. While the vicar was visiting.

'Look,' he says nicely, but his tone is clear. 'He's a boy. He gets up to stuff. That's what boys *do*.'

Some of the stuff some of the time, yes, I do concede *that*. But not all of the stuff all of the time, okay? *Okay?* We talked a bit more, of course. Well, I talked and he didn't appear to listen much. There was obviously a gulf – well, more of a well-developed mid-Atlantic ridge – between what I perceived as 'stuff' and what he perceived as 'stuff', and though he thanked me politely and assured me he would take steps to keep Harry's worst excesses to a minimum, I knew the battle of perception had been lost long before. Perhaps Will Meadows was right. Perhaps Harry was the epitome of normal well-adjusted boyhood at home. Perhaps Will Meadows was just tired of being hauled in to school and brought to account for things he considered were just not that bad. In the scheme of things, at any rate. Perhaps *I* was wrong. Perhaps I worried too much. Perhaps all sorts of things. But I wasn't convinced. Confirmed, more like. In my opinion that Harry was suffering nothing more remarkable than an absence of proper parenting, full stop and no returns. And I thought it very huffily as I watched him bound back across the car park. Especially in conjunction with the stockings. Ouch.

The sixth week of the first term of my first year as a proper, pukka, real-life head teacher and I'm still, quite remarkably, largely in one piece. Though a little thinner, it has to be said, on account of the stress.

'That's the thing,' Dorothy tells me, 'with people these days. Cash rich but time poor. I read it in the *Guardian* and it's a universal truth. There. I'm done. Step down and let's see.'

She pulls a couple of pins from between her lips and helps me climb down off the chair.

'Perfect,' she says. 'You look an absolute picture. I'm so glad you decided on the long.'

I'm still not quite sure about the long. I see myself standing in front of Dorothy's cheval mirror and I wonder what had possessed me of the notion that getting married in a floor-length, off-the-shoulder, ivory-silk fishtail gown would be just the ticket. But it *is* a late-afternoon wedding, with an evening reception, and as my last wedding dress made me look like a novelty toilet-roll cover (complete with ringlets and highwayman much-buckled footwear), I figure I'm overdue a chance to look classy. Or make a stab at it, at least. I'm not sure I'll pull it off.

'Hmm,' I reply. 'I'm not entirely convinced.'

She ignores this, sensibly, because I say it every time. 'And your hair,' she says, reaching behind me to pull out my scrunchie. 'Loose, I think. Don't you? As your shoulders are bare.'

I have the sort of hair that almost everybody is envious of because they don't have the first clue how difficult it is. Yes, it is thick and fair (okay, with a little assistance) but like my face, which feels all the time now as if it is trying to resist being wrestled into stern submission in keeping with my notions of professional gravitas, it is also the sort of hair that likes to please itself. If it decides to hang in a uniform curtain it does, but it doesn't decide to do that very often. Mainly it does what it likes. Which is mainly *not* what hair like mine does in shampoo commercials (for which lies I hold a certain someone *entirely* responsible), and I can't put it up because it will ping straight back down and I can't coif it up into extravagant swirls because then I will look like I did at my first wedding. Which for many reasons, I wish to avoid.

'Loose,' I agree. 'It's probably safer that way.'

She stands back and scrutinizes me. 'It's perfect, I agree, but God save us from "safe", dear. Remember, "safe" didn't ever do anything of note.'

Dorothy lives in the flat upstairs and has done since shortly before I moved in. She's the widow of a diplomat and has travelled almost everywhere, usually accompanied by steamer trunks and staff. But now she is here and I'm eternally grateful. Aside from her intelligence and her breathtaking skill as a seamstress, she is the balm with which I soothe away all the world's ills. She also builds doll's houses – exquisitely so – and makes cakes. Which is something I don't.

She presses a slice on me. Still warm, and dotted with a million poppy seeds. 'And I do hope you're not dieting, dear. There's only so much I can take this in, you know. And you don't want to look gaunt in this dress. You want to fill it. It's a dress that needs a bosom and a good healthy glow.'

'I'm not dieting,' I reassure her. 'I'm too busy fretting to think about not eating.' I tuck into the cake without thinking. Because I'm thinking. 'Tell me,' I ask her, 'do you think I come across as scary, Dorothy?'

'You? Not to me. Why would you think that?'

'Oh, it's just something one of the parents said. Fierce, too. Have I ever seemed fierce?' I bare my teeth to the mirror to try on fierce for size. My clavicles ping out like a pair of misplaced wishbones. I don't look fierce at all. Mad, but not fierce. But, then, perhaps it's not really about the way I look. 'Weird, isn't it?' I say. 'I'm devoting ridiculous amounts of energy to asserting my authority at the moment, but when it appears that it's working, I don't much like how it makes me feel. How strange is that?'

'Not strange at all. We all want to be loved, dear.'

'I suppose. But mainly I want to be respected. No. That's the wrong word. I know I have to earn that. *Accepted*. Yes. That'll do.' I finish the last mouthful of cake. 'Actually, I suspect I'm needled because it's a gender thing, isn't it? They're not adjectives you'd use about a man in that context. You'd say "commanding", or "authoritative". Something like that.'

'What *was* the context? Was this any parent in particular?'

'A father. A feckless father.'

'The world's full of those, dear.'

'Particularly feckless. He's like a kid himself. He lost his wife last year. Cancer. Harry's mum. Remember? The boy I was telling you about last week?'

She takes my empty cake plate. 'Then you must make allowances.'

'Yes, but how many?'

'Sufficient. No more.'

'How many is that?'

'Just enough to prevail.'

'Prevail over what?'

'His misconceptions about *you*. Hop up again, dear. The hem needs adjusting here.'

She helps me back up onto the chair, then lowers herself onto her knees once again. For someone in her sixties she is amazingly agile. When I asked her how come, once, she whooped like a call-girl and said it was all down to energetic sex. Forty years of it. Best way to keep a girl supple. I told Max about it. He was seriously pleased.

Dorothy removes and reinserts a number of pins, then sits back on her heels and smiles up at me. 'That'll do it, I think. Yes . . . Hmm,' she says, narrowing her eyes. 'You know, sweetheart? Standing up there in that gown, you look just like a beautiful Greek goddess on a pedestal.'

'Plinth,' I say, clambering down. 'You mean plinth.'

'Holly,' she says, rising from the floor with her pin pot, 'I know perfectly well what I mean.'

★　★　★

So, another not more than averagely unsatisfactory week. But as is traditionally the way, the bullet with your name on it is the one you don't see coming. If you could see it you could avoid it, couldn't you? So it never occurred to me to attach any significance to the precise timing of my leaving school that following Friday afternoon. I was rushing – it was ever thus – and if it hadn't been for the phone call from one of the governors just as I was leaving, I would have been long, long gone. My bumping into John Patterson wouldn't have happened, my being held up wouldn't have happened, and everything that happened after *that* wouldn't have happened. And 'bullet', perhaps, isn't strictly the right missile. No. That would be 'arrow'. Indisputably.

But that's what did happen. We converged in the vestibule. A bit like penguins and seals did, millennia ago.

'Ah, John,' I said, anxious to seize the initiative before he could make his escape. 'I'm glad I caught you. Your IT review. You haven't forgotten I'm going to need it on Monday, have you?'

He stopped and exhaled in a point-making way. 'No. I haven't *forgotten*, Holly, but I have rather more pressing things to get done this weekend, frankly. Like the presentation for my interview on Tuesday, for instance. There's no way I'm going to be able to get it finished over the weekend, is there?'

I don't bloody know, I thought. You tell me. No. In fact, don't bother telling me. Just make sure you get it done, you bastard.

'But I really do need it, John. You're not going to be *in* on Tuesday, are you? And I've got to have it in before half-term.'

'Exactly. So you don't need it till Thursday, do you? A couple of days aren't going to matter, for God's sake. It's not going to be the end of the world, you know.'

'Yes, I *do* know that, John. And it's not the point anyway. The point is that I would rather like to get it in *on time*. And if I don't get it from you until Thursday I will have no time to review it and finalize it, will I? And it's not as if you haven't had plenty of notice about it. It's—'

'Oh, right,' he barked. 'Like I don't have enough to do as it is. Like a full-time teaching commitment, if you hadn't noticed? Like the exams coming up. Like the small matter of sixty books to mark. Or have you forgotten about marking?'

'What do you think I've been doing for the last seventeen years of my life? Playing tiddlywinks? I know exactly what sort of workload you have.' Which was not at all the same as saying 'how hard you work'. Because he didn't. Not that hard. Not as far as I could see. Just as my mother always managed with the last of the Marmite, he made a little appear to go a very long way.

He pulled his car keys out of his jacket pocket, then flipped his other palm in my direction. 'Look, don't give me grief over this, okay?' He glared at me. 'I'll get it done when I get it *done*.'

65

Well, he could bloody well flip and flap and glare all he liked. 'John, I would really appreciate it if you'd do it by Monday. That's when we agreed and that's when I would like it.' I could feel my cheeks colouring and hoped the rain and the early-evening murk would hide it.

He smiled nastily at me. 'You'll get it when you get it,' he said, turning on his heel and ending the conversation. Then he swivelled. 'Or perhaps you'd rather I didn't get my presentation done and didn't get this job. But I imagine that's not the case. Hmm?'

And then, punch-line delivered, he did stalk off, crossing the car park in angry giant's strides and redistributing puddles as he went.

Bastard. *Bastard.* Infuriatingly, I could feel frustrated tears welling in my eyes. I stood beside my car and watched him go, still clutching my now damp pile of files and willing myself to think of some sort of rejoinder that would stop him in his tracks. Trump his little victory. Fell his bloody arrogance at a stroke. I looked angrily down at the bundle in my arms. I could even lob my 'Procedures and Protocols' file at him. Not professional, not big and not clever but, boy, it would feel so damn good. But what would be the bloody point? He'd do what he liked despite anything I said. It wouldn't be me who'd be giving him a reference. I turned back to my car, raised my right boot, and kicked one of the tyres instead.

'You all right, H?'

I spun round, startled, and almost dropped the files. It was Barry Huckley, the caretaker. Oh, God. Had he heard us?

'Oh. Yes . . . yes, fine,' I reassured him, ducking down to put the files on the back seat. 'Just getting loaded up for home.'

He glanced across the car park, where John was now sitting in his car and yammering into his mobile. Then he nodded. 'You finished inside, then? I need to lock up the front.'

'No. No, I haven't. I've got another box to bring out.'

'I'll go and fetch it for you, then. The blue one, is it?'

'Yes, that's it, thanks. It's in the vestibule.'

He lumbered off, which gave me time to snort angrily into a tissue and check my mascara in the wing mirror. Too, too pathetic. I was stronger than this.

He was back moments later with the box under one arm. I held out my hands to take it from him, but he didn't give it up. Just stood and scrutinized me in the frank, unabashed and penetrating way that only a man of advancing years who has known you since you were twenty-two and calls you 'H' can.

'It will all work out,' he said.

'Er . . . what? What will all work out, Barry?'

He glanced across the car park to the road. John's car was now just turning into it. Then he shook his head, grinned and gave me the box. 'Everything,' he said, tapping the side of his nose with his finger. 'Don't you worry, sweetheart. Just have patience.'

CHAPTER 5

Well, John bloody Patterson could go to hell. He could go to hell and rot there and if (as I chose to believe) he was so non-biodegradable, so made of bits of old tyres and rocks and cat-pee-soaked carpet tiles that he didn't rot fast enough, then he could be hauled out by Beelzebub and plunged into a vat of boiling acid, until every last vestige of his hateful, full-of-itself, rickety-rackety body was dissolved, cell by resentful little cell, from his bones. And then the Grim Reaper could ride up, put all the bones into a sack and give them to poor street children of Colombia to carve into amusingly shaped novelty tooth-picks to sell in some back-street Bogotá market and be bought by scuzzy European tourists in football shirts who would take them home and pick their toenails with them. And he would know, he would then irrefutably *know*, that he had got exactly what he deserved.

Well, it made me feel better at least. Max. On the phone. Five thirty.

'Where are you? Still at school? I thought you were going to get away early today.'

'So did I, believe me. I've just finished loading up the car.'

'Loading the car up with what?'

'What do you think? With work, of course.'

'Oh, that.' He paused to groan. 'I presume you won't want picking up then?'

'No. I won't have time to get ready. You go and pick the girls up and I'll see you down there.'

'Good day?'

'I've had better.'

'Not that boy again, I hope.'

'No. *Not* that boy again, actually. You?'

'I've had worse. So, hey, sweets, we're evens, aren't we?'

I don't know how he worked that out, except that perhaps it meant it was my turn to enjoy an especially solicitous weekend, with lots of pampering, long baths and the sort of sex that only happens to women with big breasts on Channel Five. Or perhaps not. But even though this particular weekend was going to bring the question of the Wedding Arrangements into play and could therefore not be counted on not to dissolve into acrimony, sulks and much adolescent flouncing, it *was* the weekend, which meant it wasn't work.

And work, to be fair, could have been worse. Or so I thought. In fact, I was just thinking that perhaps at least some of what I had said to Will Meadows had borne fruit, and that at least Harry hadn't been hauled into my office in disgrace during the last forty-eight hours, when I turned the corner and found myself only yards from a boy on a bicycle, careering towards me down the middle of the road. And it was only seconds after that when I realized the boy on the bike *was* Harry. Fate, it seemed, had been listening in, and had decided I should think no such thing.

He swerved to avoid me, and passed me on the right, our eyes meeting momentarily as he did so. I flicked my eyes to the wing mirror and watched his retreating back. Oh, *great*. What a corker of a headline. Newly appointed head teacher knocks pupil off push-bike. That would *really* just top off my week. But he hadn't lost control at all. In fact, he'd brought the bike to a swift stop, tossed it towards the kerb and was running back down the road towards me, full pelt. I pulled in and stopped. I could already hear him bellowing at me.

'Miss! Miss – *wait*!'

I cut the engine and opened the car door. 'Harry, what on earth do you think you're doing, riding that bike down the middle of the road in the dark? I could have hit you, for goodness' sake!'

'Miss, you've got to help me! Casper's been run over! You've got to come!'

He was clearly agitated. Bobbing up and down on the spot and gesticulating. 'Down in our road! You've got to come now!'

'Casper?'

'My cat!'

I was out of the car by now and placing my hands on his shoulders. The rain was hammering down. Running in tributaries from his fringe to his chin. I pushed my own from my eyes. 'Calm down, Harry. Where?'

'In our road! Just round the corner. He's lying in the road, Miss! I don't know what to do! Please can you come?'

'Okay, Harry. Of course I'll come. Where do you live?'

'It's just round the corner. By there!' He pointed. 'It's not far. But we've got to be quick! *Please.*'

'Get back on your bike, Harry, and I'll follow you round. Go on, then. Get going. I'll be right behind you.'

A couple of turnings later and we'd arrived at the spot. Harry leaped once again from his bike and slung it down against the verge. I parked the car opposite and ran across to join him.

'Here he is. I didn't move him, Miss,' he panted. 'Do you think he's still alive?'

I knelt down to where a cat, a sorry streak of wet fur, was lying motionless close to the kerb. There was a little blood and matted fur around the animal's hip but, although it was inert, I could feel the faint but steady pulsing of his chest beneath my fingers. 'Yes, he's alive, Harry, but I don't know how badly he's hurt. He needs to be taken to a vet. Where's Dad?'

He blinked the rain from his eyes. 'At work.'

'So who's looking after you?'

'No one.'

'*No one?*'

Stupid question. If there had been someone looking after him he wouldn't have been pedalling around Cefn Melin like a maniac, would he?

'Well, Nat is, but she's gone to her English class. She won't be back for ages. She's—'

'Nat? Who's Nat? I thought your nanny was called Liv?'

'No. It's Natali. Without an *e*. Liv was just here while she went back to Hungary. Her sister was ill. But she's back.'

I digested this confusing array of facts and frowned. 'So isn't anyone indoors then?'

He looked distinctly uncomfortable. 'No. I go to Mrs Ogden's when Nat's at her class. But she had to go to Sainsbury's.' He squatted beside me. 'Will Casper be all right?'

'Harry, I really hope so. But he does need to be taken to a vet. When is Mrs Ogden coming back?'

'I don't know.'

'A neighbour then. Or one of your friends' mums, maybe. There must be someone.'

'There isn't! I already went to Daniel's house but they're all out. And Mr Goldman isn't allowed to go in his car on Friday evenings, so I couldn't ask him, and then I saw you and . . . Miss, he might *die*! Can't you take him in *your* car? Please?' His chin was wobbling.

I stood up and looked around me, as if someone

relevant and useful might materialize though the rain. As if. I sighed. What else was there to do?

'All right, Harry. Have you got a blanket indoors or anything?' He nodded rapidly. 'Then go and fetch it, and take your bike back as well, while I try to remember where the nearest vet is. Go on. Be quick.'

And he was. I went back to the car for my mobile, but by the time I'd got as far as dialling directory enquiries, he was already back with a large tartan blanket, which I hurriedly laid out across the back seat. Then I gingerly gathered up the cat (yet another suit for the cleaners) and transferred him to it, while Harry looked on with dismay.

'Right, hop in the back with him out of the rain, and I'll see if I can find a vet.' I dimly recalled that there was an animal hospital a couple of miles away, near the barracks, and I hoped my re-collection was right. It was getting on for six now, but I assumed they must have some sort of after-hours set-up. It had been years since I'd last been to a vet. But Harry tapped my shoulder as soon as I climbed in.

'It's okay, Miss. I know where the vet's is,' he told me. 'He lives up out towards Rudry. The pink house. I know where it is, Miss. He'll be there.'

True to Harry's words, he did know where the surgery was. He'd been only a couple of months back, he told me, when Casper had had mites in his ear. And we were lucky. Evening surgery had only just started, and our sorry bundle meant we were seen straight away.

And we weren't there terribly long. The vet, a Mr Matthews, was perfectly jolly and amiable, but I have long been a good reader of non-verbal language (spending the amount of time I do with small boys and members of the teaching profession) so it was obvious, even without Rolf Harris to do it for us, that I wasn't going to need to ask the sort of penetrating questions that I really didn't want to with Harry standing there.

The vet finished the examination and placed his hands on his hips. 'There's certainly a break,' he said at last, touching Casper's leg. 'And I'll need to take a look inside to see what else. I'll have to keep him in, Harry. See what we can do for the poor chap. How old is he now?'

'Twelve.'

'Twelve! Well, now, that's a pretty good innings, isn't it?' he said gently. 'Goodness, he's even older than you! Now, you get off home and try not to fret. I'll let you know how we're doing.' He glanced at me and we exchanged a grim look.

In the end, I left the surgery my mobile number instead, and extracted a promise that someone would call me on it as soon as there was anything to tell, because Harry, by now, had indeed begun to fret. 'If my dad's not back it'll be hopeless,' he said. 'Nat's *useless* with phones. She never understands what anyone's saying.'

Which was okay by me. I was fretting too. What

the hell was I to do with the poor child? 'And speaking of your father,' I said, 'we need to get hold of him. What time *is* he due home?'

'I don't know. He's working tonight. Not till late, I think. Is Casper going to die, Miss?'

'Oh, Harry, I really, *really* hope not. He's in good hands now. I'm sure Mr Matthews will do the very best he can for him. So. We'd better phone Dad, then, hadn't we?'

'We can't. I haven't got his mobile number. It's at home.'

'Then we need to get *you* home, don't we? We can call him from there. What time did you say your nanny's going to be back?'

'She's *not* a nanny,' he said. 'She's an au pair. And she won't be back for ages. Her class doesn't finish yet.'

'Well, whatever. Mrs Ogden, then. I'm sure she'll be back by now. The main thing's to get you back and out of your wet clothes, and let Dad know what's going on. Don't worry. I'll stay with you till one of them arrives.'

Except that didn't appear to be an option. Once we got back to Harry's house, a Victorian semi with a scruffy front garden, it appeared that we weren't going to be able to get in. We huddled in the porch beside Harry's bike, while the rain continued to slide down.

'But you had a key, Harry. You went in to get the blanket, remember?'

He sniffed as he rootled feverishly in his jeans

76

pockets, of which there were many. Then he stopped. 'Oh, no! I just remembered! I left it in the kitchen!'

'Oh, Harry. *Now* what are we going to do?'

If my tone was less than patient it had a perfect right to be so. Apart from anything else, it was getting on for seven, and I was supposed to be meeting Max and the girls for a pizza at half past. But immediately I'd uttered the words, I regretted them. This was a child of ten, for God's sake. He shouldn't be letting himself in and out of anywhere. And now he'd given up the fight with his emotions and was crying his eyes out. Huge gulping sobs, which made his small shoulders heave. 'I'm sorry,' he wailed. 'I just was so – I forgot to put it back in my pocket.'

I leaned down and scooped him into my arms. 'I know, I know,' I said, rubbing his wet curls. 'I'm sorry for being cross. It's not your fault. Come on. There, there.' But he continued to howl. 'Come on, now, Harry,' I coaxed. 'Think. Is there another key anywhere? You know, like an emergency one, perhaps, that you keep under a flowerpot or something?'

He shook his head sorrowfully. 'I don't know. I don't think so.'

'What about Mrs Ogden, then? Might she have a key? If she looks after you sometimes, then—'

'She doesn't look *after* me.' Despite his distress, I could still hear a trace of indignant defiance in his voice. 'I just have to go there sometimes when

77

Nat's at her class. She lives over the back. But I told you, she's not there!'

He said this as if living over the back was a serious indictment on her worth. 'But she might well be home by now,' I said. 'Come on, we'll get in the car and drive round.'

But the house round the back was in darkness too, and there was no response to the bell. Mrs Ogden was clearly doing a marathon Friday-night shop, and once again I felt anger surge inside me. This was too much. This was bordering on neglect.

'Right,' I said finally, as the empty street stretched ahead, puddled orange from the street-lamps and curtained with rain. 'There's no point in us standing here, is there? We'll drive back to your house and put a note through the door for Natali – we don't want her panicking, do we? And then I'm going to take you back to school with me.'

'To *school*?' He looked anxious.

I checked the time. 'Yes. To school. Mr Huckley will still be there and we can call your father.'

'But I told you, I don't have his mobile number.'

'Yes, but the school does. Come on.'

He nodded and then fell silent for a moment. 'Is Casper really going to be all right, d'you think, Miss?'

His face was a picture of perfect misery. Oh, God. I really, really hoped so.

★   ★   ★

'Good Lord!' said Barry, who was walking across the car park as we pulled up and got out of the car. 'You back? I was just about to lock the front gate.' He blinked at Harry. 'Hi, Hazzer! What you doing here?'

I explained about the cat and the au pair and the neighbour and the key, and we hurried back into school before we got any wetter.

'I'm after Harry's dad's number,' I told him. 'Look, if you want to get home, Mr Huckley, then please go ahead. I can deal with the front door myself.'

He checked the time. 'You're all right for five minutes,' he told me. 'My, but you're wet, Harry. And cold. Look, you're shivering. Run along and find yourself a sweatshirt or something from the lost-property bin, why don't you?'

'I'm all right,' said Harry, sniffing.

'A biscuit and some squash then,' he suggested. Harry looked a little happier.

'I suppose you haven't had any tea, have you?' I added, flicking through the box, the phone already in my hand. Harry shook his head and Barry trotted him off to the staff room. I found the card and dialled but, once again, the phone was switched off.

The rain was hurling itself against my office window and it was cold. By the time I'd left a message on voice-mail and gone to join them in the staff room, I was shivering too. Now we'd stopped rushing about, my damp clothes were cooling fast.

Harry was sitting on the edge of one of the chairs with a glass of squash in his hand and Barry was putting on his coat.

'Any luck?'

'I've had to leave a message. Biscuits?'

'Two digestives and a mini roll.' He smiled over at Harry. 'Both already despatched.' He glanced at the clock. 'Look, I'm going to have to get off now, I'm sorry.'

'Don't worry. You go. I'll lock up the front when we leave.'

'Are you sure? Heating's gone off. It's getting pretty chilly in here.'

'Don't I know it,' I said. And he was right. Harry was shivering pretty constantly now, and it would only get colder. 'No,' I decided. 'This is ridiculous, isn't it? Come on, Harry. Change of plan. You're coming home with me.'

It was gone eight by the time we were safely installed at my flat, and by now, looking down at the forlorn little boy standing self-consciously before me, I was beginning to question whatever cock-eyed version of wisdom had persuaded me that this was the right thing to do. What on earth had I been thinking? The right thing would have been to stay where we were, even if it did mean a case of mild hypothermia. And where *was* his bloody father? I was just formulating a selection of short and pithy phrases for the benefit of Mr Meadows, when my mobile rang. And about bloody time, I thought. But it wasn't him. It was Natali. Who had, it seemed, returned from her class. I knew I could drive Harry straight back there now, but despite the chaos the situation was wreaking on my evening, I was far too angry for sensible options. I'd done it now, for one thing. And for another, it was a good forty-five-minute round trip. And even more compelling than either of those two arguments, I wasn't about to let Mr William bloody Meadows off without him hearing a few words from me. I didn't waste any time in asking Natali just exactly where Harry *should* have been, but told her the situation and that both cat and boy were safe. Harry was right. Her English sounded almost as good as my Venusian, and I wasn't sure that more than one word in five got through, but she seemed to understand that if Harry's father showed up he needed to call me straight away.

I had nothing whatsoever to put Harry in, but after herding him into the bathroom with instructions to shower, I was able to persuade him through the door that the best thing would be if he put his wet clothes outside it so I could put them in the tumble-dryer. In the meantime, I told him, he could put on Max's dressing-gown. And then I called Max.

He answered immediately. 'What's happened to you?'

'Did you get my message?'

'Kind of. What's all this about a cat?'

I explained. 'And now I'm waiting for Harry's dad to get here. We're both soaked through. I'm drying his clothes.'

'*What?* You mean you've taken the kid *home* with you? Are you mad?'

Yes. Very possibly. No. Probably. No. Definitely. 'Yes. But what else was I supposed to do?'

He exhaled. 'So, when will you be here?'

'I don't know. The father hasn't called back yet.'

'But you just said there was someone at home now. Can't you take him back?'

'Max, I just told you. His clothes are in the dryer.'

I could hear the clink of cutlery, the tinny hum of other diners. 'So, do we go ahead?'

'What?'

'Do we order or not?'

He sounded irritable and cross. His usual, perfectly reasonable, Friday-night-weary. Whose daft idea had it been to take the girls out tonight anyway? We should all have been curled up on the sofas with a takeaway. I visualized them sitting there, po-faced and scowling, wishing they could be out with their mates having fun and totting up the extra wicked-stepmother points. 'Yes, why not?' I said. 'I could be another hour.'

'Another *hour*?'

'I might be. I don't *know*, do I? Look, I'll call you as soon as we're sorted, okay? And, Max—'

'What?'

'I'm sorry.'

I could almost hear him switch gear. 'I know, 's okay, sweets. It can't be helped. One of those things. Just get here when you can.'

Harry was out of the shower by the time I'd finished, looking pink and huggable in the dressing-gown.

'Right,' I said briskly. 'Hungry? Thirsty?' He nodded. 'So why don't you go and switch the TV on while I make you something to eat?'

I made him toast and strawberry jam, and a mug of hot chocolate, and when I returned from the kitchen he was framed by the night sky, a small, incongruous form looking out across the balcony to where the lights around the bay twinkled prettily below. The rain, if anything, lent a certain blurred magic to the view.

'It's wicked out there, isn't it?' he said.

'Yes, it is,' I answered, placing the plate and mug on the coffee-table. 'That's why I like living here so much.'

He turned back towards the room. 'It's very tidy.'

'There's no one here to make it messy, is there? I'm out at work all day.'

'Was it messy when your little girl was alive?'

'She didn't live here, Harry. We lived somewhere else then. In London.'

He sat down on the edge of the sofa and picked up a slice of toast. 'I've been to London. Mum and Dad took me to Madame Tussaud's before she died. Have you been there?'

83

'Not for a long time.'

'Does anyone else live here? Does your friend Max live here?'

'Nope. Just little old me.'

He took a bite of toast and chewed for a moment. 'Our house is always messy,' he said. 'Natali's supposed to clean it and stuff, but she's not very good at it.'

I looked at him in some surprise. 'I didn't think ten-year-old boys much worried about mess. It's making it you're best at, isn't it? If the state of the classrooms at the end of the day is anything to go by.'

He looked indignant. 'I'm not messy. Well, a bit, I s'pose. But I like it when my bed's all made. My mum always used to do it. Natali never does.'

Such a little thing. But I could have wept for him. 'Then you must learn to make it yourself,' I said sternly. 'No one will want to marry you, you know, not if you can't do things for yourself.'

He let out a satisfying grunt at this notion. 'Well, I'm *definitely* not doing it, then.'

Will Meadows called ten minutes later, flustered and apologetic and not a little stressed. He was calling from the services, he told me, half-way along the M4, on his way back from London. It was almost another hour before he arrived. By this time Harry was flat out asleep on the sofa and I had wound myself up into three half-hitches and a sheep shank. I let him in, then

84

took him into the kitchen so we wouldn't wake Harry.

He slipped his car keys into his jacket pocket, then stood with his hands resting on a chair back. He had an expression of mild embarrassment on his face. Too mild, to my mind. I could feel the anger rise within me. I was almost too furious to know where to start. But, handily, he did. 'Oh dear,' he said. 'This seems to be becoming a bit of a habit, doesn't it?'

'I sincerely hope not, Mr Meadows,' I said.

'I was in town—'

'But not this town.'

He blinked. 'No. London, I told you. Shepperton. On a shoot.'

'And that's supposed to impress me?'

He blinked again. '*No.*'

'Good. Because it doesn't. You should have been *here.*'

He seemed not to know how best to respond to that one. So he didn't. He put a hand in his pocket again. 'Well,' he said. 'I really can't tell you how grateful I am. And, well . . . I'd better get him home, hadn't I? I'm sure you've got—'

'Hang *on*,' I snapped. 'Just like that? I don't think so. Do you really think I'm going to let you just waltz out of here as if you were simply five minutes late home from work? What on earth do you think you're doing, gallivanting off to London and leaving a ten-year-old child alone in the house?'

85

His eyebrows inched upwards and his chin did likewise. There was a shadow of stubble on it. Long, long day. 'I certainly do not leave Harry alone in the house,' he said quietly. 'He has a perfectly responsible au pair.'

'Who speaks about as much English as a jacket potato. Great. And that's not the point anyway. The point is that she *wasn't* there, was she? And he's zipping round the place on his bike in the dark, completely unsupervised. *And* without a helmet. Supposing he'd had an accident?'

'Oh, right. So you're saying I shouldn't let him out, are you? Christ, he's almost eleven! Or should I keep him in playing tiddlywinks till he's eighteen?'

I knew his confrontational stance was nothing to do with righteous indignation and everything to do with feeling guilty, but I wasn't about to let him off the hook that easily. Tough. I was feeling pretty confrontational myself. I was supposed to be sitting in a restaurant with my soon-to-be husband and my soon-to-be stepdaughters, not standing in my kitchen having stern words with a parent. I got quite enough of that at school. Taking your work home might be part of the job, but taking your pupils home certainly wasn't. It was way off the map. 'Don't be silly,' I snapped. 'Of course he should go out. But there should also be someone at home. And your perfectly responsible au pair wasn't. Did you know she was off at an English class?'

'Of *course* I did! She goes every week. Generally *after* I get home from work. And if I'm working late, she takes Harry round to my neighbour—'

'Well, apparently not this week, because the neighbour wasn't *there*. Christ, couldn't she have missed her English class for one week? Don't you think Harry's welfare is just a tad more important than the state of her syntax?'

'Of course I do! I told you! He was supposed to be round at the bloody neighbour's!'

'Well, he wasn't. The neighbour was at the supermarket, apparently, and your son was roaming the streets. I don't know what arrangement *you* have with her, but Harry clearly has another. One that gives him *carte blanche* to cycle round the streets in the rain when he feels like it. How else do you think he knew the cat had been run over?'

He pushed a hand through his hair. 'Look, that was not how things were supposed to be, okay? As far as I knew, Natali was going to take him round to my neighbour before she went to her class. And that he was going to stay there until she collected him. If that isn't what happened I'll have to find out exactly what *did* happen. But that's for me to sort out, okay? I did not – *do* not – knowingly leave my child without anyone to look after him. What the hell do you take me for?'

Boy, I'd need time to answer that one. 'I'm not suggesting you do,' I said. 'I'm just saying you need to take a good hard look at your childcare arrangements. An au pair is not the same thing as a nanny. Or a childminder, for that matter. Believe me, some of the au pairs I've had dealings with in my time are so witless I wouldn't want to leave them in charge of a hamster.'

'She's not witless. She's perfectly responsible.'

'Oh, right. So how come he's here with me now?'

'I don't *know*. I *told* you. I'll have to find out!'

'Which is exactly why it isn't good enough. He needs *proper* supervision. Not some endless string of girls who aren't much older than he is, with their heads full of boyfriends and God knows what else.'

I must have hit a nerve there because his expression suddenly hardened.

'Look, it may not be perfect but I'm doing my best, okay? Have you any idea how hard it is to find decent childcare for a ten-year-old boy?'

'Oh, come on. It's—'

'No. You clearly don't. Why would you? You forget, I'm a man on my own with a ten-year-old son. You work it out.'

'You found Natali.'

'Only because she lost her last job.'

'Oh, *great*.'

He rolled his eyes. 'Because they *moved*. Look, it may not be ideal, but it's only temporary, and—'

'Exactly. *Exactly!*' I spread my hands, exasperated. He just didn't *see* it. 'But what about childminders?' I said. 'Have you explored that option? If you ring the council you will find that they have a—'

'List of every registered childminder from here to bloody Treorchy. I *know* that. I've already rung most of them. You don't get it, do you? I work difficult hours. Childminders don't want children with fathers who work the sort of hours I do. They want children who get picked up by six every day.'

'Then perhaps you need to think about *changing* your hours.'

'Yeah, right. Just like that.'

'No. Not just like that. But you must surely realize that it's something you need to address.' I exhaled irritably. 'And what about family? Is there no one who could help you out a bit here and there? I can't believe there isn't some way you could—'

'Then perhaps you should think about it a little harder,' he said coldly. 'There is *no* one. My parents live four hundred miles away, and as for my in-laws . . .' He smiled mirthlessly. 'Well,' he said grimly, 'let's just say they're not an option, okay? Here *or* there. This is *real* life. There are no fairy godmothers in this equation. Just me and him. And, like I said, I'm doing the best I can. But what the hell would you know about it anyway? You may spend all day with kids, but let me tell you, bringing them up on your own twenty-four/seven is a very different matter.' He glanced around him. 'Do you *have* any children, Mrs Connors?'

'No. I—'

'I thought so. Perhaps if you did you'd be a little less judgemental.'

Because I didn't know how to deal with that particular parry, a short silence ensued. And then his face suddenly fell. 'Oh, shit. God, I'm sorry. That was out of order.' He frowned. 'Look, I apologize. I forgot. I did know. I'm sorry. Harry told me.'

'Apology accepted,' I said stiffly. 'And you know something? You're absolutely right. I don't know. Of course I don't know. But there's plenty I do know, Mr Meadows. I do know, for instance, that however difficult it may be – and, believe me, I do appreciate your difficulties – that child in there needs a whole lot more support than he's getting right now. There's only so much we can do at school. We need a bit of effort on your part as well.'

He looked so like Harry then. So defiant in defeat. 'Look,' he said slowly. 'Please don't talk to me about effort. I told you. I am *doing* my *best*.'

I squared up to him then, all out of patience. 'So you keep saying. But, frankly, your best isn't good enough, Mr Meadows. Shall I tell you something? Shall I tell you what *should* have happened tonight? I should have phoned social services, that's what.' I paused to let him take this in. Which he did. Because his mouth dropped open and he gaped at me. 'That is what I should have done,' I said. 'Just as soon as I found him. And they – not me – would have collected Harry. Is that what you would have wanted?' I gave him another moment to digest this. I had barely digested it myself. 'No,' I said, echoing his head-shake. 'Quite. So instead I've put my job on the line by doing something that is *highly* inappropriate, and left myself open to God alone knows what repercussions. It's not right that he should be here. You do know that, don't you?'

'Repercussions? What repercussions can there possibly be? I'm very grateful to you for looking after him. I *told* you.'

I rolled my eyes. What would *he* know about it? 'Look,' I said. 'You may think you're doing your best but he needs *better*. He needs stability and security. Continuity of care. Not some endless string of girls. There's no point in us trying to keep him focused in school if he hasn't any boundaries at home. He *needs* boundaries. But most of all he needs to come home from school and have someone to *guide* him. Someone to *listen* to him. Someone who actually *cares*.'

Like a mother, perhaps? His eyes burned into mine and it hit me with a jolt. Damn. *Damn.* Wrong thing to say. I cursed my insensitivity. My day for award-winning *faux-pas*, it seemed. Knocked his little barb right into a cocked hat.

'You really think—' His eyes widened. 'Christ. You honestly think I don't *know* that?' Still he stared at

91

me, his expression incredulous. 'You honestly think I don't care?'

And then, without the slightest warning, he sat abruptly at the kitchen table and covered his face with his hands. It was almost as if his legs had given way beneath him.

'Mr Meadows, I'm sorry. But it needed to be—'

He raised a hand to silence me, and I bridled again, but then I saw the action for what it was. I realized, to my horror, that it wasn't that he wouldn't speak, it was simply that he *couldn't* speak. That he was crying. Or, rather, trying hard not to. Trying to hold himself together sufficiently that he could retain at least a small scrap of dignity.

But he was coming close to losing the battle. I stared at him for several seconds, not sure what to do. I could see tiny movements in his shoulders, the bob of his Adam's apple in his throat. The tremor in his fingers where they spanned his brow, half hidden beneath the twisted skeins of his rain-dampened hair. This was an all too intimate, all too cruel humiliation. And much of it, I knew, was my fault. I had gone way too far. I'd been cruel.

I stood a moment more, torn between my instinctive urge to comfort him, and my rational reluctance to make him feel any worse.

Instinct prevailed. I pulled out the other chair. I didn't touch him, just sat down opposite him. 'I'm sorry,' I said quietly. 'I wasn't thinking. I have no right to judge you. I'm *not* judging you. I just want to *help*. That's all. I want to help Harry through this.'

It seemed that an age passed, but eventually he lowered his hands and laced them together in front of him on the table. I still couldn't see his face because it was hidden by his hair. Moments passed. I let them.

'I'm sorry about that,' he said finally, his voice level.

'Really, there's nothing to apologize for.'

'It's just that sometimes—'

'I know.'

'Yes,' he said quietly, turning to face me now. 'I don't doubt you do.' I waited for him to say something else but he didn't. He pushed the chair back instead and stood up. 'Look,' he said. 'I'm very grateful for everything you've done. And I do know what you're saying. I will try to – well.' He glanced at the clock on the wall. 'It's getting late. I'm sure you've got things to do. We'd better leave you in peace.'

That was the moment when my heart got my head in a half-nelson, because almost before I'd even gathered my senses I found myself telling him to do no such thing. That I'd make him a coffee. That Harry's clothes weren't yet dry. That I wasn't in a rush to go anywhere. That there was no earthly need for him to go.

'I don't even much like pizza,' I said.

He was patting his pockets for his keys. 'I beg your pardon?'

'Pizza. I'm not big on pizza. I mean it's *okay*. You know, in a slumming-it, watching-a-movie kind of okay. But I'm not that fussed. You know?'

He looked embarrassed. 'Er . . . right.'

'So I really have nothing to rush off for. So if you feel you want to talk about it . . .' I spread my palms. 'Well, I'm here and I'm happy to listen. That's all.'

He shifted his weight from one foot to the other. Then shook his head. 'No, thanks, but we've imposed enough on your evening as it is. I – well, I do appreciate your concern. But no.'

'I'm not saying this to be polite,' I said. 'It's just that, well . . . well, I get the feeling you have no one to talk to.' He looked a little shocked at this. 'You know. Family,' I rattled on. 'Friends. A support network. Just bits and bobs Harry's told me.'

He seemed distinctly uneasy now. A feeling I knew only too well. As if he'd bared more than enough of his soul for one evening. That I was trying to take him somewhere he didn't want to go.

Yet still I persevered. I couldn't seem to help myself. 'It's just that when my daughter died . . . Oh, I know it's not quite the same thing, but when you lose someone you love . . . well, grieving is grieving when all's said and done, isn't it? And when Emily died, I . . . well, I was like you. Most of the time I found it difficult to, well . . . really communicate with anyone about it. Not properly, you know? Sometimes it's almost like there's a sheet of plate glass between you and the rest of the world, and—'

But he was shaking his head now. Moving towards the kitchen door.

'No,' he said firmly. 'Thanks for the offer, but no. Look.' He stopped and turned round. 'I do mean it. *Thank* you. I'm grateful. Very grateful indeed. But,' he paused, dark eyes fixed on mine now, 'it really isn't any of your business.'

He said it terribly politely. *Terribly* politely. But it still felt like a punch in the face.

Enough of one, certainly, to bring me to my senses. It was almost nine o'clock and I was supposed to be somewhere else. Back in my own life. Not interfering in his.

I took him back to the living room and stood there, stiff and embarrassed, while he gathered Harry into his arms. Then I held the front door open while he carried him out onto the landing, looking at the carpet so I wouldn't catch his eye.

'Hang on,' I said, remembering, as he started down the stairwell. 'I'll get his clothes out of the dryer and I'll follow you down.'

'Don't worry,' he called up crisply. 'I'll come back for them.'

I sprinted back into the flat. I could hear the distant buzz of my mobile from the living room. Max, most probably. Wondering where the hell I'd got to. I was going to be *persona non grata* with

95

extra pepperoni by now. But it wasn't too late. I could still get there for dessert.

But it wasn't Max. It was Mr Matthews, the vet.

Will Meadows filled the doorway just as I disconnected. And saw my expression. 'What is it?' he said.

'That was the vet on the phone,' I replied. 'I'm so sorry. Casper didn't make it.'

CHAPTER 6

Saturday morning, and my head is in an altogether different species of wrestling hold on
account of my inability to know what I'm
like. The three-quarters empty bottle of wine (oh
dear) is still sitting on the kitchen worktop, along
with the three-quarters empty glass (oh dear, oh
dear), the three-quarters empty box of mint
Matchmakers (oh *dear*) and the seven-eighths
empty tumble-dryer. The towel that I used to rub
Harry's head dry is still tongue-hanging half in and
half out of the door.

'Yes or no?' says Max, irritable without his
dressing-gown. 'If you'd rather I didn't meet up with
her you only have to say. I don't want this to turn
into an issue. I just want to get this bloody nonsense
sorted out once and for all. Jesus! As if there's any
way I wouldn't want my own daughters at my
wedding. What planet is the woman on, for God's
sake?' He tugs at the cord of his pyjama bottoms
and follows me into the kitchen. 'Hey, you all right?'

I went to the restaurant as soon as they'd gone
– ditched the suit, pulled on jeans, didn't stop for
a shower, just got in the car and drove there

through the teeming rain. I went because the flat suddenly felt so empty after they'd left, so full of woe and ghosts and uncomfortable echoes, that not to have gone would have plunged me into the sort of self-pitying torpor that I have spent the last eight years trying not to remember how to do. So I went. I had an ice-cream sundae with extra mocha sauce and Tara told me she liked my jumper. Which was progress.

To say that I'd had a number of misgivings about the events of the previous evening would be like saying a tornado is a bit of a breeze. True, almost all of them centred on the five minutes of largely insignificant conversation I had had with the man who had been trying not to weep in my kitchen, but it's often the ostensibly insignificant details that have the most significance of all. He had told me it was none of my business. Why is that phrase always so difficult to hear? It was wholly insignificant that he'd told me his wife's death was none of my business, and monumentally insignificant that it caused me to feel piqued. But even so. Even *so*. And the cat had died and now Harry would be bereft all over again, and I wished so very badly that Casper had made it through the night. But why, oh, why hadn't I just done what I should have? If I'd driven Harry home once the au pair had called I wouldn't have launched my cruise-missile invective, and I wouldn't have had to suffer the indignity of having been told *anything* was none of my business. I could have hauled Will

Meadows into my office on Monday and told him he was feckless in a professional manner. In a suit, with my stern face on, and from the safe haven of my desk.

I flip-flop my way across the kitchen and grope in the drawer for the packet of Ibuprofen. There is also the small matter of propriety. God. As *always*. Though propriety is probably the wrong word. Protocol. Procedure. Whatever you want to call it, the fact is that I shouldn't have taken a pupil home with me in the first place. According to Rule 117, sub-section 11, clause B and a quarter, it was highly inappropriate for me to take a pupil home. Would have been even if a blizzard had been raging. I have spent a good deal of the night considering this, because the Child Protection Act is one that any intelligent person in a professional capacity ignores at their peril. It is not a sensible thing to do. It makes that person vulnerable to all sorts of un-savoury possibilities and leaves them open to what-ever mad accusations the child in question – or their parents, more correctly – might, for whatever reason, lay at your door. It is a position one does not put oneself in lightly. It is unprofessional. It is very bad practice.

No matter that it was absolutely the right thing to do. No matter that the alternative wasn't.

I turn on the tap and fill a glass with water, then flip-flop across to the table and sit down. 'I shouldn't have done it,' I tell Max.

He rolls his eyes and pulls out the other chair. He

knows what I'm talking about. 'Too right you shouldn't,' he agrees. He sits down opposite me and puts his elbows on the table top. 'Look,' he says. 'This boy. This Harry. Don't you think you're getting just a little bit too involved with him, Holly? I mean, be honest. Would you have done all that last night if it had been any other kid?'

I shrug. How should I know? I haven't been in that position with any other kid. But I know what he's getting at just as much as he does. And it's not only Harry now, either. I have spent almost as many hours fretting about his father. There's a saying – a kind of creed – in the teaching profession: if you want to get your head round a child, you can do a lot worse than take a good long look at the parents. And now I have, I can't stop fretting. Feeling guilty. Feeling sad. *Feeling*, full stop. Not good. And not even helpful. His problems aren't any of my business, as he made very clear. But Harry's *are* – in so far as they affect his school life. 'But he's *not* any other kid, Max. I know he's not my responsibility, but he's formed an attachment to me and I think I can help him. So I *should* help him, shouldn't I?'

'Look, I appreciate *that*. It's your job, isn't it? But there's help and there's help, as you found out last night. I'm just saying you don't want to get too personally involved with a problem kid, that's all.' He gestures towards the living room. I can't see, but I know what at. At the heap of paperwork still sitting on the coffee-table. 'You have plenty on your plate as it is.'

I know what he's saying, but it doesn't change anything. I have *this* on my plate now as well. 'He's not a problem kid, Max. He's a kid with some problems. There's a difference.' I rub my hands across my eyes and groan. 'God, I shouldn't have drunk all that wine last night.' I get up and go round to where he's sitting across the table and weave my arms round his neck. 'No,' I say, decided. 'You're absolutely right. It's the weekend. I'm off duty. I shall put it all out of my mind.'

He tips his head back against my chest and I can feel the prickles of his hair through my pyjama top. *His* pyjama top. 'I'm sorry,' I say. 'Subject emphatically closed. Right. About Catherine. Look, I really don't mind, okay? I think it'll be good if you talk to her. Whatever. Take her out to lunch or something. Do whatever you feel you need to. It's going to be a perfect day and there's nothing she can do that will spoil it for us. But if she won't come round you must promise me you'll back off a bit and give in gracefully if you have to. It's crazy to have the girls upset, isn't it? If she's going to give them hell for being there, we'll have to sort something else out, won't we? Take them out for a treat in the evening or something. It's difficult for them, Max, being pulled both ways all the time.'

He reaches his own arms up and pulls my head down towards his.

'Take *her* to lunch?' He kisses me. 'She can bloody well whistle. Besides, I know a woman not a million miles from here who deserves taking out to lunch a *whole* lot more.'

'That sounds nice.'

'But not just yet. First we have to implement your hangover cure.'

'Oh, yes, Dr Stapleforth? And what would that involve?'

'What do you think, sweets? Us going straight back to bed.'

In the interest of professional detachment, I did not seek out Harry as soon as he returned to school on Monday morning, but John sent him along to my office just before playtime anyway, as he had brought in something for me. A carrier-bag with Max's dressing-gown in it. I thanked him and put it on the floor beside my desk, hoping John hadn't asked what it was.

'How are you?' I asked him.

'I'm okay,' he replied, shrugging. Then he pointed to the bag. 'There's a card in there,' he said. 'From my dad.'

'Dad okay?' I asked, before I could stop the words from emerging. Rats. It wasn't my business how 'Dad' was feeling, was it?

'He's sad,' Harry said, after some moments of deliberation. 'But okay. He's not *sad* sad, like he is about Mum and that. He's going to go and get the ashes from the vet's this afternoon.'

I did a double-take. 'Ashes?'

'Casper's ashes. They put them in a box for you.

Did you know? You can have their name engraved on a thing on the front.' I nodded. 'Beast, isn't it? Did you have your little girl cremated?'

I hadn't. I couldn't bear the picture the idea put in my head. I shook it now. 'No.'

'My mum was cremated. We put her ashes in some flowers in the park. We're going to get Casper's ashes and put them there too.'

'I'm sure she'd like that.'

He nodded. 'She will. She can have Casper to keep her company now, can't she?'

He gave every impression of having bounced back, as children so often seem to. But I knew that by now he had probably learned to keep his grief tucked away where no one could haul it out for inspection. Like a conker in his pocket. 'Yes, she can,' I agreed. 'And I'm sure she'd like that very much.'

'And I've written her a letter. And told her all about it. I told her how you took us to the vet's and everything.'

'Good, Harry. *Good*. I'm glad you've done that.' I thought for a moment. 'Look, now you're here, sit down for a minute, will you? I need you to tell me the truth about Friday. It's very important, okay?' He looked glum at this, but perched him-self on the chair as directed. 'I need to know exactly who was supposed to be looking after you on Friday evening, Harry. I know you told me Mrs Ogden was supposed to be, but if that was the case, I want you to tell me why she went to the supermarket and left you riding around on your bike. Okay?'

'But she—'

'Think before you answer, Harry. Do you think it's likely I'd believe that Mrs Ogden, who I know is a very responsible grown-up, would go off to the supermarket and leave you on your own?'

'No.'

'So how come you told me that was what happened?' He was silent for a moment, chewing his bottom lip and making little semi-circles on the rug with the toe of his trainer. 'Only I spoke to Mrs Ogden first thing this morning and she says she'd spoken to your father earlier in the day, and that she'd *thought* she was going to have you, but that when she called Natali to see if you were going to have tea with her or not, you told her that Natali wasn't going to her class after all. Well?'

He stopped playing with the floor and pushed out his lower lip. 'But I *hate* going there.'

'And why is that?'

'Because Lauren and Katie suck.'

Lauren Ogden was Mrs Ogden's daughter. I had established that there were two Ogden children in the school. Lauren was in Harry's year but I didn't know her well enough to judge whether she sucked or not. Which probably meant she did. We had several Katies. I made a note to myself to find out which one. Not that it mattered much, really. Most girls suck when you're a boy and you're ten.

'And does your father know how much you hate going there?'

He shook his head. 'No.'

'You haven't told him?'

'No.'

'Why, Harry?'

'Because he'll tell me not to be stupid. He doesn't understand about Lauren and Katie.'

'You don't know that, Harry. You try him, okay? You might be surprised.' He shrugged. 'Anyway, how come Natali didn't answer the phone?'

'Because she was in the shower.'

'So as far as she was concerned you were still going round there.'

He nodded. 'I pretended I was.'

'But doesn't Natali normally take you?'

He looked affronted at this. '*No*. I'm nearly eleven. I walk.'

'Which is quite old enough to know that it's wrong to tell lies, Harry.'

He stuck out his lip again. 'But I *hate* it there. And I'm big enough to stay at home now anyway.'

'I'm sure you think you are but that's beside the point. You weren't *at* home, were you? Suppose something had happened to you?'

His expression told me that he'd heard this already. I didn't doubt it one bit. 'I'm sorry, Miss,' he said.

'And I'm sorry about Casper, Harry. And I'm also very glad I was there when I was, believe me. But I want you to promise me you won't do something like that again, okay?' He nodded again. 'Because if you want to be trusted – want Dad, and Natali, and all the teachers here, for that matter, to treat you like a grown-up – then it's up to you to prove that they *can* trust you, isn't it?' He'd heard all this before as well. And recently. I could tell. 'Now then,' I said. 'Back to class.' I stood up. 'Before Mr Patterson thinks I've decided to keep you locked up for the rest of the day. And don't think I wouldn't.'

He smiled a wan smile. He was up and almost out of the door when he turned again. 'Miss, can I ask you something?'

'Yes, Harry. What?'

'Is sterile like clean?'

'Sterile? Yes, it is. Very much so. If something is sterile it's super-super-clean. Even under a microscope. No bugs or germs at all. You sterilize instruments when you do operations so the person you're operating on can't pick up any bacteria or viruses. And babies' bottles. That sort of thing.'

He nodded. 'I thought it was something like that.'

'Why d'you ask?'

'Oh, it was just something my dad said. About your flat.'

After Harry had gone I picked up the bag with the dressing-gown in it and pulled out the envelope inside. It contained a small square card with a watercolour picture of a bunch of anemones on it. Inside, it read,

Dear Mrs Connors, thank you so much for your care and concern on Friday evening and please accept my sincere apologies for the stress and inconvenience you have been caused. I have spoken to Harry and he assures me he will not do anything so irresponsible again. I am also currently looking into alternative college arrangements for my au pair and I am confident something like this will not happen again. Once again, my apologies. Yours truly, Will Meadows.

He'd underlined 'happen'. I could hear his voice say it. I shut the card and put it away in a drawer. He wasn't my business, after all.

CHAPTER 7

I don't know why it bothered me so much, but it did. Okay, taken on its own, it not being my business was fair enough. Patently, not everything *is* my business and Will Meadows had a perfect right, an inalienable right, to tell me so, even if I did feel affronted about it. So that was okay. I could cope with it. Just. But there was also the small matter of me having bared my soul to *him*. Okay, not much, but even so, I had tipped the balance and brought about an uncomfortable inequity in our relationship. Made myself feel vulnerable. Embarrassed, too. Okay, only a teensy bit, and to someone who probably couldn't give a fig, but every time I thought about what I'd said to him about me, I cringed. It was, I fancied (albeit somewhat prosaically), akin to walking down the high street with my skirt caught in my knickers. I felt I'd exposed too much of myself. And this to a man who, it now transpired, had decided my flat was sterile. A double insult. A double whatever it was that blighted one's generally good opinion of oneself. I was not a helper, a carer, a person blessed with intelligence, grace, compassion, wisdom, a posh office, a few letters after my name and all that. No. I had been unmasked as a fraud. I was the very worst kind of superior, know-it-all, interfering do-gooder, and with a bad eye for colour as well. Or carpets. Or even cushions. How did I know? What exactly *had* he meant?

'Oh, come on,' said Toni. 'It's not *that* bad. I've heard a lot worse.'

'About me?'

'No. Not about *you*. God. You're paranoid, you are! Here, take that and chuck it in the bin for me, will you?'

Half-term and I'm in hospital. Not as a patient, but as Keiran's so busy, I've agreed to come along for the ride while Toni has her latest MOT. It's been a long time since I've been in an ante-natal clinic, obviously. And things have changed a great deal. There's a sort of DIY system in operation round our way these days. You turn up with your notes, and before you see the doctor, you go off and weigh yourself. Then you check your urine sample using one of the strips provided. Toni's urine, the little squares on the strip inform us, is negative for anything nasty today. I put the strip into the bin and follow her back to the waiting room. There's a film showing on a video about how to put a baby on your breast when you've had a Caesarian. You tuck them under your arm. I remember it well.

'Anyway,' Toni says, sitting down with a huff and a puff, 'why would you care? I don't imagine Will

Meadows is the last word in style gurus, do you? And why would you worry about what *he* thinks of your soft furnishings? Hey, he's a sweet bloke, but he's still a bloke, isn't he?'

I wished she wouldn't persist in this 'sweet bloke' line of hers. He was all sorts of things but he wasn't a 'sweet bloke'. Not to me, anyway. He thought I was sterile. Well, sort of. I shifted in my seat and crossed my legs irritably. 'But it would be okay if he'd just said, oh, I don't know, that it wasn't his sort of thing or something. But *sterile*. It's a bit of an emotive word, isn't it? It's like he's really saying something about *me*. And after all the bloody time and attention I've given his son. I mean it's a bit off, isn't it?'

'But you don't *know* what he said, Hol. Just the one word, remember. Perhaps he lives in a tip and this Harry of yours started prattling on about how grand your place was and—'

'*Grand?* My flat? What's grand about it?'

'Okay, okay. Don't get touchy. Wrong word. Smart. Stylish. Chic. *Homes and Gardens*. Whatever. The point is that you don't know the circumstances. And you obviously really intimidate the poor guy. He even said as much, didn't he? Don't forget that.'

I was still stalled on chic. 'That's rubbish, Toni. Did he look intimidated to you when he saw us? I don't think so.' And then the picture of him sitting at my kitchen table resurfaced. Had *I* done that? Really? Surely not. Surely it was simply the—

'Well, I *do*,' she persisted, cutting through my thoughts and, in doing so, reminding me not to think them in the first place. 'And don't look so shocked. You *can* be intimidating. Once you're in character, you'd probably intimidate me if I didn't know what you wear under your skirts.'

'Support tights and sensibly big pants. Always.'

'Utter rubbish. Anyway, enough of your self-indulgent whining, woman.' Only Toni can say things like that to me and get away with it, which is probably why I love her so much. 'I have something very, very important to ask you.'

'Which is?'

'Which is . . . since we're here, and it seems a good place to do it, I wanted to ask you a very big favour. If you'd consider being my birth partner, in fact.'

'Me? But what about Kei—'

'No! Don't say a word! *Wait!*' I waited. 'Keiran and I were talking about it last night and we've reached the conclusion that he would be best employed in a mainly external-cum-consultative role.'

'Come again? What sort of a role is that?'

'One where he waits outside while I give birth and then the midwife goes out and consults him. *Just* outside, mind you. Not getting slaughtered in the Dog and Trouserleg or anything. I do want him *there*. Of course I do. But in a strictly hands-off capacity. I mean, he's keen and all that, but he's not terribly good with body parts and screaming and I don't want to have to be worrying that he's going to throw up all over the staff. Plus I read an article the other day that said that women who have other women as their birth partners do statistically way better on the agony front than the ones who just wheel in their other halves. And I'm all for that. Wouldn't you be? Anyway – no, don't say anything yet – I thought long and hard about it, because I am all too aware that this might be something you won't feel very comfortable with, what with Ems and everything, and I wouldn't want you to say yes to it if it would cause you even the tiniest amount of *angst*, but there is no one, *no one*, I would rather have holding my hand and I would be eternally grateful if you said yes. There. I've finished. You can speak now. What d'you say?'

'Oh, Toni, it would be an honour. A joy, in fact.'

'Really?'

'Yes, *really*. I can't think of anything more lovely.'

'You won't find it difficult?'

'What's to find difficult?'

'You know very well.'

'Well, that's just where you're wrong. I'm not made of porcelain. Well, perhaps I used to be, but when I broke I went and got myself mended. Refired in the kiln that is getting over things. Right?'

'Get you! You're exceptionally philosophical today. Hold up. That's me. You want to come in and have a prod?'

★   ★   ★

112

Dorothy went to Montpellier for half-term. Her son, his wife and their two children live there, in a *Year in Provence*-style rustic French villa, though he doesn't write books. He makes wrought-iron tables. She hasn't brought me back a table, though she threatens to often. Instead she's brought truffle oil and a big box of chocolates, and she says I look like I've been working too hard. 'So what did you get up to?' she asks me, over muffins, Sunday night.

I'd quite like to tell her I've spent much of it fretting about Harry and Will bloody Meadows and being called sterile and feeling all agitated about having made him cry. I wish I felt I could, because I'm sure she would have something soothing and sensible to tell me, but as I can't quite bring *myself* to believe that's what I've mainly been doing, let alone her, I decide not to. Instead I say, 'Er, let me see. Worked on the school development plan, had my highlights done, went and had a facial with Toni, worked on the school development plan, bought a blow-torch, torched – no, incinerated – some crème brûlées with it – dark muscovado is *not* a good idea, I have to tell you, Dorothy . . . er, worked on the school development plan, went with Max to look at a hotel just outside Usk . . . er . . . did I mention the school development plan?'

'What exactly *is* a school development plan?' she asks reasonably. 'It seems to loom very large in your life.'

So instead I tell her about school, about John Patterson and my suspicions about him, and how frustrating the whole situation is at work with him, and how I'm not feeling on top of things yet, and how the job has turned out to be so much more than I thought it would be and that suddenly I don't feel I have anything like as much wisdom as I thought I had, and lots of other get-it-off-your-chest stuff like that.

'And how's your tragic widower?' she asks me, once I've finished.

'Pardon?' I say straight back, eyes wide. 'My *who*?'

But Dorothy just smiles and sips her tea.

CHAPTER 8

And now I'm back in my suit and *in situ*, and the world is full of daffodils and sunshine and the promise of spring. But my own spring of vernal enthusiasm is soon to be tapped, because almost the very first thing that happens on Monday morning (the actual first being that I spill half a mug of tea over the school development plan) is a fight in the playground at playtime.

The first I know of it is when Glenda, looking altogether the worse for having apparently spent her half-term having root-canal work and stippling her lean-to, bursts into my office. 'There's been an incident,' she pants. 'Can you come?'

Which I do, of course, to find John Patterson (looking all the worse for having presumably spent his half-term working on his presentation for yet another interview and/or in clinches with Clemency) playing post-match referee between the two protagonists, who are, in no particular order of exasperatingness, one Owen Rhys-Woodruff and one Harry Meadows. Oh, joy. What a surprise. What a lovely start to the rest of the term. As I approach, sending onlookers skittering for cover, I see that the former has a bloody nose and is crying and the latter – dry-eyed – sports a badly ripped sweatshirt and an expression of still simmering rage.

'Thank you, Mr Patterson,' I say, glaring hard at both of them. 'Mrs Heaven, would you take Owen and Harry to the medical room, please? I'll be along in a few moments. Thank *you*!'

Just two things form the main tenet of the post-fisticuffs protocol. One is that you always conduct the interviews with a witness, and two is that you work on the need-to-know principle. The principle being that in almost every case where ten-year-old boys are concerned, all you need to know is that everything they tell you will be lies.

Nevertheless, and as John is my witness, I go through the usual homily about telling the truth before fixing Owen – to whom I have granted first audience – on the end of the sort of sympathetic, understanding, motherly gaze that is designed to disarm, and as such stands the best chance, albeit still a slim one, of eliciting at least some vague semblance of the facts.

'So, Owen,' I ask him nicely, 'why were you fighting?'

'He hus *hing* he!' he says, through his tissue. 'He hing he hirst! It hog *hin*!' Hmm. Yes. This much I do believe. It is not Owen's style. Way too direct.

'And why do you think Harry hit you?' I ask.

He lowers the tissue. 'Dunno, Miss,' he grunts.

We go on in this vein for a few unproductive minutes before I usher him out and haul Harry in.

He does little to flesh out the facts with a selection of now standard Harry staples. ('He was bothering me, Miss, he was annoying me, Miss, I don't know, Miss, I don't remember, Miss, he's a liar, Miss, I'm saying nothing without my solicitor present, Miss. And am I not, pray, entitled to a telephone call?')

No, the facts, as is often the way in such travails, come from the witnesses John and I have gathered up. Girls, I'm very pleased to see. Girls, to a man. Girls are always ready to dish the dirt. I think it's called having good communication skills.

What happened, it transpires, is that Harry had been crying. Had been doing so, here and there, before half-term as well. 'About his cat, Miss. And Owen's been, like, *really* nasty. He swore, Miss. He called Harry the F-word this morning. And he hid his lunchbox behind the computer. We saw him. We told him, Miss. Didn't we? We told him we'd tell.'

Hmm. Much good *that* did. After I had finished the interviews, written up the incident report and meted out a unilateral 'outside my office every playtime till Thursday' punishment, I sat down at my desk and rang Will Meadows to let him know what had happened. I half hoped he'd be un-available somewhere so I wouldn't have to speak to him. So I could huff and harrumph my way back to feeling self-righteous and vindicated about having given him hell, instead of what I did feel (and kept coming back to *ad nauseam*), which was that, with every justification in the world, he ob-viously didn't think much of me. Which made me just – damn it – so *mad* with myself. Because, well, so *what* what he thought of me? Why the hell did it matter? It was in *my* good offices that *he* needed to be, wasn't it? Not the other way round. But he answered his mobile on the second ring, and his voice, deep and polite and full of concern, had me right back in Wicked Witch of the West Land again.

I told him that Harry had been involved in a fight, that he wasn't to worry, that Harry was okay bar the odd bruise, that it was nothing to be too concerned about, that another child had, according to what I'd elicited, been taunting him over the loss of his cat, that I had spoken to both boys, that I had explained to Harry that if Owen was troubling him he should have gone to his teacher (yeah, right), or to me, or a dinner lady, or a friend – told *someone* – and that losing your temper and getting involved in fights was never the right way to deal with your problems and that I hoped this would be the first and last time I would have to have him in my office about it, that I hoped he *would* come to me if he had any more difficulties of that nature, that they had made up (well, sort of), and that, well, he might want to sit Harry down and have a chat with him about it this evening. Just see if he might open up a bit. Talk about the importance of managing his anger. Reiterating what I'd said to him earlier about *telling* someone. Talking it through a bit. That sort of thing.

I'd said almost all of it before he said anything much back.

'I'm very sorry to hear that,' was what he did say. And he sounded it too. Sounded so, so sad. 'But what about the other boy? Is he okay?'

At which point, taken that he should bother to ask, I surprised myself by deciding to forgive him unreservedly on the germ front. 'Yes, he's fine,' I reassured him. 'Just a nosebleed.'

'Good. Right. Will do. I'll sit him down and have a good talk to him this evening. Thank you for calling.' And he rang off.

I put down the phone feeling strangely flustered and upset.

So, to cheer myself up, I rang Mrs Rhys-Woodruff. And she went, 'Eek! Oh! Oh, my baby! Shall I come and get him? Oh! Eek! Oh, oh, *oh*! How could you let something like this *happen*? That dreadful *boy*! Oh! Oh, my poor lamb! Is he wounded? Oh! And with his piano examination coming up and everything! Oh, oh!'

And so on. I wondered if perhaps I should quiz Owen further and get both families in so we could sort this thing out. But not twenty minutes later her husband called and insisted on seeing me forthwith.

I don't do forthwith, as a matter of principle. And the principal reason for invoking such a principle is that Rule 68, sub-section B (amended) makes it clear that where parents like the Rhys-Woodruffs are concerned it is never a good idea to promote the impression that you generally have nothing better to do. And if it doesn't say that, it certainly should.

'Fine,' I said firmly. 'Wednesday would suit me.'

Wednesday it is, then, and when Wednesday comes along, it occurs to me that every teacher should have a Mr and Mrs Rhys-Woodruff in their life. Indeed, they should be wheeled out often, as part of the training. Mr and Mrs Rhys-Woodruff are the yardstick against which every other set of parents can be measured and found not to be wanting. Naturally I am not afraid of Mr and Mrs Rhys-Woodruff. Individually, jointly, in whatever configuration. I am not afraid of Mr Rhys-Woodruff because he is a buffoon, and I am not afraid of Mrs Rhys-Woodruff because she isn't scary. She's all vapours and swoons and hand-flying-to-mouth stuff. Though Mrs Rhys-Woodruff, I think, with childish satisfaction, is a little bit wary of me.

Today I have the full complement. A brace of Rhys-Woodruffs in my office. And though it's pleasing to go with the wildfowl analogy, I suspect that within the confines of their own cosy world-view, it is not they but I that am the quarry this afternoon, and that the best-case scenario for the Rhys-Woodruff camp is to take me home slain, between a Labrador's teeth.

But I'm prepared for them. I am also minus Glenda (more root-canal work – does she sport a Grand Union?), minus John (another interview), and plus Mrs Cairns, supply teacher from Hades, so I am also, it has to be said, rather testy. It's off-season for terrorizing teachers today.

'Good morning,' I say brightly, as I usher them in. 'Thank you so much for coming in to see me today.'

I haven't said this with the intention of putting them off guard. They know as well as I do that it was they who demanded to see me. But it obviously does, because Mrs Rhys-Woodruff glances nervously at her husband.

I take my long hard look at the parents. Owen Rhys-Woodruff is a gifted child. I suppose it's not unreasonable to think that I might, one day, come round to believing there is a nugget of truth in there somewhere, because I have certainly been told it often enough. He's only difficult because he's bright. He's only moody because he's not being stretched. He's only struggling with his language skills because he has been at the mercy of indifferent teachers who fail to understand his intellectual frustration and, *quel surprise*, how very gifted he is.

I know Owen Rhys-Woodruff has a gift in there somewhere. Every child does. But it is buried beneath many layers of unrealistic expectation – a reclusive beast, fearful of its worth to the world. I also know, because I have done lots of research and have now had it corroborated by at least three other, independent, if diminutive, witnesses, that Owen Rhys-Woodruff's favourite pastime right now is not to seek out and nurture that gift but, rather, to chant 'Harry Meadows loves Mrs Connors' whenever the opportunity presents itself and 'gay boy w★★ker' whenever time is short.

Strange to think that in this John Patterson and I share an edgy but definite accord. Much as Harry gets up his nose and under his skin, Owen is the bane of his existence, the Rhys-Woodruffs, *en masse*, his nemesis.

I consider Mr Rhys-Woodruff as he lowers his very large frame into one of my very small chairs. Mr Rhys-Woodruff may, for all I know, have the intellect of Einstein. But the man I see before me exhibits little evidence of breathtaking mental acuity. He is bullish and bombastic and, whatever his IQ, he has the emotional intelligence of an ant. Less, even. At least ants work as a team. Mr Rhys-Woodruff is the sole proprietor of Absolutely Bathrooms, *the* name in stylish sanitaryware. Thus Mr Rhys-Woodruff is no doubt well versed in the social mores of the domestic-plumbing industry. I don't know what those are exactly, though it presumably involves the sort of skills that Mr Rhys-Woodruff excels in: being *the* name in anything must be testimony to that. He is also a bully and a bore and a tyrant. But Mr Rhys-Woodruff gives the school money. And is big golfing pals with Mr Pugh.

Mr Pugh is currently the chair of the governors. This is how it works and it was ever thus.

Mrs Rhys-Woodruff, in happy synchronicity with Mr Rhys-Woodruff, is similarly engaged in commercial endeavour. When not zooming round Cardiff taking Owen places to better himself, she runs a little interior-design outfit called Just Penny (which is her name, though it doesn't escape my notice that 'Just' is a different kind of tag from 'Absolutely'). As Just Penny, she tweaks the living spaces of the well-heeled and well-connected from her neo-Gothic home-office up the lane near the woods. But she's not at all like him. She's actually, surprisingly, encouragingly normal. But she does as he tells her and what he generally tells her is that Owen, her precious, her one and only child, is altogether more academically able than he is. If I got her alone, I think I'd make progress. I'd be able to make her see that the private tutoring, the five-days-a-week after-school-activity habit, the relentless pursuit of grades, captaincies, prizes and plaudits are not doing Owen much good. That all they do is give him an ego the size of Ayers Rock, paradoxically close-coupled with the self-esteem of a slug. That everyone, him included, would be happier all round if he could be what he is, rather than constantly striving to be what Mr Rhys-Woodruff would like him to be and never quite measuring up. Mr Rhys-Woodruff has always been clear on that point, apparently. No son of his is going into bathrooms. Oxbridge. Medicine. And if not, the Law. I smile at Mrs Rhys-Woodruff as she sits beside her husband. She knows what I know, even if she doesn't admit it.

'It's not good enough,' says Mr Rhys-Woodruff, without preamble. 'We're not happy. Are we, Penny? We're very concerned.'

'No. Er, yes,' she says. 'We're very concerned.'

I nod sagely. 'Have you had a chance for a chat with Owen about Monday?' I ask nicely.

'Yes,' says Mrs Rhys-Woodruff. 'And we're—'

'*Very* concerned.' Mr Rhys-Woodruff adjusts his pink tie. 'And what we want to know is what *you*'re going to do.'

I spear him on the end of what he's least expecting. A smile. '*Precisely*,' I say, beaming fulsomely at him. 'That's *exactly* why it's so good to have a chance to talk to you both. The incident itself is, as far as I'm concerned, over and forgotten. Boys at this age – well, they sometimes have difficulty expressing themselves, don't they? But, like you, I *am* concerned about the ongoing situation. I think Owen does, perhaps, have some minor behavioural difficulties that do need—'

'*What?*' says Mr Rhys-Woodruff, visibly inflating.

I lift a hand. 'If I could finish?' He deflates a little. 'I'm concerned, as I'm sure you both are, that Owen is expressing himself in ways that are not wholly conducive to good relations in the playground at present. And while I fully appreciate that it was the other child who started the fight—'

'Fight?' pipes up Mrs Rhys-Woodruff. 'But it wasn't a fight! He was beaten up! Beaten up by—'

'*That boy*,' says Mr Rhys-Woodruff, who likes, it seems, to finish her sentences for her. 'And don't give me any of that about his mother dying—'

'I wasn't about to. I—'

'Bullying,' he barks at me. 'That's what it is. Plain bullying. And I'd like to know exactly where the school stands on this. I've had—'

'Yes, bullying,' I cut in again, because if he can, I can. I address myself to Mrs Rhys-Woodruff now. 'It's not a word we're fond of at Cefn Melin, Mrs Rhys-Woodruff, but it's certainly true that aspects of Owen's general behaviour lately have been giving us cause for concern.'

'*What?*' says Mr Rhys-Woodruff again, more loudly. 'You're not seriously trying to tell me that *Owen* is the one doing the bullying here? I think not, Mrs Connors. I think *not*.'

Oh dear. It's going to be a long day.

And not just for me, as it turns out. The clock wheezes round to three thirty, and when the phone rings in Glenda's office, I'm on my way in there to ring the buzzer anyway. I pick it up.

'Is that you, Hol?'

'Toni?'

'Yes, it's me. Thank God I caught you. Help! The bastards won't let me out!'

CHAPTER 9

For a while I think I must be having a phantom pregnancy because by the time I've driven all the way across Cardiff to Toni and Keiran's place, found the key beneath the bay tree, opened up, gathered some gear for her, stopped off in Sainsbury's for supplies and driven on to the hospital, I have a gnawing pain in the pit of my stomach. But by the time I've walked the mile and a half from the multi-storey to the maternity department, it's gone, and I realize I'm just being fanciful. It's probably nothing to do with anxiety transference and everything to do with the slice of bara brith and cup of tea I gulped down hurriedly before I left, in the interest of not offending Mrs Grace, who is one of the classroom assistants, and who's been off since October and is due back next month. She came in with it specially, to celebrate her hysterectomy. And when she asked where JP was and I told her at an interview, she mouthed, 'Fingers crossed', at me so no one could see. I don't know what she knows, but it seems I have an ally. I think I'm going to like Mrs Grace.

And how *could* I think it could be a phantom pregnancy? As if. Toni really does look very different from me now. Despite the blotchiness of her face and the dark circles beneath her eyes, she looks every inch what she is: a radiant woman in the plump bloom of pregnancy. And for the tiniest of moments I am envious of her. I feel all thin and crabby and too spiky in my suit. Like a wizened old parsnip to her velvety peach.

But the moment soon passes. I'm so relieved to see her looking okay.

She's been put in a side room because the gynae ward's full, and they didn't want to put her in the post-natal ward because it's full of babies who are safely on the right side of the womb. And she's asleep. Sleeping like a baby, in fact. Though I've no personal experience of the truth of that analogy. Emily never slept. Was a terrible sleeper. But right now I'm grateful to have had those extra hours. More to the point, to have *enjoyed* those extra hours. I never minded the night watch. I'm glad about that.

I stand and study Toni, unsure whether I ought to wake her or not. Not. So instead I start to unpack what I've brought.

'God, get me,' she says, coming to in moments, despite my tiptoes. 'I keep dozing off. Why didn't you wake me, you noodle?'

'Because you obviously need the sleep,' I tell her sternly. I hold pyjamas aloft. 'Where d'you want these?'

She nods towards the bedside cupboard, then eases herself into a sitting position, falling eagerly upon the copy of *Harpers* I've brought. She's not much of a mother-and-baby-mag fan, on the grounds that they'll make her feel all inadequate and compelled to go shopping for stuff in Baby Gap. She pats the bed. 'Thank you *so* much. You're such a sweetie. It must have been a huge hassle for you, dragging all the way down here. I'm really sorry. I know how busy you are. It's just that Keiran's running some bloody IT seminar, and I didn't know what else to do. And now they've told me they're going to scan me – any minute, I think, I've got to drink *all* this bloody water – and I feel sick to my stomach and the sound of this bloody monitor is driving me absolutely bloody insane, and I'm really, seriously, *horribly* fed up, and I'm scared, and I need a hug.'

I've finished unpacking the holdall now so I sit down on the edge of the bed and hug her as instructed. She smells of Chanel mixed with hospital blanket. Now her eyes are open I can tell she's been crying. Though I'm not about to mention it. She'd only deny it. 'But why have they kept you in?' I ask her instead. 'What's the problem exactly?'

She pulls a banana from the bag I've put on her bedside table. 'My bloody blood pressure,' she says, beginning to peel it. 'It's high. Not *that* high, but they want to be on the safe side and keep an eye on it.' She smiles ruefully at me. 'What with me being so *ancient* and everything. And with Mum and that.'

Toni and Max's mum has Alzheimer's disease. She lives in a nursing-home somewhere near York, and she doesn't even know who I am. Well, she does, because she knew me from college days, of course, but not now. Not as in who I am to Max. When I visited with him, she became very tearful. She thinks he's still married to Catherine. So that's how we've left things. 'Mum?' I say now, confused.

'With her having diabetes.' I nod. Of course. 'I am *such* a klutz for mentioning it. I mean she was, like, in her *sixties* when she got it, for God's sake. So it's not like it's even relevant. But, well – oh, I know they think they have to, but I just so *hate* it in here. I can't stop listening to *that* bloody thing.' She nods towards the monitor, from which a lead snakes to her belly. 'B-dm, b-dm, b-dm, b-dm. It's horrible, isn't it? It's like I'm frightened to move – did you find that? – in case it stops.' I nod. She takes a bite from the banana, then flips the skin back and frowns at me. 'God, I could kill for a drink.'

'Finish that water, then,' says a stern female voice, and I turn to see a nurse standing just inside the door. She smiles at us over an armful of sheets. 'Porter's just coming with a chair for you, lovely.' She comes round the bed and frees Toni from her monitor. Then she disappears again and Toni picks up the glass.

130

'But why were you back here anyway?' I ask her. 'You only just had your last antenatal. Your next shouldn't be for a month or so, should it?'

She shakes her head as she downs the last of the water. 'I had to come in for the diabetes tests. I've been here half the bloody day. You have to drink stuff, then hang around, then pee, then drink some more . . . It's a real pain. And I'm way behind on work as it is.'

'You mustn't think like that. This is far more important.'

'Don't you start. I *know*. That's probably why I have high blood pressure.' She puts the plastic glass down. 'Tsk. I ask you, do I *look* like the sort of person who'd have high blood pressure? Anyway, they *took* my blood pressure, of course, and hey presto, here I am. And now I'm going to have my scan today instead of next week and Keiran, as always, isn't here to hold my hand. Great, eh?'

'Can't he get here?'

'He's on his way. But the unit closes soon and I very much doubt if he'll make it in time. He's been up in Llandrindod. I can't see it, can you?'

I take her hand. 'Toni, don't fret. *I* will hold this for you, okay? But you never know. There's still time.'

She squeezes it. 'No, there's not. Here comes my porter.' She pulls the sheet back and swings her legs round, wincing, while I move out of the way to make room for the wheelchair. 'Tell me,' she says, directing her big, brown-eyed smile towards him. 'You have

131

speed cameras anywhere in this hospital of yours? Because you really are going to have to go some, believe me. I'm going to need to pee out Lake Michigan. And *soon.*'

When I finally got home, Max was already there. Standing in the kitchen, glass of red at his elbow, the kiss-the-cook apron I'd bought him for Christmas double-tied round his waist, chef-style. He was still in his suit trousers and he was peeling shallots.

'Good day?' I asked.

'So-so.' He put down the knife and reached into the cupboard for a glass. 'Go on, then. Let's hear it. What's the big drama?'

We were supposed to be meeting up at six thirty for a drink, but when I'd phoned to let him know, he'd been in a meeting with some clients, and then I'd been at the hospital so I couldn't call back. I'd had to leave him a message about Toni on his mobile.

I told him what had happened while he poured me some wine. It was almost eight now and it felt overdue. Hospitals do that to me sometimes. 'She's had her scan and they're keeping her in overnight, poor thing. Her blood pressure's still up.' I accepted the glass. 'Thanks. God, but it's such a stress for her. I hope everything's going to be okay.'

He returned to his peeling. The sweet-sharp tang filled the air. 'She'll be fine,' he said. 'You know what she's like. She has the constitution of a rhino.'

And when he said this, I thought he meant 'you know what she's like' in the sense that she was particularly robust. Which she wasn't: she was just very good at pretending.

'That's as maybe,' I said, climbing onto the stool at the end of the worktop, 'but she's still quite old to be having her first baby. They have to watch things like that.' I took a sip of the wine. It tasted strong. Furry against the roof of my mouth. 'Anyway,' I said, 'I told her that if they don't let her out, I'd pop along tomorrow lunchtime and see how she's doing.'

He stopped peeling. 'Holly, don't you have enough to do?'

I laughed then, because I still didn't twig. 'When do I ever not these days?' I quipped.

'Quite,' he replied, not laughing. 'Where's Keiran?'

'Oh, he got there in the end. Otherwise I dare say I'd still be there. But he's got to drive back up to Llandrindod tonight – he's lecturing on some sort of course, and—'

'Has he?'

'Has he what?'

'Has he *got* to go back?'

I blinked at Max, because there was something so pointed in his tone that it finally cranked me into gear. 'Well,' I said, 'not "got to" as in "absolutely *must*", I'm sure, but, you know, it's difficult for him. And, anyway, *I'm* here if she needs anything, aren't I? And—'

'Perhaps you shouldn't be.'

'What?'

'Perhaps *he* should.' He put down the knife and lobbed the last shallot at the bowl of water in the sink. There had never been much love lost between Max and Keiran. Nothing specific. There just wasn't any bond. Before I'd come along they'd seen little of each other. Not a whole lot more than I saw of my own brother. Different lives, different life-styles. Funny how the recombination of relation-ships throws people together in such an arbitrary way. He started gathering up the papery shards on the worktop. 'Perhaps if you *weren't* here, he wouldn't be so quick to hotfoot it out of town and let you do all the running around.'

'*What?*'

He clasped the little pile in his hands and put his foot on the bin pedal. 'I'm just *saying*,' he said, 'that perhaps it wouldn't do any harm to keep in mind whose baby this is.'

I put down my glass while he untied the string round his waist and pulled the apron over his head. I was shocked. What had brought this on? 'And what,' I said levelly, 'do you mean by that?'

He sighed a big, heavy, okay-let's-not-fight-about-it sigh. 'Look, I just think you ought to keep it in mind, that's all. I know you like to run around looking after everyone, sweets, but there *is* a limit—'

Clever, clever. 'Sweets', so definitely not row-mode. Which was fine. I really wasn't in the mood for a row. I just wanted to fathom this curious turn of events. Was this about Keiran, or was it really about me? 'Er, what's brought all this on, Max?' I asked him nicely. 'Is this because I didn't make the wine bar? Look, I'm sorry, but what did you expect me to do? She's my friend.'

And his little sister to boot. 'Look,' he said, 'I know you worry about her – I do too, of *course* I do – and I know you want to help out. But I don't think you should feel you have to drop everything for her all the time. It's Keiran's job. He's got to learn to pull *his* weight.'

Such speechifying. 'Max, I wasn't dropping everything. *Anything*, in fact.'

'If you say so.'

'I *do*.'

'Then that's fine. You look tired, and I just thought I'd mention it, that's all. Keiran's got to understand that . . .' He stopped then, and frowned. 'Look, let's leave it, shall we? Now, are you going to get off your arse and lay the table? I'm going to pop to the off-licence and get some more wine.' And he smiled then, and kissed my cheek, and said, 'Get the griddle pan on too, can you?' and the moment had passed. Which was fine with me. Because I *did* understand where he was coming from. Sort of. He was tired and he was tetchy and though I was sure he *was* anxious about Toni, his equilibrium was precious, and a large part of that had always centred on me. I had been the port in his post-marital storm. His rock and his refuge, his place of uncomplicated peace. *His*. Not Toni's. It was probably that simple. As simple as anything between siblings could ever be.

Which had always been so, but suddenly it felt a little stifling. After he'd gone, I went into the living room and found he'd tidied up the slight disarray I'd left before work. Straightened the magazines, replumped all the cushions, and put the hastily drawn curtains back behind their tie-backs. And even though I felt bad about it, I went round and changed them all back to how they'd been. Except the curtains, which I closed, feeling guilty. To maintain the equilibrium. Shut the world out for Max. Perhaps, I thought idly, I was having a moment. Perhaps I was beginning to learn what I was like.

CHAPTER 10

I would have made a good mistress, I think. If that had been my bag, which it never had. Not because I had particularly superior moral principles about it – these things are never black and white, after all – but because my nature was such that I would have found it all too simple to look after a man whose wife didn't understand him. I'd feel sorry for him and want to help out. Which is a pretty half-baked notion, clearly. I would never knowingly get involved with someone else's man. But to Max I was in many ways *like* a mistress. That much was clear. Though we had got together long after he and Catherine separated, if not before his decree absolute, I think I fulfilled – was still fulfilling – almost that role. I was without any sort of complication. I loved him, pampered him, made him feel good about himself, provided succour from the bloody post-divorce battlefield, and wanted nothing but uncomplicated love in return. In short I was a find. Or so Toni always told me. But, then, she often remarked on how lucky Max was. Too much, and a bit too enthusiastically, to my mind. I was lucky too, because these things worked both ways. Max didn't trespass on the life I'd left behind me, which was how I liked it.

So despite my moment of irritation about it, I pretty much put the Toni-Max niggles from my mind. Toni had made her escape from hospital, all was quiet on the home front, and my mind could go back to my work, so it did.

The following Friday year six went on a school trip. Which, of itself, is nothing of great note. Where once, a school trip was something you did annually if you were lucky, and usually consisted of walking in an excitable crocodile to the local post office and back, the range and scope of the average school's off-site activities these days is breathtaking, eclectic and happens almost half-termly, so this one was remarkable only in the sense that everything that happened after it happened *because* of it, and without it might not have happened at all. I nearly went on it myself because John was away yet *again*, this time on some sort of education-authority seminar for *angst*-ridden deputies with murder on their minds. Okay, it wasn't that, but it might as well have been. But, as ever, the paperwork mountain won out so Mrs Cairns went with Clemency. Which was fine by me because Clemency needed the sort of experience that only six hours in charge of five dozen children let loose in the middle of nowhere could bring. And she'd be fine, I knew. Whatever the gulf in our affections for JP, I was beginning to find that I quite liked Clemency. Whatever she got up to in her private life, she had the makings of a good teacher.

A head herself, perhaps, one day. If that was her plan. If eloping with Laughing Boy wasn't.

So I had a quiet Friday, and Clemency got the duck stuff. And sometimes I find myself wondering where I'd be if I *had* gone on the school trip. Somewhere other than I am now? I wonder.

But that's not what I was thinking when Glenda put her head round my door that Friday afternoon. Right then I was thinking your regular Friday-afternoon thoughts. Like how much weekend I'd have left to myself once I'd waded through the new directives on the application of sun creams at playtime, the white paper about EU link-school initiatives, the new LEA listening-skills programme and the PTA meeting minutes (of which there were screeds). Not very much. Perhaps Max had been right.

I looked up. 'It's Miss Bright on the phone,' Glenda trilled.

Despite her bright tone, her lip was curling, and it wasn't anything to do with the dentistry. It was becoming tedious – her and Clemency were pretty much not speaking – but I wished she wouldn't be so poker-faced about it with *me*. I knew it wasn't my business (having been so recently reacquainted with that concept) but the whole atmosphere thing was plain wearing at times. So she didn't approve. Fine. But it wasn't *her* business either. And if it wasn't her business then it was just plain old gossip. And if so, she should do the decent thing and spill the beans.

I picked up the phone in my office.

'Oh, Mrs Connors,' said Clemency, 'I'm *so* sorry to bother you, but we've got a bit of a problem.'

I imagined a sick child. It generally was. Coach trip plus sweets plus over-excitement plus more sweets . . . 'What sort of problem?' I asked.

'Well, the thing is . . . how can I put it? We . . . um . . . seem to have mislaid a child.'

'Ri-ight . . .'

'And I wasn't sure what best to do. We've got all the children gathered together, and the manager is going to have his staff make a thorough search and everything, and I'm sure we'll track him down – I mean, where can he go? There's nowhere *to* go, is there? But I wasn't sure if I shouldn't call the parent or something, and the police, and . . . well . . . *should* I?'

She was beginning to sound as if she might lose *it* as well as the child.

'No, no,' I told her calmly. 'You keep searching. Don't worry. Leave all the phone calls to me. Which child is it?'

'Harry Meadows.'

Of course. It would be. Who else? 'Cool head in a crisis, remember,' I told her. 'He won't be far away. Keep looking. I'll be on my way in ten minutes.'

It's an hour's trip by coach to where they've gone today, but I manage to make it in a scant forty minutes. Quick, yes, but still way, *way* long enough to imagine the worst-case scenario – in colour – then to double it, treble it, take away the number

I first thought of, divide by two and arrive at something nasty. I know it won't be, I *do*. I know I'm simply following procedure. It happens all the time. They are *always* located. But my imagination doesn't care. It is now Harry-hotwired. And, as such, it does as it likes.

But, happily, it's wrong. When I pull into the entrance of the Happy Valley Wildfowl and Wetlands Centre the first thing I see is Harry Meadows.

The first thing, that is, bar the coach, the fifty-seven other children, the five members of the Happy Valley Wildfowl and Wetlands Centre staff (all looking very cheerful in their appliquéd yellow T-shirts), Clemency, Mrs Cairns, the trio of parent helpers (Mrs Williams, Mrs Shah and Mrs Rhys-Woodruff, naturally), a constable, an Alsatian, a woman in a rain hood, a man heading off with a wheelbarrow full of manure, the coach driver (smoking) and a Canada goose.

But he is the first thing I properly *see*, and the relief floods through me like melted chocolate, loosening the knot that has strangled my gut. 'Mrs Connors!' cries Clemency, breaking away from the pack and covering the thirty or so yards between us at an impressive lick, pulling Harry along in her wake. The constable peels off as well. Plus the dog.

'I would have called you back already,' she pants, as she approaches, 'but you can't get a signal here. I was literally *just* about to go in and use the phone in the centre.' She gestures. She is

141

pink. She is still, as my mum would have said, all of a lather. She is post-traumatic stress syndrome in a yellow cagoule. 'And now you've come all this way, and we've had the police out and everything for nothing. But we've literally, *literally*, only just found him.'

'Well, three cheers for that!' I smile down at Harry. 'Don't *worry*. You did the right thing in phoning, Miss Bright.'

'That you did,' says the constable, who seems very jolly. A breath of air with the dog probably brightened his day.

'So,' I say cheerily, 'what happened?'

What happened, or so Clemency tells me, somewhat breathily, is that after lunch – after they'd done their little tour of the visitor centre, answered all sorts of penetrating questions about the ecology of the wetlands, the lifecycle of the damsel fly, and so on, they were split up into groups – eight to a teacher or staff member or parent (in Harry's case, Mrs Rhys-Woodruff – hey, *great* choice, Mrs Cairns), then sent off with laminated sheets and instructed, quite reasonably, to scour the wetlands for wildfowl (which they were to identify and mark on their sheets with the natty write-on wipe-off pens provided). So Mrs Rhys-Woodruff took her group off as instructed, lost half of them (the Harry half) somewhere out at the far side of the lake, found them again (now minus Harry), sent Owen and the others off to find him again, failed, gave up, hurried back to Clemency and her group, at which point Clemency raised the alarm, mobilized all the staff and rang me. Then, having corralled the other children into a largish gaggle back in the visitor centre with the lady in the rain hood, everyone else began searching the environs in earnest.

During which time Harry, who had been in one of the hides at the far side of the lake with three other boys (who had, it seemed, disappeared) had dropped his write-on wipe-off marker pen, which had rolled between the planks that made up the slatted floor of the hide (which was set on a sort of jetty over the lake) and plopped down onto the muddy bank below, at the lake's edge. Thinking he'd probably be in trouble if he didn't bring it back (it *was* rather natty after all) he'd left the hide and climbed down under it, the better to get to the muddy bank and reclaim the pen, which was how he got his trainer stuck in the mud at the edge of the lake and also why, having established everyone else had gone off without him, he had decided to make an unscheduled stop at the toilet block over by the far play area (which, strictly speaking, wasn't open till April) so he could wash his trainer so he wouldn't get into trouble for that either when he got back and, yes, he *had* heard someone calling him when he came out but they were, like, *miles* away, and just as soon as he realized people might be wondering where he'd got to, he'd hot-footed (and wet-footed) it back to the visitor centre, only to find it deserted except for the woman in the rain hood (who ran the tea room and gift shop, and gave him a gobstopper), the policeman, the goose and the dog. Who was called Sally and was a sniffer dog, apparently, which was lush because she mainly did drugs. And he was very, very sorry. But he *had* got the pen back. And was his dad going to, you know, like, kill him?

'No, Harry,' I said, with more confidence than I felt. I had just dragged his father from the middle of a dub, apparently, which sounded like something one should only be dragged from kicking and in extremis, if the girl who took the call was to be believed. 'I'm sure he won't kill you,' I told him. 'But you do know why all of this has happened, don't you? Because you wandered off on your *own*.'

'But I *didn't* wander off on my own, Miss. We were all in there. And they just, like, left *me*.'

'Well, you should have gone with them.'

'But I was doing the birds, Miss. All they wanted to do was throw stones at the ducks.'

'I did not!' said Owen Rhys-Woodruff, who had heard him.

'Yeah, you did,' said Harry. He said it quietly, almost under his breath, and with the weary air of one who knows there's no point, and thus can hardly be bothered, and in doing so secured my unconditional belief that what he was saying was absolutely true.

But I was now becoming conscious of the time. The debrief would have to wait.

144

'We will discuss this tomorrow,' I said, frowning hard at both of them. 'It's getting late and all the parents will be arriving at school soon. Miss Bright, time to get them back to school, yes?'

By the time I'd finished helping Clemency gather up the children's sheets and pens (pausing only to place a reassuring hand on Mrs Rhys-Woodruff's arm and tell her she *really* mustn't feel in *any* way responsible), Will Meadows's car, for which I'd been scanning the entrance at intervals, was pulling into the car park. I watched him climb out, take in the scene, notice Harry, and then how his body language echoed mine of just minutes before. He'd sounded calm when I'd spoken to him, but he no longer looked it. What terrible scenarios must have spooled through *his* mind?

He jogged across to meet us and I explained what had happened while Clemency began getting the children back on board.

The tension was draining out of him almost visibly. 'Well,' he said, ruffling Harry's hair absently and speaking in a tone that, to his credit, did not betray any hint of how strung up he must have been, 'no harm done, at least. Shall I take Harry back with me, then?'

'If you'd like to,' I began. 'If—'

'*Da-ad!*' hissed Harry. 'I'm not coming home, am I? I've got to go on the *coach*. It's Jack's party. Remember? His mum's picking us up from school.'

He blinked at his son, then nodded. 'Oh, of course. Yes. That's right, isn't it?' He turned to me. 'He's at a friend's house for a sleepover tonight. Birthday do.' He turned back to Harry. 'But what about that wet trainer?'

'It's okay,' said Harry. 'I've got my DCs in my back-pack, haven't I. *Remember?* I'm going to get changed when I get there.'

'But what about your socks?'

'*Da-ad*,' said Harry.

'Well . . . okay, then,' he said. 'Well. Have a good time, mate.' He stood smiling for a moment, and I knew, I just *knew*, that he wanted to hug him, but he didn't. He reached out to pat his head instead. Then he looked heart-breakingly lost and self-conscious as Harry, without noticing, climbed up the coach steps.

I turned away quickly. Busied myself by giving Clemency a super-big hug and reassuring her again that she'd done exactly the right thing, and that I was *really* pleased with her, and that she must remember that it was our job to plan for the worst, not just hope for the best. Then I helped get the last of the children back on to the coach and counted. Twice.

'I'm sorry you had a wasted journey,' I said to Will Meadows, as I climbed back down and we waved them off together. I felt inexplicably *so* agitated being around him. Conscious of a strong sense of unfinished business. But *why?* It was all done and forgotten, wasn't it? By *him*, it

146

seemed, anyway. But now he was here that wasn't how it felt. I'd forgotten how disarming a presence he was. Or had I remembered that right? Had he grown? We started walking back towards his car. 'But I felt I had to call you,' I carried on briskly. 'In this sort of situation we always like to act sooner rather than later.'

'Absolutely,' he said, nodding. 'The right thing to do. Don't worry. It wasn't a problem.' Then he glanced at me and his mouth curled into a grin. 'Though I have to admit, it was a *slightly* stressful drive.'

Moments later we reached his car, and he pulled his keys from his pocket. He was wearing the same jacket he'd had on the last time I saw him. Heavy black leather. And newish, I figured. Though it looked pretty worn, it manifestly wasn't, because I kept getting traces of its warm animal scent. 'I know,' I said. 'Me too.'

He nodded. Fixed his eyes on me. 'Well, then . . .'

'So,' I said, uncomfortable under his scrutiny. 'Better get back.'

'Yeah. Me as well. Well, um . . . thanks.'

'Whatever for? I'm just sorry you . . .'

'*Don't* be. I *told* you.'

'Okay. Right, then.'

'Right.'

'Right. 'Bye.'

I watched him get into his car, none the happier for having seen him (and substantially less so for my dire inarticulacy), then turned as he drove off and walked quickly back to thank the nice policeman and his dog. That done, I went into the visitor centre with the manager, signed his incident log (does *everyone* have one?), phoned Glenda to tell her all was well and that the coach was on its way back now, thanked the manager and his staff for their help, then headed back out to my car, got in, pulled out, and began the long drive back to school. With luck, I'd make Cardiff before the rush-hour got going.

Or so I thought. And why wouldn't I? Drama done for the day.

Not.

Where good or bad fortune is concerned, I've always figured that there's probably some sort of celestial score sheet on the go. In the dark early days after Emily's death, I embraced religion in a way that I never have either before or since. Though the thrust of my imprecations to the Lord at that time were generally mostly of a 'Why *me*?' (as opposed to the 'Why *not* me?') variety, as time has gone by I have assimilated my reasoning into a kind of personal (if batty) cosmic theory, and reached the comforting, if misplaced conviction that bad things, like cold sores, are probably shared out among us. And that perhaps I'd already had more than my share. That things could never – *would* never – be any worse. I was thinking big, life-changing things at that time, of course, but as the years have trundled on, my ongoing relationship with the concept of destiny has expanded to

148

include almost every aspect of life. Mine, from that point, I reasoned, was well overdue to be a charmed one. And in as much as you can sensibly correlate the one with the other, the sheer scale of my tragedy seemed to me to be the reason why other, less life-changing but nevertheless still significant, bad things had never been directed my way. I had never been burgled, never broken a limb, never had my handbag ripped from my shoulder in a drive-by mugging, never grown a disfiguring wart on my nose. And this was also, I imagined (by an impressive leap of logic, admittedly), the reason why I'd never had a puncture. This last is probably of little note, I imagine, to a person who has never had a puncture themselves. It certainly never has been for me. Every time I drove past someone toiling with a wrench at the side of the road I would think, Thank goodness I've never had a puncture. Not in a smug way. Not even in a particularly focused way. Just a fleeting thought, something that enters your head and leaves it again immediately, rather like when the opposite motorway carriage has a ten-mile tailback and you think, Thank goodness I'm not going *that* way. Thus punctures had become one of those things that I had largely ceased to think about. Like testicular cancer, or going bald, or meeting a sticky end pearl fishing off the Maldives, it was simply not on my list of things to worry about.

Yet here was a puncture. My own personal

puncture. And even as I stood and studied it, stupefied, I was already thinking, Why now? Why here? Why in a lane in the middle of nowhere when I'm in the car on my own and have never had dealings with wheel nuts or a car jack in my life and there's no Max on hand and nothing in the way of passing traffic and even if there was it might be a dangerous, Texas chainsaw, in-bred kind of person who is not to be trusted and when, moreover, I've just had my nails manicured in readiness for the Perkins and Stapleforth Ides of March ball?

Why *me*, in fact? I stood and looked at it for several seconds, as if by squinting my eyes just so it would become something entirely different, like maybe a dip in the camber that was just giving the *appearance* of a puncture, or a trick of the light (which was beginning to fade), or the product of me never having looked at the contours of my tyres before now. But no. It was a puncture. It had to be a puncture. The tyre was as flat as the tundra.

I stood a second or two more, then said a rude word very loudly. And then I said it once more to be sure God was listening and would know without doubt that I was not best pleased with Him. Then I hastily apologized, because I didn't wish to displease Him to the extent that he laid on a thunderstorm too. Then, calmly (cool head in a crisis, remember?), I got back into the car and reached down for my bag. Worse things, I told myself sternly and with conviction, almost *always* happened at sea.

Which is probably nothing to do with the fact that mobile phones don't work out there, obviously, and much more likely to be due to drowning and sharks, but just the same, I'm sure it doesn't really *help*. Just as it had never occurred to me that I might one day have a puncture, it had also never occurred to me that, having had one, I might find myself marooned in the sort of mealy-mouthed, geologically spiteful landscape in which mobile phones would be rendered useless. Belatedly, and adopting the sort of wry frown Inspector Morse had so made his own, I remembered Clemency's words about hers. But no signal, no problem, I told myself stoutly. It couldn't be more than a mile or two back to the centre. I would head off down the lane – heels a-clack, skirt a-swishing – and ask to use their phone instead. I gathered up my bag, locked the car, remembered about the hazard warning lights, unlocked the car, switched them on, locked the car again, remembered about the red warning triangle that was clipped (purely for decorative purposes up to now) to the underside of the boot lid, unlocked the car again, opened the boot, got it out, dusted it off, locked the car again, then set off back up the lane, congratulating myself on my doughtiness of spirit, and counting out fifty careful strides as I did so, then erecting my little triangle on the nearside of the road.

But I *was* right about the celestial score sheet,

I think, because I hadn't gone more than half a mile when I was nearly but not *quite* mown down by Will Meadows, by virtue of my having veered off towards the hedgerow to take a rejuvenating look at some lily-of-the-valley nestled in the grass.

'What on earth are you doing here?' he yelled, once he'd shuddered to a stop, leaped rangily out of his car, and run back up the lane to where (blinking and also now scowling) I stood.

I blinked some more. 'Right now? Mainly I'm offering up a prayer of thanks to the Almighty that I am still on this earth.'

But it had to be said that, boy, were my feet glad to see him. So I took off my scowl and replaced it with a smile.

'God, I'm sorry,' he said, smiling back apologetically. 'It was a blind bend. You just kind of reared up,' he gestured with his hands, 'out of nowhere.'

I contemplated the image of myself rearing up, and found it pretty much impossible. 'I'm not rearing,' I told him. 'I'm trudging. My car's back down the lane there and I have a puncture. And how come you're here anyway? You left way before me.'

'Ah, yes. And then I promptly got lost.'

'Don't you have Sat Nav on that beast car of yours?'

He shook his head. 'I wish. I'm pants at navigation. I used to rely on Wife Nav too much. I get lost all the time. Ph.D. level lost. I can go somewhere six times and still not find my way back there. So. Where are you headed? Far?'

This admission, I decided, was rather appealing in a man. 'To find a phone,' I said. 'I can't get a signal on my mobile.'

He fished in the inside pocket of his jacket and pulled out his. It was bijou, in that reverse-phallic thing men always seem to go for. He flipped it open and peered at the display. 'Me neither.' He glanced around him. 'Must be all the trees.'

'And the happy valley, of course,' I said, a touch ruefully.

He nodded. Then he clapped his hands suddenly. 'But today's your lucky day, methinks. Here I am. A knight in shining armour, come to your rescue.'

I smiled. 'You have the hair for it.'

'*And* the horsepower. Though regrettably not the armour. I find it tends to rust in these inclement climes. So. Shall I come and change your wheel for you, ma'am?'

I hadn't thought of that. But now I did, I found I didn't want him to. I didn't know why. It just didn't feel right. I coloured. What on earth had possessed me to mention his *hair*? 'No, really,' I said quickly. 'I don't want to put you to any bother. I was going to go and ring the RAC.'

'It's no bother. *Really*. I'd be happy to,' he said.

I shook my head. 'That's very kind of you but a lift back to the centre will do me just fine.'

'You sure?' he said, and this time I nodded. 'Well, okay, then. Up to you. Come on,' he said, beckoning. 'Let's go round up the horse.'

We walked back to his car, then drove on past mine, whose tyre was still clearly punctured, then turned round at the next junction and retraced our steps. But when we got back to the centre it was to find that a low chain had been slung across the entrance to the car park and that the only sign of life that didn't sport a beak and webbed feet was the man with the wheelbarrow, now empty, who was wheeling it up a path in the distance that led to a low huddle of sheds. We stopped at the chain, got out and called to him.

'Aye?' he said, turning on the path as we straddled the chain and began to approach him. 'We're closed,' he added helpfully. 'Four o'clock. Off season.'

I looked at my watch. It was now twenty past. 'Isn't anyone here still? We were hoping to use the phone. I've got a puncture, and I need to call the RAC.'

He set down the wheelbarrow and peered back across towards the visitor centre in the gathering gloom. 'I doubt it,' he said, then pointed. 'No lights on.' He scratched his chest. 'They don't hang around this time of year.'

'And you don't have a key?' asked Will, though it wasn't really a question.

The man shook his head. 'Not to the centre. I'm grounds.'

'Is there somewhere nearby where we could use a phone? Pub? Shop? Petrol station or something?'

'There's always the Shearers in Pontyffosfelen,' he said. 'It's about two mile up the road towards Llanpandy. Take a left. You can't miss it.'

Oh, yes, we could. Another ten minutes elapsed before a road sign with anything approaching the right selection of consonants came into view. But we'd found life, at least. There was a ribbon of houses, some now lit, with drawn curtains, a shop and, as promised, a pub.

And a pub with a payphone, so I fished out some change.

I was through in the blink of an eye to a human, but the news wasn't good.

'How long?' asked Will Meadows, as I replaced the receiver.

'About an hour, they think. She said I'd get priority as a lone female and everything, but they didn't think it would be much less.'

I called Glenda, then, to let her know I wasn't going to be back after all. She told me that the coach had just returned to school, and the children had all been collected.

I put the receiver back on its cradle, then thought, and picked it up again. I should call Max as well. So I did. But Max was in a meeting with some VIP clients. Was it urgent? I told his secretary no, there was no point in worrying him. I wasn't due to see him till later anyway. And even given the hour's wait, I'd still be home before seven. Hardly worth bothering him about.

Will Meadows, who'd been studying the menu on the wall while I made my calls, turned now and said, 'You really want to wait an hour?'

'You never know. It might be less.'

'I doubt it. Look, call them back and cancel. *I'll* change your wheel.'

'But . . .' But *what*? 'But it's such an imposition. It's not so long to wait. Besides, don't you have to be somewhere?'

He shook his head. 'Nope. Come on, where's the problem? Let me change your wheel for you.'

Yes, Holly. *Yes*. Where exactly *was* the problem? The man was offering to do me a favour, wasn't he? Changing wheels was like lawnmowing and dustbins. Sure, I'd do it if I had to, *could* do it if I had to, but given a man in the immediate vicinity, then they could if they wanted to. It was bloke stuff, after all. And I hadn't been about to do it myself, had I? So it was hardly as if it was an affront to my feminist principles.

'Or would you consider it an affront to your feminist principles?' he said. Then he raised his brows. '*What?* Go on. What's so funny?'

I shook my head. 'Nothing. No, *really*. It's nothing. Okay, then. Yes. Thanks, Mr Meadows.'

He pulled a face. 'It's *Will*.'

'No, it's not.'

'Yes, it is.'

'No, it *isn't*.'

'Yes, it *is*. Make the call. I *insist*.'

That was why I didn't want him to do it. *That*. Because because because because *because*. But now he was going to, and I'd have to swallow whatever it was that was sticking so stubbornly in my craw. So I did, and we were back at my car ten minutes later. It was growing dark now, the last wisps of pink turning a deep, smoky mauve. At least I'd had the good sense to pull in at a passing space, and he'd parked his own car in such a way that it would protect him from any oncoming traffic, but even so, it didn't feel like a very safe place.

'Will you be able to see okay?' I asked him anxiously.

He nodded. 'No worries. I have a very large torch.'

He did too. And a very large tool kit. And he knew where my jack was. And he knew what he was doing. Within minutes he had the car up and ready for its op.

'You got the key?'

'What key?'

'The key to the locking wheel nut?'

'Oh. I hadn't thought. Yes, I must have, mustn't I?'

He held his hand out. 'Well, then?'

'Oh, yes. Right. Keys.' I passed him the bunch and he went quickly through them. 'This'll be the one, I imagine.' He squatted down again and tried it. Sure enough, he'd been right.

'I've never had a puncture,' I told him, as I watched him.

'Tell you what,' he replied, with a smile, 'nor have I.'

I almost told him about my theory then, but it made me think of his dead wife and I certainly didn't want to go there again. So instead I asked him how he came to be so good at changing wheels.

'Oh, I'm good at all sorts of things. Most of them without much practical application, admittedly, but I do make a mean shepherd's pie, and when it comes to mechanics I'm definitely your man.'

The thought made me start. A man. Not my man.

My mother had another mantra. Little known generally. 'Sugar and spice and all things nice,' she'd say, 'but you're just a little heavy on the chilli, my girl.' I didn't know about chilli so I thought she meant chilly. Which I wasn't, because she always made me wear a thermal vest. I must have been about fourteen before the penny dropped. She'd say it to anyone who remarked on my cuteness. As people often do about blue-eyed blonde little girls.

'*Much* too heavy on the chilli,' she'd always say, when I cheeked her or got into some row about nothing very much. I was, she said, a hot-headed and confrontational child. Never able to let anything go.

158

And though I didn't see myself like that, it seemed she had a point. 'I'm so sorry,' I said now, apropos of nothing.

I hadn't meant to say anything. I hadn't wanted to go there, had I? But I couldn't seem to help it. It was just seeing him there, kneeling on the damp road, being so friendly and helpful, whistling to himself, taking control, wielding the wrench so confidently, getting his hands dirty for me, being capable, being sweet. Not being feckless at all. I didn't know why I so needed to confront it. But it had been building up all afternoon and I just knew I had to. Just knew I *must*. And *now*.

He looked up at me, his hair curling damply round his jawline, his shaggy brows converging in enquiry. 'You what?'

'I said I'm sorry. Very sorry.'

He smiled up at me. 'I told you,' he said. 'I'm happy I could help.'

I shook my head. 'No,' I said. 'I don't mean that. I mean I'm sorry for all the things I said to you on the night Casper died. It's been playing on my mind ever since. I was unkind to you, and I'm sorry.'

He sat on his heels now and pushed his hair from his forehead with the back of his hand. Considered me a moment, his expression difficult to read in the gloom.

'You don't need to be,' he said. 'It all needed saying.'

'No, it didn't. Well, okay, *some* of it might have, but it wasn't what I said, it was the way that I said it. I was out of order. I was completely unprofessional. I ranted at you, basically. I was cruel.'

'*Cruel?*' He looked surprised. Then he shook his head. 'No. You're wrong. You weren't that. Not at all.' He fixed the wrench onto one of the nuts and started turning it. He'd taken off his jacket and was working in his T-shirt. I could see the muscles in his forearms bulge and tense.

'I was just so *cross*,' I said, grateful his attention was mainly elsewhere. 'Cross with you, cross with myself, upset about Harry . . . and I was so damn busy being furious about it all that I never stopped to think about you. Not really. I can't begin to imagine how difficult these past months must have been for you. You were absolutely right,' I said. 'I *was* being judgemental. I had no right to be but I was.'

He removed the first nut and handed it to me, then went on with the next. I stood and watched him self-consciously, hands stuck up my jacket sleeves, the cold of the Tarmac seeping into my soles. It was fully dark now, the torchlight a creamy yellow halo fuzz around us. It was a good twenty seconds before he replied.

'That's not how it was,' he said, to the tyre. 'Sure, we had a few words, but as *I* remember it, mainly you were very concerned.' He paused. 'Very kind,' he added gruffly. I watched him pause again. Watched his brow crease as he thought. Then he frowned and glanced up at me. 'But, as you might have noticed, I'm not too good with kind.'

The second nut came off and I automatically pulled one hand from my sleeve to take it. He plopped it into my palm to join the other. His fingertips were icy. Cold as the metal. I wanted to say I knew *just* what he meant. But we'd been there already. Beware of the dog.

'Then you must have a selective memory,' I said instead.

'No,' he said. 'I have an almost photographic memory. Goes with the territory. And you *are* wrong. You know that, don't you?' His gaze was locked onto mine now. 'Do you want me to tell you what I really remember about that evening?'

'I'm not sure I do. But something tells me you're about to.'

'Yes,' he said, turning away to fit the lever onto the third nut. 'I am.' He grinned up at me as he turned it. 'Since we seem to have fetched up inexplicably on the *Trisha* show. What I *really* remember about that evening – no, that's wrong. *Not* just that evening. Pretty much every encounter we've had since I met you—'

'Is?'

He stopped and exhaled before speaking. 'Is that you're the first person I've come across since my wife died who actually, *genuinely* seems to care about Harry.' He passed me the third nut and smiled at me now. 'You know that? Sure, everyone's been very supportive, of course they have. And, yes, I know the school, and even that Mrs . . .' he flapped a hand. 'What was her name?'

'Mrs Plum.'

'Mrs Plum. That's the one. Her. They've all been great. Can't fault them. But you,' he waggled the wrench at me, 'you're different from them. You really do seem to *care.*'

'Of course I care. It's my *job* to care. And who wouldn't? He's a lovely little boy.'

He didn't answer straight away. Instead he set to work on the last nut, freeing it with one powerful yank on the wrench. 'Hey, of course he is – here, grab that, will you? – he comes from good stock. And though he'd kill me for saying it – so don't you go telling him – little boy or otherwise, he has a bit of a thing about you.' He gave me the last nut, then sat back on his haunches, his expression now serious again. 'Look, don't get me wrong. I'm not working on the principle that anyone else even *should* care. But I don't think you have any idea just how grateful I am that you do.'

He stood up then, and pushed his hand through his hair. And then he looked straight at me, his face half in shadow, his eyes glittering amber in the torchlight. 'Because I might have neglected to let you know that,' he said quietly. 'Like I say, I'm not so good at dealing with people being kind to me.'

Nor was I. I was *hopeless.* It was just that, unlike him, I seemed to have forgotten that I wasn't. And

162

now it had come back to me just how *very* hope-less. All in a rush. Several seconds ticked by. I felt distinctly uncomfortable under his gaze. 'You've got me all wrong,' I told him, as he handed me the wrench, then squatted down again to pull the wheel off the car. 'I may be fond of Harry, but I wasn't being kind. Not a bit of it. I thought you were completely feckless.'

He heaved the wheel off, and rolled it alongside the car to the back, where he leaned it care-fully against the bumper. Then he laughed, which disarmed me some more. 'Well,' he said, rising, 'you were probably right about that.'

I followed him along the flank of the car. 'No, I wasn't. That's just my point. I *wasn't*.'

He turned to face me again and now I could see my own eyes reflected in his. 'Hey, I'm not about to argue with you,' he said. 'Not while you're the one holding the wrench, anyway. Come on, Mrs Connors, let's get this spare wheel out, shall we?'

'Oh, go on, then,' I said. 'Call me Holly, if you must.'

I don't know why I said that. I just slipped out. As well it might. He was changing my wheel, after all, and to have him call me Mrs Connors felt all wrong. It made him sound like the hired help. We exchanged a smile then, the barrier broached, and that, I guess, should have been that. *Was* that, to all intents and purposes. I'd cleared the air, I'd apolo-gized. Cue end of existential *angst*. Except it's a funny old term 'all intents and purposes'. Rather an opaque concept to get your head round. Just saying it seems to imply something else, even though it shouldn't. My intention had been to apologize to him, my purpose in doing so to make me feel better about myself. Bring the little cache of discomfort I'd been carrying around with me out into the open and spirit it away. And now I had, *ergo* job done, that *was* that, wasn't it? But it wasn't. Couldn't be. I was still Harry's head teacher, Harry was still one of my pupils. And now his father had edged his way into my consciousness too, in a way that he had had no business to do. I watched him rub the grime from his hands against the front of his jeans, press the boot-release catch, pass my crate of paperwork to me, brush a curl from his eyes as he lifted up the carpet. And as I watched him, I thought about how sad and lonely he must be. About him going home to his empty house, his childless, wifeless, hugless home. I visualized him picking up some microwave rubbish for his dinner (or making a little shepherd's pie for one – even worse), then going to bed and sleeping with nothing but his dreams to keep him warm, living out every day hoping that the next would be easier, and it touched my heart. Didn't break it, because that's melodramatic and silly. But touched it. Nudged it. Spoke to it some-how. At the very least, it made it sit up and take notice. There are lots of words for feelings of that nature, obviously. Sympathy, empathy, compassion, concern. I could choose any one. Because they all seemed to fit.

'Okay,' he said, 'spot the deliberate mistake.'

'What?' Off in my reverie, I was now looking at the moon.

He snorted at me then and pointed to the boot. 'Do'h. As in "Holly, where *is* your spare wheel?"'

And we both burst out laughing. Just couldn't *stop* laughing. Because even though it plainly wasn't anything to laugh about, it seemed so uproariously funny.

And perhaps that was when I should have realized what I'd missed. That there was no choice to make. That the feeling chose me. And though I didn't see it then, it was none of the above.

CHAPTER 11

'Well now,' said the barman, looking up from *TV Quick* and placing two pale Popeye forearms on the pitted dark-wood counter. 'You two back? Stopping for a drink this time?'

We'd stopped laughing eventually, of course, because grown-ups tend to have that irritating but necessary compulsion to think beyond the next thirty seconds of their lives. Perhaps we'd all be a lot happier if we didn't.

I absolutely couldn't believe it. But there was no rational reason for my disbelief. The blind faith most of us have that our spare wheels will be sitting snugly *in situ* at all times is often exactly that: blind faith. I don't think I'd ever once looked into the place where my spare wheel, apparently, used to live.

'God, it must have been when the car went in,' I told Will. 'Couple of months back. I had a bald patch on one of my tyres. But why would they have taken the spare out?'

'Could be any number of reasons. Perhaps they put the spare on the car.'

'But why didn't they put the other one *back*?'

'Er . . . because it was bald?'

'Well, why didn't they put another one in there?'

'I imagine they meant to. But perhaps they didn't have one in stock and they were going to get one. Perhaps one of them had a fall-out with your great-auntie Matilda and they saw this as the perfect opportunity to get you back. Perhaps the tyre person has a ten-second memory. Like a goldfish. Who knows? Look, no matter. Your car's not going anywhere, is it? Let's drive back to the pub and call the RAC. There might be a garage open somewhere and they can pick up a tyre for you *en route*. What gauge are these?'

I rolled my eyes. 'You may not be feckless, but you're definitely thick,' I told him. 'You really think I'd know something like *that*?'

'One tries to keep on one's toes,' he told me sniffily. 'It's very easy to offend women where cars are concerned. For all I know you might be Cardiff's answer to the Simonite sisters.'

'The who?'

'Or perhaps not. Don't worry. I'll check on this one.'

So he did, and I wrote it down on the back of my paying-in book, and then I climbed into the passenger seat of his racy yellow car and we drove back to the pub in Pontyffosfelen, where I called the RAC again and explained what had happened, and they told me they'd send a recovery truck.

It was too late to pick up a tyre now, they told me, but the truck would be with me as soon as they could manage and would take both my car and me home.

'To the garage, in fact,' I said to Will, as I replaced the receiver. 'Makes more sense. They said he'd drop me home afterwards.'

'Excellent,' he said. 'So we've another hour to kill. How about we stop here for a drink?'

Despite the merry nature of our exchanges, my brief epiphany at the roadside had left me somewhat raddled. Not because I had worked out what was *really* causing me to have become so arrested by his presence. Oh, no. Not a bit of it. Altogether different antennae were twitching. Like, here was someone who was pressing the exact same buttons in me that Harry already had. Like I ought to put out the 'road closed' signs or something before I took *him* on as a project as well. Because I didn't want my heart being spoken to like that. Didn't want the hassle of having to feel sad on yet another person's behalf, thank you very much. I had quite enough to be going on with fretting about Toni. I could do worst-case ante- and post-natal scenarios standing on my head, and I didn't want my head traumatized further. Even so, I couldn't help it. Suddenly the clarity of his features had sharpened; they had resolved themselves into discrete points of focus, and once focused on (try as I might not to) they had, without warning or reason or intention, become ever so much more than the sum of their parts. So that now, as I looked at him, I saw something else as well as Harry's feckless father. I saw a man with the weight of the world on his shoulders, burdened by grief and with no one to love him, who was having to play Harry's father *and* mother, operate his own washing-machine and ball his own socks. Which – despite equality, despite feminism, despite every kind of logic – was (as every woman, despite *herself*, knows) very dangerous territory indeed. Nothing like a large dose of personal tragedy to make a woman see a man through a soft-focus lens. Had he suddenly become the sweetie to whom Toni had alluded, and who, up to now, I hadn't managed to see? It's funny the way these things happen sometimes.

Funny, disquieting, but I managed to hide it. One learns, as a member of the teaching profession, that what's happening inside isn't always best reflected by the expression one paints on one's face. Was hiding it still as I nodded a brisk yes, and let him guide me back towards the barman. It was nothing more significant than the whimsical musings of a woman in thrall to a tragic widower with a wheelbrace, an empathetic take on bereavement in general, and a rather overactive imagination.

'Indeed we *are* stopping for a drink,' announced Will, to the barman. And with the sort of uncomplicated smile and merry tone that betrayed not a hint that he had the least idea about his newly revised status as principal-tragic-figure-in-my-life. He raised his brows at me. 'Holly? What would you like?'

'I'd like a coffee, I think,' I said, turning to the barman. 'Do you do coffee?'

Apparently yes, and he said he'd bring it over, so we took Will's drink – a Coke – and found ourselves a copper-topped table in the corner. It sported six little beermats, all carefully arranged, like place settings for a pixie *soirée*.

Will pulled off his jacket and said he had to visit the men's room, and only moments after that, a beeping noise started up.

It was coming from somewhere close by, and I realized that it was probably his jacket. Beep-beep, beep-beep, beep-*beeeeep*, it went. As it didn't seem appropriate to start delving into his pockets, I had a bit of a delve in my handbag instead, while I waited for it to stop beeping. Which it did, just as Will reappeared.

'Your jacket,' I said, gesturing, as he crossed the small distance between the door and the table. 'I think it's trying to tell you something. I thought you might have a text, but my phone's still out.'

He grabbed the jacket and rootled around in an inside pocket. As he did so, the beeping noise started up again.

'Ah,' he said. 'That's not my phone. That's my Palm Pilot.' He pulled out something plastic a little larger than a playing-card and scrutinized what I assumed was the display. Its light lent a greenish tinge to his chin. 'Ah,' he said again, tapping his finger against the screen. 'Of course. Look, sorry, I've got to go and make a quick call. Won't be a tick.'

He went back to the payphone while I poured milk into my newly arrived coffee. I could see him still, partly obscured by a poster that was fixed to the door and listed all the upcoming football fixtures that could be seen via satellite and the landlord's largesse (and with free roast potatoes) in the ensuing weeks. I could see the left side of his lean torso, his long legs. His feet. He was wearing exactly the same style of basketball boots as the ones Harry had worn into school, and a picture of them shopping together formed in my mind. The sort of picture, embellished by a heavily populated M and S background, that had the two of them, lone males, bobbing in a sea of permed harpies, all a-fret in a Saturday afternoon mid-season sale. Which was patently stupid. M and S didn't *sell* boots like that. I wondered what sort of structure their Saturdays had. And he really *was* thin. Was he eating enough? But then it came to me that the whole business of wondering such things came under the category of 'things I must avoid because I know what I'm like'. So I stopped myself wondering. And the tick trundled by. Perhaps a tick and a half, even, but then he was back through the doorway, all smiles. 'Sorry about that,' he said.

'Everything okay?'

'Forgot the time.' He smiled again and picked up his glass. 'Just something I needed to cancel. No problem.'

I put down my coffee cup. 'Cancel? Look, if I'm holding you up . . .'

'No. Not at all. Just a guy I'm supposed to be meeting up with. Nothing important.'

'Look, if you have to get off, it's not a problem. I can easily ring the RAC and have them meet me here instead.'

He shook his head. 'No, really. It's all sorted now.'

I picked up my cup again and looked him in the eye, frowning. 'I thought you told me you didn't need to be anywhere.'

He held up his palms. And held my gaze. 'Okay. You got me. It's a fair cop. I lied.'

I didn't know what to say to that, especially in tandem with his expression, half smile, half challenge, which made me drop my eyes. I swallowed a mouthful of coffee instead and wondered quite why I should find it so difficult to accept that he might do that for me. I wished he wouldn't. I *really* wished he hadn't.

'I wish you hadn't,' I said. 'I feel awful now. What with us losing Harry and everything, I feel like I've comprehensively hijacked your day. You didn't need to—'

'Yes, I *did*,' he said firmly. 'I owe you one.'

'No, you don't.'

'Yes, I *do*. And even if I hadn't, I would have

done it in any case.' He drew breath as if to emphasize his words. Then he leaned forward a little. 'Because I *wanted* to, okay? Because I like you and I wanted to help you out. Why on earth do you have such a problem with that?' He looked baffled. 'Look,' he added, 'if it makes you feel any better, it wasn't anything *that* important. Just a guy I have to run through a storyboard with. Nothing that won't keep till tomorrow.'

'But it *shouldn't* have had to. That's exactly my point.'

He winked at me. 'Shall I tell you something?'

'What?'

'My decision, okay? And I'm staying.'

Oh, dear, oh, dear. I really had to move this conversation along. All these should-haves and would-haves, all this unsolicited chivalry, all this uninvited reading of uncomfortable thoughts. He was looking altogether too pointedly at me, I decided. 'So tell me,' I said quickly, 'what exactly *is* a storyboard?'

'Pretty much what it sounds like,' he said, changing gear now, and nodding behind his half-empty glass. I watched his Adam's apple rise and fall as he tipped and drained it. 'It's the story. Of whatever you're making the film about. Told frame by frame. In pictures. So you can see the thing visually and establish your shots.'

I'd never thought of the average washing-powder ad in terms of a story, so I said that as well.

He put down his glass. 'Pretty much everything

you see on film is a story of one sort or another. Doesn't matter if it's a five-second promo or a three-hour movie. The basic elements are still the same. You have a script, you have a treatment, you have a crew, you have a story. You're still essentially trying to achieve the same thing. To get your point, your product, your *raison d'être*, if you like, across through a visual medium. Doesn't matter whether what you're doing is trying to sell, explain, or entertain. The mechanics of it don't change.'

He moved his arms about a lot as he talked. Always seemed to, I realized. He was perpetually animated, sprung and restless, as if possessed of an irritating surfeit of energy and thus constantly straining at an invisible leash. I nodded. 'And that's what you do.'

'Yup. Pretty much.'

'Sounds a million miles away from what I do.'

'I guess it is. What you do for a living actually matters.'

He said it entirely without emphasis. Just as a statement of fact.

'Oh, you shouldn't say that,' I said.

He shrugged. 'Why not? It's true. Which is not to say I have any issues about it. Or that I'd want to do anything different. But you should sit in on a post-production meeting some time. Once you realize that a dozen people can argue to the point of violence over something as insignificant as the typeface they're going to use beneath a packshot – and, believe me, I've seen it happen – then you kind of get a handle on the word "superficial".'

As you did when bereavement came to visit, it occurred to me. Oh, yes, I knew all about that. And he was right. Had I been asked to find a word to describe what I had hitherto thought of the advertising industry that would probably have been the one I'd have chosen. But to agree with him would have been rude. And unfair. 'I didn't go into teaching because I wanted to save the world,' I told him instead. 'Any more than you do what you're doing because you didn't. I went into teaching because I thought I'd be good at it. Though only after a painful process of elimination. I spent most of my childhood planning on being a movie star, but regrettably no one else shared my vision. The most I ever made was shepherd number four. I was generally cast as a tree.'

He clapped his hands then, just as he had at the roadside. 'Well, today's your *double* lucky day then, I'm pleased to tell you.' He did a little cigar flourish with the Palm Pilot pointer. 'D'you still wanna be in the movies?'

'*Me?*' I shook my head. 'Er, no. Not any more. The movies can manage quite well without any input from me.'

He sat forward in his seat then, resting his elbows on his thighs, his fingertips touching between them. 'No, no. I *mean* it, Holly. Seriously. I'm working on some treatments for a TTA recruitment campaign, and I'm in need of a tame headmistress.'

The TTA was the Teacher Training Agency. It had never occurred to me he might do that kind of work. 'It's "head *teacher*",' I corrected him, smiling. '"Headmistress" makes me feel like a hateful old hag. Not that I want you to run away with the idea that I'm a pedant, or anything.'

He smiled back and rolled his eyes. 'Forgive me. Did I say *tame*? What was I thinking? Okay, head *teacher*. So. How about it?'

'Depends. To do what? Why exactly do you need one?'

'Because I need a school, basically. Staff. Children. Nature table. Games. You know. Best-days-of-your-life stuff. Dead poets and all that.'

'Dead *poets*?'

'You know what I mean. The whole childhood-idyll thing. D'you get a lot of low mists on the playing-field this time of year? Don't worry. You don't have to answer that. I was going to ask you about it a few weeks back, actually, but after the business with Casper I decided it might not go down that well.' He smiled.

So did I. His was catching. Like measles. 'You were right about that,' I said.

'But now?'

I folded my arms. 'You still haven't said. To do what? Gambol in the mist spouting Wordsworth?'

'If you think it'll make you happy. No, it's nothing too arduous. Not much to camera. I'm thinking more in terms of a montage of images. Tell you what. I'll have to come in and take you through the concept board.'

I was struggling to keep up. 'Which is like a storyboard, right?'

'Kind of, but different. It's not sequential, of course. Because it's all about the—'

'Concept.'

'You got it.'

'And what's yours?'

'Pretty fluid right now. It's still very much a work in progress.'

A little bit like Harry, I thought. A little bit like Will.

'Like me, eh?' he said ruefully, which brought me up short. I didn't know if he meant the same thing as I'd been thinking, but it didn't make any difference. I'd thought it, and he'd said it. He *was* it, and I'd *seen* it. I was being sucked in, despite my every good intention. And the whole thing felt, well, inexorable, somehow.

By the time we got back to my car it was dark as only the countryside can be. Dark and growing chilly now, settling into night-time, the hedgerows all spiked with early-spring growth that danced along the tops like so many rows of paper dolls. The RAC man, who was already there, was a riot of reflector strip that almost fizzed against the dark. He whistled appreciatively as we climbed out of Will's car.

'I always wanted a Morgan,' he said, adopting the quiet reverence men reserve for bosoms and bottoms and cup-final wins.

And cars, of course.

'Me too,' Will agreed gravely. He flattened a palm downwards at his side. 'Since I was *this* big.'

'And now you've got one. She's a dream to drive, I'll bet.'

'A dream,' Will confirmed. Then, after the appropriate period of silent worship had been observed, they sighed as one and gently stroked the car's wing. Strange creatures, men. But it still made me smile. My dad had had an Austin Westminster automatic. He used to announce it in the same reverential, hushed tone. I must have been six or seven when he bought it. 'It's an Austin Westminster automatic,' he'd say, if somebody should admire it.

'And with real walnut tables in the back!' I used to add. I thought them quite the nattiest things I'd ever seen. I didn't know anyone else with little pull-down tables in the backs of their cars.

And then he'd fluff my hair and grin and say, 'Oh, go *on* with you. You and those tables!' Crazy. As if he really thought no one had noticed just how bursting with pride *he* was. This was just like that. That same dreamy look was right there in Will's eye. As if he couldn't quite believe he should ever be so lucky. It made me feel wistful, but it made me smile too.

It didn't take too long to get the car loaded up, and what time it did take, I spent sitting in the cab of the RAC truck, having only half grudgingly conceded to their joint insistence that they'd do it between them without any help from me. It felt like only a matter of minutes, in fact, before we were bowling comfortably along the lane back towards the M4, Will's tail-lights an ever-diminishing pair of tiger eyes ahead of us. It was only when we got to the garage in Cardiff that the last hitch in a day full of hitches became glaringly apparent. The biggest hitch of all, had I but figured it out.

'You going to write them a note?' the RAC man said, once he'd lowered the car onto the forecourt.

'Yes,' I said, opening my bag. 'I'd better do that, hadn't I?'

He nodded. 'Best thing's to wrap it round the keys and stick it through the letterbox. You can ring them first thing and fill them in.'

Which was a perfectly good idea except for one small detail. The fact that the keys weren't in my bag. It didn't take me more than a moment to realize why. Because I hadn't been the last one to have them. Will had. I remembered him having them when they'd loaded my car. I didn't remember having had them back. Because I hadn't. They would still be where they'd been then. In his jacket pocket.

'Oh, well,' said the RAC man, while I scribbled my amended note. 'You'll have to pop them along in the morning, won't you? Car's not going anywhere. C'mon. Let's get you home, love.'

There was nothing to be done about it. Although I'd added Will's mobile and home numbers to my phone list on the night that Harry's cat had died, I knew there was no point in calling his home yet, and he wasn't answering his mobile either. So I left a message telling him not to worry about it, to have Harry drop them in to me on Monday, I didn't want to inconvenience him any more. I'd have Max bring his spare set with him later.

Except I'd already missed Max. There was a message from him on the answerphone when I got in, saying he was popping round to Catherine's to sort out Tara's computer, and that he'd come on to me at about nine. Which meant he'd have to bring them tomorrow instead. Or go back for them, which was sure to put him in a mood. I drew the curtains to shut out the night then, cursing my stupidity, took myself off for a shower.

I was just towelling my hair when I heard the entry-phone buzzer. Max, a little earlier than he'd anticipated, I thought. He had a key, of course, and he usually used it. But although he generally let himself in downstairs, he always stopped and buzzed before he came up and let himself into the flat. I didn't know what he thought I'd be up to. Perhaps nothing. Perhaps it was simple propriety, and once we were married he wouldn't do it any more. Of course not, I thought, as I slipped into my bathrobe, because I wouldn't be living here any more. I wished I could begin to get my head around that.

But Max didn't appear, and a few seconds later the entryphone buzzed again. Not Max, then. I crossed the room and pressed the intercom button.

'Hello?'

'Well, hello there! It's your friendly neighbourhood key-return service.'

'Oh!' I said. 'Will!' Gracious me. *Will*. 'Oh, right,' I said. 'I'll come down.' Except I was still in my bathrobe, so I couldn't. 'Er, no. No, I won't,' I said. 'You'd better come on up.'

I had a matter of seconds to change from bathrobe to clothes if I wanted, but I decided not to bother. This wasn't the sort of bathrobe to inspire impropriety, after all. It was floor-length and powder blue, designed for drying, not deflowering. It was the bathrobe my mother had bought me the Christmas before she died. A bathrobe with all the sexual allure of a teabag.

The door went, I opened it, and there was Will Meadows. Standing in the corridor looking dark-eyed and tired, but still as Bob-a-Job cheerful as when he'd almost run me down.

'One set of car keys, duly returned.' He looked at them, then fished in his pocket. 'Ah. No. Sorry. Those are mine.' He tried his other pocket. 'Hang on . . .'

'Will,' I began, unsure whether I should be asking him in or not, 'you didn't need to come all this way, you know.' I ushered him over the threshold, via hand signals, and he took two polite steps into

181

my tiny hallway. It was gloomy, so I flicked on the light. 'Come on. Come on in.'

'No,' he said. 'I'm not stopping. Just wanted to drop your keys off. I wasn't sure you'd have a spare set.' He tried his inside pocket as well. 'Nope. Palm Pilot. Well, I presumed you would have, but I thought, well, you know, just in case.'

He moved on to patting his jeans pockets, and I waited, realizing I should have thrown on something after all, because I was being made all self-conscious simply by the *concept* of the bathrobe, a point that hadn't figured in my thinking, alas. 'Well, that's sweet of you,' I said. 'I feel such a fool for forgetting them.'

'My fault. I didn't give them back to you, did I?'

'No, mine. I should have thought.' He had the right keys in his hand now. 'I'm not normally so scatty. Not scatty at *all*.'

He didn't give them to me right away. Just exhaled and narrowed his eyes as he considered me. 'I wasn't thinking so for an instant,' he said.

I pulled the lapels of the bathrobe together. 'Well, I'm very grateful.'

'And you're very welcome.'

'But you shouldn't have. I mean, coming all this way . . . You could have rung. I do have a spare set. I left a message on your mobile. You could have had Harry drop them in to me on Monday or something.'

I was only gabbling at such a rate because I had come to realize that every time I stopped speaking there was some sort of time-lag thing going on. Like when the TV anchorman in the studio goes across to some foreign correspondent and there's a satellite delay and they seem not to hear for a moment. Just stare into the camera. That thing. *That* thing. It was almost imperceptible, but definitely there.

'I know that,' he said, still holding my keys. 'I picked up your message at the lights at Coryton. But when I called back, you weren't answering.' His eyes flicked towards my wet hair and back. 'In the shower, I suppose. Anyway, I thought . . . well, what the hell? I was in the car anyway, wasn't I? It was no problem to drive over here first.'

As if it wasn't an extra forty-five minutes on his journey. As if it were just round the corner. As if he really had nothing better to do. But, then, perhaps he *didn't* have anything better to do. Apart from the someone he was supposed to see about the something or other he had to run through on his storyboard, perhaps his weekend stretched ahead of him as one endless veldt of regretful introspection. Perhaps he stalked the rooms of his house colliding with ghosts. And no Harry, even. Not tonight. Just him and his grief rattling around together. Lonely. It might have been the work of imaginative extrapolation, but so much seemed to me to be going on behind his smile. Was he waiting for something? Was he hoping I'd press him to have a drink? But I couldn't. Max was due. Shouldn't anyway. No.

Still he held the keys. Still he stared into my eyes. 'And at some speed,' I said, lowering my gaze and taking renewed refuge in gabble. 'I've only been back about a quarter of an hour myself. If that. That's pretty impressive going for someone who has a Ph.D. in getting lost. I'm amazed you even remembered where I live.'

He held out the keys to me then. Finally. *Finally*. And, still clutching at the lapels of my bathrobe for security, I put out my left hand to take them. An ordinary, workaday, unremarkable exchange. One set of car keys from his hand to mine. But his fingers brushed my skin as he placed them in my palm.

It was just an accidental whisper of skin against skin, but a lingering whisper, as if it was being shot in slo-mo, and I found myself looking up again and colliding with his gaze. I didn't mean to. And I probably should have been on my guard. I mean, hello? Was I *awake* here? Had I not seen the signs? But you *do* look at someone, don't you? When they give something to you? You glance up and smile, you nod, you acknowledge. Move your eyes from the person to the something and back. That's the way it works, isn't it? It's usual. Normal. So I had no reason to suppose this would be any different. But as my eyes meet Will's now, they somehow got stuck.

Stuck good and proper, like a wheel in a snow-drift. Spinning and spinning and kicking up sparkles, but making no progress except to sink deeper in.

He lowered his hand, I closed mine round the keys, but our eyes remained fixed for what seemed like an age. Four seconds? Six? A whole handful of heartbeats.

'Funnily enough,' he said softly, 'I'm not.'

CHAPTER 12

'She does look lovely, doesn't she? Absolutely stunning.'

This is Max, who is talking to his partner, Trevor Perkins. Who nods at me. 'Oh, yes. Lovely,' he agrees.

'Lovely,' says Trevor's very lovely wife, Molly. She smiles politely, perfect teeth emerging from behind the lip gloss. 'Where did you find that beautiful dress?'

I got the dress from Dorothy. Well, not so much got as borrowed. Dorothy has lots of evening dresses, almost all of them gorgeous, almost all of them the sort of frocks that one doesn't generally aspire to wearing when one has been living on a teacher's salary all one's life. This one, which is humming-bird green and shimmers with gold bead-work, last saw service at a ball in St Kitts. It has danced with an ambassador by a Caribbean shore-line. Which is quite something. It *is* a beautiful dress.

Friday night. Just a handful of heartbeats but, God, I was in the most appalling flap. It couldn't have been more than six seconds or so, but six seconds is a very long time when you are making unblinking eye-contact with someone who is not telling you their life story, trying to get an eyelash out of your eye, or explaining the mechanics of a toaster. In terms of packing an emotional punch, it is the most meaningful thing you can do with a spare six seconds, let me tell you. Because eyes don't mince words or attempt *double-entendres*. They tell it like it is and are quite without guile. They knock giving flowers into touch, for certain.

Though the detail eludes me, it was probably the sound of Dorothy coming out of the lift that brought it – whatever 'it' was – to an end. And brought it to and end that it might not have had in mind. Which is something I'm having more than a little trouble getting my head round.

The lift is just round the corner of the corridor from my flat, in the opposite direction to the stairs. In any event, she rounded the corner, Will blinked and said, 'I'd better be off, then,' or something, then Dorothy said, 'Oh, good evening!' and Will was obliged to turn and say, 'Good evening,' back, which of course obliged me to say, 'Will, this is Dorothy Bates, my neighbour,' and to Dorothy, 'Dorothy, this is Will Meadows.' *My what?* Then they both said, 'Hello,' and 'Nice to meet you,' and 'Goodnight,' and then Will went down the stairs and I bundled Dorothy inside.

'He looks just like a gentleman pirate,' she observed, as she entered. 'What a very handsome and charismatic young man.' She turned then, and smiled. 'I do see what you mean, dear.'

'What d'you mean what I mean?'

'Well, all right, not so much what you *mean*. Just, let's say, why you're so taken with him.'

'Taken?' I snorted. 'What on earth are you on about?' But even as I blustered and tutted and went, 'Nonsense!' the blood was charging through my body like a runaway train.

Max has already had two pints of beer and I can smell it on his breath as we make our way through to the ballroom. The place is dripping with wildlife. Every five yards there is a pillar with a vase from which ridiculously big marshmallow-laden branches erupt. There must be one mighty cross blossom tree out there somewhere. Which I find myself feeling is a terrible waste because blossom doesn't last once it's cut.

'Lovely,' he says again. And I wish he'd stop doing it. 'D'you think anyone would notice if we slipped off and skipped dinner?'

'Oh, be*have*, Max,' I say, a bit snappily. I'm sure he doesn't notice, but I do. *I* do. 'Have patience,' I add quickly. But I add it too late. Half a minute too late.

'Beg pardon?' he says.

And then he adds, 'Ah! Hello! Here's the Rhys Woodruffs! Hello there, you two! Are we okay for drinks?'

I do a double-take, as they do. Then we paste on some smiles. Oh, lovely. Just lovely. More wildlife. *Fab.*

If Mr Rhys-Woodruff had been born sixty or seventy-odd years earlier, he would have owned a coal mine, for sure. A coal mine, a watch on a chain and a walking cane. Not stick, mind. Cane. Topped with a duck head or a rearing cobra. He has that florid look so beloved of Victorian novelists. A big bullish Bounderby to Trevor Perkins's Gradgrind. A roly-poly figure in gaiters and waistcoat. Grizzled greying hair, a booming laugh, a touch of gout. He would have fitted in well. Been a Colourful Character. But the twenty-first century is not his best arena. In his bow-tie and DJ he looks what he is: a rather bombastic and arrogant overweight company director, who probably thinks the can-can girls that dance across his shirt front mark him down as a bit of a wag. He has reined in his girth with a black satin cummerbund. His shirt is leaking out underneath.

'Well, well, well,' he says now, as if inspecting a U-bend. 'Mrs Connors! How the devil *are* you?'

I think he has been drinking as well. Everyone's been drinking. Everyone *is* drinking. And why wouldn't they? It's Saturday night. It's a *do*. Except I'm not. I dare not. If I drink I might relax. If I relax I might think. If I think I might think things that will make me feel stressed.

'I'm very well, Mr Rhys-Woodruff,' I tell him politely, once the shock has subsided. What luck, to find I am to spend my Saturday evening in the company of my favourite parents. He explains

189

that we've met, Max explains who he is, they both explain the intricacies of their client/lawyer relationship. And everyone says, 'Goodness! What a very small world!' Except it's not. Cardiff is not a big place, and it shouldn't come as any surprise that Absolutely Bathrooms would retain absolutely the best lawyers. And Perkins and Stapleforth are unquestionably that.

'And, puh-*lease*,' he booms heartily. 'It's *Dafydd, okay*?'

So we're all on first-name terms tonight. How very chummy.

Dafydd has been seated three along from me. To my left is Trevor, to his left is a Mrs Irma Swindells (who is fairly aged, smokes cigars, and apparently breeds goats), and to her left is he. Mrs Rhys-Woodruff (beg pardon – *Penny*) has fetched up next to Max, which puts her across the table from me, behind yet more flowering cherry. Despite the thicket, I can hear her telling Max all about new developments in flame-retardant upholstery fabrics, which I know he will greatly enjoy.

Tell the truth, I wasn't much looking forward to coming to the Ides of March ball, even before Friday's traumas when my head became disconnected from my shoulders in so alarming a fashion. By Will Meadows, in what I've decided must have been some sort of drive-by mugging of the emotions. *No*. No, it wasn't. It was Dorothy who did it. Dorothy who put into my head the notion of being 'taken with' him. Oh, God. Whatever. Before *that*, at any rate.

It was nothing specific that was putting me off – I hadn't known the Rhys-Woodruffs were going to be there, had I? – just that these corporate things have a way of making you irritable. The having to wear oddly shaped items of scaffolding-type underwear, the mincing around in heels, the cloying powder-room fumes. The diabolical music, the chicken 'n' peas dinner, the having to dance to Abba with insufferable old gropers, the having to talk endlessly, endlessly, *endlessly* about the demise of the eleven plus, the state of young people's grammar, and why they don't seem to teach the three Rs any more. I sometimes wonder if I shouldn't attend these things incognito. 'Oh, you're a head teacher? Really? Tell me something, will you? Where do you stand on times tables?'

Like tables – times or otherwise – Ides are simply representational tools, of course. Though less re-presentational than numbers, perhaps, because dates back then were a great deal less rigidly defined than they are now. A bit like train timetables are these days. I never did get my head round the Roman calendar set-up, but that much I do know. When I was younger, I used to think Ides were monsters of some description. You had to beware of them, so it made perfect sense. But it's like April Fools Day, or Friday the thirteenth. And the only relevance it has to Trevor's late dad's charity is that he used to hold an annual fancy-dress party for his neighbours in March, and generally insisted on togas. Such was cutting-edge partying back in the sixties. And with the amount of key- and wife-swapping reputed to have happened, the toga was perhaps the best facilitative tool.

Anyway, I have been right to beware the Ides of March because we're not long into the starter when Dafydd Rhys-Woodruff leans across the table and says, 'That reminds me. Can I bend your ear about selection later on, Mrs C?'

I'm not sure *what* reminds him or, indeed, how much later on he means, but it's certainly something to look forward to. Not. In the meantime, Penny Rhys-Woodruff has the whole table in thrall, by virtue of the fact that she once saw Laurence Llewellyn-Bowen in a lift.

'In Selfridges. Or was it Harrods? No. Selfridges. Or was it? Anyway, he was wearing that jacket I've seen him in on television. There's very few men that can get away with *toile de Jouy*. But he can. He's ever so much more macho in the flesh, you know. Just oozes testosterone. *Oozes* it, believe me.'

'Who does?' barks Dafydd.

'I was just saying, love. Laurence Llewellyn-Bowen.'

'Looks like a bloody ponce to me.'

'What's *toile de Jouy* when it's at home?' asks Trevor.

The main course passes in similar fashion. Seated as I am at the apex of two disparate conversations, I have a choice of interesting topics to dip into.

And by the time dessert arrives, I have learned two important new things. One, that the secret of success with *toile de Jouy* stencilling is mainly a question of intelligent sourcing, plus attention to detail in the brushwork, and two, that the secret of slaughtering goats is just a question of having a grip like a docker and an extremely sharp eleven-inch knife.

Lovely. But once the table has been cleared of dessert and of those among us who won't feel their evening is properly under way until they've leaped up to flail around to whatever tune is best accessorized by community air punching and lots of really bad singing, i.e. almost all of the women and such men as are properly in touch with their feminine and/or gay side (and/or Max, who has been hauled onto the dance floor by the unexpectedly lithe – and grippy? – Mrs Swindells), my conversational opportunities are about to become altogether less free-range, because Dafydd hops across the three seats that separate us, ignites a small cigar and asks me where I stand on the abolition of grammar schools. As I know exactly where *he* stands on this issue (not at all happy about the fact that he will have to pay dearly for any sort of education that will not bring his delicate child into close contact with the 'sort of children who have head lice and bloody crack dealers for parents') I elect, despite my earlier enthusiasm for debate, to hop straight up onto the diplomatically safe fence.

I tell him that while I appreciate their academic

strengths I do feel there are some issues for society as a whole if such a large percentage of it are written off at eleven, especially in today's technologically advanced society, where there simply aren't the quantity and range of manual jobs available that perhaps there were fifty years ago, in conjunction with the relatively longer period of full-time education that is nowadays the norm – and to be encouraged, of course – and in tandem with the fact that expectations are greater for the whole of society these days, and not just for the élite, I am not sure that it is entirely right and just that we should make decisions that might affect the whole of a person's life based on the decidedly tenuous premise that every child reaches an equivalent developmental milestone at the age of eleven, regardless of background, sex and genetically determined maturation rate.

He adopts a tobacco-filtered scowl, then sniffs. 'One of those lefty liberals, then, are you?'

Oh dear. I should have seen that coming.

To be in the company of a 'lefty liberal' obviously holds entertainment value for Dafydd Rhys-Woodruff. Either that or he's determined to wind me up. Whichever, in the space of a scant twenty minutes, we've moved on from lefty liberals and their deleterious effect on manners, morality and, that old standard, 'standards', to the manifest deficiencies of the state education system and the 'fact' (his word) that modern teachers are all wets, and don't know how to discipline kids any more. (This last is via a comment concerning one Master Meadows, which I manage to ignore, but nevertheless duly file, in short-term memory folder D, sub-folder 17: 'Don't worry, I've got your number, all right, pal.')

It has to be said that Dafydd Rhys-Woodruff's is a view so often expressed for my benefit that under normal circumstances I wouldn't bother to rise to it, but tonight, for reasons various, it gets right up my nose. Which leads me to observe that as I, despite having owned several bathrooms, would never presume to know anything much about the intricacies of plumbing, why does his having produced Owen lead *him* to suppose he is more qualified to judge *my* profession than I his? To which he replies, 'Look, love, it's simple. I've got a brain in my head, see?' to which I reply that perhaps he ought to deploy it before opening his mouth.

And so on and so forth. All merry banter. But somehow, in less time than it takes to fashion an attractive *toile de Jouy* firescreen out of a length of unwanted wallpaper, some gaffer tape and a hairdryer, I realize our banter is becoming rather less merry, and that we've fetched up at Poles-apart Central, a place most sensible people don't visit often as it leads to a siding nearby called Mutual Hostility. Bugger political correctness, I've decided. Bugger the fact that he's one of my parents. There are some things, some stances, some varieties of pronouncement, that simply cannot pass unremarked. Something like that, anyway. It's a knee-jerk thing mainly. All I know for sure is that we're now talking about hanging, that he's informed me I'm 'naïve to the point of imbecility, God help us', and that I've told him, in no particular order of unpleasantness, that he's ignorant, cruel and anachronistic. All *terrifically* politely, of course. Oh, and his cigar has gone out.

A silence ensues while he attends to his butt and I whoop silently at my coup. His look of barely concealed bafflement and intent on diversion makes it perfectly clear that he wouldn't know an anachronism if it was fired, via a trebuchet, straight up his left nostril. *Un point* to *moi*, Mr Big.

But there are, it seems, no more points to be scored tonight. There have been several comings and goings while Dafydd and I have been talking, but as they've only been happening at the edge of my attention, several seconds now elapse before it sinks in that not only has all other conversation ceased but that Max is pulling a face. And that Penny, Trevor, Mrs Swindells and Mrs Trevor are all looking at us too, anxious to hear his response.

Which is not forthcoming. As is often the way with the sort of heated debate that happens at these functions, the point has been reached where the only course of action is either to agree to differ and call it a day or start swapping swear words and fighting. So, as if by tacit agreement (one thing we do agree on), I find myself now smiling gaily at him, and him at me. And having failed to relight his cigar, he stabs it instead into a nearby ashtray, says, 'Yey!

Robbie Williams!', yanks his startled wife from her chair, and the pair of them hot-foot it to the dance-floor, while I pour myself a fresh glass of mineral water, and cut myself a small piece of Brie.

And that was that. I dare say I would have thought little more about it were it not for the fact that an hour or so later, post much of the manic dancing and while Max was doing the rounds and saying his farewells, I happened upon Dafydd as I was coming out of the ladies', on my way to get my coat. It was Max, in fact, to whom he was talking.

'Spirited old filly, that one, eh?' he was saying. 'I'll bet you have to keep her on a very short leash.'

They were out of sight, beyond the screen with the table plans on it (no *toile de Jouy* here, just your standard-issue blue hessian), and I paused, waiting to hear Max's response. But he said nothing. *Nothing.* Just laughed some sort of laugh, and one of them, I couldn't see which, clapped the other on the back. Dafydd, I imagined. And did Max roll his eyes? I could imagine him doing it. Going 'Tsk! Women, eh?' Or something like that. Not an edifying thought.

I swept past them and went off to the cloak-room. Evidence, I thought grimly, that Penny Rhys-Woodruff hadn't always sourced *quite* so intelligently.

Even then, although I was faintly peeved about Max's failure to produce a spirited rejoinder, I didn't much care. A stupid man, being stupid. Nothing new there. I even smiled to myself about it. There are few things more gratifying than putting in their place people who deserved to be put there. End of evening. Subject closed. What a goon. What a moron. What a joy that, come the summer, Owen would be leaving, and thus my acquaintance with his father would end.

End of story. I thought fleetingly of sharing what I'd heard with Max, but decided against it. In some ways, being described as a spirited old filly by the likes of Dafydd Rhys-Woodruff was something about which to feel pleased. His was clearly a world where women did as they were told. Do him good to have his feathers ruffled now and again. And I certainly wasn't looking for an argument with Max. I thought he was quiet walking to the car because he was tired. Or slightly drunk. Not drunk, as it turned out. Though he handed me the car keys, it was more reflex than anything. He was perfectly lucid as he got into the passenger seat.

'Well,' he said, reaching for his seat-belt as I slipped off my sandals to drive barefoot, 'thanks for that.'

Well. What a miscalculation I'd made, to be sure. 'I beg your pardon?' I said.

'I said thanks.'

'What for?'

'I'll know who to call.'

'I beg your pardon?' I said again, mystified at his tone.

'If the day comes when I find my client list just a little too large and unmanageable and in need of a trim, I'll know who to call.'

He was being sarcastic. He was being unpleasant, even. I could have said, 'I beg your pardon,' again. But I didn't because I was tired, the balls of my feet were on fire, and I couldn't be doing with silly games. So instead I decided to go at it head on. I said, 'Stop being obscure, Max. If there's something terrifically important you want to say to me, I wish you'd just do it, okay? I'm tired.'

'Oh, I don't doubt it.'

'There you go again! What *is* it?'

He shook his head slowly from side to side. I could see him do it out of the corner of my eye. Then he turned to me. 'You don't even know, do you?'

I started the engine and pulled out into the road. 'No, Max. You're right. I don't even know.'

'Then there's no point in me telling you.'

'Max, you are beginning to sound like my mother. Look, if you've got something to say, then—'

'Yes, Holly, I have, as it happens. Like, what the hell was all that *about*, for God's sake?'

'All what?'

'Christ. All that nonsense with Dafydd, of course!'

The penny dropped. Or, rather, didn't. Not quite. Not yet. 'Nonsense?'

'Yes, nonsense. I've never been so embarrassed. What the hell did you think you were doing?'

'I *beg* your pardon?'

'You heard.'

It did now. God! He was telling me off! *Me!* I may be confrontational but I'm not generally that quick to anger. So I was perhaps as shocked as he was to hear the tone of my reply. 'Yes,' I snapped back. 'But I thought I heard *wrong*. For a minute there I thought you might have failed to notice that I don't happen to be one of your *children*!'

We drove the rest of the way home in silence.

Guilt is one of those things that can creep up on you unexpectedly. In my case, at this time, it wasn't just because I'd had ten minutes to spool back and rerun my run-in with the pugnacious plumber. Wasn't just because I knew my state of mind was less unruffled than normal. It was Max and his silence. A silence that was the result, I just *knew*, of him digesting and accepting that he had no business speaking to me as if I was one of his daughters. Which should have made me feel all self-righteous and huffy, but instead made me feel fifteen. Yes, of *course* he would have been embarrassed. Max was not the sort of person to draw attention to himself. Outside the necessaries inherent in his profession, he was the sort of man who'd consider it the height of bad manners to wait in the road for someone to vacate a parking space if so much as one car was held up behind him. I swung the car into the drive and killed the ignition. Still he said nothing. And there was something so stiff and pained in his demeanour that I immediately regretted every last thing I had said to Dafydd Rhys-Woodruff, from 'good evening' onwards, and possibly before. Perhaps it was time to rein in.

'Look,' I said, while I wriggled my feet back into my sandals, 'I'm sorry, okay? It's just that he's such an infuriating man. I didn't—'

'He is also one of my clients, Holly,' he said levelly. 'What on earth did you think you were trying to do?'

Max didn't raise his voice. Max doesn't raise his voice.

I did. Rein in or otherwise, I found, to my dismay, that I couldn't help it. 'Trying to do'. What the hell did *that* mean? So off I went again. 'I wasn't *trying* to do anything! I was just having a dis—'

'Row with him.'

We both got out of the car. '*No*,' I said to him, over the roof now. '*Discussion* with him, Max.'

'Row with him, Holly. You should have been in the audience.'

I rounded the bonnet and fetched up beside him on the pavement. 'Look, I'm sorry if I got a bit heated, but, frankly, he deserved it. The man's an arrogant, pompous, opinionated dick, and if the bottom drops out of the sanitaryware industry I shall be first in the queue waving a flag at his wake.'

Max blinked then. Twice. Then took his car keys from me and stalked off past me up the steps to the front door.

'But he *is*,' I persisted, following him. He turned just as I reached the second to top step and flung out a gesticulatory arm with such force that, for a second, I thought I was going to end up in the berberis. With all the spiders and slugs and the coils of cat poo that Max's cat, Cleopatra, who generally ignored me, habitually left under the hedge.

'What the hell's that got to do with it?' he snapped. 'He's a client, for God's sake. You know? Like – hello? – one of the breed that pays my salary?'

I gripped the handrail and pulled myself back to the vertical. 'Oh,' I said. 'That makes a difference, does it?'

'Of course it makes a difference! I don't know how things operate in your line of work, but in my line of work it entails treating him with a modicum of respect!'

We lurched, as one, into the hallway. A pair of Tara's trainers blocked our passage. Max almost went headlong and automatically I grabbed him. It was the way he shook off my arm, above every-thing, that did it. As if I was a cockroach that had scuttled up his sleeve.

'What do you mean, my line of work?' I demanded. 'Believe me, forbearance is my middle name.'

'Oh, right. So you thought you'd save your venom till you weren't at work, did you? Till you had the chance to embarrass *me*. Well, thanks. Thanks a lot.'

I rounded on him by the newel post, still unsure

what had got into me this evening. 'Look, I said I'm sorry, didn't I? Yes, I'm a little cross with myself for rising to it and, no doubt, come the morning, I will regret having done so. But that's *my* prerogative, okay? Not yours. Max, I am not in your employ. What I choose to say to people is none of your business.'

He poked his own chest. 'It is when you're out with *me*.'

'*What?*' He just couldn't see it. Wouldn't. He continued to glare at me. 'Oh, right,' I said. 'Is that so? Well, forgive me for being thick, but since when was it written that there were rules of engagement here? Perhaps I missed something somewhere, but I wasn't aware of any rule that said I couldn't have an adult discussion with a fellow human being without consulting you first. I do apologize. Perhaps you could have your PA email me the protocols so that next time I happen to fetch up at a dinner dance with you I know how to behave, should one of your clients happen along. Hmm? Yes? That might be best, mightn't it? Wouldn't want to let my appalling opinions stand between you and a fee. Or, better still, why not be on the safe side and tie me to a lamp-post somewhere on the way in. Hmm?'

I glared right on back, then stomped into the kitchen, not so much off the back of a flourish or anything, but simply because I was cross as hell and I wanted to go off in a self-righteous flounce. Childish, I knew, but I didn't care. Why should Tara and Sasha have a monopoly here? But my moment was short-lived, because he just shook his head and followed. Always shook his head and followed. I wasn't allowed flounces any more than they were. I had to take things or leave them because we didn't do 'scenes'.

His expression was back on the right side of cross. Damage limitation, as ever, with Max. He said, very calmly, 'Holly, this is stupid,' which, of course, made me feel it all the more. What else can you feel when you're trying to have a huff, and the person you're engaged in trying to have a huff with points out just how silly you're being?

'Okay, *okay*,' I agreed, kicking off a shoe. It sailed across the kitchen and landed in Cleopatra's litter tray, spraying gobbets of grey gravel high into the air. I turned, lit on his troubled blue eyes, and felt all the fight in me begin to ebb away. 'Tell me, Max,' I said more quietly, 'do you believe in the death penalty?'

He rolled his eyes. 'Why are you even asking me that? You know I don't. You *know* I don't.'

So why hadn't he said so? It was something, I realized, that I really wanted to know. It hadn't occurred to me at the time, but now it did. He'd been listening, hadn't he? Why hadn't he so much as offered it up as an opinion? Instead of pulling disapproving faces at me, why hadn't he, at the very least, made it clear to Rhys-bloody-Woodruff that he was with *me* on that point? Why? But I didn't need to ask him because he already knew what I was saying.

'Look, Holly—' he began.

But I couldn't be bothered. It was already done. 'No, no. I understand. He's a client. I understand, Max.'

'There's a world of difference between agreeing with someone and maintaining a diplomatic silence,' he said, looking offended.

Yes, I thought. As I'd witnessed myself later. 'Did they teach you that at law school?'

'Holly—'

'Oh, ignore me,' I said, all at once overcome with the sadness of it all. It was a question of loyalty and I felt he'd let me down. He didn't even realize and I couldn't begin to explain. Either about that or what he didn't know I'd overheard. 'It's not you,' I said instead. 'It's him. I'm cross with him and I'm taking it out on you, that's all.' And as I said the words, I knew that most of them were true. Most, but not all, because that *wasn't* all, was it? And thinking that, thinking of the whole ridiculous muddle that my head was in right now, I felt dishonest and shameful and disloyal. Sorry for him, standing there, looking so off-kilter, totally oblivious to why I'd been so testy. So anxious now to make everything right. No, we didn't do scenes and we didn't have rows. Ours was a harmonious union at all times. That was one of the reasons I loved him so much. Wasn't it?

'Look, why don't I make us a coffee?' I said. 'No. A cup of tea. Nice and strong. Yes?'

'I'm sorry, sweets,' he said, reaching for the

kettle ahead of me. 'It's just that it's so unlike you to—'

'I know,' I said, chewing on the uncomfortable realization that it *wasn't* so unlike me. Not really. Only unlike me when I was around *him*. 'I don't know what got into me either,' I lied. 'That's the truth, Max. Just been a stressful week, I guess.' I went across the kitchen and squeezed his arm. 'And, listen, you should be so lucky. I've got to face the bloody man at the school Easter Fayre. He's doing the bran tub, God help us. Shift up and I'll get some cups out. I'm parched.'

He did as instructed. 'I don't know what to make of you sometimes. D'you know that?'

'I know that. And, Max—'

He turned.

'I'm really, really sorry.'

'No, I am. I shouldn't have got cross with you about it. I should have been more supportive, shouldn't I?'

I shook my head. 'No, you shouldn't. I'm not a listed building.'

He put his arms round me. 'But solid as a rock, even so.'

And as he was saying it, I was wishing that he wouldn't. I wished he'd say something else. Something more meaningful. Like 'I don't know what to make of you, and I want to find out. Has something got into you to make you so snappy? Are you okay? Shall we sit down and talk?'

But he wouldn't. Too risky. I might just say yes.

And, to be fair, he had more than enough problem women in his life. I plucked my sandal from the litter tray and shook it off in the darkness. I should try to get to know that cat, I thought. But I couldn't. It was never at home.

CHAPTER 13

I made an appointment to see Will-and-his-concept-board at nine forty-five the following Thursday morning. Despite my reservations. Which were many in number and eclectic in form. Having reservations about things is, as everyone knows, an important adaptive response. It's why children don't like sprouts or spring greens. They taste pretty vile, *ergo* they might be poisonous. My first and most powerful reservation had occurred at about two p.m. on the Monday, just as soon as Glenda said, 'I've got Mr Meadows on the phone for you that Harry's not up to his tricks again is he typical just when I was beginning to think that boy was beginning to behave himself but I might have known it was too good to be true what with Friday and everything did you ever get to the bottom of that by the way Mrs Cairns was telling me there was some sort of to-do on the coach coming back and—'

'Put him through,' I said, largely deaf to her bustlings and twitterings because the blood was pounding so hard in my temples that it was fogging up my ears. Oh, the peculiarities of the autonomic nervous system. Which is a fine old thing to find yourself thinking on a Monday and testimony, perhaps, to one of my mother's favourite mantras, which was that a university education is never, ever wasted. Even if, in this case, it was my brother's and not mine. Adrenaline didn't feature a great deal in my syllabus, but I do recall him telling me that one of the first experiments he performed at university was on the dissected heart of a frog. A dead frog, but one held in a kind of suspended animation, so that the heart – clamped and waiting – was still responsive to stimuli. Wired up, as well, so those responses could be measured, and my brother could thus push back some new scientific frontier.

There wasn't much frontier-pushing going on, as it turned out, but I do recall him recounting how when you dripped adrenaline onto said heart with a pipette, it chuntered away like its little life depended on it, which was a shame, given that it was being sold a dummy all along. So this lunch-time, my *Frusli* bar arrested mid-bite, I knew adrena-line, with its annoyingly autonomic disregard for my intentions, had fetched up as a visitor in my day.

Had I remembered? Will asked me. Had I given it some thought? Did I think it was feasible to do something in a week or two? Was I going to need to consult with the LEA about it? Check our insurance? Speak to parents? Jig my schedule? And, most importantly, could he come into school later in the week to run through such treatments as he'd already been playing with? By then, he said, he'd have roughed out a storyboard too.

'As soon as that, eh? That's absolutely perfect!' announced Clemency, by whom I had taken the speculative step of running this possibility only that morning. 'It ties in well with our transition phase project. D'you think they might be prepared to help us with making a bit of a mini-movie of our own while they're here? Nothing major or anything. Just that I remembered that EU link meeting I was at the other week. We could maybe put something together for our link schools on the website. What d'you think? That would be quite ground-breaking, wouldn't it?'

So Clemency had been pretty productive. She was certainly nothing if not full of ideas. My own feelings, once I'd digested the adrenaline rush, the telephone call itself, the two pieces of Mrs Grace's home-made lemon drizzle cake and the probable level of my diastolic blood pressure, were a little less focused. I had already spent not a small portion of the Saturday night/Sunday morning interface locked in silent debate with myself about Will Meadows and whether I should or should not devote any further time to fretting about the implications of that look we'd exchanged. Were life the fair and biddable thing of fairytales instead of the cruel and indiscriminate beastie it had proven itself to be thus far in mine, I'm sure I would have reached something useful by way of an answer. Like forty-two, or five-eighths, or πr^2. Something

I could work with, at any rate. But all I could arrive at was a sense of unease that he was so very present, so very often, in my thoughts.

But why, I reasoned stoutly to myself, did that matter anyway? After seeing *Braveheart* (okay, two and a half times) Mel Gibson had been in my thoughts a great deal. Who did things like that hurt? Dorothy was right. He was a good-looking man whose circumstances struck a chord with me, that was all. A romantic male lead in a rom-com made flesh. A flirtation. A bit of whimsy. A harmless diversion. And if I'd got myself a tad carried away with the damsel-in-distress bit, so what? Why worry about it?

If it had really been *that* big a deal I could always have said no to his coming, couldn't I? And I hadn't, and wouldn't, for the logical reason that to do so would not only have made me look pretty foolish but would also make more of the thing than it warranted, endorse the idea that seeing some more of him was not a good thing to be doing. Yes, I decided. Dorothy was right. I was just a bit taken with the *idea* of Will Meadows. Which just goes to show that a university education doesn't always cover all the bases.

Harry came to school that Wednesday sporting an oversized badge that said, 'Yo, dudes, I'm eleven' on it.

'It's my birthday,' he told me, breathing in gulps after his sprint across the playground to find me.

He pushed hair from his face in exactly the same way his father did. Ploughing the curls into furrows with his long, slender fingers. Pianist's hands, as my mother would have noticed. Except Harry's were grubby and poster-paint speckled. And the last time I'd seen Will's they'd been blackened by grease.

'I can see,' I said, sipping at the mug of coffee I'd brought out into the playground with me. It felt chilly for April and I should have worn my coat. 'So,' I said, cupping the mug in both palms, 'are you going to have a party?'

It had been a very long time since I'd organized a party. For Emily's fifth birthday, we had hired the local community centre, a female clown called Dot the Spot and, as a last-minute addition, a bouncy castle. We had twenty-two children, about a hundred balloons, and a girl called Matilda slipped over on a Smartie tube and sustained a hairline fracture of her wrist.

I knew which bone once. Knew the mother well, too. We used to go to Tumble Tots together. Her name was Alison, and when I last saw her, Emily had been gone six months, and she was heavily pregnant with twin boys. Matilda was with her and she spotted me and waved. I waved straight back, but Alison, head down, affected not to see me, and they crossed the road at the pelican crossing before I got there. I suppose I was hurt, but I didn't mind that much. Sometimes it was better. Sometimes, for a time, I found it a relief. We still swap Christmas cards. They called the boys Ben and Jerry, which I presumed must be some sort of joke. But I've never liked to ask in case it wasn't. As I walked with Harry now, I wondered about Matilda. She'd be a pretty thirteen-year-old – almost fourteen. So many birthdays. So many parties. All her Barbie years already over and done.

'I'm way too old for parties,' Harry told me, with a sniff. 'We're going go-karting.'

'Really? I'm sure that'll be fun.'

''S okay,' he said. 'I really wanted to do paint-balling, like Rhys is doing for his party, but there weren't any spaces. They could only do it when I'm up at Gran and Grampy's.' He sighed. 'Sucks, doesn't it? I wish I didn't have to go.'

I stopped walking and turned to face him. 'Why don't you want to go, Harry? Don't you like visiting your gran and grampy?'

''Sokay,' he said. 'But there's, like, nothing to do there. And I can't take a friend or anything. Grampy's too tired for having friends. I don't see why. Nanny M let me take Scott with me last time. We had a wicked time. But there's, like, no one at Gran and Grampy's. Well, there is. There's this boy who lives at the end of their road. But he's really lame.'

On the perhaps spurious grounds that to under-stand the dynamics of Harry's family life might offer me useful insights, I found myself carefully extracting and analysing all the salient points from this narrative. Nanny M. So that would be Will's mother. And there was a dad around too, hadn't he

213

said? And they lived four hundred miles away, I remembered Will mentioning. A long, long way. Scotland? The Lake District? So Gran and Grampy would be Harry's mum's parents. The ones who had lost their daughter, and who weren't so far away. I tried to imagine how things must be for them. Was Harry a ray of light shining down into the dark well of their loss, or was it painful to be around him? 'Oh, I'm sure you'll have a fine time,' I told him. 'I'm sure your gran and grampy will have lots of treats planned for you.'

Harry sniffed. 'Yeah. Prob'ly. I don't go there much any more, so I s'pose they will.'

I wondered why he'd volunteered this particular bit of information. 'You used to, then?' I asked.

He nodded. 'Gran used to look after me when Mum was at work. But then Mum stopped work. You know, when she got ill. And then, after she died, we got Petra to come and live with us.'

'Petra?'

'She was the first one. She was from Prague. She had a tongue stud. And pink bits in her hair.'

'And what happened to Petra?'

'She went back. To go to college. So then we had Susie for a while, and then when she left, Nat came. She was already here anyway. She was Petra's friend. And Liv's. But Liv's gone to live with her boyfriend now.'

'It all sounds very complicated.'

'Nah. Not really. It was at first, because Petra was, like, *such* a dork. She was fun and all that, but she couldn't cook or anything. Gran still used to come and stuff then, though, so it was all right.'

'But she doesn't now,' I said. *Why* not?

He stopped and shook his head thoughtfully. 'Not for *ages*.' Then he walked on beside me. 'Not since France. I've only been a few times since then.'

'France?'

'When we went on holiday in the middle of the night.'

The words rolled off his tongue as if joined by invisible dashes. As if they'd been spoken together many times before. 'What, you and your gran did?'

He grinned at me. 'No. *Dad* and me, of course.'

'Now that *does* sound exciting.'

He walked backwards to face me then, gesticulating as he did so. He was so like his father. I wondered what sort of career lay ahead of him. 'It was. It was wicked. He just, like, woke me up and I had to pack all my stuff and then we got in the car and drove all the way there.' He swept his arm in a low arc in front of him. 'All the way in one go. Through the tunnel and everything, and all the way to the seaside at a place called Cannes. It was wicked. We went jet-skiing.'

'That sounds brilliant, Harry.'

'It was. Except my gran went ball*is*tic.'

'About the jet-skiing?'

'About *going*.'

'Didn't your dad tell her?'

He shrugged. 'I dunno. I thought so.' He drew his brows together. 'Yes. He must have. She knew we were going. She was there when we went. But she was mad anyway. Because I missed all my year-five tests.'

'Well, well. Lucky you, eh?' I drained my coffee, intrigued. 'So now Nat looks after you instead.'

'It was best for my dad, with work and everything. And Grampy retired so it was best for them too. And it's, like, better because she lives with us so it's easier. So I don't go there much now.'

All worked out, then. All sorted. 'It does seem a shame.'

'No, it's not. It's okay. Nat's safe.'

'Safe?'

He rolled his eyes. 'You know, Miss Cool.'

'That's all right, then.'

'Yeah. She's coming karting. She's good.'

Mrs Grace came out and rang the bell for the end of play. I gave Harry my empty coffee mug to take back to the staff room, and made my way thoughtfully back to my office. Family relationships always sounded more complicated when described by a child, but Harry had clearly been brooding on his visit, and I would have liked to know why. I would have to ask his father when I saw him. Or not. Or not. *Holly*, or NOT.

CHAPTER 14

Rule 151, sub-section H (see accompanying notes on procedure), states that if you intend doing anything in school that involves outside agents of whatever persuasion then on-your-own-head-be-it. Though why they need a rule for it is beyond me. Whenever you do anything that isn't written in blood on the termly curriculum planner you must expect the unexpected and prepare for the worst.

John Patterson, unsurprisingly, thought the whole idea ridiculous, irritating, and an inconvenience to his SATs preparations. Which was fine by me, because I didn't want to involve him in it anyway. For one thing, Harry was in his class, and I didn't feel it appropriate to feature him too much in the proceedings, and for another, the less I had to do with John Patterson, the better both of us liked it.

'He's just peeved,' said Mrs Grace, whose springy step and jolly demeanour she put down to the miracle of HRT. 'Peeved because it isn't anything to do with him, that's all.'

Perhaps that was John's problem. Testosterone

depletion. Or, indeed, his own personal form of HRT. Head Teacher Relationship Trauma, perhaps. But yah, boo, sucks anyway because everyone else thought it was a great idea, the LEA included, so by the time Will arrived on the Thursday with his enthusiasm and boards various, there was a definite air of excitement in school. My own reservations, now dusted off, analysed and painstakingly catalogued in their various compartments, I had put to the back of my mind. Best part of a week on, I now reasoned that whatever little frisson had happened between me and Will Meadows was no more than that. And if our continuing involvement meant his continuing involvement with Harry and the school, then it could only be a good thing for both of them, couldn't it?

Though I did think it might be a little awkward, seeing him again. He, after all, wasn't privy to my musings. Or I to his, for that matter. He might well make some discomfiting gesture towards acknowledging what had passed between us the previous Friday evening. But I needn't have worried. He didn't do or say anything untoward. Just smiled his usual friendly smile and was so altogether businesslike that I almost felt embarrassed for getting into such a fret. What had I been thinking? Imagining, even? This was *work*.

And it seemed he'd been busy.

'This,' he said, manhandling an oversized portfolio folder in front of him and undoing the zipper with a flourish, 'is essentially what we're about.' He then explained, with the aid of a number of sheets, diagrams, cartoon-strip pictures and lots of energetic gesticulating, that the main thrust, the core message they were trying to get across, was that teaching was the sort of profession where every two days were different. This was to be achieved by the filming of a variety of segments, to include a wide range of activities from storytime to a rugby match to dealing with incidents in the playground to extra-curricular activities to assembly and so on.

'What about sick?' I asked. 'You haven't mentioned sick yet.'

'Sick?'

'There'll be some before the week's out. Trust me.'

'Okay,' he said, writing 'query sick seg' on his jotter and winking at me. 'But *aside* from sick, what is it that puts most people off a teaching career?'

'Where d'you want me to start?' I said.

'Anywhere you like.'

'Okay,' I said. I was beginning to enjoy this. 'The pay. The stress. The parents. The stress. The pay. Did I mention the stress, by any chance?'

'You got it. We've got a basic misassumption that we're trying to dispel. That teaching's a pretty dead-beat kind of job. Crap money, crap prospects, heaps of shite from parents – oh, I'm sorry . . .'

'Don't be. It's true.'

'Present company excepted, I trust?' He looked suddenly a bit bashful, then cleared his throat. 'Too much paperwork, yes? Too much prescriptive stuff coming down from on high. And you're right. Too much stress. They flagged that up big-time.'

'Don't I know it.'

'And basically little in the way of reward – crap money, as you said, kids you can't discipline, parents who don't support you.'

'You've done your homework.'

'Not me. As I said, it's a clear brief. So what we're working on is this. You've seen the army recruitment ads, right? We're working with a similar core premise. And this is aimed at a specific audience. What they're trying to do is get more mature people interested in retraining. People who've perhaps become disillusioned in other careers, people who are looking for something that will challenge and fulfil them.'

'Clemency Bright comes from industry. Lots do now. You know, post kids and everything.'

'*Exactly*. Anyway, the way we plan to do that is to contrast an average day in a school with an average day in an office. I'm going with a call centre on this because it's topical – very now. So we're going with a montage of soundbites, with strong visuals, and splicing them back to back. So, if you look here,' he tapped a felt pen against the first of a page of images, 'we've got, say, morning assembly, whatever kind of thing you'd do, I don't know, singing, someone reciting something, then we switch to the call-centre girl's first call of the day. You know "Good morning! Bloggs, Bloggs and

Bloggs, can I help you?", then a pause, then, "Sir, can you spell that for me?" and cut to – I don't know. Noisy classroom, lots of movement. Colour. Sound. Teacher at the blackboard—'

'Whiteboard.'

'D'oh. *Whiteboard*, then. Anyway, spelling, or something. Then cut to . . . "And if I can just take your address," then back. Outside. Nature walk. That kind of thing. In the woods. You go on walks to the woods, don't you?' I nodded. 'I was thinking habitats, things that live in the stream maybe. Again, lots of noise and colour, but some close shots with the teacher maybe having something in her hand. The kids' faces and so on. And then we go back to the call centre, and by now it's late morning and she's looking a little glazed, you know? And this time we've got her saying, "And what seems to be the problem?" and "If you could spell that for me" again, then we cut to lunchtime. Eating with the kids – chatting about stuff. Then in the playground, kid with a cut knee, or crying about something . . . we'll have to see what shapes up. You got any good actors? Anyway, doing the whole counselling, problem-solving bit, then back to the call centre – same thing again, this time just a half-second visit. She's sitting in a staff room – several other clones in there. All staring into space and biting into shop sandwiches. Then back, maybe some science or something – we'll shoot lots and see what works best – and then counterpoint to her back at her desk, stifling a yawn, looking at her watch, "And what seems to be the problem?" And then back to school. Coats on. Teacher clearing up. Stretching. Smiling to herself about something a kid's drawn, that sort of thing. We're going to close on the tag line, "Good day at work?"'

'Wow,' I said. 'Harry was right.'

'About what?'

'Steven Spielberg eat your heart out.'

'You like it?'

'I love it.'

His smile was one of such genuine pleasure that I realized for perhaps the first time since I'd met him that here was someone who loved what he did. That however sad his night-times, however lonely his life, every day was a good day at work.

Glenda, whose demeanour suggested she had not had a good day at work since the introduction of the computerized dinner-money spread-sheet program in 1987, knocked on the door at precisely that moment. She said, 'There's a call from the school nurse,' then she mouthed 'about the headlice.'

'I'll take it in there,' I said, following her out. 'Won't be a tick,' I told Will.

Of course, he didn't get the joke because he hadn't heard the first bit. 'Absolutely.' He nodded. 'No probs. I'll pack up.'

I was gone about five minutes, and when I returned, he had put away all his flip-sheets and paraphernalia and was standing with his back to me, one hand stuffed into a jeans pocket. He seemed to be looking out of the window.

At the click of the door he turned to face me and I could see he held a framed photograph in his other hand. One he'd picked up from the sill. I looked at the photo, and he looked at me looking at it. I expected him to ask me who the picture was of, but obviously he'd already worked that one out. 'Hope you don't mind,' he said, taking his other hand out of his pocket and pointing at the glass. 'You know, I was just wondering. Do you still find it hard sometimes? Sitting in here day after day, watching all the other children grow and change?'

I was a little shocked by the directness of his question, but not so shocked that I wasn't tempted to correct him. Tell him that I spent much less time sitting in my office than he might suppose. But he'd see that soon enough in any case. And thinking the thought was only a displacement activity. He was still looking at Emily's picture, waiting for my answer, his long fingers cradling the small frame in his palm.

'I've only been here three months,' I said. I crossed my arms as I spoke, instinctively preparing for what might be coming. It was so automatic, this bracing of myself – as if I was on an aircraft plummeting towards the ocean – that I uncrossed them again deliberately. 'So there's not been masses of growing here just yet.' I paused, but he

223

didn't reply. Just looked at me harder. 'Yes,' I said finally. 'Of course I will. But not often. And only very fleetingly then. It's been eight years, after all. So it's okay. It's almost, I don't know, cathartic in a way. It's okay.'

He narrowed his eyes. 'You said that already.' Then he put the photograph carefully back on the windowsill, paying particular attention to getting its angle just so.

I felt a keen sense that there was something else I wanted to say to him, but I couldn't work out what it was. So I reached for the sheaf of papers he'd left on my desk. He was pushing his arms into the sleeves of his jacket, considering me as I considered the notes on the paper.

'She had your eyes,' he said, peering to inspect mine.

I felt self-conscious and had to look away. 'Yes. Yes, she did.'

'Your eyes but not your nose. Yours is kind of retroussé, isn't it?' He glanced at the picture again. 'Her dad's nose, was it?'

I looked too, and now I found myself smiling. 'Ah,' I said. 'You guessed right. Her father had a, um . . . significant nose, for certain.'

'Thought so.' He grinned at me. 'Emily's had all the makings of a real Glenn Close corker, didn't it?'

My surprise must have registered, because his own expression changed suddenly. As if he, too, had registered something. That he might have put his foot in it – misjudged the tone of my response.

But he hadn't. He really hadn't. My surprise was genuine, but born of something altogether different from what he might have thought. Not that I was offended by his words. Far from it. Here was someone talking about Emily as if she'd existed as a person. Not exalted as an angel, spirit or ghost. As something that had been real in my life. Real and imperfect and human. It was guileless on his part, I was sure. But lovely. I couldn't remember another occasion since she'd died when anyone had mentioned her nose.

'I used to lie awake at night worrying about it,' I said, smiling to reassure him. I picked up the photo now – I'd not considered Emily's nose in so many years that I no longer even saw it. 'You can tell, can't you? Even at the age she was then. You know, even the day she was born it showed. I remember my dad sitting there – he was holding her at the time – and saying, "I knew you should never have married that man, Holly. She's going to have one hell of a conk on her, you know that?" And I laughed so much I thought I was going to burst all my stitches.' I laughed at the memory then, and Will laughed too. And the rest of it came at me in a rush. The sweetish smell of the ward. Baby talc, nappy sacks, the brand of nipple cream I liked. My mother saying, 'George! *Really!*' Colin walking in at precisely that moment and wondering what we were all giggling about. It was so powerful, so unexpected, so altogether pungent a memory that I had to put down the picture,

225

lest it bite me. 'Listen to me,' I said to Will, who was looking at me now with an expression that made me feel laid bare and flustered. Exposed. I needed him gone. 'What am I thinking?' I said. 'Telling you all about my *stitches*, for God's sake. Look, I don't know about you but I'd better get on.'

He dipped his head. Picked up the portfolio case. 'You're right,' he said. 'Me too. Monday week, then. Yes?'

I walked across to open the office door for him. 'Monday week. We're all very excited about it.'

He nodded and started to go through it, then turned. 'Oh. I almost forgot. Will it be okay if Harry has a day off school? Friday week? The one before term ends? Only he's staying with his grandparents over Easter and they're going down to spend a few days with his cousins in Brighton. His aunt's driving up to collect them.'

A couple of tots from Reception were changing their reading books at the low shelves outside my office under Glenda's watchful eye. I nodded at Will. 'He told me.'

'Did he?'

'Yes. And that's fine, Wi— er . . . Mr Meadows. As long as you put it in writing. You know, rules.'

His hand was on the door jamb and he tapped it twice before he went through it. 'No probs. I'll bring it in with me when I come. Till then, then, Mrs Connors.'

We exchanged a different type of look. A conspirator's grin. 'Till then, then, Mr Meadows,' I said. 'Thanks so much for coming.'

I went back into my office and watched his progress all the way across the playground and out to his car, which was, as I'd asked, not parked on the zigzags but across on the far side of the road. Then he glanced back, surprising me, and raised his hand to wave. I started to lift mine, then changed my mind. With my head bent, I decided he was far enough away that I could pretend I hadn't seen him.

There are many, many cupboards in Cefn Melin Primary School. As well as the capacious cupboards that reside in the corner of most of the classrooms, there are, let me see, the stationery cupboard, the PTA cupboard, the other stationery cupboard (the one you must be in if you're not in the other stationery cupboard), the PE equipment cupboard, the cupboard for the cleaning equipment, and the cupboard in which we keep all the costumes for shows that industrious parents have made over the years. We could put on *Bugsy Malone* meets *Goliath in Wonderland* with *Oliver's Army*, who would naturally be *très misérable* without turning so much as a hair. With a seven-foot chipmunk, whose provenance eludes me but which predates both of my sojourns in this school.

There's also the cupboard in the medical room. Which houses both the main fuse board and the other photocopier (the one you must be using if you're not using the other one). Every school should have a second photocopier. Teachers spend more time queuing to photocopy stuff than in almost any other activity. Though perhaps there's no need for that to fetch up in Will's film.

As head teacher I get priority status at both photocopiers. Not because anything I want to copy is, *ipso facto*, more urgent than anything anyone else might have, but because it has long been the practice at the schools I have worked in to say, 'Can I jump the queue? This is for . . . [insert name of head teacher].' Which works like a charm every time.

But as someone had already programmed the photocopier when I came in to use it (it was spewing out vast quantities of something or other and was set to spew vast numbers more), I went into the cupboard to use the other. My need was simple. Shortly after Will had left, JP had stomped into my office (*sans* the common courtesy of knocking, and very much *avec* the net result of dissipating all the happy charm that still lingered in there, plus Will's woody aftershave, which was a shame), and announced that as he had an important presentation to write for his next upcoming interview (his personal presentation being such that I was inclined to agree with him for once) he could no longer commit himself to all these after-school activities. Thus, and after heading off another rant about his Hellish Bloody

Workload by agreeing with him, I now had to make twenty-seven copies of a letter saying that due to unforeseen circumstances, Mr Patterson would not be able to run junior rugby until after the Easter holidays. Glenda's job, really, but she'd been doing the dinner money, and as rugby was tomorrow – thanks, John, *really* helpful – I thought I'd better do it myself. But as the paper-jammed sign was glowing, it was first necessary for me to curse whichever member of my staff had snuck out without fixing it, then open the back end and do something constructive with whatever was in there.

There are two schools of thought on the use of school copiers. The first has it that you pull out the manual whenever the occasion calls for it and familiarize yourself with the functions of all the colour-coded levers, knobs and buttons inside. You 'get to know your copier'. You understand that the word 'reset' has more meanings than 'snow' does in Inuit. You speak photocopierese. The other is that as every copier is a law unto itself and whichever copier-whisperer in an over-all fetches up in school whenever things look moribund, there is little practical use in learning photocopier husbandry, one copier's 'reset' being another copier's cyanide pill. This school, of which I have long been a student, says that if you lever every visible lever and tug, you've a fair chance of making things right.

It was to this task that I was attending when

I became aware of two people entering the medical room. They were Clemency and Glenda, and they were speaking very quietly indeed. I couldn't make out everything they said because of the other machine's chuntering, but what little I did catch was disquieting. Glenda, quite clearly, said, 'Actually, I happen to think his marriage is very *much* my business,' and Clemency barked back, 'And by that I assume you're trying to say it's not *mine*?' To which Glenda said, 'Precisely,' to which Clemency went, 'Pssh!' to which Glenda responded, 'You really have *no* idea, do you? You think you do, but you really don't have *any* idea. So don't come all high-minded and self-righteous with me.' To which Clemency said, 'There's more people than you know who are . . .'

Which I presume meant they'd left. Which was galling.

As was the fact that Glenda had obviously finished the dinner money and by rights should be fixing this bloody thing – not stalking the medical room handing out sermons. I brooded for several minutes by the machine. Should I say something? Do something? Confront Glenda again about what she knew? Confront Clemency? I really wasn't sure what, if anything, to do. The truth was that I found the whole sorry business so unutterably depressing that perhaps I didn't *want* to know any more. It was manifestly (as the saying went) none of my business, and would only become so if it impacted in some way on school life. And as the only person whose work seemed to be suffering was John's, there seemed little practical reason for getting involved. He had another interview. God willing, he'd be gone soon. And perhaps we'd hear no more about it.

Anyway, I have decided I have enough problems of my own. Two of which are sitting in TGI Friday with me now. Tara is the eldest. She is fourteen, almost fifteen, with poker-straight hair the colour of butterscotch and long, coltish legs that she generally encases in black tights. I don't think I've ever seen her legs without them. She's a very pretty girl but in a very angry mood. Sasha, who is just thirteen, couldn't be more different. She has her father's wiry curls, is generally softer, less angular, and where Tara bristles with pubescent indignation about life, Sasha is pliable, generally more smily – although with her own hormonal upheaval now on the horizon, it's perhaps only a matter of time. They are mine for two hours, possibly more than that, and neither looks terrifically pleased.

Earlier in the week, Max and I had spoken about the possibility of taking them away for a few days over Easter. We had no particular plan in mind, just that we might book into a hotel somewhere and spend some time doing things they'd enjoy. We'd toyed with Alton Towers, the West End – get tickets for a show maybe – or the coast perhaps, if the weather looked promising.

As it turned out, the coast had already been vetoed. Buckets, spades, sand in their sandwiches. They, like, *so* didn't do that kind of thing any more. Fair enough, I'd thought, albeit in secret. I didn't much do it either. It always made me so sad. But the other options had elicited both enthusiasm and disagreement so tonight was to be the night when we made our final choice. But it wasn't necessarily going to be an amiable meeting, Catherine having dropped the bombshell to Max on the Wednesday that she and the girls had had a chat and she must regretfully inform him that they had decided they didn't want to come to our wedding. She was sorry and all that but she knew he'd understand how they felt. Max was er . . . let me see . . . not best pleased. No. Apoplectic. That's a better word.

And now it's Friday evening, and he is also not here.

'Look, what could I say?' he'd said plaintively, an hour back. 'This is a really important client, Holly. I'll stay for a couple of drinks and then I'll make my excuses, okay?'

I was tempted to remind him that his really important client was way less important than the two daughters he only got to see for what amounted to little more than a day or so a week, but I didn't because who was I to stand in judgement? I had no experience in these matters, did I? Plus he'd go all hurt and *angsty* and tell me not to drum it in what a crap father he was. 'Okay,' I said lightly. 'We'll see you when you get here.'

Of course, by now I have decided that I'm not altogether sure this isn't a wheeze to get the girls to spend some time alone with me. I so wish they'd want to, but I can quite see their point. Being with me feels like a betrayal of their mother. I accept that. These things take time.

Max, of course, hates Catherine and loves me, so he has little patience with the time factor. It upsets and annoys him that they're so offish with me. He doesn't seem to understand that it isn't *about* me. It would be the same with anyone, and I don't take it personally. Although, seeing their expressions when I suggest we have fruit cocktails, it's wearyingly hard.

But I don't agree with Max that we should meet this wedding thing head on. It seems to me the very last way to approach it. I know I have almost no wisdom where the emotional maelstrom that constitutes the internal life of the average teenager is concerned, but despite my usual default position that frank exchanges of views are generally the best way to deal with differences, this is one situation where I feel less confrontational tactics are needed. Patience, in fact, that it will all come right in the end. The wedding date is still four months off, and four months is a long time in the life of a child. More than that, I feel that maintaining an atmosphere of loving acceptance will be altogether more constructive than Max's position: that as his girls are being blatantly manipulated by their mother it's his duty and right to put them both straight. 'Get them on side', as he put it.

I am, it has to be said, somewhat dismayed by his choice of terminology. Keen as I am to form a bond with Sasha and Tara – hopeful as I am that we can become friends – I don't want to approach it on the basis that their mother and I are the coaches of opposing football teams. Without having had a similar experience of my own, I find it hard to fathom Max's feelings where Catherine is concerned. That he detests her is obvious, but his ill-concealed enthusiasm for pointing out her failings to the children whenever the occasion arises makes me uncomfortable. Isn't that sort of thing usually the preserve of the 'wronged' party? I know it's not black and white, but I don't want to be a part of it. I just want this unhappy period to pass.

But ten minutes into my (necessary) glass of wine and their two diet Cokes, I am right in the firing line regardless. I'm not even sure how the subject came up. Oh, yes, I am. We were talking about holidays. About how Catherine's told them if they were expecting to go on one then they'd better ask their father if he has any spare money after paying for his extravagant wedding. That was the gist of it, if not the exact words. The exact words are now being uttered by Tara, to whom a promise had been made some two years ago that their father would take them to Disneyworld. He, of course, has reneged on the deal.

Which is fair comment. I take her point. 'I'd love to go to Disneyworld too,' I tell her. 'Perhaps we should work on Dad between us, eh?'

She eyes me carefully, as if she is weighing me up. It must be so hard being nice to the person whose mother tells her daily is the cause of her distress. 'So would my mum,' she says pointedly. 'She's never been either. She'd like to take us herself but she can't afford it, can she?'

Sasha looks as uncomfortable as I feel. I think fleetingly of Will Meadows's fierce tag. Right now I feel about as fierce as a ball of cotton wool. And much more like a hapless defendant in a dock.

'I understand that—' I begin.

But Tara hasn't finished. 'We should have been going together,' she continues. 'As a *family*. Except you came along.'

I am almost speechless at her total lack of inhibition in how she speaks to me. I know teenagers like to shock, but it's such a contrast to how children speak to me at school. But I maintain my level tone and unflinching expression. I understand where she's coming from. I almost think I should be glad that she's able to articulate it. Better that than all this unspoken hostility. At least it will open up a dialogue.

Some dialogue. 'If it wasn't for you,' she says, 'Dad would never have left us.'

Now I do speak. I have to put her straight on

this one. 'Tara,' I say gently, 'that isn't true. I didn't start seeing your dad until after your mum and he split up. You *know* that.'

She plucks at her straw and takes a short pull on it. 'And we're supposed to believe that, are we?'

I can almost hear her mother saying it to her. 'Yes, of course,' I say, shocked now at such bile. 'Because I'm telling you the truth. Your *father* has told you the truth. All along.'

'No, he hasn't,' she responds. 'He's a *liar*. I know because Auntie Antonia told us.'

Toni? 'Told you what?' I say.

'That you knew him before.'

Things, somewhat grimly, are making sense. 'Tara, I don't know what she's told you, but you've got it all wrong. You've misunderstood her meaning. I did know your father before, but only because Auntie Antonia was my friend at college, and your dad was her brother, and that was years and years ago. And I didn't really know him as such, just bumped into him from time to time. I didn't see him more than a handful of times. Just if he happened to be around when I was at your gran's with your auntie, that was all. And I certainly didn't see him after I left college. Not at *all*.'

'So *you* say.'

I can't believe I'm hearing what I'm hearing. No wonder they don't like me. They have it all figured out. I stole him. That's what they think. 'Yes, I do say, Tara, because it's the truth,' I say firmly.

Sasha looks at me sharply. 'If he hadn't met you he would still be with Mum,' she says.

'Sasha, I—'

'I hate you,' she says.

It's going to be one very long evening.

CHAPTER 15

I don't know where I got the notion, but I think I expected something altogether more dramatic. Winnebagos, catering vans, makeup girls, people holding clapperboards and klaxons. In reality it was just three days and three people. Will, of course, plus a man called Mitch, who was a cameraman, and another called Ewan, who I assumed was a soundman because he held the furry caterpillar most of the time. There was no mention of makeup – either as verb, noun or a room one went into for a buff-up.

Unless you were being filmed, you'd barely know they were there. And as I wasn't being filmed much (to my knowledge, at least – except for one story-time stint and a self-conscious assembly) I dare say I wouldn't have seen much of them, except that on the Friday Mrs Grace came along to my office after first play.

'I'm so sorry to bother you, Mrs Connors,' she said, 'but Mr Meadows wants to do some filming with Miss Woolf's class in the playground, and I thought I'd better come and check with you because he wants to use the trolley.'

'Trolley? What trolley?'

'The science trolley. The one outside John's classroom. I think one of them wants to sit on it.'

'*Sit* on it?'

'So he said. To do the filming. I thought I'd better check.'

So off I went with Mrs Grace to the junior corridor. Will and Mitch were standing in the open doorway that led out onto the playground, deep in some sort of technical discussion.

'Ah,' said Will, smiling warmly as he saw me approach and causing my cheeks to flush. 'The very person. D'you think there's any way we could borrow this? Take everything off it first, of course. And we'll put it all back, naturally.'

'What for?'

'I want to get a tracking shot of Miss – what was her name, Mitch? Miss Wolf, that's it. Her. She's got a bunch of tweenies all dressed up as vegetables over there.' He gestured across the play-ground to one of the demountable classrooms.

I nodded. 'They're rehearsing their class assembly, aren't they, Mrs Grace?'

She nodded. So did Will. 'That's the one,' he said. 'Anyway, I want to get a tracking shot of her leading them across the playground. You'd nor-mally use a dolly on a rail for the sort of shot I'm after, but we can improvise and have Ewan pull Mitch along on this just as easily. If that's okay with you.'

I said I didn't see why not. Because I didn't.

As you would. More dot. Fool dot. Me dot dot dot . . .

'Well, I do!' barked John Patterson, in my office, not two hours later. 'And who gave them permission?' He didn't pause for either a breath or an answer. 'You see?' he snapped, jabbing a finger towards the door. 'This is precisely why these sort of people shouldn't be let loose in a school.'

'John,' I said, putting down my pen and rising wearily from my paperwork. 'What exactly has gone missing?'

'The thermometers! I've spent half my bloody lunch break setting everything up, and now they've disappeared! Typical!'

Huff bloody puff, and bloody so on.

So off we went, back down to the junior corridor. As promised, everything was back on the trolley. Except the box of thermometers.

'Are you absolutely sure they were on here to start with?'

'Of course I'm sure. I checked this morning.'

'Well, might Clemency not have them? Weren't they working on conductors last week? Perhaps she's following something up.'

He gave me the sort of look that might have had the word 'Weedol' as a trademark and been a high performing garden-centre stock line. 'I told you,' he said slowly, as if to a moron, 'I checked this morning. This morning they were here and this afternoon they are gone.'

So off we went to find Will, who was now filming a game of rounders. And back we all came to the trolley.

'Thermometers,' barked John. 'Box of about thirty. Plastic. Right here. Middle shelf. With a lid on. Says "Ther-mom-et-ers" on the side.'

Will shook his head, politely ignoring John's tone. 'I don't recall it,' he said, 'but everything we took off we put back on again. Absolutely everything.'

Another squirt of Weedol headed off in his direction. 'So why isn't it *here*, then?'

'Because it obviously wasn't there in the first place, John,' I told him. This was getting ridiculous. Yes, it is. No, it isn't. You're a liar. No, *you* are. Okay, then. Wanna fight? Stick 'em up.

'Honest, mate. *Everything*,' Will said again. 'I mean, we can check with Mitch if you like, but—'

'So someone *must* have taken it,' I said. 'Have you tried the other classes? Let's send one of yours out on a scout for it, shall we?'

'I told you. I have already done that. Four children, to be precise.' He stuck four fingers up. 'To ask "Have-you-got-the-box-of-thermometers?" We have been round the whole school and no one has, okay? It was here and now it's not. And it's now twenty to two and I've got an experiment to do. Except I can't, because these *people*—'

For 'people' read 'invertebrates'. 'John,' I said, feeling like a teenage girl who's invited her new boyfriend to tea only to find her father is in full-on old-git mode, 'if Mr Meadows says he put everything back I believe him. He's absolutely no reason to—'

'Well, of *course* you would,' he said nastily. 'You've got your fifteen minutes of fame to think about, haven't you? If you weren't so dead set on getting on the telly, perhaps this school would function as a school instead of as a bloody film set.'

Will had half opened his mouth at this point, glanced at me and shut it quickly, then moved his gaze to follow mine. A small child had come round the corner with a box in her hands.

As any infant-school child might when it finds itself in the junior-school corridor faced with the head teacher, the deputy head teacher and the strange man who's been wandering around doing stuff with a man with a giant caterpillar, she froze.

I hoped the two flaming spots on my cheeks would look pixie-ish and cheerful. I smiled at her. 'Hello, Millie,' I said warmly. 'Can I help?'

'I've got this to put back,' she said, proffering the box shyly.

'*Ah!* The ther-*mom*-et-ers! *Lovely!*' I cooed at her, savouring every last spoonful-of-caviar syllable. 'Just what Mr Patterson was looking for! Well done!'

'What class are you in?' John said to her gruffly.

'Mrs Pugh's, sir,' she offered, 'but she's poorly so it's Mrs Cairns today.'

'I know *that*,' he said, which impressed no one and only served to make him sound younger than she was. 'But what did Mrs Cairns want the box of thermometers for?'

'She didn't, sir,' said Millie. 'She wanted the box of pitettes.'

'Pi*pettes*,' I corrected her automatically.

'Yes,' she said. 'That's what she wanted. But I bringed the thermometers by mistake. We didn't know until now so she told me to come and see you and bring them back.'

I reached down to get the pipettes for her. Her chin had started wobbling. 'Don't fret,' I reassured her. 'It's very easily done. The boxes are the same, aren't they?' She nodded forlornly. 'Off you go, then. Mrs Cairns will be waiting. Tell her Mr Patterson says thank you very much.'

'*Jesus*,' said John, once the child was out of earshot. Then he stalked back to his classroom, thermometers in hand.

'Bloody hell,' observed Will, who had not been dismissed yet. 'He's a real barrel of laughs, that one, isn't he?'

I was so incandescent with fury by now that I didn't even pause to consider exactly which form of unimaginable and bloody misfortune I would most like to observe befalling John Patterson. Which, when you're dealing with someone so infuriating, was probably all for the best. Otherwise I might have been tempted to think one up and put it into practice straight away. After all, the kilo weights were but inches from my twitching fingers. Instead, I waved Will back to his rounders and marched up to John's classroom door.

And opened it. 'Mr Patterson? A moment outside, if you wouldn't mind.'

Out he came. I bade him close the door. He did so.

'How dare you speak to me like that?' I spat, albeit softly. 'How bloody *dare* you speak to me like that!'

He looked so shocked I thought he might break with tradition and blurt out an unguarded 'sorry'. But no, ever braced on the sand in the middle of the colosseum, he raised a 'go on then, bring out the lions' finger instead. 'Now, *listen*,' he began. The front of the man! But if he thought I was going to listen to any more along those lines, he was very sorely mistaken.

'No, *you* listen,' I barked at him. 'And you listen good. *I* run this school and *you* are my deputy. I care sod all for how much that irritates you, frankly. It's a fact and there's nothing you can do about it. On the other hand there's lots I can do about *you*. I have tried being nice. I have tried being understanding of your circumstances. While you, on the other hand, have been plain nasty. Fine. Whatever gets you through the day is okay with me. You go ahead and be as unpleasant as you like to me in private – I'm way past worrying about your good opinion – but you speak to me like that again in front of the staff or visitors or the children or *anyone*, and I'll take personal delight in seeing your head on a block. Got that?'

Clearly not. He sneered at me. 'For God's sake,

stop being so melodramatic, will you? We're not on *EastEnders*, you know.'

'Oh, there's no melodrama here, John, believe me. Just facts. If it's soap opera you want, perhaps you should try looking a bit closer to home.'

'What the hell d'you mean by that?'

Ah! How absolutely *fab*. A 'John' moment, if ever there was one. I wheeled round and stalked off, leaving his brain to commence whirring. 'You heard,' I threw over my shoulder.

Protocol 57B in the Management of Horrible Employees directive didn't, regrettably, say anything about driving six-inch nails into the tyres of staff cars. I knew this because I'd been having a quick cram of the literature.

One more thing. Just one, I thought, and I'd more than have his head on a block, I'd have his personal science equipment in a mincer as well. And he could shove the whole box of thermometers where the sun didn't penetrate. Take his temperature as well while he was at it.

It was gone five and pretty much everyone had gone home. And as the cleaners were yet to arrive, John's, mine and Barry's were the only cars still in the car park. So, when I heard the rap on my office door I fully expected John's head to appear round it. Apology or rant – I was ready for either. Past caring either way. Stupid cretin. But it wasn't John, it was Barry who came in. 'Found this,' he said, holding a small black plastic something up in front of me. 'Not seen it before. Thought it might belong to one of those film chaps.'

I recognized it straight away because I had seen it before. I held out my hand and Barry placed it in my palm.

'I think it belongs to Mr Meadows,' I told him.

'What is it?'

'A hand-held computer.' I told him. 'It's called a Palm Pilot.'

'Just as well I spotted it, then,' he commented. 'Half an hour and I would have shut up shop for the holidays, wouldn't I? And it wouldn't have been piloting anything. I'll leave it with you, then, shall I?'

I nodded. Yes, I said. He could leave it with me.

The mobile answered after the first ring. 'Don't tell me,' Will said. 'You're having second thoughts and you want the tape erased.'

'I'll reserve judgement till I've seen it,' I told him. 'But in the meantime I've got something you might want.'

'Well, that certainly sounds like the kind of offer a guy doesn't get every day of the week. Am I supposed to guess what it is?'

I didn't manage to answer right away because I was too busy gaping at my reflection in the computer monitor at what I'd just said to him. My mouth was so totally at odds with my brain at the moment. 'Your Palm Pilot,' I went on quickly. 'At least, I think it's your Palm Pilot. Looks like yours. Or do they all look the same?'

There was a moment's silence, presumably while he performed a quick audit of his pockets. 'God, you might be right,' he said. 'Does it look a bit chewed in the top left-hand corner?'

I looked. It did, bless him. 'Yup,' I said. 'It does.'

'Then I'll be up for it right away. You going to be there for a while?'

'I was just about to leave,' I told him. 'Are you far away?'

'No, I'm at home. I can be there in five minutes.'

'Well, in that case I'll drop it off to you on my way home.'

'But you don't know where I live.'

'I hope I do. Your son attends my school, remember?'

'Of course.'

'And I've already been there once, haven't I?'

'You have?'

'With Harry.'

'Of course,' he said again. 'Of course you have. Casper. Well, if you're sure you don't mind.'

'I'm sure. I'll be driving right past the end of your road, won't I?'

'Then thanks. That's really kind. I'll see you when you get here. Hey, by the way, meant to mention but I missed you.'

'Mention what?'

'I heard you say "sod", Mrs Connors.'

'God, you *didn't*.'

'I did. After lunch. To that teacher. I'd left my shades on the bench and had to come back.'

I heard him chuckle. 'Anyway, turns out I was right, eh?'

'About what?'

'You *are* pretty fierce.'

At which I laughed as well. Then denied it. Commented, even, that I sometimes wished I felt as fierce inside as I obviously looked on the outside. Which kind of set a bit of a tone, looking back. Though I wasn't thinking that as I climbed into my car.

The house looked different in the sunshine. Perhaps it *was* different, even. Had shaken off the dark days to embrace another summer. A rank of tulips, blackish-red frilled ones like the combs on a row of cockerels, thrust tall from among a cloud of forget-me-not along the path edge, and the rectangle of lawn, previously just a dank space in the teeming March rain, was close-cropped, diagonally striped, frozen-pea green. Will's car sat alongside it, a streak of sunshine in the driveway, its wipers pointing skywards, standing proud from the windscreen, and the brickwork drive was dark with recent moisture. There was an empty bucket with a sponge in it beside the open garage door.

An internal door at the back of the garage stood ajar, but I ignored this and stepped onto the front porch. There was no doorbell, but a substantial brass knocker, which I lifted and lowered twice.

He was at the door in moments. 'That was quick,' he said.

'It's hardly far.' I held out the Palm Pilot. He was wearing the habitual jeans and T-shirt combo, the latter teal blue and faded, raw edged along the sleeves and hem. The chain round his neck glinted dully here and there beneath the collar. A shaft of sunlight silhouetted him in the doorway. The kitchen beyond him was modern and white.

'I can't believe I left it. It's like a fifth limb. Where was it?'

I shrugged. 'I have no idea. The caretaker spotted it. Anyway—'

'Oh, I'm sorry.' He took a step back. 'Where are my manners? Come on in.'

I took a step back as well. 'I'd better get off home, actually. Lots to do. I'm supposed to be going out in an hour.'

'Just five minutes, go on. Have a cup of tea or something. I've already put the kettle on. I've got something to show you.'

I made a performance of looking at my watch, even though I knew the time almost to the minute. I don't know why. I suppose there just didn't seem to be a plausible reason why I couldn't commit five minutes of my time to this. Even less why I shouldn't. I just *felt* I shouldn't. My eyes lit upon a huddle of things on the stairs. A packet of razors, some toothpaste, an antiperspirant aerosol, a plastic bottle of green shower gel. Recently bought and on their way up to the bathroom, I supposed. That was it. That was really what it was. That I didn't want his domestic life laid bare before me like this.

All his choices. These mugs, those pictures, that brand of soap. 'I'd better not,' I said, uneasy with the sense of intimacy that had begun to crowd and jostle me. 'As I said, I'm going out. Swimming.'

He crossed his legs at the ankle and considered me as he stood there, one hand still on the latch, the other holding the Palm Pilot. *Déjà vu* in reverse, without the wet hair and bathrobe. I dropped my gaze and began to turn. 'Oh, *come* on,' he said. 'Aren't you even going to ask me what I've got to show you?'

I shrugged again. 'I assumed you must mean something to do with the filming.'

'Of course I do. I've been taking a look at it. Come on. Aren't you just *itching* to see it? *Everyone* is always itching to see themselves on film. So don't deny it.' He raised a finger and leaned forward a little. 'Don't *worry*. The camera loves you, Mrs Connors. Really does. Come on. What's the rush? A few minutes is all. Let me make you a nice cup of tea.'

With hindsight, I like to think it was for his benefit that I did so. He did look awfully keen to show me what they'd done. But he was quite right, of course. I *was* itching to see it. So I stepped inside while he stood back to let me pass. The front door shut behind us with a sigh.

There was a great deal of muddle in the rest of the hallway. Battered-looking boxes, much adorned with labels, long cylinders, metal cases, big boxes, bearing numbers, on wheels.

'Sorry,' he said, as I threaded my way round it. 'Off to Prague in the morning. On a shoot.'

'That sounds nice. What for?'

'A bank, as it happens.'

'In Prague?'

'You've never been?' I shook my head. 'It's very pretty. Pretty buildings. Kind of Vulgaria-ish. You know? The child-catcher? *Chitty Chitty Bang Bang?*'

I nodded. 'Vaguely. I haven't seen that since I was about seven.'

'Then you must see it again.'

But who with?

The kitchen was clean and clear of clutter. Altogether much less messy than I'd anticipated, which was clearly rather silly of me. Max was the most pathologically tidy person I knew, so why should this other male person be any different? It was just an impression, of the kind that are so easy to form: two males, one rather young, a domestically inept au pair, no wife, no *mum* around to tut and declutter and make shopping lists and pin important bits of paper to notice-boards, no collection of tins ready for recycling on the draining-board, no small assemblies of ingredients out in readiness for preparing a meal. But my impression had been as wrong as it was illogical. For sure, there was evidence that ano-ther life had been lived here in abundance, in the gnarled and knotty pelargonium on the windowsill, in the stack of Tupperware containers on the corner of the worktop, their curl-edged

251

labels clearly long ago written and affixed, in the meander of stencilled ivy that traced a route round the cupboards – I don't know why I knew, but I just *knew* she'd done that. But there was also evidence of fresh new domestic endeavour. A pile of recently ironed tea-towels, a cake tin with a Post-it note exhortation to 'keep out!', a shopping-list-in-progress with a ballpoint on top of it sitting next to the tear-off part of a letter I recognized as being from my very own school. Will opened a cupboard – the inside exemplary in its neatness – and picked out two plain scarlet mugs.

'You use the same tea as me,' I said, as he reached for the packet.

'Other way round,' he said. 'I saw it first.'

I smiled, charmed and self-conscious in about equal measure. 'Harry get off all right?' I asked. Better to make conversation rather than fixate on all the domestic detail of the regeneration of his life. It was almost as if I was storing a long list of items that I could regurgitate in a memory game. The beige china cat bowl that still stood on the corner of the worktop, the Wild Flowers of Wales tea-towel, the picture hook on the wall with the pale patch round it. What had hung there? Why wasn't it hanging there now? He turned from where he was swooshing out a big brown teapot in the sink. No teabags in mugs here. Proper tea, plain and strong.

'He did,' he said, nodding, then turned back to

rinse the teapot. His head was tipped forward and so was his hair, but a single twist of his Caramac curls remained coiled in the nape of his neck.

'He told me he wasn't much looking forward to it,' I said. He turned, and if I'd expected him to look surprised at this I'd have been wrong. He didn't look surprised, but he wouldn't be drawn either.

'It's difficult,' he said, frowning. 'Skimmed or normal?' I told him skimmed. He nodded, and crossed the room towards me. 'Shove up, then,' he said, nudging me with his hip so he could get into the fridge.

'He told me about France,' I said.

Will's brows converged. 'Did he now?'

I nodded, judging it safe to nudge the conversation along. 'I've always rather fancied jet-skiing. Does it feel as dangerous as it looks?'

Now he did look surprised. Not necessarily bothered, but surprised.

'You two do have some chats together, don't you?' he said.

'And you do seem to get up to some adventures.'

He looked quizzically at me, then began pouring milk into the mugs. 'He told you all about our little jaunt then, did he?' I nodded again. He pulled a petulant face. 'It was pretty childish of me,' he said, 'taking off with him in the middle of the night like that. And irresponsible too, what with school and everything. Probably the craziest, most impetuous thing I've done in a long time. But I'm

253

glad I did it, even so. It was the right thing to do. It was needed. We had a really good time.' He put the milk back into the fridge and picked up a chrome caddy. 'Plus it sorted some stuff. More than any amount of talking had done. And, boy, had we done some.'

'With his gran?'

He seemed to hesitate over his choice of words. 'There'd been problems.' The kettle spouted steam and he glanced at it. 'But not any more. Not since then. Right. Water's boiling. Come on. Shove up again.'

So I shoved, moving across to the adjacent bank of units. In doing so, my eyes fell upon something I hadn't seen before. A large photograph, eight by ten, a soft-focus studio affair, stuck to the side of the freezer. I recognized her straight away from the pictures Harry had shown me. The lush swathe of inky hair, the dark eyes, the full mouth. So unlike Harry, should you glance superficially, but for the oh-so-familiar curve of her smile. He'd inherited that from his mother, for sure. Attached to the photo, with a torn length of Sellotape, were two feathers. Starling? Blackbird? I wasn't sure. Black, at any rate. The barbs were clustered at intervals along their lengths, as feathers get when they've been out in the elements for a while.

'She was very beautiful, wasn't she?' I heard myself say to him. I couldn't take my eyes from her face.

'Yes,' he said slowly. 'Yes. Yes, she was.' His voice

was toneless. Low. He was pouring water into the teapot as he spoke and he didn't turn round.

'Are the feathers particularly special?'

I caught his nod. 'Harry found them last week,' he said. 'Where we scattered her ashes. He wanted to keep them. I think he liked the idea of them coming to see her. As if she'd called them to her. To keep her company, he said.'

I inclined my head too, but said nothing more. The image of the two of them visiting her resting-place had taken shape in my mind and I had ground to a halt. Just as people so often used to do with me. He was silent too while he stirred the tea.

'I'm sorry,' I said at last, recalling how awkward he'd been with me before. 'I shouldn't ask. You don't want to talk about her, do you?'

Now he did look at me. 'No, no. It's fine. It's fine, *really*.'

He looked haunted now. Visited by ghosts. 'Sure,' I said. '*Good.*' But it wasn't.

The tea poured, he led the way back into the hall and then into a smallish back room, clearly a work-space of some seriousness. There were three separate screens, a profusion of computer hardware, a printer, other things that I had no idea about, grey boxes in some number, some plain and some with arrays of dials and switches, all of them cabled up to each other, and all, I imagined, generating substantial computing power. The window was dressed with a pale blue roman blind, which had been pulled down, presumably to keep out the sunlight. The back of the house was west-facing. I could feel the fuggy warmth of the stationary air. The room looked as if it had not long ago been decorated – divested of all the painful bits so he could concentrate on his work? There was one chair, a ladder-backed kitchen one, at the main area of desk, and he now pulled another, a swivel chair, beside it, then patted the latter and bade me sit down.

In here, in this new space, he looked altogether less haunted. I sat. 'This is where it all happens, is it?' I asked.

He placed his mug of tea on the desk beside him.

'God, no. This is just where I play about with stuff. The business happens in the office and the edit suite. It's down near the bay. Not a million miles away from where you live, in fact. All I'm doing at the moment is sorting what we've got, getting some sort of overall running order in my head. I'll be starting the edit proper when I get back from Prague, end of next week, week after. I'm hoping to snatch a few days with Harry when he comes back.' He was playing with his mouse, bringing different screens up as he talked, while a reel of tiny pictures moved along the bottom. None of it made much sense to me, but then he clicked again and an image of something happening in the school hall appeared.

We watched five or ten minutes of footage, much

of it unconnected, here Clemency, wreathed in a bower of spring clematis, explaining plant reproduction to a group of pleasingly rapt-looking children, there Mrs Cairns organizing teams for a game. He'd captured things happening in the playground that I wouldn't even have considered, nuances of expression, a solitary girl looking close to tears, two tiny children squatting with a stick by the storm drain, a bigger boy, in closeup, examining the contents of a tissue. Cerys Woolf with her vegetables, striding across the playground, just like Boudicca going into battle. It was powerful, arresting, so much cleverer than I'd imagined. And all this for a thirty-second ad?

The next scene – if that was the terminology – was back in one of the classrooms, and suddenly I was looking at an image of myself. My voice sounding odd in my ears. It was one of the year-four classrooms, with both year-four classes crammed in, some at my feet on the carpet in the reading corner, others seated behind or on desks. I was reading to them. Wednesday, then. Must have been Wednesday. Last period on a Wednesday I read to year four while Sue and Naomi, their teachers, got together to plan for the following week. It was something I'd implemented when I'd started at the school, a chance for me to get back into the classroom a little, and a means of generating useful non-contact time for them together.

'This was *Bambi*, right?' Will said.

I nodded. He hadn't been in there with me that

afternoon. I vaguely recall he'd been off doing something on the field. It was his friend Mitch who had set up shop in the corner. I remember being only dimly aware of him after the first few minutes. You get so used to being watched in that situation – advisers, inspectors, students and so on – that you learn how to filter it out and just teach. Plus it was *Bambi*, like he said, so the filter wasn't even needed.

My mother had bought me the copy of *Bambi* for my eighth birthday. I can remember ripping off the wrapping paper as if it were yesterday. A heavy hardback, yellow cover, that I unwrapped in bed, very early on the morning of my birthday while we were on holiday in Bournemouth. The first page – *Bambi: a life in the woods*, by Felix Salten, and underneath, in my mother's fancy hand, the words '*to our dearest little girl on her birthday. Eight already! Heaps of kisses, your ever loving Mummy and Daddy.*' I didn't register *Bambi* as 'Bambi' in those days. Not the cinemascope *Bambi* everyone knows now. Those were still the days when video hadn't been invented, and a trip to see a Disney film was a precious and unusual treat. I must have read in bed, that morning, for over an hour. Pages and pages and pages. And then again, that evening, when my mother sat on my bed and read some more of it to me. It didn't matter that she no longer needed to. She enjoyed reading to me and I liked being read to.

Bambi was special because it was the first book

that made me cry. It was perhaps the most precious book in my possession, and even before Emily was born, I'd looked forward to the day when I would be able to sit and read it to her. Just as my mother had read it to me. Just as one day she might sit and read it to *her* daughter. Such a very easy pleasure, predicting the future. It's living strictly in the present that demands all the skill. Perhaps that was it. Perhaps it was because I started thinking about my mother. It must have been *some*thing that set me off. Something more than the thought of my long dead daughter, surely. After all, I'd been reading this book of mine to children for many years since then. Perhaps it was because I was in the unnatural position of being outside looking in on myself. Perhaps it was the children's expressions as the camera panned across them, picking up, perhaps, nuances that I might not have seen. Perhaps it was because Bambi's was such a painful journey, a story that was so overwhelmingly about loss, about death. And that, sitting so close beside Will, in the half-light, the enormity of Harry's loss had hit me so hard. And Will's *too*. Perhaps it was the photo in the kitchen. His reticence in the face of such manifest pain. Perhaps I was more wound up than I'd realized about arguing with John. Or all the trouble with the girls. I was still smarting from their words. Perhaps *every*thing. Who knows why these things happen? All I knew was that, to my consternation, I could hardly bear to watch myself any more. That I'd become ridiculously overwhelmed by emotion. That my throat felt constricted and my eyes had filled with tears. I sipped my tea, mortified. I kept looking, sightless, at the screen. I didn't dare blink because I knew if I did the tears would slide straight down my cheeks. But almost as I thought that, they over-flowed anyway. Thank goodness, I thought, for the dimness of the room.

'You read beautifully,' Will was saying, totally oblivious, his voice deep and close over my own on the screen. I sensed him glance in my direc-tion. Felt the light and shadow change. 'You know,' he said lightly, chattily, even, 'when I played this back last night I got so into it I almost rang you up and asked you to read me some more. Now there's a new take on phone sex, eh?'

I was aware of his mouth forming a grin at the edge of my vision. His laugh. His hand coming up to brush away a rogue coil of his hair. I placed my mug carefully on the desk in front of me, then dipped my head and fashioned what I hoped would come out as part cough, part sniff, part response to his comment, while plucking up my bag from where I'd put it on the floor. But when I lifted my head again he was looking straight at me.

'Hey, hey. You okay?' he said. '*Holly?*'

When I was young and self-conscious and had nothing much to cry about I went to the cinema with Colin to see *Kramer versus Kramer*. I'd already read the book, so I should have known what was coming. Should have opted for an aisle seat. Should have bought a stash of tissues. As it was, we were mid-row and all I had was a sleeve. I sniffed, people looked. I snuffled, people huffed. So, not wishing to compound the toe-curling embarrassment further, I stayed put, gave up my attempts at staunching the flow, and just let the tears drip-drip-drip from my chin. But I'd shed so many proper tears since – so many buckets of the sort of tears that come out of you so hot and insistent and mindless of anything that's going on around you – that I'd forgotten the other kind existed. *This* kind. This well of unexpected, and largely self-indulgent, leakage. Here. Now. In front of *him*.

'Look at me!' I said briskly. I made some dabs at my cheeks with the back of my right hand.

'I *am* looking at you,' he said quietly. 'And you're crying.'

Do people do that as a rule? Isn't there some other sort of best practice one should adhere to when faced with situations like this? Aren't you supposed to make like you haven't noticed? And if that's not an option – if it's really that evident, snot flying about, sound effects, great well-springs of saline – isn't the thing then to go for it, big-time? Shouldn't you scoop up the crier and hug them to your bosom or something? Not point out the blinkin' bloody obvious, surely. But Will didn't make any sort of move towards hugging me to his bosom. Perhaps if he had, albeit paradoxically, an altogether different atmosphere might have prevailed. I could have sniffed into his T-shirt while he patted my back. We could have laughed it off, drunk our tea, gone back to the film. But no. He didn't *do* that. Instead, unspeaking, and looking frankly bewildered, he placed his left hand on my forearm and squeezed it very gently, all the while searching my face with his gaze, presumably in the hope that he might spot a clue. The moment stretched and deepened. A whole chasm of embarrassment opened between us. Crying in front of people is just so excruciating.

'What's the matter?' he said finally. '*Why* are you crying?'

Which was a fair point, because I was as clueless as he was. 'I don't *know*,' I said, which in some senses was true. Hey, there's plenty of candidates. Take your pick. Plus crying gets easier the older you get. You top up the tank every time life smacks you in the face so it gets ever easier for it to overflow. Just the same as with stress. I had a healthy stock of both. So I drummed up my own diversion, shrugging and sniffing, explaining how silly it all was, saying how these thigns crept up on you at the most unexpected moments, didn't they? That it really wasn't anything, it was just seeing myself on screen, I supposed, seeing the children's expressions, seeing my *own* expression, remembering how much I'd loved the book as a child, how I was probably feeling a bit sorry for myself. Hard day, hard week, hard *term*, all things considered, and that I'd come over all sentimental and silly, and that he mustn't worry. Which twittering was all fine and great and gave me a chance to brush away the tears and make light of everything and stop him looking so penetratingly at me, except that these things often work out to be not so fine and not so great, because the more you try to understand why you're crying, the more, sometimes, it seems to make you want to cry. Seems to work every time with me.

'Look at me!' I said again, snapping the words out staccato-style, as if somebody had just stepped on an old seventy-eight. 'Dear me, what am I like?' I rattled on. 'Don't worry, normal service will be resumed at any moment.'

Whatever normal service was. Normal sure wasn't *this*. I was suddenly consumed by a powerful yearning to be somewhere else altogether. As I'm sure he was. He'd invited a mad woman round.

He removed his hand from my arm and now reached across me to pull open a desk drawer. There was a muddle of stuff in there: paperclips, Sellotape, pencils, stubs of chequebooks, but there was also a packet of tissues in the corner, with just one left, which he pulled from the plastic.

'You know,' he said, sliding the drawer shut again, his wrist only inches from my knees, 'you shouldn't feel like that.'

I took the tissue and dabbed it carefully beneath my lower lashes, collecting up black speckles as I went. 'Like what?'

'That you must pull yourself together all the time. That you mustn't allow yourself to cry. You should. Crying's good for you.'

And he would know, I thought. He would *so* know about that. Did he do all his under cover of darkness, stifling the sound with a pillow so Harry couldn't hear? Which thought made me well up all over again. I sniffed again from behind the tissue. 'Is that what you tell Harry?'

'That's absolutely what I tell Harry. Well, no. That's not strictly true. There are times, lots of times, when he does need to be able to hold himself together. When it wouldn't help . . . what with him being a boy.'

I nodded vigorously. Swallowed. Let a heavy sigh escape from my lips. I didn't mean to. But some other part of me prevailed. It came out all by itself. 'It really gets to me, you know.'

'What does?'

'Seeing your Harry. Sometimes I catch sight of him and . . . well, sometimes – doesn't seem to matter what he's doing – he just gets this look, and it's almost as if I can *see* the pain ambush him. Can see it cross his face and I could weep for him, I really could. It shouldn't happen to a child. It shouldn't happen to anyone. It just feels so arbitrary, so cruel and unfair.'

'I know,' he said. 'It's been pretty tough for him. But we're getting there, you know. He's *fine*.'

I balled the tissue in my hand. 'I know that. I *do* know that. But it still plays on my mind all the time. It's almost as if something's happened to me since Emily died. As if I've grown a whole new extra set of nerve endings. Hyper-sensitive ones.' I smiled ruefully at him. 'Specific to their genesis. Super-conductors for other people's grief.'

He nodded. 'New heartstrings, perhaps.' Then he laughed. 'God, that sounds cheesy.'

I didn't laugh. I grimaced. 'It's a bloody good description. I can't seem to help them getting tugged at all the time. I look at you too, you know, sometimes, and I think back to that night when you were sitting there in my kitchen, so upset, and then that plays on my mind as well. How you're coping, if you're okay, how you must feel so lonely sometimes, how . . .' I found myself looking earnestly at him. 'I do know how it is,' I told him. 'I know how hard you find it to talk about her. I can see it in your face. But you should try to, you know. I *so* know that, Will.' Now it was my turn to touch his arm. 'I so worry about you, bottling it all up the way you do.'

He looked at me, wide-eyed now. 'You worry about *me*?'

He spoke the words so quietly I almost didn't hear them. And then I did, and embarrassment washed over me once more. So I nodded. I shrugged. I balled and unballed the tissue. I told him I'd preferred it when I thought he was feckless. Then I realized I shouldn't have said that either. Why was I *saying* all this? Had the manoeuvre been physically possible I'd have been

265

looking at myself in a pretty wide-eyed fashion. 'I'm sorry,' I said at last. 'Listen to me, will you? I don't usually burst into bouts of uncontrollable tears like this.'

Still that look. Still those eyes. 'Like I said, perhaps you should.'

'I don't think so.' I shook my head. 'Much less expound all this bloody pocket philosophy. You must think I'm such a flake.'

'I don't think that at all,' he said firmly. 'You cry all you like. There's no one here to see you, is there?'

'Yes, there is. There's *you*.'

'Why on earth does that matter?'

'Because . . . because, well . . . because it does. I've no business sitting here grizzling in front of you. You, of *all* people. I don't think I've felt so embarrassed since . . . well, since I last felt so embarrassed. Which was . . . God, I don't know, but it can't have been that long ago because the feeling is horribly familiar.' I gestured towards the screen. 'And I'm not sure I should watch any more of that. It's obviously bad for my health.'

'Or good for it,' he said. 'Depends on your viewpoint. And there is really, *really* nothing for you to feel embarrassed about. Not with *me*, Holly. Me, as you pointed out, *of all people*. Here . . .' He leaned in towards me and drew the back of his index finger beneath my right eye. My wet skin felt clammy against the warmth of his hand. He lifted the other then, performed the same gentle manoeuvre on my left eye.

266

'What must I look like?' I asked. 'What must I *look* like?'

'You look . . . you look . . . I don't know, *anguished*,' he said. He cupped my face in both hands now and stroked my cheeks with his thumbs. He shook his head minutely, looked intently into my eyes. 'Don't feel anguished,' he said. 'There's no need. There's no need to worry about me, *really*. No need to feel anguished. Please don't.'

I thought he was still wiping off my mascara, I really did. And then – I don't know when – I realized he wasn't doing that any more. How long? How *long*? I'd lost all sense of time. I began counting elephant seconds in my head. One elephant, two elephants, three elephants, four. I'd reached eight when his lips met mine.

CHAPTER 16

Excusable transgressions. That was the expression. We had this kind of code on the go, Toni and I, when we first became friends. The finer details elude me now, but in essence it was simply a handy reference for the right way to conduct relationships; our own and that of the boys we (and they) were lucky enough to have relationships with.

The things you do when you're young.

Okay. Transgressions, sub-section: 'Very Excusable'. Number one was being drunk, for definite. Almost everything that happens between lips is excusable when you've had a few drinks. But only at night. That was important. Ante-meridian transgressions weren't ever excusable. No one normal went off the rails before lunch. Not unless they'd shared a bed the night before, of course. But we were studious girls, both fresh from our A-level studies. Transgressions back then were much more likely to involve not getting your homework in on time. But this was the real world, and transgressions *now*, given that we were prepared to allow the possibility in the first place (which we were – we'd just got to college – we wanted to *live*) could be plotted as a graph, with the usual two axes, that of the extent of the transgression (call it y) and that of the quality of the mitigating circumstance (call it x). Toni had been seeing a mathematician at the time.

I didn't want to dwell on the y axis. So I didn't. I wanted to forget. What I wanted to dwell on was, frankly, a reason. A reason why I'd done as I had. I mentally thumbed through the card index file. A kiss was an excusable transgression not only if *you* were drunk, but also if *he* was drunk, or one of you'd been at the dope, or if you were at a party (everything was okay at a party), or you'd recently had a row with whichever then boyfriend, whose ire you had every justification to inflame (this excuse didn't count if the kissee had a girlfriend: the notion of a sisterhood hadn't quite found us yet), if you fancied his friend and the friend had failed to notice, if you'd just passed – *or* failed – an important exam. Or been involved in a trauma. Almost forgot that one. Toni had kissed the biggest saddo in the union bar on the night she heard her dog had died.

Two terms into college the code fell by the wayside. By then Toni was seeing an astronomer from Wantage, who read her poetry daily and stole her heart. Only for a term, but she emerged a proper grown-up, and the whole thing was rendered redundant.

But there was nothing to make light of on

this most verdantly springlike of spring evenings. Nothing. I was driving on autopilot, my knuckles forming two arcs of white fairy hillocks on the steering-wheel in front of me, all the way from his home to mine. I hadn't been drunk. *He* hadn't been drunk. No party. No exam. No recent trauma to recount. No dozy friend to impress. Not a single mitigating circumstance whatsoever. No. Looked at any which way, the facts didn't change. This was not an excusable transgression.

But transgression it was. I hadn't so much as peered over the clifftop to check out the drop. I'd simply launched myself over the edge like a fool – just surrendered myself to whatever was to be. Surrendering yourself to something is, as the expression itself indicates so succinctly, an impulsive, wicked, all-consuming kind of thing to find yourself doing. No surprise, then, that I was seriously stunned. Worse than that, I had, as I didn't like to dwell on but probably should have expected to be the case from the outset, kissed Will Meadows every bit as much as he'd kissed me. Not that it had been a triple X kiss. Far from it. But even as the qualities of kisses various came to me, it occurred to me that, as kisses went, that was precisely the problem with this one: it had been its tenderness that had made it feel so very bad. His lips had touched mine with as gentle an impact as that of a feather falling not very far onto a velvet cushion or a bed of fluffy moss. It had been such a slow and sweetly chaste meeting of mouths that, had it not been for the fireworks it had set off inside me, it might have been transplanted into Victorian fiction, and not a single note of it would have jarred.

If that had been that. If that had been *all*. But, God, how we had lingered at this kissing. Had we got on with it, crushed, bruised, panted, moaned, groaned and thrashed about a bit, then perhaps, just perhaps, I could have dredged an element of reckless impetuosity into my stew of regret, watered it down with a big slug of heat-of-the-moment, sweetned its taste with a slosh of end-of-term mania and made it feel altogether less damning. But no no no no no, it simply wasn't like that. We dallied, we dawdled, we tarried awhile, we *hung about* in this kissing glade of ours. How can any two people spend such a long time just, well, touching each other's lips with their own? Just touching, disconnecting, varying the angle a bit, touching again. It made no sort of sense. It didn't seem to have a purpose. It wasn't going anywhere. No A to B sexual impetus. It just *was*. Like stopping in front of a painting that appeals to you. Checking out the colours, the brushwork, the perspective. Drinking in its every tiny nuance before moving on.

And then, so much later, so damningly much later, we stopped kissing each other and drew apart. We shared two lungfuls each of the heavy air that hung between us, and Will took his hands from my face. Slid them down over my shoulders, along the

271

outsides of my forearms, then fanned the fingers of both hands and encircled my wrists. My own hands – hands that, only seconds ago, had moved among his curls, confirmed their wiry softness, touched the baby smooth cleft at the back of his neck – were, as if now in denial, in my lap. He moved his to enfold them.

All of this wordless still. His face was inches from mine. Near enough for me to see that he still looked bewildered. As if he was trying to fathom what had caused him to act in the way that he had. Enough for me to see that, nestled between the amber, there were narrow grey streaks in his irises too. The grey of a raincloud. My attention to detail overwhelmed and surprised me.

He opened his mouth then. Moved his hands. 'I've been imagining kissing you,' he said, 'a great deal.'

He spoke as if the idea had only just occurred to him. Was that so? I wasn't sure. I had certainly imagined kissing *him*. Imagined it lots. His expression was changing. His hands moved on mine. I pulled my eyes from his and looked into my lap. 'I'm engaged, Will,' I told him. 'I'm getting married in October.'

He said not a word, but as I looked up at him, I met his astonished gaze on its way down towards my hand. He uncovered it and held it on the palm of his own. The ring had become twisted. It was a little too large. I turned my palm up and the diamond winked. I swivelled it back twenty times a day or more. I'd not yet got round to having it made smaller. I must do that, I thought. I really, really must.

I could hardly bear to meet his eye. He looked so shocked, so appalled. 'I had no idea,' he said. 'I never thought. Not once. I didn't even notice.'

I pulled my hand gently from his grasp and tucked it inside the other. 'Why should you have noticed? You wouldn't have been looking. I didn't tell you. It wasn't relevant, was it?'

'No,' he said. 'I guess not.'

I forced myself to look him in the eye and said, 'I don't know what happened just then, Will. I just . . . I was upset . . . and there you were . . . and, well, everything, really. And then . . .' I frowned. Lowered my eyes.

'And then?'

'I don't *know*, Will. But it shouldn't have happened. I'm sorry, but it shouldn't. I think I'd better go, don't you?'

I stood up then, and the tissue dropped from my lap to the floor. He picked it up. His face was a mask of disbelief, mirroring mine.

Though for entirely different reasons. He cleared his throat.

'Your tea's gone cold,' he said.

I swam forty-eight lengths, fast and furious, head down, four strokes to each breath instead of the normal three, so I came up right-sided for air every time, which felt strange. And exhausting. I was gasping. The breathing pattern didn't suit me.

273

But still I swam on. I couldn't make myself stop. Just one more. And then another. And another and another. Till my thighs were on fire and my temples throbbed.

We usually swam in tandem if the pool wasn't busy, chatting as we went about nothing very much. But tonight in moments I had half a length on Toni. Toni's always been a strong swimmer – stronger than me – but when I finally paused to gulp in air I could see her at the other end, sitting on the side, feet in the water, looking weary. She waved. I mouthed, 'Last one,' then ploughed back.

When I reached her and took off my goggles, she said, 'Bloody hell, Hol, you on something or what?'

I told her I had a headache, that I'd thought a hard swim might help to clear it. That if she didn't mind I'd head straight off after we got dressed. No drink, if that was okay with her. She was tired herself, she said.

We parted soon after, and as I watched her walk to her car, I realized – not for the first time, but definitely for the worst time – that marrying your best friend's brother had its drawbacks. I could have done with my best friend to talk to right now. But I couldn't. On this one I knew she wouldn't be at home.

But Dorothy was. There was a Post-it note on the front door of my flat when I got home. It said, 'If you get a moment, dear – BEADS! Dxx'.

Dorothy has beads to rival any haberdasher. A

selection of tins – travel-sweet tins, tobacco tins, tins that used to hold cough pastilles and pins – each with their own distinctive remnant of scent, all labelled, and stored in a candy-striped box. New additions, such as those she had bought for my dress, sat alongside them in their clear Perspex boxes. Had I been a child I would have been in heaven. As it was, did perdition beckon? I couldn't remember the last time I'd felt so *bad*.

I'd showered at the pool so there was nothing much for me to do except stand in the middle of my living room and do endless action replays in my head. Which was just what I didn't want to do. Instead I went and chucked my swimming-costume and towel in the washing bin and went straight up to Dorothy's flat.

She was sitting, as ever, in the big tapestry armchair in the corner. It was part of a suite; there was also a little sofa, both with elaborate hunting scenes woven into the cloth. Copses, leaping horses, jaunty-looking figures in red jackets. Not that you could see a great deal of the chair. My wedding dress, as if to remind me of everything I needed to remember, was a waterfall of glossy cream spilling over her knees onto the floor. The patch of carpet at her feet was covered, as always, with some sheeting, extending the sense of fluid grace around her, giving the tableau an even greater air of good. As if it was an oil painting entitled *The Night Before the Wedding* or a pen-and-ink study, an Edwardian lithograph, with a caption that read, perhaps *Toiling in the Service of the Bride*.

The wicked, wicked bride. 'Shall I put the kettle on?' I said.

By the time I got back into the living room, I felt better. It was less oppressive up here with Dorothy. The warmth, the occasional phut-phut of the fan heater, the mindless sorting of bugle beads, sequins, crystal orbs. The counting, organizing, comparing of colour and shape, the passing of beads, Dorothy's easy chat. Losing myself in something mechanical, something that would reroute all the frazzled scraps of thought. Or so I hoped. Guilt can be a terrible bully.

And I wasn't even sure what I felt most guilty about. The kiss? That was the number-one candidate. Or that I'd led Will to believe it had been the natural and right thing to do? Or worse still – worse *still* – that it *had*? Oh, Max.

'So, how's your week been?' Dorothy asked, delving into the box of beads I held out for her. 'The film thing at school go okay?'

I hadn't seen her since the first day. The Wednesday. What a long time ago it seemed. I told her it was fine, that it had been fun, that I'd had a sneak preview of some footage. That I'd been to Will's house and he'd shown me what he'd done. I could tell her that much.

'And was it good?' she asked.

'Yes. Yes, it was. Even better than I thought.'

'So you're pleased.'

'Yes.'

'And how is *he*?'

It was, I didn't doubt, the most innocent of questions. But my expression must have indicated my confusion because Dorothy had affected her penetration expression. She had a fearfully good nose for hidden agendas. 'I meant how's he getting *on*?' she added. 'His difficulties with his son. I know you've been worried about them. Are things any better at home?'

Home. *His* home. Rule eight million and seven. I must not tell Dorothy about having kissed Will. A thousand years ago, when Emily was a baby, I remember having a big row with Colin. A stupendous, free-wheeling, unstoppable juggernaut of a row. It ended, as these things often do, with him leaving. Not leaving as in stopping to pack-your-case leaving but stomping out in high dudgeon and driving off into the night. In my immaturity I decided I wasn't having that, so I went huffing to my mother's. There I sat and I ranted. I disgorged every last spark of anger, along with simmering resentment and not a small quantity of bile.

By bedtime it was fine. He came to get me. We made up. It was soon, as is best, all forgotten. But for the longest time after, though the row was forgotten, my mother's memory of it was still sharp. As were her looks at Colin. I came to wonder if she'd been taking notes.

This was different. No loyalties at issue. Dorothy,

dear as she was, wasn't my mum. But the principle of not spreading unrest still held good. If I
wanted to work this thing out of my system, I'd
be best employed *not* sowing the seeds of it in hers.

I said, 'Yes.' Then I nodded. 'They seem to be
anyway. Harry's much happier in school. And
Will's . . . Well, it's not my business, is it? I don't
know. But yes, I think so.'

Dorothy plucked a pinch of tiny pearl beads
from the tin, then speared them, one, two, three,
with her needle. She didn't speak again until she'd
drawn the needle through the fabric. Then she
rested her hands lightly in her lap. 'You've got a
bit of a crush on that one, haven't you?' she said.

Whaaat? I gaped at her. 'God, Dorothy,' I said,
and I believe I even laughed. 'God, is it really that
obvious?'

There. I'd admitted it. Well, some of it, at any
rate. Dorothy smiled in satisfaction, and even as
she did so, I began to feel differently about it. Not
the chill dread of revelation I'd expected, but a
welcome surge of understanding. Of relief. That
was all it was. A silly crush. And put like that,
it didn't sound remotely as damning as it had
felt. I'd had a crush on a horse once. A big bay.

'Thought so,' she said. She didn't say any more
for a few moments. Just finished the piece she was
sewing, then stabbed the needle and thread into the
arm of her armchair. I asked her once why she didn't
get a pincushion. 'Why ever would I want to do
that?' she'd replied. 'Isn't life complicated enough?'

She said the strangest things sometimes. There were times when I found myself awake and wondering about them at four in the morning. She had nothing strange to say about this, however.

'And?' she asked me.

'And what? It's just thrown me a little, that's all.'

'These things always do.'

'I know. I wish they didn't.'

'Darling,' she said, 'you don't seriously suppose that marrying Max is going to mean you never find another man attractive, do you?'

'No, of course I don't.'

She looked sharply up at me. 'So there's no need to get yourself into a tizzy over it.'

'I'm not. Well, I am, but not for the reasons you might think. I just . . . oh, I feel awful, to tell you the truth, because . . . well, because I think he's attracted to me. And, well, oh dear. I inadvertently gave him the impression that there might be something between us. He didn't know I was engaged, you see. He thought . . . well,' I stood up, 'I just feel a bit bad about it all. What with everything.'

'I *see*,' she said, threading a new bead onto her needle. 'Bit of a delicate situation, then. I thought you were looking pale.'

I digested this as I went into the kitchen to make tea. I didn't feel pale. I felt hot. Hot and rather bothered. It was as if some hitherto hidden part of myself had been coaxed out of some shadowy recess of my personality and was still sitting in that room with him even as I thought it. And that if I didn't manage to reclaim it it would be out for good, and I wouldn't get it back into its box.

I reached for the kettle and there was Dorothy, in the doorway, arms folded, studying me. 'That's all, then, is it?'

'Yes,' I said. 'That's all.' The steam rose in a Paisley whorl between us. I looked at the kettle then put it down. 'Have you got any wine?'

'There's a merlot in the sideboard.'

'That'll do. I'll replace it tomorrow.'

'Don't be so silly.' She turned. 'I'll get it. You fetch the corkscrew and some glasses.'

You calm down in the end. Once you've put temporal as well as spatial distance between what you've done and what you're going to do next, you calm down and get things into perspective. You step outside the heat that's been licking at the walls of the kitchen and you look back coolly on the current state of play. The kiss was done, and I couldn't undo it. All I had to undo now was the misunderstanding. That and the tangle of un-bidden sensations that had me wishing I could kiss him again. They weren't to be trusted. Of that I was sure. As was Dorothy, even in her ignorance of the fact.

Dorothy, older and less hot-headed than I was, had not got where she was today (i.e. comfortable, content, unshockable and wise) without having lived a little along the way. Though she had been happily married for much of her adult life, she had endured her fair share of trauma. She had lost two babies, she had sat through six nights of horror after her son had an accident on his motorbike and nearly died (he still has a marked limp) and, most pertinently, she too had fallen victim to a crush. A brief period of unimaginable passion for a man called Nathaniel, a diplomat colleague of her husband's. While they were living in Malta. For a whole half a year. When she was the age I am now.

A ridiculous age for an infatuation to take hold. But it had. 'So, what happened? You had an affair with him?'

'Heavens, no. In my head I consumed him in every way imaginable and, yes, we met often, even kissed a couple of times. But I never did anything that could be called infidelity. And my name's not Lewinsky, so you can exclude that one too. We never made love. But the wanting, the aching, was almost as good.'

'And how did it end?'

'He was drafted elsewhere, and I got over it,' she said. 'It was, after all, just a collision of circumstance and geography. Marcus and I were going through a fallow patch – Seb was an unimaginably terrible teenager, and Marcus was away a lot, I was restless and under-occupied – all rather mundane, but a Molotov cocktail of small dissatisfactions and niggles. And Nathaniel was in similar straits. His wife was unhappy away from home – it was his first foreign posting – and she was back and forth whenever she got the chance. It was as commonplace, no doubt, as every other mid-life crisis, but we came together, discovered a glorious, mutual, almost animal attraction and, well, it was, shall we say, an excitable time?' She sipped daintily from her glass. 'Proximity is an interesting thing to contemplate, isn't it? I dare say that the probability was equally as great that I *wouldn't* have met someone whom I found myself adoring so passionately, in which case I'm sure I would have muddled on through the grim bit anyway, and got back on an even keel with Marcus in the end. Or maybe not. These things do have a tendency to make one self-analyse and soul-search, so perhaps because of him I got through my marital doldrums altogether more quickly than I might have, had I not been forced to confront it. Don't *worry*. It's just a flight of fancy. And his circumstance. Men are always at their most captivating when they let you see their vulnerable side. Things will be fine. It will be the same for you.'

'But it's not at all the same for me, is it? I'm not in any doldrums. It's not as if I've been with Max for years and years and have become bored. I haven't even married him yet! What on earth am I doing flirting with another man when I'm just about to head up the aisle?'

'Do you love Max?'

'Of course I love Max!'

'Then there's no problem, is there?'

'But there is. There's still Will to consider, isn't there? I just feel so bad that I might have led him to believe that . . . I feel so desperately, desperately sorry for him, Dorothy.' With that terrible forlorn expression on his face. That he'd got things so wrong. Why on earth hadn't I *told* him?

Dorothy rolled her eyes. 'I'm sure he'll get over it, Holly. I'm sure it's nowhere near as serious as you think. And remember, it's feeling sorry for him that got you here in the first place.'

'I know. But I still feel awful.' It was so hard, trying to explain without actually explaining.

'Well, don't. Just accept that he's struck a chord with you, that's all. One that Max is unable to strike. It's perfectly understandable that he should get under your skin.'

'I know. That's what I keep telling myself. It's just sympathy, isn't it? I mean, I know he's attractive, and of course that's a factor, but you're right. It's mainly his situation. I know that. Sympathy.'

Dorothy shook her head. 'That's precisely where you're wrong. You don't sympathize with him, Holly, you empathize. There's a whole world of difference between the two states.'

I found myself smiling at this distinction until I was reminded of my conversation with Will about heart-strings, which wiped the smile straight off my face. 'Oh, I'm good at empathy,' I said, sitting down heavily on the stirrup-cup scene. 'I can do it with my eyes shut.' I considered my glass. 'That's the trouble. I *have* been doing it with my eyes shut. If I'd had them open in the first place I wouldn't have walked into all this, would I?'

'Walked into having this man think you have feelings for him, or walked into how you feel about his feelings for you?'

'I don't know. Don't start blinding me with science. I just feel I've got involved when I'd no business doing so, and now I've let him down. That's all.'

'Let me put it another way,' she persisted. 'All this.'

'What?'

'You said, "walked into all this".' She took another sip of her wine. 'Tell me. What's *your* definition of "all this"?'

But the answer to that question would have to wait, because just as Dorothy asked it her phone rang in the hall. Her friend Hester, from the Dolls' House Club she belonged to, with details of some upcoming event. Her voice floated into the living room. Talk of guest speakers, new products, discussion about fellow members' projects. All so safe and ordinary and worlds away from kissing. But, I wondered, did a pulse of passion still throb sometimes in her breast?

She came back in with my handbag, which I'd dumped, as I always did, on the side table by the front door.

'Been beeping,' she said, passing it to me before she sat down again and reached for her needle. 'I would have shouted, but it stopped before I even realized what it was.'

'Probably Max,' I said, fishing for my mobile. Said it automatically, without thinking. Max was entertaining clients. It was probably *not* Max. I found the phone. One missed call, it told me. I pressed the button. No, it had not been Max.

The display said Mr Meadows. It looked alien. As if I was holding someone else's phone. I couldn't remember typing it in. But I could certainly remember 'Mr Meadows' as a concept. How quaint it was that I should have entered 'Mr' in the phone. Not 'Will', but 'Mr', as if hammering home my point. *That* father. *That* man.

I put the phone back into my bag and put the bag down on the floor. 'Max,' I told Dorothy, finding the lie, though unpalatable, the only realistic option in my current frame of mind. I knew I was close to telling her the truth. 'I'd better ring him back before it gets too late. In fact, it is getting late. I'd better leave you in peace. Shall I give you a hand with the dress?'

Dorothy drained her glass and looked at me. Considering, I judged, whether I was on the verge of saying more. Then she shook her head. 'No. You get off downstairs, dear. I'll carry on with this for a bit.'

'Are you sure?'

'I'm sure. Get on. Sleep well.'

*   *   *

285

It would be fine. Just as long as I kept a sense of proportion about what had happened. By the time I got back to my flat I had decided that perhaps I needed to explain myself better. The image of Will's face kept overlaying itself on my consciousness. His astonishment on finding out about my situation, the embarrassment that had followed so hard on its heels. Had I really made myself clear enough earlier? In my mind's eye, I'd done anything but. I'd sat there like a dummy with his hands in my lap, my mouth saying one thing, the right thing, for sure, but my body saying quite another.

I should ring him, I thought, tutting to myself. I must return his call and tell him I am very, very sorry that I had found myself attracted to him, but that I loved my fiancé and that it had been one of those wrong-place, wrongtime things. Come on, Holly, I thought. What things would those be? I could already hear the lack of conviction in my voice. Worse, I could already imagine his expression as I did so, and though I wasn't about to flatter myself that I was anything more important in his life than a woman who had been kind to him and for whom – perhaps as a consequence, even – he'd felt what could well have been the first stirrings of physical desire since losing his wife, the idea of rebuffing him again made me cold with a feeling I couldn't put a name to. It just felt all wrong.

But wasn't that just my excess of empathy

muscling in again? Of course it was. I stabbed at the various buttons that would bring me to his voicemail message. I would phone him and put him straight because it was the right thing to do. It had been an aberration and needed nipping in the bud.

Suddenly he spoke. Close up, cradled against my ear. I felt hot. I felt cold. He'd got it right. I felt *anguished*.

'It's me,' he said. 'God, I hate talking to these things. Look, I just wanted to apologize for what happened earlier. I feel such an idiot, Holly. I had absolutely no idea.' I know, I thought. I *know*. I heard him take a breath. 'But it's funny, isn't it?' he went on. 'The whole protocol thing we talked about that time. Remember? I keep on coming back to it. You giving me all that stuff about surnames. Remember? And I remember thinking – wow, this is one uptight woman! But you knew I was thinking that, didn't you?' He laughed then. But it seemed forced, self-conscious. Had he been sitting alone in his house when he called? 'So,' he said. 'Phew, eh? All change now, Mrs Connors!' Another pause. A longer one. 'I'm sorry,' he said again. 'This isn't something to be flippant about, is it? Look, I'd love to be able to tell you I didn't know what came over me, but I'd be lying. Well, not so much lying – I didn't write a storyboard for this happening, I can tell you, but I can't deny I hoped it would, Holly.' His voice seemed so near. I felt hot again. Nauseous. I realized that I hadn't eaten since twelve. 'It's just I had absolutely no idea about you and, well, whoever it is you're marrying. No idea at all. Zippo. And I just kind of got the idea that you and I . . .' A sharp outbreath. The longest pause. The *longest*. Three heartbeats. 'Anyway, all it is . . . well, I just wanted to let you know that you don't need to worry. Or be embarrassed when you see me. It's history, okay? Protocols re-established and all that.' He cleared his throat. 'Call me if you want to. I'll be up, okay? Night.'

Click. 'End of message . . .'

I'd sat down on the sofa at some point. And I continued to sit, staring out at the impenetrable black of the bay. The moon was almost full. Creamy and mottled, slung high in the sky. Big as a beach ball. Such a strange way of thinking. How big was enough clear blue sky to make a shirt? Five thousand miles worth? What would that make my beach ball? I couldn't think of anything spherical that was big enough. Except a comet. Which didn't feel metaphorical enough. Wasn't so far from being a moon itself, in fact. Will. Oh, poor Will. I'm so *sorry*. I weighed the phone in my hand for a few moments more. Then, decided, I scrolled through and dialled.

Seven long rings. I almost gave up.

Then a click. 'Hello, you! What time d'you call this? That sister of mine been keeping you out on the tiles?'

I stood again now. Walked over to the window.

Pressed my forehead against the cool glass as I spoke. 'Are you in bed?'

'Almost. Everything okay?'

'Everything's fine.' The words formed a cloud just in front of my lips. I licked at it. 'Just thought I'd ring and say goodnight.'

'You sure? You sound funny.'

'I'm fine.'

'You've not had too much to drink?'

'Do I sound like I have?'

'Not in the least.'

'Have you?'

'*Oh*, yes, sweets. Indubitably so.'

I moved my head. Wiped the smear with the sleeve of my sweater. 'You can still say "indubitably".'

'I'm a well-preserved drunk.'

'You mean pickled.'

'Yes, pickled. Yes, I'm certainly that.'

'Go to bed, then.'

'I was just about to. I told you.'

'Then I won't keep you up.'

'Good. Nighty-night, then.'

'Sweet dreams.' I frowned at my reflection in the window. Would *I* dream?

He yawned. 'I'll see you in the morning, sweets.'

'Not too early, I hope.'

'Oh, don't worry. It won't be.'

'Go on,' I said. 'Get yourself off to bed.'

'I would have been there already, but this strange woman phoned me. Just wait till I tell my fiancée.'

Just before I got into bed, I made a point of

289

putting my phone away in my handbag, and my handbag in the kitchen. Just in case Will called again before he went to Prague.

The clock hands marked the hours, oblivious to me. I slept with my head beneath the pillow.

CHAPTER 17

We weren't going away with the girls after all and, all things considered, I was glad. I felt bad enough about my episode of moral turpitude as it was, without having to bolt on the hooked nose and the broomstick.

In any case we'd not planned anything as yet. We had only just climbed back up to the place we'd been before the wedding embargo 'I hate you' fiasco. We were all teetering, to be sure, but we were just about there. Max had explained again, the girls had apologized, and I'd done my usual Mary Poppins all-singing-and-dancing, all-forgiving routine. And I *had* forgiven them. I could understand how they felt. Our trip was still on, though the plans were loose. We'd see what occurred to us. What the girls fancied. Ease our way back into easiness with them. No point in rushing what couldn't be rushed.

'I understand.' This had been me to Max on the Tuesday. My lovely Max, who made me feel anchored, safe and in control again. Banished the wellings of unfocused panic, and reminded me that my situation wasn't like Dorothy's. No doldrums here, just a future together. It was echoes from the past that had stirred our calm waters. I could quiet them again. That was all I needed to do.

We'd been having lunch in one of those places in the bay that are forever changing hands. Bitsy food, curious mock-shipboard artefacts, tailored women with straightening-iron hair. Him, suited and sharp, having slipped away from work, me, footloose, demob happy, in holiday mode. And I *was* okay. I was too busy with paperwork not to be. I was occupied. More settled. It had just been a kiss, that was all, and here was my Max, and I loved him. It would all be fine. I could see my way clear of this blip.

'I just feel,' he said, though he'd said it once already, 'that it'd be best. You do agree, don't you?'

I said yes, I did. That I thought it best too. His mother was poorly. She was going to have to have an operation on a part of her anatomy that women my age don't like to think about too much. And as a consequence she was even worse than usual. Confused and afraid. Toni was already up there with her. Max could do second shift, starting Thursday after work. With the girls in tow. Might as well take them. Plenty of other relatives to catch up with nearby. A couple of second cousins – boys – they were fond of. They could do York. See some sights. *Talk.*

'But best if I don't go,' I had already said, before he could.

He had frowned and nodded. Looked so relieved

that I knew it had been weighing heavily with him. 'You don't think we should tackle it head on, then?' he'd said.

'No, I don't,' I said firmly. 'But this'll be a good opportunity for you and the girls to talk on your own.'

'I know, sweets.'

I put my hand over his. 'I'm not offended,' I told him. 'I'd rather this than ram it – ram *us* – down their throats at the moment.'

'I feel bad, even so. It shouldn't have to be like this.'

'Max, whoever said this was going to be easy?'

'You're sure you're okay about it?'

'I'm sure. Max, I *understand*.'

And I did. But I was still a bit upset. Not that I wasn't going up north for Easter, simply that I hated that they hated me. Simply for the mantle I had no choice but to wear. Simply for the fact that there was nothing I could do.

But now it was Thursday, and I had shaken off the rain-clouds. It wasn't me they hated, just the concept of me. As well they might. And here was Max, straight from the office, to spend a happy half an hour with me before he picked up the girls. No rainclouds allowed at this time.

'Happy Easter!' he announced, from behind a cloud of spotted Cellophane, balanced on one leg while he shut my front door with his foot.

Flowers. And a preposterously large Easter egg. No, two. 'This one's from Sasha and Tara,' he said, handing it to me first. 'By way of a peace-offering.'

'Really?' I took it from him, my spirits lifting. 'Well, that's sweet of them.' I had already got them both a little something. Agonizing in Miss Selfridge. I'd already given the parcels to Max to put in his case. 'You didn't tell them—'

'*No.*'

'Okay, *okay*. Just asking.' I checked my watch. 'You stopping for a coffee, or what?'

'Or what,' he said, winking as he shrugged off his jacket.

Which was fine. He had such a lot on his plate. The least I could do was send him off with a smile.

A scant twenty hours later, I was certainly not smiling. Why, oh, why did it have to be like this? Because they'd journeyed up late, I hadn't called that evening and now I was phoning to check they'd got to York okay. Only Max didn't answer his mobile. It was Sasha.

'Hello,' I said cheerily. 'Journey not too arduous?'

No, she said. Did I want to speak to Dad? Only he was in the shower. Should she have him call me back?

'Yes, please,' I said. 'By the way, thanks for the lovely Easter egg. I've been dreadful. I've eaten most of it already.'

A pause. 'Pardon?'

'My egg,' I said again.

'Oh, yeah,' she said. 'Right. Yeah. 'S fine.'

Max called ten minutes later. 'Look, I'm sorry, okay?'

With hindsight, it had been so obvious I couldn't believe I hadn't twigged it the minute I'd clapped eyes on it. How could I have been so naïve? 'Max, if you're going to buy me something and pretend it's from them you should at least let them in on the secret.'

He groaned. 'I know,' he said unhappily. 'I know . . .'

'Max,' I said gently, 'don't do it. Please. It doesn't help.'

'I did tell them, last night.'

'Max, you know what teenagers are like. They probably only take in one word in three if it issues from the mouth of a parent. And it's not the point anyway. You shouldn't do it because it doesn't help. You are not their PR manager. Or mine, for that matter. We'll work things out between us, okay?'

Silence.

'They don't *want* you giving me peace-offerings on their behalf. It'll just make them feel even more resentful of me. Don't you see that?'

'No, I don't, Holly. Because that's ridiculous.'

'No it *isn't*. It just makes them feel even more manipulated. They don't want to be forced to like me. Don't you understand that? It just makes them feel even more insecure. That your approval of them is all bound up with them being nice to me when they clearly can't *do* that yet. They have too much to blame me for.'

'You? But you haven't done anything! It's *me* they should be blaming!'

'Yes, *we* know that, Max, but they can't do it. They *love* you. So they blame me instead because what else can they do? They need to transfer it to me because I don't matter to them. Can't you see that?'

There was, to my consternation, the sound of an irritable sigh from the other end of the line. Perhaps it was that. Perhaps it was everything. Perhaps it was because he hadn't pulled me up on my rash assertion that they should blame him and that I knew he had just filed it away resentfully, but when he said, 'Oh, and you're the expert of course,' so peevishly, I responded in a way I had no business to do.

'No!' I said. 'But neither are you, Max. And I know which of the two of us *should* be.'

'I beg your pardon?' he said, an edge to his voice now. 'I'm trying to *help* here.'

'Well, you're not,' I said. 'You're just making things worse.'

'Fine,' he said coldly. 'Point taken.'

He called me later, of course. Apologized. Wanted to know what I was up to. Apologized again. I apologized back. We sorted it all out. Smoothed over the new cracks. But they'd widened, even though we couldn't see them.

'He never really could do hands, could he?'

Tuesday morning and Dorothy and I were up

in the city centre, strolling around the gallery at the museum. Killing time before the art lecture we were going to, which Dorothy had seen advertised in the paper. We were mindful of the time: there was a queue, by all accounts. He was a TV celebrity, our artist-cum-lecturer.

At the sound of the voice, I twisted my head. If nothing else, the sensation of unexpected warm breath against the side of my neck had sent a shiver down my spine. The first thing I saw, however, was a small male person, a head shorter than me. Black sweatshirt with skulls on it. Grin. Check. Curls. Check. 'Hello, Harry,' I said.

Another twenty degrees brought me round to the origin of the voice. A lot taller. Leather jacket. White T-shirt. No logo.

Curls. Check. No grin. Then yes grin. Yes, *eyes*. I took my gaze off to make an inspection of the parquet flooring, in case it turned rogue and let me down. 'Hello, there,' he said. 'Happy Tuesday.'

And down, down, down came the whole flimsy edifice. The edifice of artifice I'd built for myself. With a powerful demolition-ball whump in my stomach. At least, that was what it felt like, but I could ride it out. It was only chemicals, after all. Nothing more.

So here we were, back with the adrenaline again. Scientists have long banged on about it, haven't they? So much so that almost anyone over eleven would be able to answer perfectly should you care to ask them what it was for. For muscles, of course. For flight or fighting. I could fly now, for sure – to 'Evolution' or 'Seventeenth-century Ceramics' – but that would just make me look barking. On the other hand, fighting felt almost inviting. I could pummel his T-shirted chest with my fists, knee him in the groin, perhaps. Kick him in the shins. 'How dare you be such a goodlooking pirate! There should be a law! Be gone, I say!' I might be thrown out but my single most powerful adrenaline-fuelled thought was that at least it had that touchy-feely, hands-on appeal. And I had never been one to wimp out of situations.

'Hello,' I trilled back, surprising myself. 'How was Prague?'

He drew a hand over the top of his head. 'Hot.'

'Really? I guess I never thought of Prague as a hot place.'

'Hits the low thirties all the time in the summer.'

'Really?'

'Uh-huh. You here for the – oh! Hello!'

'Hello,' said Dorothy, who'd been looking at a Sisley.

'Dorothy,' I said, 'you remember Will, don't you?'

'Will?' She nodded. 'Of course. Yes, I do.'

'And this is Harry,' I said.

'Pleased to meet you,' Harry said, politely extending his hand to be scooped up by Dorothy's. I caught Will's flush of pride. He caught me catching it. I looked away.

'So, Harry,' I said, 'did you have a good trip?'

'It was safe,' he said. 'Me and Matt went quad-biking.'

'Wow,' I said.

'I've been on a quad bike,' said Dorothy.

'Really?' said Will, who, of course, didn't know Dorothy.

'A friend of my son has two,' she said.

'He lives in France,' I tacked on, for no particular reason.

'I didn't drive,' she told Harry. 'Just had a go on the back.'

Harry nodded a natural-order-restored sort of nod. 'I drove,' he said gravely. 'It was a special off-road course.'

'I'm sure you did,' said Dorothy. 'You've a touch of the Barry Sheen's about you.'

Harry glanced from her to me. 'Right, then,' said I.

'Well,' said Will, frowning.

'So,' said I, frowning too. 'Very nice to see you both.'

'You too,' said Will.

'See you in school, Miss,' said Harry. 'I'll bring my photos.'

'Yes,' I said. 'Do that.'

'Toodle-pip!' said Dorothy, which made Harry laugh.

When I get home from the museum – I dropped Dorothy off at her friend Hester's, round the corner – I switch on the TV and there's an advert on. It's for a car and I remember Toni telling me about it. It's an advert Will made, and the car is driving round a city. You can't see the driver very clearly. Short dark hair, thirties, unshaven, a generic Everyman, a good-looking guy. Will is so much not a generic Everyman good-looking guy. He is cut from a singular mould. That shaggy mess of hair, those heavy-lidded eyes, the loose-limbed lean sprawl of him whenever he sits down, the valleys and hillocks of his sinewy arms. I wonder where he stood while this was being filmed at his direction. I toy with the idea because it appeals to me. His direction. I picture him leaning against the wall of an adjacent building, the comedy checklist of clipboard, megaphone, baseball cap, sneakers, all present and correct. Him barking orders. Consulting his notes. Shouting, 'Cut!' or 'Go again!' The car is small, playful, chunky-looking. Orange. Here, there and everywhere, among architecture that is unmistakably Eastern European. Prague? I cannot name a single building in Prague. Is there a famous opera house, museum, cathedral? All I know of Prague is that men go there for stag nights. I recall one of the younger teachers – Naomi? – telling me her brother had gone to Prague for his.

The ad has gone now and is replaced by another. Then another. Air-freshener. Cat food. Bio-active yoghurt. An endless parade of things you can buy. And my mobile is ringing.

Because the wonders of technology mean that

as well as a flashing telephone icon there are also the two words 'Mr Meadows' illuminated on my phone screen, I have a choice. I can choose not to answer it. I can have Mr Meadows leave a message after the tone. The non-interactive, therefore nonhazardous option. I choose to answer it, because I'm beginning to feel mightily cross with myself. And stupid. Like I haven't any control. How ridiculous.

'Hello, Will,' I say firmly to the phone.

When I still had my old mobile, thousands of people had newer, better ones so there was a period when I never knew who was ringing me but when I rang someone they'd say, 'Hello, Holly!' I'd say, 'How did you know it was me?'

It feels a bit like that in reverse, that rather knowing, 'Hello, Will.'

We don't need the preamble any more, that's the thing. You know who's ringing you before you even answer. Which is fine, because he doesn't seem to want preamble anyway. He says, 'Can we get together?' straight away. Just like that. I say, 'Um,' because I'm still a light year behind him. For all my doughty resolve, I don't know what to say. I'd thought we'd chat. About everything but. Politely, one step removed, as if the kiss hadn't happened. That was surely best, wasn't it? But now he has reneged on the deal. I add, 'Look, Will, I don't *know* . . .' Because I am floored. My brain can't think of a single other thing to say.

Yet his can. '"Don't know" as in diary commitments?' he replies. 'Or "don't know" as in not sure you should?' Then he waits. He isn't doing this the way I think he ought to. Sounds so much on a mission it feels scary.

'"Don't know" as in . . .' I can't decide how to finish this. The TV is talking to itself in the corner. A cartoon. I pick up the remote with my free hand and switch it off. 'As in . . . well . . . the thing is, Will—'

'Look,' he says, 'I don't want to make you feel uncomfortable, Holly. I just wondered if you'd like me to take you down to the edit suite and show you what I've done. That's all. But it's up to you. I just thought that as Harry's at some paintballing party tomorrow, and it's good for me, that if you haven't got anything on you might like to take a look before I show . . .' He reels off a name I don't recognize. The name of the advertising agency who commissioned it, I presume. He tells me it doesn't matter if I can't – he can let me have it on DVD at the start of next term. That nothing's finalized yet, if there's anything I don't feel happy with. It's just that—

'Well, it's just that I can book some time down there tomorrow afternoon. If you'd like me to pick you up and take you with me then great. If not, well . . . that's fine too. Your shout.' He pauses. 'I don't want to make this a big deal. Make things difficult for you or anything.' I can hear the subtle change in his tone as he says this.

Hesitation and anxiety. He is waiting for my answer. 'Okay,' I say. I say it very clearly because I am thirty-nine years old and I can deal with a crush. Deal with it well enough that I don't have to embarrass him any further. If he can be grown-up about it so can I. And he's worked so hard on what he's done. And he wants to show it off. 'Okay. Yes. I'd love to see it, Will,' I say. 'What time would you like to pick me up?'

CHAPTER 18

One o'clock. Tuesday. And the sun is looking smug in the sky. As it has every right to. It has shown its face, dried up all the puddles, made everyone's day a little easier on the eye. I woke early, dressed in jeans and a vest top, although it's only April. The air, even at seven, had that haymaking smell. I did paperwork all morning. It felt like all day.

Will has the top down when he arrives to collect me. We're all of like mind when the sun shines in Cardiff. That's what it is. We're in thrall to radiation. I've got the patio door open and when his car pulls up in the road below I'm standing out in the sunshine on the balcony, with my pots of pansies clustered gaily around me. There's a mug of freshly brewed coffee in my hand and I must look, I think ruefully, a bit like the irritating woman in the brochure the agent gave me when I viewed the apartment. I wave, but only quickly, suddenly self-conscious: I might have given him the impression I'm looking out for his car, and I hate that idea.

We had just one conversation, Dorothy and I,

after we saw him at the museum the previous day. She said, 'That's *it*. I've remembered who he reminds me of.'

'Who?'

'That actor. The one in the film about two out-of-work actors. You *know*. What's his name? Not the tall one with the coat.'

This was an hour or so after. We'd been coming out of the lecture theatre. I processed her words and arrived at a conclusion. '*Withnail and I*,' I said, almost automatically. 'Richard E. Grant.'

'*That's* the one. But not him. The other actor. *Him*.' She'd turned to me then. 'Paul someone. You know. One of those brothers who are all actors. McGann. That's it! Don't you think?'

It didn't seem Dorothy's sort of film, somehow. But then I thought, Why assume that? Wasn't that judging a book by its cover?

'Who?' I said. 'D'you mean *Will* does?' And I was jolted to realize how wholeheartedly I'd been dreading her mentioning his name.

And I'd thought I'd got away with it.

'Of course I mean Will does,' she said sharply. 'Who else?'

I said I'd thought she'd meant the man who'd been giving the lecture. He'd been long-limbed, ponytailed, a bit of a catch. She said, come on, did I really? I said, 'Yes.' I was a bit terse and we didn't discuss it any more.

But he was back in the front of my mind now. After he'd called me, after I'd deconstructed my reasoning, after I'd properly persuaded myself that I was going to see him out of basically guilty/altruistic Mother bloody Teresa of Poona or wherever reasons, after I'd made so little progress with the report I was writing that I had to accept my mind was irretrievably elsewhere for the evening, after I'd dithered about ringing and cancelling the trip, after I'd showered, cleaned my teeth, taken a Sunday supplement to bed, after I'd slept a scant hour, after I'd spent another listening to the rain doing drumrolls against the window, I made a decision. I was lying to myself; I was pretending motivations that were not honest. And I was not going to run away from this feeling any more. The more I ran away, the harder it was to remove it to a quiet corner of my brain. If I could do that, so my reasoning went, it would be out of the way and wouldn't bother me so much. Avoidance is a great tactic for some things (wasps, shellfish allergies, John Patterson, fudge) but for others it intensifies the anguish (flying, escalators, fear of public speaking – my mother's habit of not making car journeys with right turns put many thousands of miles on her clock and meant it sometimes took her an hour to travel five).

And this was true of my feelings for Will Meadows. I'd done the right thing in agreeing to see him. If I couldn't avoid him for ever, and I couldn't, then I'd best face up to the non-avoidance bit now. If I had any hope of ridding myself of this crush, I had to face him.

And now he was outside my home and my heart was hammering at the sight of him and I wasn't so sure I had thought the right thoughts after all. I *should* avoid him. Avoid Him At All Costs. But here he was, and there was nothing else to do but go down and speak to him. Having gone back inside to dump my half-empty mug and pick up my bag, I stepped back onto the balcony to tell him to stay where he was because I'd be coming right down. But he'd obviously assumed that because he was in his car, shades off, eyes closed, face tilted towards the sun. His mouth was making small movements to lyrics I couldn't hear and his fingers were thrumming on his thighs. Dorothy had been right about Paul McGann. Sort of. But not exactly. Will looked mainly like himself. I went back inside, then out of the front door and locked it behind me. I went down on heavy legs. This was hopeless.

I'd forgotten my sunglasses, so I had to go back for them. I'd come down the stairs out of the building into the street and across the road. Will had opened his eyes, even though he couldn't have heard me, leaned forward to turn down the stereo, flipped his sunglasses back over his eyes, smiled broadly and patted the passenger seat. And I realized I had forgotten my sunglasses.

My unscheduled dash back upstairs meant that I was panting a little as I slid in beside him, and a little more frazzled than I'd planned.

Which made me feel more resolute. 'Look,' I

said, twisting in my seat and hitting my head on the sun visor, 'we have to deal with one thing before we go, okay?'

'Okay,' he said, grinning as he took off his sunglasses again. He had a smudge of stubble on his jaw. A plaster on his thumb. I wondered how he'd hurt it. He was wearing the red basketball boots again, laced half-way up and left untied. His jeans were blue-black and looked professionally distressed. He'd made a move as if to switch on the ignition, but now he didn't. The key fob swung idly beneath the wheel.

'The one thing,' I said, 'being that I don't think we've properly got things straight about what happened at your house.'

'Oh,' he said. 'Ri-ight. Did you not get my message?'

I nodded. 'I did get your message, but I just thought I ought to clarify things.'

'Right, Miss.'

'Will, please don't.'

'I'm sorry.' He stopped grinning and held up his hands. '*Really*. I'm sorry. Go on.'

Saints *alive*. I gobbled some more breath. 'Will, I just wanted you to know that I am so, so sorry about everything. Sorry that I've given you the impression that you and I were – well, that's probably the wrong way of putting it, isn't it? But you know what I mean. And I'm sorry.'

'I told you,' he said. 'I understand, Holly. It's history.' He grinned at me. '*Hist*-or-ee, okay?'

'No,' I said, 'you don't, Will. That's just it. I'm a great deal more upset about all this than you probably imagine. I love my fiancé dearly. I am dumbstruck about what we did. What *I* did. I still can't quite believe I—'

'Hang on,' he interrupted. 'It was *me* who kissed *you*.'

'Yes, but I kissed you back.'

'I know,' he said. 'I remember it well. But, Holly, these things *happen*.'

I shook my head. 'No, they don't, Will. Not to *me*.'

He didn't reply. Almost as if he knew he didn't need to. *Up to now*, I kept repeating in my head. Up to *now*.

Bull by horns, Holly. Go on. Just say it. 'Will, I'm not going to deny it. I do find you attractive. I find you very attractive, and now I've got to know you as well and what with everything that's happened to you, I—'

He groaned. 'Don't say it.'

'Say what?'

'That you were feeling sorry for me, Holly. Come on. Don't kick a guy when he's down.'

The dismay in his eyes was all too painfully evident, at odds with his jocular tone. But he was partially right. Not that it had anything to do with the kiss, but it was there, all the time, a dull pulse of compassion. Dorothy had been right about vulnerability. It elicited a universal feminine response. But that was not for his ears.

'Will, believe me, you don't know how much I wish it were that simple.'

'So it's not, then?'

'*No*. I mean, *okay*. I'm sure it played its part in the beginning. It must have, mustn't it? But now . . .' I stopped speaking while a teenager rattled past on a skateboard. I was becoming muddled as I strove to find words that wouldn't hurt his feelings. But this needed nipping in the bud, didn't it? 'Look,' I said at last. 'You're absolutely right, these things *do* happen. But it shouldn't have happened to me, Will, for whatever reason. And it certainly won't be happening again.'

If there was one time I really didn't want to feel like a teacher it was now. But that was just how I did feel. And just how I sounded. Like a dried-up, judgemental, authoritarian old bag. What was with the 'certainly'? Who was I convincing? But he didn't seem to notice. Just inclined his head in assent. 'I told you,' he said, 'it's done and forgotten. Yes, I got to hoping we might be . . . Well. Whatever. Turns out we weren't. I'll get over it, okay? Hey, I'm even pretty flattered.'

'Flattered?'

'That I have such a powerful effect on non-kissing women.'

'Will, please don't be flippant.'

'I wasn't. I *mean* it. I—'

'Then don't make light of it.'

'Hang *on*,' he said. 'I thought that was exactly what you *wanted* me to do.'

'I do. But you talk as if it meant nothing. It wasn't like that. It was complicated. It's very *upsetting*.'

'But I thought it did.'

'What?'

'Mean nothing.'

'Will, for *God*'s sake—'

'Okay, okay, okay. Look, I'm *sorry*. What else can I say to you? Conversation over, okay?'

'Okay.'

'Okay.'

Now he started the car and the engine growled awake, and it occurred to me that all I had to do was open the door and get out. That was all I needed to do for it to be truly done with. It was that easy. Yet I didn't. Instead I put my hand on his forearm, and said, 'So why did you call me, Will? If you already knew that? Why did you really come here today?'

He depressed the clutch, engaged the gear, checked the road for cars. 'To go take a look at this little movie,' he said. He adjusted the mirror and pulled out into the road. We were several yards down it when he added, 'See? For precisely the same reason you did.'

It's a funny old thing, feeling as if you've been kidnapped. But it was just a little like that, that short drive through the back-streets to the edit suite. Neither of us said anything, and it occurred to me as we pulled up outside that I could, perhaps should, have taken issue with his comment, but what was the point? It was out now, our mutual attraction. These things did happen. Men and women fancied each other.

We parked in silence. But it was a natural and undemanding silence. The sort of silence that occurs entirely unselfconsciously when two people are engrossed in the same train of thought.

'So,' Will said, as he killed the engine, 'here we are, then.' He seemed to have moved into a different gear now. There was so much unspoken stuff going on that I didn't feel able to formulate any credible response. I was here. He was right. I was here and didn't need to be. Part of me wanted to make a run for Grangetown, but the other part counselled a different route. He was hurting. Bereaved. A touch embarrassed, no doubt. I even smiled to myself as we got out of the car. And here I was feeling sorry for him again.

But our visit to the edit suite wasn't yet to be. Almost as soon as we entered the forbidding brick building it became clear there had been a problem. Will had gone off to speak to someone about it and returned to explain that a rush job, shoehorned into this morning, had developed a major problem and would now overrun.

'So we've an hour minimum to kill. Hour and a half, more realistically. What d'you want to do? You okay to wait?'

Oh, God. With *him*? What would we do? Should I invite him back to mine? Should I just have him drop me home? No, I couldn't do that. It would be terribly rude. What, then? I hadn't planned on this big chunk of time together.

'I don't know,' I said. 'Um . . .'

He smiled a fetching smile. 'It's a beautiful day,' he said. 'How about we go for a walk?'

Yes. That would be fine, I decided. I actually did feel easier around him now we'd been straight with each other. Huh. As if *he* hadn't been straight all along. It was *me* with all the hidden agendas on the go. Yes, I thought. I could kill an hour and a half by going for a walk with him. It wouldn't hurt, surely. It might even realign me in my correct position in his life. Perhaps persuade him to talk a little more about his. It hadn't escaped my notice how adept he was at talking about my life while deflecting all queries about his. I knew that because *I*'d always been so good at it. 'Yes,' I said. 'A walk would be good. We can talk.'

'About Harry?'

'If you like. Among other things. I was thinking more you.'

'Uh-oh,' he said. 'We're not back on the programme now, are we?'

'Programme?'

'You in official head-teacher mode.'

'*No*. Don't be stupid. Do I look like I am? But I know almost nothing about you.'

'But enough, it seems.'

'*Will!*'

He tutted, then smiled. 'Lighten up, will you?'

he said. 'I'm only winding you up. Tell you what. You ever been to Llangorse-on-Sea?'

That is probably what it is as much as anything, I decide. That, like Harry – *because* of Harry, even – I can't stop myself feeling a sense of responsibility for this man. It's taken me a while to get my thoughts round it, but I watch him now, walking so carefully back across the causeway from the little café where he's fetched tea for us, and I feel a powerful jolt somewhere deep inside me that this man's happiness matters to me. For no good reason whatsoever, but that makes little difference. It's as simple and as complex as that.

It took no more than fifteen minutes to drive the short distance to the headland, and he parked the car mere inches from what looks like the cliff edge. It's not. Walk around the front of the bonnet, as I've done now, and you can see the wide shelving below.

He approaches now with care, glancing up only sporadically from the cups. The steam is curling up from them only to be whisked away horizontally on the air. I am berating myself all of a sudden. I could just as easily have asked for a Pepsi. So much easier to deal with. But he's here now.

'We used to come here a lot,' he says, handing my tea to me, 'when Harry was little. Fly kites and stuff. Play footie on the beach.'

I take the polystyrene cup from him and nod. His hair's all snakes in the breeze. He's thoughtful now, sipping his tea, staring out over the sea. I wonder about the silver silver of scar tissue that runs in a curve over the back of his hand.

'Funny,' he says, 'isn't it? I can see him down there, you know.' He gestures towards the sand. 'Can picture him toddling across that patch of beach.' He mimes a rocky two-year-old walk. Then he stops. 'And I can remember, clear as if it happened yesterday almost, turning to his mum and wishing him just a little bit older. Not wishing his life away, exactly, but thinking ahead. Always thinking ahead. When he's a bit bigger, we'll do this. When he's a little older, we'll do that. And here he is, eleven, and I'm not sure quite where the years disappeared to.' He lifts his arm, sweeps it across the foreshore. 'He's not even here *now*, is he?'

We lapse into silence, fielding our own bitter-sweet memories.

'That's the real bitch,' he says, and I'm not sure if he's saying it to me or to himself. 'That he's had to grow up so bloody quickly. I catch his expression sometimes and it's almost as if there's this little old man looking at me. I wish I could get it back for him, you know? Just a little more time when things could be right, and normal, and carefree. Well, as carefree as they ever were. But it's too late now. I mention the kite, the beach, the park, and it's always, like, "*Da-ad*, do we *have* to?"'

'You don't have to try and get it back for him,' I say. 'It's gone now. It's not what he needs any more. He needs to go forward. Get out there and move on to the next bit.' I glance across but Will is lost to me again. I wonder who else he sees running carefree across the beach. 'You know, I go on, 'the bit where you're a sad old git who doesn't understand anything about anything.' Shades of Sasha and Tara. The bit Max lives in now. I find myself wondering where they are now. How Max is. But it's a surprisingly detached kind of wondering. Them there, me here. Two independent units.

Will is grimacing now. 'Don't be fooled by the wrinkles,' he says, though he has hardly any. 'I'm just *so* not ready for that bit. Funny, isn't it? I never really thought about having kids. Harry wasn't exactly planned. But I never saw him as an only child, either. Now I've got where I've got, I realize I haven't had enough of the first bit yet. I know it's selfish, but, well, you know, that's *it*, isn't it? I've squandered so much of his childhood and it's too late to do anything about it. I was rummaging in the roof of the garage the other day, and I found his half-finished go-kart.'

'So finish it, why don't you?'

'Oh, it's way too late now. He'd never get into it. I should have finished it for him at the time.'

'Your wife was ill.'

He nods. 'Yeah. That, and me never being there, of course.'

'So make him another.'

'He doesn't want another. He already told me. Not some manky one I made out of odd bits of wood. Says it all, really, doesn't it? I want to make up for what he's lost of his childhood. He wants a go-kart from Argos.'

Both of us laugh. But the breeze whips away the sound and now he's not laughing any more. As our eyes meet I can see his brain whirring, and I know he's remembered Emily and what will come next.

'Shit,' he says, '*Shit*. Oh, God, Holly. I'm such a bloody idiot. I just didn't think.'

'Oh, for goodness' sake,' I snap, because that tends to be the best way to do it. 'Don't go all maudlin on me now, *please*. Come on. Drink your tea and let's go for this walk.'

He keeps apologizing. Doesn't matter how much I try to point out that my circumstances don't have any bearing on his, that it's okay for him to say things like that and he shouldn't beat himself up for being a less than perfect father. He's good enough. That's all he needs to be. But he keeps banging on. And I wish I'd never encouraged him to talk in the first place because the more he opens up to me, the more surely I get sucked into his life. I want to comfort him, cuddle him, counsel him.

Take care of him. And however much I try to dampen the feeling deep in my stomach, it's telling me I want to do it in ways I'm fairly sure Mother Teresa never went in for. At least, not that made the press. I can feel a blush coursing up my neck to my face, but thankfully he doesn't notice. 'I just wasn't *there* for him enough,' he's saying. 'You know? It was only when Caitlin . . .' He pauses. Scans the skyline. 'Well, when she became ill, I guess, that it came home to me how much time I *hadn't* spent at home with my family.'

Caitlin. He's said her name to me. I mouth it to myself, try it for size. Then I shake my head. 'You couldn't help that.'

'Of course I could. I worked such ridiculous hours. Still do.'

'But that's your job,' I say, 'and it's his future.'

'But I could do other kinds of work. More regular hours. Poster stuff. Local. But I find the idea so hard.'

'Will, that's perfectly normal. You have a career that you love and are good at. You shouldn't torture yourself about it. It may not be ideal, but you're coping. And it's going to get easier, isn't it? As time goes on. And Harry's *so* proud of you. You should hear him. You've nothing to feel guilty about.'

He stops on the path and puts his hands on his hips. 'Wow,' he says. '*Wow-ee*. You've changed your tune.'

I stop on the path too, breathing heavily because we've been walking uphill at some speed. He's right, and I'm shocked, and I don't know what to say to him. But it seems I won't have to. Either side of the path wild flowers are growing in profusion, speckling the spring greens with dolly mixtures. He leans across, pulls a tendrilly stalk out at random, a guileless smile playing on his lips. 'You know what this is?' he asks me.

'Er, a flower?' I say. 'Botany's not my strong point.'

'It's common vetch,' he says.

'Is that right?'

'Yes, it is. Hey, try not to be too enthralled, will you?' He holds it out for me to take. 'Come on,' he says. 'I've just had an idea.'

'That sounds ominous.'

'No, really. Let me take you up to the point. Won't take much more than forty minutes there and back. It's a bit of a climb, but the view is something else. And you look fit enough.'

The something else, it turns out, involves a hike up the side of a near-vertical ravine and a wind-raked route march across an exposed headland, with nothing but meadow grass and early bees to keep us company. Almost everyone who isn't on holiday, I realize, will be holed up at work being useful, and this afternoon I'm just being. It's quite a nice feeling – or would be, if I weren't here with Will. His presence at my side is like permanent white noise.

Constant. Intrusive. It makes it difficult to concentrate. Plus his wife is here with us. I can feel it. Am I part of a catharsis this sunny afternoon? Should I be here at all?

When we get to the top I wonder at his telepathy skills because he grabs my hand and squeezes it as he leads me to see the promised view.

'I really *am* sorry,' he says. 'You know. Going on and on and on. I get rather self-absorbed sometimes. You just have to tell me to shut up, okay?'

I want to tell him I see that in his face, but I

don't. I wonder if he has anyone to talk to, with whom he's shared his loss, apart from Harry. I don't know, but something tells me he keeps his feelings hidden from the world. Which makes me feel even more acutely close to him. 'You've every right to be self-absorbed,' I reply, gently but firmly reclaiming my hand. 'You've been through a very difficult time.'

'But it's selfish,' he says, 'droning on at you, of all people. Doesn't matter which way I look at it, I can't imagine how I'd go on if I lost Harry.'

You, of all people. You, of *all* people. You, of all *people*. We've been here before. We're two of a kind, us. Both dog-tagged by our previous history. 'There you go again,' I say, rattled by his relentless pursuit of my sore bits. 'Don't you think that's precisely why you do? Haven't you already said as much to me, in fact? Anyway, it's not a question of imagining, Will. You just do. You just *did*. Not Harry, thank God. But come on. You did lose your *wife*.'

He shakes his head. 'It's not the same.'

I don't answer this, because I know that losing an aged parent is not the same as losing a partner and losing a partner is not the same as losing a child and also that I'd be talking to a wall. That he's seeing in me things that aren't there. That the boot has slipped to the other foot. That, curiously, he feels sorry for *me*. I stop walking. 'Will, can I tell you something?'

He turns. 'Shoot.'

I sit down on the grass. 'I'm not one of the Tolpuddle martyrs, you know.'

He sits down beside me. 'I never said you were.'

I hold up a hand. 'Which means I don't need anyone walking on eggshells around me and apologizing all the time. I don't want anyone to tell me I'm putting on a brave face. I'm just someone who had something bad happen to them. It doesn't confer on me any special qualities of goodness or wisdom or piety. It only informs what I feel and think in so far as it makes me sad occasionally to think of all the things I'd looked forward to doing with my daughter and which will not now be a part of my future. But that's not all I'm about, Will. It's a part of me, yes, but it's not *all* of me. Far from it. I don't wallow in it. And I wish you wouldn't either. I don't want to be defined like that.'

'Like what?'

'As this tragic person. This person who is *making the best of it.*'

He looks a little confused. As well he might. I'm getting ranty. I know it's because I feel vulnerable around him but I see him looking at me with the same compassion in his eyes that he probably sees in mine and I hate it. My life is just fine. I'm happy. And I don't like his laser-beam stare. 'But isn't that exactly what you *are* doing?' he asks.

My biceps are becoming fatigued from the strain of holding up my torso, so I uncurl myself and lie flat on the grass. All I can see now is sky. I tuck my hands behind my head. I think seriously about his question, which no one has ever asked me before. Were my mother still alive, she would ask it, worry away at it, not be satisfied till she knew it wasn't true any more. But she's not alive, so I don't come under that sort of scrutiny. That's it, I think. *That*'s how Will makes me feel. Scrutinized. Like he's not at all convinced by the finish. Like my dad used to be about 'modern ruddy houses'. 'Humph,' he'd say. 'It may look okay, but that timber's probably been out in the rain for six weeks.' I wonder what Will is trying to see in me. I wonder if it's the same thing I've seen in him, after all. 'Now and again,' I say. 'I'd be sub-human if I didn't. But that's all.'

He nods but doesn't answer, and neither of us speaks for a moment. There are mare's tails tracing wisps across the face of the sun, and I squint so I can make out the corona behind them.

Then he says, 'And how about your fiancé? Are you making the best of it with him?'

Even though I'm still looking upwards I can see well enough from the corner of my eye. He's looking at me. It's the first time my engagement has been mentioned and I find it uncomfortable to hear that word from him. And the implication. I open my mouth to be all indignant about it, then close it. The lady might find herself protesting too much. So when I open it again it's to say mildly, 'Of course not.'

He says, 'Uh-huh.'

I turn my head to face him now. 'Uh-huh?'

'You don't go there much, do you?'

'I didn't say that.'

'But you don't, even so.'

'How would you know?'

He's on his back and looking up into the sky now as well, a thick blade of grass clamped between his teeth. But now he turns his head too. I can see my sunglasses reflected in his, my eyebrows inched up in enquiry above them. I'm glad I can't see his eyes. He smiles, showing me his teeth.

'You don't cut yourself a lot of slack, do you?'

I find myself coming over all Anne Robinson at this. 'Slack? What are you talking about?'

Now he takes off his sunglasses, stares right past mine and into my eyes. And then, in one slow, deliberate movement, his arm spans the two feet or so of grass that separate us, he takes hold of the bridge of mine and pulls them off too.

'There,' he says, the grass moving in his mouth as he smiles. 'Now we're both naked.'

I force myself to keep looking at him. 'You didn't answer my question.'

'I know,' he says. Then he takes the stem from between his lips and tucks his palm under his cheek. Then he picks another. 'How did your daughter die?'

The sun feels white hot on my face. 'Of meningitis,' I tell him. 'She was five years and three months old. One minute she was under the weather, a bit drowsy, a bit flu-ey. And the next she was dead. Well, not quite the next minute. It took five hours. That's all.'

I stop speaking, not because I'm finding it difficult, but because other people quite often start drawing their brows together about now. I hate that. I watch his face.

'Life's a bitch,' he says quietly.

'Yes.'

'And then?'

'And then what?'

'And then what happened?'

'You mean you want a précis of the whole last eight years?'

'And then what happened with *you*? How d'you get from there to here? What happened with your marriage?'

'Ah. *That*. We-ell, let me see. It was okay at first. We managed to inhabit our mutual hell quite companionably for a time. After a year or so we even decided to try for another baby. We'd lost one when Em was three. So we did, and I got pregnant, and then I had a miscarriage, and then I fell to pieces all over again, and then I got scared, and then, let me see . . . I decided I didn't want to put myself through it again, which, looking back, was pretty pathetic of me. But there you go. You never know what you're made of till you're tested, do you? So I fudged. I made excuses. I kept saying "soon". But I knew I didn't mean it. And I threw myself into my work big-time. And bit by bit we got to this stage

– without me noticing, looking back – where I was working pretty much every hour I had, and Colin was working pretty hard as well. Except his motivation was different. There wasn't a great deal to come home for. And then the inevitable happened. He met someone.'

I pause again, but for different reasons this time: in all the years I've spent analysing the aftermath of our tragedy, it's only now that I have described the depressing arc of my own culpability without embellishing it with justifications and excuses for myself. It just was. It went wrong. We didn't love each other enough to see it through and move on. 'He's remarried now. She's called Dawn, which feels just right, you know? They have a boy. He'll be three now.' I pluck a clover flower. 'I hold nothing against Colin,' I add, almost defensively. 'Nothing at all.'

'That's good.'

'It is. But I didn't plan it that way.'

'Even so. Now I guess it's just yourself you have to deal with.'

'I beg your pardon?'

'Like I said, cut yourself a bit of slack.'

'I don't know what you mean.'

'Yeah, you do.' His expression softens. The challenging edge leaves his voice. 'I might be wrong, but I get the impression that you don't allow yourself any. That you put an awful lot of energy into scrunching that part of your life into a ball and burying it in a hole in your head.'

'And that's wrong? You really think it would be *helpful* to wallow in it?'

'No. But you seem to have this whole wall round yourself. How can you be happy if you're not prepared to let anyone get close to you?'

'Er, excuse *me*. Who said I wasn't happy?'

'Well, are you?'

'Yes.' I add a 'very' as well, but too late. Like a belated dollop of mortar in some pretty dodgy brickwork.

'Okay,' he says. 'Fine. If you say so.'

'And what would you know about my personal relationships anyway?'

'What you've told me.'

'Which is?'

'Never mind. Chin up. Move on. Stuff like that.'

I lie and take this trio of soundbites on board, rolling the stem of the clover between my thumb and index finger. He watches me do it. He's waiting for me to speak. But he's right. I *am* naked. And I don't want to answer his question. I'm not even sure what he's trying to say. And then I think I am. And it makes me feel anxious.

'Since when did you become Claire Rayner?' I say instead.

'I didn't. I'm Will Meadows. And I'm right.'

'Okay. If you say so,' I parrot at him, like a petulant child.

'And that's all you've got to say?' he says.

'Yes, it is.'

'See?'

'See what?'

'I have your number, Mrs C.'

He picked me a bunch of different flowers. Cranesbill and willowherb and bird's foot trefoil and pea orchids, the whole local flora pretty much accounted for. He'd leaped up when he'd spoken those words to me, and I was overwhelmingly glad of it. I had thought he might cover the distance between us and put his arms round me. Kiss me, ravish me. Take me. And part of me had been wanting him, waiting for him to do it.

I got up too, then, diamonds dancing before my eyes. I scrambled to my feet, brushed the stray straws and burrs from my jeans and followed him across the headland, having to walk faster than I wanted to keep up.

We talked flowers. He named them as he picked them. And I was shocked: 'How do you know all this stuff?'

'Because I'm such a funky, post-modern, altogether well-rounded kind of guy.'

'No, *how*?'

'Because my mum used to run a nursery. And in the summer she would be working pretty much flat out all day, and I'd have to go and hang out there with her after school. They had these big plant books in the back room. *Common Weeds and Their Habitats, The Wild Flowers of Great Britain.* I'd spend hour upon hour drawing them. No telly to watch, you see. I even made a book, which won a competition. Here. Another commoner. That's comfrey. Won a ten-shilling postal order. Which I believe I spent mostly on sweets.'

I took the stem he handed me and added it to the bunch in my hand. 'I didn't imagine you like that.'

'Like what?'

'You know, your childhood. The nursery and everything. Your parents. I suppose I saw them as altogether more Bohemian. Your mum as an opera singer, maybe, or a sculptor.'

He laughed so loudly at this that a red setter that had been bounding along in the distance stopped dead in its tracks and wheeled round. Then he said, 'I'm sorry, but I'm going to have to disappoint you. She's really very ordinary and suburban. Makes flapjacks.' And then he said, 'Go on. What about my dad? What did you have him down as?'

'I guess something similar. A chess-player, maybe. Something erudite in publishing. Or a pianist.'

He shook his head. 'You know what's just struck me?' he said. 'That's one hell of a lot of imagining you've been doing about me.'

Oh, God. Did I fall into that one! As I would. Idle speculation is best left unarticulated, as I know only too well. I think about what he's told me on the drive back to the edit suite. Funny the way you can identify a category of person and then decide it's the one they fit into. We don't talk much in the car – trying to second-guess the script of the next bit in our heads? I know I am, and

328

I wonder if that's the fundamental difference between us. That he is what he is what he is. That what he does is so inextricably linked with who he is that he spends not a moment wondering about the relationship between those two things. Didn't I used to be like that? But now it feels like an alien state. I seem to exist in a constant state of checks and balances. Might I have done this? Might I have become that? Toni's words return to my mind. What I do is a job, not a lifestyle statement. Part of me but not all of me. Yet I seem to have become one of those people who finds themselves chronically anxious that people don't see beyond it to all the other aspects of me hidden underneath. As if the me I present to the world is the only safe option. As if another me, given half a chance and the courage, might one day wriggle her way out and demand to know what the hell I think I'm playing at. And then the whole house of cards might come crashing down.

I think of Max who, like Will, is what he is. If Max suffers existential *angst* then I'm a teabag. I doubt he'd even know what it is. Which makes him the opposite of Will, but also very like him. He isn't confused. He knows who he is. It's me who's got myself into a muddle. I straighten my legs in the footwell and stretch.

'Good nap?' asks Will. It's the first thing he's said since the motorway.

'I wasn't asleep.'

'Oh. I thought you were.'

329

'Just had my eyes shut.'

'So *you* say.'

'I *did.*'

But now they're open. And I'm wide awake.

This is how it happens. This is how you cause the fabric of your life to unravel before your eyes. You make a rogue decision and, as a consequence, you set a dangerous process in motion. All you have to do then is ensure that every decision you make subsequently is a rogue one. From when did I do that? From the Palm Pilot. Everything before that was happenstance and fate. After that it was all down to me. Well done, Holly. You have become the orchestrator of your own sorry destiny. But you're a poor deity. You're heading for an F grade.

'Go on,' I find myself saying, as we sit in the car. Saying it even as I'm assimilating the awesome dimensions of my stupidity in doing so.

The engine is still running and we're parked outside my place. We've been to the edit suite, seen all the different bits of footage condensed, connected and made into something so perceptive and inspiring that I remember why I do what I do. I'm fulsome in my praise. So much so that he gets shirty. 'Ease up a bit, can't you?' he says, as we watch. 'It's kind of what I do. It's *supposed* to be good.'

And a mate of his is there, and says, 'Yey! Golden Lion!' and Will turns round and laughs an easy, blokey laugh, then tells his friend to go f**k himself, remembers I'm with him and is mortified. And I laugh and tell him I'm going to give him a detention. To which his friend says, 'Result!' which makes me blush and go quiet, because it's plain that his friend thinks there's something between us, and Will's rueful glance at me makes my stomach turn over. And now we're here and the day's over and the sunlight is fading, and I wonder what he's planned to do till Harry gets home.

'Go on,' I'm saying. I'm saying it in response to what he has just said to me. And what he's just said – 'I don't think so' – is by way of a response too. To what I asked him before that, which comprised nine little words. 'Why don't you come in for half an hour?' I think I might have added 'for a cup of tea'. Alluded to biscuits, even. God knows. It's all gone. All I know is that my saying so was also a response of a kind. To that tricksy little circumstance/geography equation that Dorothy outlined so succinctly before. I don't want the day to end yet.

But he's standing his ground. Now who's changed their tune, eh? 'Come on,' I coax. 'Or do you have something to rush back for?'

He tells me that Harry's being dropped home at about ten. It's now ten to seven, I point out. He gives in. But he doesn't want a cup of tea. A glass of water will be fine.

Because it's still so warm my flowers are drooping. After I've given Will his glass of water, I go back into the kitchen to find a vase. I have one in a cupboard that will be perfect. A cut-glass bud vase I inherited from my mum. An anniversary present, though I can't recall which. If she and Dad were still alive, I find myself calculating while I rummage, they would have been married for forty-seven years. I managed seven with Colin. How long was it for Will? I climb up and get the vase down. Run the cold tap.

When I return to the living room he's standing, looking out at the dusk that's beginning to daub its fuzzy blush round the bay, clutching the glass of water close against his chest, like a shield. He turns, frowning when he sees my reflection in the glass.

'Holly, I was twenty-two when I met my wife,' he says, without any prompting from me. 'Twenty-two. That's all. Which puts me eighteen years out of the loop, give or take. And hopelessly rusty. This is a whole different country.' He gestures towards me with the glass, then puts it down on the coffee-table and walks round it. 'A whole different landscape,' he adds, as we meet at the edge of the rug. 'And I don't have a map, I'm afraid.'

Geography again. And I'm a whole different country. If I had any sense I'd *be* in one too. He takes the vase from me, complete with its little posy. 'They'll perk up,' he says, 'in a little while.'

'I made sure the water was really cold,' I tell him. 'And I don't know what you're getting at, Will.'

I'm sure I do, but he's only inches from me now

and my brain cells are all in a tizz. He starts to lift his other hand, then lowers it again. I can feel the tips of my fingers tingling. Getting the vase down from the top shelf in the kitchen, most probably. All the blood rushing back.

'That's because I didn't put it very well,' he says. Then he frowns again. 'Because I don't know how to.'

'Put what very well, Will?' I hear myself say. The tingling's easing now. I ball my hands. There's a perceptible hum coming from outside. An engine. The bay boat, disgorging its last passengers of the day.

'What I want to say to you.'

'Just say it.' The words come out almost without my knowing it.

'That's the problem, I guess. I don't even know if I *should* say it. I didn't even think I *would*. But since this afternoon . . .' He looks fraught. Little-boy-lost fraught. 'Look, *you* know how *I* feel, but what about *you*? Christ, Holly, I am *so* confused. Look, I know actions are supposed to speak louder than words, but should I be convinced by what's been happening here? Am I really *reading* you right?' He lifts an arm again. Points to the door. 'Or do I go?'

The blush beyond him is turning to violet, then plum. The strings of fairy-lights are coming on outside even as I watch. His other hand is still clasped round the neck of my bud vase. He is looking pensive. Beautiful too.

333

'Those would look nice on the mantelpiece,' I say. He blinks at me, then turns, takes three strides, puts the flowers where I've told him. I follow his every movement with a kind of appalled fascination, aware, even as I watch, of the grave implications of what I'm about to say. But it doesn't seem to touch me, even so.

Then we're back, face to face, as the indigo presses in. My head is full of Max now. A hot, spitting cauldron, a violent swirl of regrets. But I've never felt so sure about anything as the feeling that's rising up inside me now.

'So?' he says.

'*No*,' I whisper. '*No*. You don't go.'

CHAPTER 19

When I wake the next morning there's a seagull on my windowsill. Enormous webbed feet, splayed to give him purchase on the narrow ledge. They're such big birds, seagulls, so loud and cocksure and arrogant. If they could speak they would all sound like sailors. All *avast!* and *ahoy there!* and *shiver me timbers!* and they'd smoke reedy pipes and down flagons of foamy ale. It's a funny thing, anthropomorphism. All seagulls are Jolly Jack Tar types, male, like moles and rhinos, motorways and mountains. Whereas the wildflowers Will gave me – now sitting on my dresser – are all, indisputably, girls. Yes, even the thistle is female. I turn over, sniff the scent of him on my pillow, feel something catch in my throat.

I haven't been anywhere like this in my life. I have been to so many uncomfortable and painful places. But not here. Wherever it is, it is not a nice place, made nastier still by the fact that there's no one to blame for my being here. That I put myself here. I wasn't seduced. I wasn't drunk. I certainly wasn't coerced. I knew what I was doing and still put myself here. I clutch at the duvet and decide to give myself another hour before I get up and look myself in the eye. I'll wake up again, soon, and I won't have gone away, but I'm not ready to face me yet. I breathe deeply. Sniff again, as the seagull wheels away. He doesn't much care for me either.

'I've got to go to London first thing,' he had told me, before he left. 'For a meeting about a campaign I've tendered for.' He was taking Harry with him, he said, and then they were going to drive up to his parents for a few days. He was holding both my hands in his as he spoke. It was nine thirty, time he was off. He was frowning again. Saying how he wished he didn't have to go. How happy he was. How wonderful it had been. How alive I'd made him feel. Stuff like that. Twisting-the-knife stuff. Asking when it would be okay to call me. *If* it would be okay to call me. What was going to happen? What did I want to do? Kissing my lips, my cheeks, my closed eyelids, my fingertips. I didn't take it all in. I said I didn't know, I didn't know, I didn't *know*. I was in no fit state to think.

I had been in no fit state from the moment I asked him to come up to my flat. No, no. Before that. From the moment he called me. No, no. It was earlier. From the moment I'd seen him at the museum. That was it. That was when I conceded. Tried it out for size and found it fitted so well. But certainly when we got back to my flat. Physically, achingly, unstoppably so. The term 'weak at the knees' is not a cliché for nothing. Though they didn't buckle right off and send me reeling, even then.

There was a period of ten, fifteen seconds, perhaps, when a different, dispassionate, rational, engaged-to-be-married me resurfaced. It said, 'Christ, Holly, what have you just *said* to this man?' A period where I stood and watched my words sinking in. A period where his expression moved through almost every shade and nuance imaginable: disbelief, then belief, then uncertainty, then joy, then the unmistakable contours of tenderness, desire.

At which point I said it again. Because I passionately didn't want him to go. 'No,' I said. 'No, Will. You don't leave, okay?' So he didn't leave. He gathered me into his arms and held me instead. For five minutes. Ten minutes? No. Longer. Much longer. We just stood there holding each other for so long. As if that was all he needed. Just to hold. To be held.

'You smell of Harry,' I'd said to him. 'You smell of his school sweatshirt.'

'No,' he said. 'Wrong. He smells of *me*.'

'We're not supposed to touch the children,' I said, my cheek against his T-shirt. 'Did you know that? You have to be checking yourself all the time. It's okay with the little ones – if a child is crying you give them a cuddle, of course you do. It's automatic. But not the older ones. With them it's hands off. Always. Proceed at your peril. And it's a terrible thing because it's in the older ones that you usually see it.'

'See what?'

'When they need a cuddle.'

'It feels so good to be holding you,' he said, into my hair. 'It feels so long since I've held a woman in my arms. Thank you,' he said. 'Thank you, thank you, thank you.'

How had we got from that place to this one? How had it happened? I just have this whole fuzz of unconnected pictures. A storyboard with some of the frames gone astray.

The next time I wake up is even more horrible. I used to have this dream all the time, and in it I lost Emily. A universal dream, I'm sure. I'd be transferring my shopping from trolley to car boot, thinking I'd strapped her into her seat, but then I'd realize she'd gone. The details varied but the dream never did. I'd run round and round and round, but I wouldn't find her. I'd call for help, I'd get it, but still I wouldn't find her. And then I'd wake up, sweating, terrified, sobbing, and the feeling of relief was so intense it made me weak.

I kept having it even after Emily died. When the business of waking, especially in the first few weeks after her death, was already the most exquisite form of torture. I'd clamber slowly up to consciousness. And I'd have *forgotten*. And then I'd wake properly and the hollow dread that I still had to go on would close in. And on nights when I had my getting-lost dream as well, I'd have a whole other layer of hell to negotiate. I'd wake, bathed in horror, then come to from the dream. I'd feel the relief, then come to again.

It stopped a year or so later. I guess because I could no longer lose her.

I haven't dreamed my losing-Emily dream in years. Perhaps it's my punishment. Perhaps there'll be more. I fling off the duvet angrily and get out of bed. I realize the reason I've woken with a dream on the go is because I've *been* woken. It's the phone. I know it's not Will because he only has the number of my mobile. It might be Max. My mind bunny-hops through a string of time and date hoops. They're due home tomorrow. Not today.

But it's not Max, and my heart slinks grate-fully back into its hidey-hole. It's Naomi: she needs to be able to get into school because she wants to put up the background for her summer-term display. It's Vikings. I remember doing Vikings. The *Daily Norseman*, our very own in-class Viking tabloid, full of tales of pillage (though not rape – they were eight), the construction of longboats, the *Ride of the Valkyries* – Wagner blasting out so loud one afternoon that my then head, a miserable, close-to-retirement old curmudgeon, came stomping down the corridor, saying, '*Please*, Mrs Connors, could you try to keep it down? There are teachers in this school who are trying to do some *work*.' I never did have it out with him, and now I wish I had. Na-na-nee-na-na. Ignorant old fart. I hope he knows I got my headship a lot younger than he did. And then I feel sad that I did. Because now there are way too few eight-year-olds and Vikings in my life.

I tell Naomi I'm going to be there all day Friday, if she can hang on till then. I tell her I might even have time to give her a hand. She says, 'Really? I'd enjoy that,' and seems to mean it. Which cheers me up a bit.

I shower then. Dress. Try to get some semblance of the day under way. But it's as if my brain is on autocue replay. Sitting on the end of my bed and tying my trainers, I can see my way back into last night through the mirror. See Will sitting right here where I am now, pulling on the red basketball boots, tugging at the laces, bending down to tuck in the trailing ends.

'Why don't you do them up all the way to the top?' I'd asked him. 'Does it make them too tight?'

He'd laughed and stood up, crossed the room and drawn me against him. Back in his T-shirt he smelt like Will again. Like Harry. No, like *Will*. Every fibre in me now said I shouldn't let him hold me any more, but I breathed deep, even so, because I knew I'd have to make it last.

'No, dozy,' he said. 'Because I'd look like a dork.'

'Er, *how* old are you?'

'It's not a question of age. It's a question of cool. Which, as everyone cool knows, is not age-dependent.'

'But doesn't Harry mind?'

'Doesn't Harry mind what? Me being cool?'

'No. You wearing the same footwear as him.'

He looked shocked. 'Should he?'

'Isn't that usually how it goes?'

He shook his head. 'Not in our house. Anyway, aren't I supposed to be his hero?'

'Oh, you are.'

'Quite right too.'

'I think it's beautiful,' I said.

'Beautiful?'

'You and him. The way it works. The way you are together.' Stupid, but another thing to make me want to cry. He couldn't see that because my head was hard up against his chest. But I knew he could tell. I just *knew*.

He squeezed me closer. 'You're lovely. You know that?'

I am not. I am so completely not that any more. I have done something so morally reprehensible I cannot consider myself with anything but disgust. I sit up straight and consider my surroundings. My feet in my not particularly cool trainers. My smart yet unremarkable mauve and grey bedroom. The two hand-blown glass vases on the windowsill with their bedrock of silver sand and their topsoil of lavender beads. The candle garden Will found so hilarious a concept ('It's a *what*?' 'It's like, well, a *garden*. Of *candles* . . .'), the shimmery voile at the window, the family photos on the wall. The wardrobe full of power suits and sensibly heeled footwear, the upper-echelon perfumes, the tightly woven two-colour geometric rug. I imagine my teenaged daughter sitting in here with me now and messing it all up. With neon tights, piercings, mad jewellery, scowls. Borrowing my hairbrush. Trying on my lipstick. I don't mean to, but I let myself anyway.

For a brief time, we were a Laura Ashley pair. Almost any print they made into both a size twelve and a twelve months, because I knew the time would come all too soon when she wouldn't be seen dead in anything I liked. As I was with my mum. As girls so often are.

I spend five minutes crying noisily for Emily, which shocks me. Then a whole half-hour curled on the bed, crying for myself.

Then I head off upstairs to find Dorothy.

CHAPTER 20

We'd made a plan, Dorothy and I, that on the Wednesday – can it really be Wednesday already? – we'd mosey into town and look at stuff. Wedding stuff mainly: sugared almonds, disposable cameras, rose petals, cake boxes. Then we'd meet up with Toni outside her office, and go for lunch somewhere nice. I hadn't seen Dorothy since the previous week because she'd gone to spend Easter with her family in France.

So concerned about the fragility of my composure was I that I rehearsed my opening line under my breath all the way up the stairs. But I shouldn't have bothered. She opened the door, took one look at my face, then said, 'Gracious me, sweetheart, what's happened to *you*?', then 'Oh, no. Don't tell me. Come on. Come in.'

At which point proper time started up for me again. Proper time, proper life, proper planet.

Because the rain – that I'd missed altogether – had stopped, we decided we wouldn't sit on the hunt this morning. Instead, Dorothy made coffee while I went outside and wiped down the two chairs and table, and we gathered up cups and

343

saucers and a plate of chocolate digestives and went and sat on her balcony. It's higher than mine and two along laterally so it has a markedly different view. From Dorothy's balcony you can see the local primary-school playground. It's note-worthy, I recalled reading somewhere, because the staff speak something like ten languages between them. I sat clasping my coffee, licking the choco-late off a biscuit, and wondered if any of them spoke a language I understood. Like Hell and Damnation. Or Lost Soul.

You can only see the place where Will's car was parked yesterday if you stand at the edge and look down. It was not from here that Dorothy had spotted him in any case. She had seen his cark parked there when she got back from the airport. 'The taxi driver even remarked on it,' she said. 'It's very distinctive, isn't it? I must admit, I wondered.' Wondered what? I wondered. 'And I thought about calling.'

'But you didn't.'

'No. I decided not to. Should I have, perhaps?'

I put my cup down on the little table and my head into my hands. I was too cried out for crying, but my throat was on fire and my temples were throbbing. The sun was too harsh.

'It wouldn't have made any difference,' I said dully. 'Nothing would have. Nothing.'

She inclined her head. 'So come on,' she said gently. 'What happened?'

I told her. Detail by agonizing detail. That we'd

talked, that he'd held me, that we'd talked a bit more. That we'd watched all the stars come out, standing on the balcony. That we'd talked about Emily. My mother. Him and Harry. How he'd cut his thumb clearing his washing-machine filter. 'And then I slept with him.'

'Okay,' she said, nodding. 'Uh-huh.'

The pictures were all lined up in my head. But still the gaps. How *had* it happened? Here the two people, standing. Silent. Arm in arm. Here his hand at her temple. Her head leaning in to his touch. Her face lifting to greet a kiss. Even then, even *then*, it had felt right still. Okay. And then something had happened. Some subtle shift of feeling. And here a new picture, shot in closeup, well lit. The frenzied movements, the quickened breathing, the unseemly ripping off of clothing. The clamouring of desire, like the thud-thud-thud-thud of an approaching helicopter.

'I *slept* with him, Dorothy. I still can't believe it. I just couldn't seem to stop myself.'

That too. The conviction I'd felt that here and now I would and I should, *would*, make love to this man. That making love to him was the only right thing to do.

'I think I lost my head,' I continued. 'God knows why. God knows how. It was just this thing that's been going on between us. Been building and building and building. And I thought it was, I don't know, safe. Just, you know, to hug each other. Just that. Just connecting. You know?'

Dorothy's mouth was shut at this point, but her expression said a great big fat no. Because how *could* she know? I was talking in five shades of garbage. 'But it wasn't safe, was it?' Her expression sat and waited. 'Because then the next minute suddenly it *was* about that. About *sex*. I mean, how stupid can a person be? I mean, he's a man and I'm a woman, and I – *we* . . . God, Dorothy. I've never done anything so bad in my life.'

She opened her mouth. Shook her head. 'Bad is hardly the right word. These things are never that simple.'

'Oh, but they are. I could have done the right thing and not slept with him. I can't pretend I'm not attracted to him, because I *am*, but I still could have done the right thing. Which makes me bad, however much I try to persuade myself I'm not. Let me see, I've tried out wicked, evil, dastardly, unforgivable, calculating, sordid, low-life, unforgivable . . . Oh, I said that already, didn't I? No matter. They'd all do, wouldn't they? But bad feels best on my tongue. *Bad*. I mean people don't just fall into sleeping with people by accident, do they? Not in real life. I keep telling myself I was overcome by some terrible, unstoppable mania, but if I believe that then I must also believe I've lost all control of myself. And I haven't. I didn't. I just decided I was going to do it and I did. *Me!* You know something, Dorothy? As of yesterday morning, I had slept with four men in my entire life. Four. I have never had a one-night stand. I have never even come close to having a one-night stand.'

'Was that what it was, then?'

'*Yes*. No! Oh, God. I don't *know*! It didn't feel like that at the time, but in the cold light of day . . . I mean, what must I have been thinking? I love *Max*. Why have I done this?' I picked up a second biscuit. I loved Max, but still I was like a bitch on bloody heat. But I didn't say that to Dorothy, even though she wouldn't have blinked. I didn't say it because, although it was undeniably true, it vexed me even more, because I knew that I *hadn't* been kidding myself. I hadn't started out with making love to Will in mind. Not at any point. Yes, we had kissed. Yes, he had moved me, but the idea of having sex with him had registered as being no more actionable a notion than owning a Rolls-Royce, or buying an island off Fiji. Not as something that might actually *happen*.

'God! Listen to me!' I said, leaping up and almost choking on my mouthful of biscuit.

'You didn't say anything, dear.'

'Because it doesn't even bear articulating, Dorothy. God, I'm so *stupid*! You know what I'm doing? I'm sitting here trying to persuade myself that I had no idea it was going to happen! Like "Good grief! What a shock! I'm having sex with this man! Who on earth would have seen *that* coming?"'

Mrs Harrington, who lives on the ground floor and keeps a gecko, was walking along the road down below. I could see the bobbing of her little

347

raspberry pink angora hat, and the sudden snapping up of her head underneath it. She looked appalled. I ducked backwards. Dorothy suppressed a smile. I lifted two fingers upwards and grinned wanly at her.

'Twice,' I mouthed mournfully. 'It was twice.'

Dorothy drained her coffee cup – she's one of those amazing women who can drink scalding fluids in seconds flat. 'I think you're being a little hard on yourself, dear. I'm sure you *didn't* see it coming. Well, not until, ahem, biology kicked in.'

'I wish biology had kicked *me*. Oh, Dorothy, what am I going to *do*?'

'Well, that depends on how you feel about him, doesn't it? In relation to how you feel about Max.'

Which is precisely why I am so grateful to have Dorothy in my life. She is ever calm. She understands me. She does not make assumptions.

'Ah,' I said, dimly aware that tears were falling from my eyes again quite without direction from me. I sniffed. '*That*.' Because it was this that had kept me awake for almost all of the night, and too terrified to answer the phone. I toyed with the idea of a third biscuit, but didn't take one.

'How I feel about Will,' I said, sniffing again and rubbing my face with my sleeve, 'is terrible. *Terrible*. Guilty and terrible and sad.' Sad because it wasn't only Will. It was everything around him too. Harry. His wife's death. My pathetic need to be of use to them. To help them. The way that everything to do with him, despite my reluctance to accept it,

348

seemed to connect me to bits of me I didn't want to revisit any more. Guilty because I didn't think I'd ever known sex as astoundingly passionate and *right* and take-your-breath-away *wow*. It was all too scary and visceral and so not where I wanted to be. It was losing my head in the most frightening way imaginable. Like taking psychedelic drugs.

'So that's it, then, between you.'

I stared at her, stupefied. 'Of *course* that's it! How could you think otherwise? I'm engaged to *Max*, Dorothy. I love him. I *told* you. Oh, God. I feel awful.'

'Sweetheart, I know you love him. But are you still *in* love with him?'

I didn't even need to think. My response was automatic. Max was everything good that had happened in my life. It was finding Max that had driven all the bad things away. Whereas finding Will had only served to bring them all back again. '*Yes*,' I said. 'God, yes. Of course I'm still in love with him. Wouldn't this all be so much less of a mess if I wasn't able to say that? Wouldn't it?'

'Yet still this has happened.'

Yet still it had. I nodded morosely. 'But it's not about Max. It was never about Max. It's just un-finished business. That's it. Unfinished business. I think I just got caught up with the emotion of it all. The whole— Oh, I don't know. But you were right, you know. It's the empathy thing. Having something in common. Me indulging myself maybe. It's been so long since I've been able to talk about

Emily . . . No, no. It's not even about Emily. But it's not about Max. Oh, God. What do I do, Dorothy? I can't *tell* him.'

'I'm inclined to agree with you there. I can't envisage a circumstance where you'd help anything by confessing. Your conscience, maybe. But your conscience will have to cope.' She watched Mrs Harrington turn the corner. 'And how about Will? What does Will have to say?'

Will. Oh, God. Will. 'I haven't spoken to him yet. I can't bear to face him. He'll think . . .' Oh, God, what must he be thinking?

'But you must. And you must tell him what you've told me,' she said. 'Put him straight. And tell Max nothing about it.'

'Just carry on as if nothing had happened? How can I do that with my head in this mess?' I put it into my hands again to protect it from the sunshine. And the thought of the wedding. Catherine. The girls. Panic engulfed me. 'God, Dorothy. We're supposed to be getting married in four months!'

Dorothy sat and considered me. 'Perhaps you shouldn't.' She lifted her hands to forestall my next panic. 'Perhaps you should slow things down a bit. I know it's none of my business, Holly, but given everything that's been happening – and I'm not just talking about you here – would it be better to wait a little while?'

'Postpone the wedding? I can't do that! He'll know something's wrong!'

'Holly, something *is* wrong. What's happened with Will is a symptom – don't you see that? – something you need to get out of your system. It seems to me there are several things that you would do well to get sorted beforehand. Would a few months make so much difference? You've told me more than once how distressed Max is about his and your relationship with the girls. Quite possibly it *would* be best to go ahead and hope that they'll come around afterwards, but on the other hand, what if they don't? How is Max going to feel then? How are *you* going to feel?'

'But Max will be devastated!'

'If Max loves you, he'll see the sense in waiting. I'm sure he'd rather that than have everyone unhappy.'

'But all the work. The preparations. The plans. The *dress*.'

'I really think you're old enough to appreciate the fact that fear of changing arrangements and inconveniencing people is not a good reason to gallop down an aisle.'

CHAPTER 21

On the next day, Thursday, I'm making sense. I've been seduced by a surfeit of misplaced emotion. Been carried away on a current of self-indulgent feelings that I'd no business swimming around in in the first place. Mistaken. Misguided. A classic case of displacement. A metaphor, clearly, for the whole muddle of insecurities I have about making such a big change in my life. And now I see that for what it is I feel better. Enough to realize that addressing it is the first step in dealing with it. Enough to begin to take control.

I have a text message from Will on my mobile, which I delete. It says, 'Can I call U? If so, WHEN? X x x.' I have an answerphone message from Max, 'Hi, sweets, I'll try your mobile.' Which he's already done. So I delete that as well. I have a sudden thought and, with a silent yelp of panic, I remove the vase of wilting wildflowers from the dresser in my bedroom, wash the vase, put it back in the top cupboard, deep-breathe to try to slow my heart rate. Like a yogi.

Who, everyone knows, is smarter than the

average bear. And good at all things wily. Good at raiding the hampers of unsuspecting picnickers. Food. I have to think about food. I've asked Max to come here straight after work. I know he's gone to work because he told me so this morning. He was dropping the girls off at their mother's, going home, getting changed, then going to work. I asked him if the trip went okay. He said it did. I asked him how his mum was. He said she was so-so. But we couldn't really talk because he was driving when we spoke and he didn't want to be arrested. I have a wild moment wondering how *I* could be arrested. Just to take me away. Save me running. Dinner. Dinner? I decide there's no point.

I get another text message from Will at five thirty. Just '???'. Why no longer the calls or the voice-mail? And then I understand, with a grim shudder of recognition, that he's simply, and sensibly, observing what he deduces to be a new set of rules. He's now become someone whom I might find it uncomfortable – hazardous, even – to be taking a call from in company. Even though not a word has passed between us since he left here, we are nevertheless complicit deceivers. Though he has no one to deceive, of course. He's the one without guilt. He has done nothing wrong. And if he has, it's only the perfectly reasonable response of a man in possession of all the usual male urges. A man, moreover, to whom this woman has given every intimation that she is interested in seeing some more of. Why shouldn't he believe my engagement is a sham? Why shouldn't he hope that's the case? But it's not. What got me to where I am with Will is altogether too fraught and too complicated and too unreliable a cocktail of emotions. Just as I'm quite sure is the case with him too. I know I will have to make contact and tell him. Make him see it for what it is. I love *Max*. I care for *him*. And I don't want to lose him. I didn't mean for this sexual frenzy to happen to me. I want my life back exactly as it was, please, God. The thought of what I've done fills me with fresh waves of self-loathing. I've never cheated on anyone. Two timed *any*one. *Ever*. And now it's special-offer day. Two for one. Toot-toot.

When you know someone well, it doesn't take much to grasp when they're about to impart something serious. The first thing Max says to me is, 'Sweets, you look dreadful. What's up?'

Yet the curious thing is that I don't even know that myself. Not yet. I have taken Dorothy's words on board about Tara and Sasha, but I have no plan. I am trying for normal. I am trying for calm. But now he's here and it's all I can do not to throw myself prostrate at his feet and plead forgiveness. Seeing him reminds me of all the things I've been so conveniently forgetting every time I have clapped eyes on Will. What a good man he is. How important he is. How much I need him to keep me sane. My usual confrontational style now deserts me. I've been busy confronting this thing for two days. Now

I just want it to go away. But it isn't going to. *He* isn't going to. And he looks so worried.

We don't kiss. He's too distracted. We sit down. I try chit-chat. But he's not having any of it. He wants to know what's wrong. Why I'm so pale and preoccupied.

'Because I've been thinking,' I tell him, 'about the wedding. And wondering . . . Oh, I don't know, Max . . . I was just wondering if we shouldn't be thinking about, well . . . what with everything—'

'What about the wedding?' He looks terrified now.

'With everything that's going on at the moment. Your mum, Toni, work . . .' I'm flapping my hands now, making shadow puppets, moving them in ever-increasing arcs in front of me. As if to expand such reasons as I can cobble together to fill the gaping hole that is his mouth. But despite everything, I can't mention his girls. Convincing though it might be, it makes me feel too dreadful. It would be, it *is*, too convenient. 'I was thinking that perhaps it might be a good idea to move it back a little. Till things are more sorted. Your mum and everything. Till Toni's settled with the baby, perhaps.'

There. It's out. It takes a few seconds for it to settle in the air between us, before it is spirited away on the turbulence caused by his response, which is something along the lines of '*Whaaaat?*'

All the colour is now disappearing from his face, and for a moment I expect him to crumple in a faint. Which is patently stupid. Max would never do that. But I might. The enormity of what I've just suggested is pressing down hard on my lungs. I make a conscious effort to slow my breathing. 'I don't know how to explain, Max. Really I don't. I, well I've been thinking about everything while you've been away, and, well, I think more and more . . .'

'What the hell has Toni got to do with *us*?'

'It's not just Toni. It's—'

'Or my mother, for that matter?'

'Max, she's *ill*.'

'And if you were planning on waiting for her to get better, you're going to have a mighty long wait.' He stands up now, starts walking back and forth across the rug. 'I knew things weren't right. You've been so strange lately. I thought it was wedding nerves, but it's more than that, isn't it? It's been ever since you started this job of yours. Everything was fine till you took over at that bloody school. All the stress. The changes. The responsibility. I don't know. You tell me. What is this all about, Holly? Christ, I'm home five minutes and you land all this on me! What the hell's *happened*?'

His eyes bore into mine, bleak and un-comprehending, and once again I'm almost overcome with the need to tell him. To be truthful. Tell him I have half lost my mind. I don't know what has happened to me. Just that something has. But his mobile rings. And it's Catherine, I can tell, in some cruel twist of fate. He stands up and barks at her, sounding snappy and irritable. 'Is it urgent?' Yes. *Yes*, it *is* urgent, it seems. He strides across the living room, away from me, to talk to her, looking out over the bay, his back stiff.

My heart is in my boots, and I don't know what to do. He carries on talking. Something about the girls. Some row or other. Some difference of opinion. Some more-of-the-same incident about which he needs consulting. Or chastising. Or berating. Probably some combination of all three. Ordinarily I'd be close to him. Close enough to empathize. Close enough to stroke his forearm as he talks to her. Let him know I'm there. That he has me on his side. But now I'm looking at his back and he's not turning.

The call ambles on. And on and on. No, he doesn't think it would be a good idea to go round there. No, he isn't going to ground Tara. She'll have to sort this one out her bloody self. If she didn't spend so much time putting crap in the girl's head, perhaps she would treat her with a little more respect. For perhaps the first time I feel sorry for Catherine, trying to make her life work. Lonely, bereft. All at sea without the helmsman Max so unquestionably was. Trying to relearn the instruction manual, bit by stressful bit, while all the while sailing through a force-ten gale. I've never felt any discomfort at her continuing need for him in her life, just a sobering sense of the contrast between my good luck and her bad. I hope she finds someone to love her. I really do.

We're not so different, I'm sure. Just at different places in our lives.

Yet to Max I am so, so, *so* different from Catherine. I am an independent woman. I have my own home. I have no relatives to take my attention away from his needs. Which makes him sound selfish but he's not. He couldn't be more loving, attentive or caring, but that was the deal with us. That I was not like Catherine. That was what has made this thing work. I am in control of my life. I have a flourishing career. I am not needy. I am what I am. On his side, in his camp. I am, always, his port in a storm.

And wasn't that very inequality of need exactly what I had been looking for? To be emotionally self-sufficient and invulnerable, but to nurture my strength in being needed by someone else? I think that often. I act on it often. I respond to it often. Christ, isn't that exactly why all this has happened with Will? And isn't that precisely what he was getting at about me? I am genetically programmed to do so, I think. Rewired, at the very least, since Emily died. My need to be needed must be nigh on insatiable.

And yet . . . couldn't that be it? That I don't *feel* very needed by Max? Isn't it more that we inhabit separate, mutually independent emotional landscapes? Yes, he thinks he needs me, but we think lots of things are indispensable when they're readily available to us. Take them away and it's surprising how often we find we can manage without them. My central heating, for instance. When it broke down, I just wore more clothes. Used blankets. My car. I walked, saw the scenery, got up earlier. When the corner shop closed down, I shopped elsewhere. Max thinks he needs me, but does he? Doesn't he just want to be with someone who doesn't make emotional demands on *him*?

And who is the perfect woman he loves so much? Isn't she just a badly photocopied me? A me with all the sound and colour turned down? Quiet and undemanding. Easy on the senses. Is that what I want to be? Is that who I *am*?

He presses the end-call button on his phone and turns around. 'How long?' he says.

'What?'

'How long d'you want to wait? You seem to have got everything else sorted in your mind. I just wondered if you had a new date pencilled in on your calendar. Something to run by me. Hmm?'

'Oh, Max. I don't have *anything* sorted. I just wanted us to talk about it, consider giving things a little more time to settle down.'

'Give *what* time to settle down? Your job? My mother's brain cells? My sister's hysterics? Holly, this is about *us*. Not *them*.' He walks towards me. 'About us. Us as a *family*. You and me. The girls, and . . .' He looks down at the phone, stares at it, then waggles it in front of me. 'Bitch,' he says. '*Bitch*.'

And I think he means me. It's a good half-second before I realize he doesn't, but by then my expression has given me away.

'Not *you*,' he snaps. 'God! When is this ever going to end?' Then he sits heavily beside me on the sofa. 'This is really about Tara and Sasha, Holly, isn't it?'

Because I have to accept that this isn't about the difficulties we've had with the girls, my denial sounds less than convincing. Unsurprising, then, that he isn't convinced. 'It *is* the girls, isn't it?' He's nodding to himself. 'This is my fault. I've handled everything wrongly with them, haven't I? I should have been more loyal to you.'

I try again. 'Max, it's *not* that. It's just, well . . . yes, you're right, I'm not finding things easy, but they're still only *children*. It's not a me-or-them situation. They're hurting. But that'll change in time. When they see they haven't lost you. They feel so insecure. It's difficult being a teenager at the best of times, isn't it? It's not anything you've done or not done. It's—'

I stop, because his expression has altered. As if the mists have parted in his mind to reveal something new. And it seems they have. 'Children,' he says. 'You having another one. That's what this is really about, isn't it?'

How did we get to *this*? It was never about children. And yet now he's brought the idea into my head, I find myself wondering. *Is* that it? *Is* it? Have I been barking up the wrong tree all along?

Once Harry's no longer in my life, will I need to find another Harry to take his place? And another? Will I always be searching for surrogate versions of Emily to tend? Other tragedies, other Wills to support? Have I been trying all along to fill the hole she left behind? This hole I've always denied was even there?

I don't recognize this me. She's a new incarnation. But is that why this marriage feels so doomed all of a sudden? This sense that I'm bolting a door on the past? Is that what it's really been with Will? A need to find a family that will welcome me gratefully into its bosom? The thought is so much at odds with my perception of myself that I can hardly digest its implications. Amazing how insightful we can be about others while remaining so clueless about ourselves.

But already I can see the truth in what Max says. Marrying him does mean that's it. No more children in my future. And although no conscious part of me is actively brooding on the prospect, I see that another, sub-conscious, part of me has always refused to rule out the idea.

I am almost forty. I cannot imagine it happening. I cannot even imagine wanting it to. But at the same time I'm far from acceptance that it won't. I'm now so far away from the me I thought I was that I don't know what to think any more.

'You've changed your mind,' Max says flatly. 'About having more children. Is that it?'

'No, Max. Not consciously. But – God. I don't *know*.'

'I can't do it,' he says. 'I can't even begin to contemplate it, Holly. You know that. I'm too old. I'm forty-six, for God's sake. I can't start again.'

'Max, I'm not *asking* you to. I love *you*. Having children of our own wasn't part of the deal. But maybe I didn't think it through enough. About how I'd feel at this point. How *final* it all is. Maybe I do need things to be better with the girls before I'm ready to accept that that's it. I don't know. I need time to get things straight in my head. Get used to the idea. That's all.'

He stands up again now. Slowly. Deliberately. A horrible stillness carved into his face. 'But supposing you don't, Holly? Supposing you *don't* get used to the idea?'

'Max, I will. I *know* I will.'

'Sure,' he says. 'Fine, then. Tell you what. Keep me posted.'

He stalks out into the hall and opens the front door. And although there is nothing to suggest it in his demeanour, he slams it behind him with such violence and force that the vase of eucalyptus I had on the hall table crashes to the floor, spewing glass beads across the carpet. The vase breaks. But very neatly. No shards.

There we are then. It'll be *fine*. If he loves me, he'll understand. If he loves me, he will accept it's best to wait a little while. If he loves me, he'll calm down, digest what I've said to him, call me, fix up to see me, talk everything through. We'll get back as we were and the girls will come round, and his mother will make a miraculous recovery, win *Mastermind*, tell me I'm the (other) daughter she always dreamed of, and every pig in the world will take flight in delight.

I telephone Max as soon as I estimate he has had time to get from my place to his. There's no answer. I leave a message. I say, 'Max, please. Can't we talk?' I telephone him on his mobile. It's on divert. I leave another message. I say, 'Come on, Max. We're not going to get any further with this if you won't talk to me.' I telephone him at the office the next morning. It's on voicemail. I leave another message. I say, 'Max, I don't want any more children, okay? I just want you to understand what I'm trying to tell you. To explain how I've been feeling. Why I'm anxious. I know you're upset, but refusing to speak to me isn't going to make you feel better either. Please call me.' But he doesn't. Not a peep.

On Monday morning Toni rings me. I'm in the middle of an appraisal with the special-needs adviser, so I call her back.

'Holly,' she says, 'what the *hell* is going on?'

Because I'm such a creature of habit, I tell Toni I want to go swimming, as per usual, so she has no choice but to come with me or not see me. She chooses the former, though everything in her manner suggests she is angry with me.

I swim twenty stressed lengths to her floaty half-dozen. When she lies on her back her belly's like a beach ball and her chin's a little mound in her plump, creamy flesh. I'm not sure if it makes me feel better or worse. Her body seems alien these days. And provocative. Ever more provocative to be around. My own torso, made sleeker daily by food being such a chore and a side issue, feels humbled by its bouffant proximity. Whatever the genesis, there is something so blameless, so dripping with virtue, about a woman who is carrying a child.

'Tell me,' I say, while we're still in the water, 'what he's said. Is he all right?'

'Hardly,' she snorts. 'He's beside himself, Holly. Poleaxed. Bewildered. Wouldn't you be? He's on the phone for half an hour at a time.'

When we had met outside the leisure centre I had decided that I wasn't going to allow Toni to bully me. Quite apart from the fact that this was between Max and me, quite apart from the fact that I would dissolve into a puddle of tears within seconds of any attempt at interogation on her part, quite apart from the fact that I had been living like the Grinch for almost a week now, deleting Will's messages, not answering my mobile, dreading the sound of his car engine below, quite apart from all *that*, I knew one simple truth: that I must not let myself be harried into a corner and blurt out the truth about Will. Things were bad enough for Max and me as it was. And none of it, I reminded myself firmly, was any of her business.

But my business had been Toni's for almost all my adult life, so it was hard to make it not so. Painful. Ours was a relationship I craved to take ownership of this. Were it anyone but Max, she would have been helpful and wise. But Max was her brother and I had betrayed him, and if I told her about Will, I would burden her with a secret she would find traumatic to keep. So, not-her-business was what it had to be. The awful thing about lies and clandestine liaisons was that they made you lie more. I didn't want to have to tell Toni any lies so I told her that I wasn't about to discuss Max in his absence. She said fine, so let's swim. So we did.

Which has taken us as far as my enquiry. No further.

'So, what has he said to you?' I ask her again.

'Not a lot,' she says, stirring the water with her fingers. 'I'd called about Mum. I was leaving a message. He picked up half-way through.'

I felt confused. Half an hour at a time saying what, then? Nothing of substance. Just sharing his bewilderment and shock. 'He won't talk to me at all,' I tell her.

'So I gather,' she replies. Then she inhales deeply, stockpiling reserves, and adds, 'I can't say I'm in the least surprised. I mean, Holly, I'm sure you have your own agenda here, and I know you're not happy about Sasha and Tara—'

'That's not true, Toni. They aren't happy about *me*.'

'And what do you expect?' she snaps. So sharply and suddenly that it brings me up short. I want to make her see that I've been as patient as a saint, that I've always been understanding, that I've always tried my best. But I can't say it now because I'll sound as if I'm whining, trying to make myself seem better than I am. And, anyway, I thought she knew that. It upsets me that she doesn't. 'I mean, Christ, Holly,' she continues, 'when did you ever get the idea it would just be you and him trotting off into a sunset? He has other people to think about beside you. As well you knew when you started seeing him.'

Which so takes my breath away I am unable to speak. Toni? Telling *me* that? The world has gone mad. Or I have.

'If that's your interpretation of the facts, Toni,' I tell her, 'then you *clearly* don't know how things have been.'

'Oh, I'm sure your interpretation *would* be different. But from where I'm standing it sounds to me like I've got things figured about right. And I think it's pretty lousy of you to do this to him, Holly. Especially now.'

Belatedly, guiltily, I remember their mother. Which makes me feel awful, and perhaps explains her anger. She's right. This *is* a bad time. For everyone.

'Look,' I say, 'I'm sorry to cause so much pain, believe me, but—'

'Too right you have,' she says. 'To do this to him now,' and she points towards her stomach, 'and to do this to *me*.'

I am suddenly, unexpectedly, filled with anger. Why can't she accept that my reasons are valid, that postponing the wedding might be the right thing to do? 'I can't believe you just said that,' I say to her. It's a whisper. I daren't raise my voice in case it leaps straight to a shout.

She seems oblivious to this. 'Holly, it's true!'

'Toni, this is nothing to do with you. It's about me.'

She glares at me. We must make for an interesting sight, both waist deep in water, squared up like a couple of sealions. 'I knew it,' she says. 'This *is* all about my baby, isn't it? How can you say you're not being selfish?' She shakes her head. 'My *poor* brother. He said as much. He always knew this would happen, you know.'

'*What?*'

'He said it to me when I found out I was pregnant.'

'Said what?'

'That he thought you might end up like this. God! Now it's come true. As if he hasn't got enough on his plate with the girls! Since when did you get to be so heartless?'

'Heartless? That's a bit over the top, isn't it?'

'That's not how it looks from where I'm standing, Holly.'

She says this in such a superior tone that my

hands bunch into fists. 'Then perhaps you should stand somewhere else,' I tell her. 'Because if you think Max is the only one suffering here, then your view is severely restricted. Christ, Toni, I thought you might at least *try* to understand.' I spring out of the pool as she lumbers to the steps. 'Toni, I thought you were my friend.'

She doesn't say anything. She doesn't need to. Her silence says everything for her.

It's dark by the time I get home from the leisure centre, but I know something's up even before I'm fully through the front door to my flat. Know because I've put my foot on something unyielding, and it's not a free sample of soap. I feel for the light switch and move my foot as I do so. It's a key ring. I recognize it. It has a heavy metal fob on it that came from some hotel in New York where Max went to visit some clients. I reach down and pick it up. Both keys are there. Outer and inner front doors. He's been here.

I make a small inspection. Gone is the dressing-gown. Gone are the CDs. Gone is the collection of male toiletry items that are the exact duplicates of the ones he has at home. Gone are the spare shirts, the spare ties, the spare jumpers. Gone is the hand-held electric coffee-whisk contraption that was part of his elaborate after-dinner ritual. Gone is the copy of Liddell Hart's *History of the First World War* that has sat for months, bookmarked by a postcard of a donkey, on the floor at the side of the bed.

I am, it's mostly agreed, a sensible person, so I must now do the sensible thing. I must take a deep breath. Three or four, maybe. Then I must go into the kitchen, make myself a cup of tea and press on with the amendments to the school development plan, which waits for no man, and will brook no excuses, and lies in wait at the bottom of my blue plastic box. Except that I don't. I do that other thing I've become so good at again lately. I immediately burst into tears. I am so tired of crying but it seems to be the only thing in my repertoire just now. Uncontrollable weeping – the response *du jour*. I cry my way through all five rooms in my flat, then I cry my way back out into the living room and across it so I can cry at the dark sky like a wolf atop a canyon. Then I cry my way back into my bedroom and sit and cry on the bed, until the sight of myself in the mirror on the dresser becomes one of such shoulder-heaving pathos that it's distracting, which makes me realize that my crying has become a matter of self-indulgence and self-pity, neither of which are qualities that make me feel better. I opt to dry my eyes and drink a big glass of wine, so I can overlay regret with the sort of raggedy, *faux*-optimistic cognitive gymnastics that will persuade me that it-is-all-for-the-best. I'll feel bad first thing tomorrow for sure, but I decide that feeling hungover for half of tomorrow morning is preferable to feeling wretched for the whole of tonight.

As I pad along to the kitchen, what strikes me with most force is that I will need to make no comparable visit. I had nothing at Max's place. What started out as a conscious decision in the interests of diplomacy, an acceptance of the girls' fragile sense of belonging in his new home, an appreciation of their space and how I must not invade it, had, in the almost two years of our relationship, quietly morphed into an unspoken status quo. Max's house belonged to Max and his daughters. I visited, I stayed over, I even cooked there occasionally, but my domestic detritus, my clothing and books were not in residence without me. I recall one occasion, after some sort of function, when I'd left behind a silver bangle. I'd taken it off before we left for the do because it felt a little hefty on my wrist. It was returned to me by Sasha, several days later, when I happened to be driving them on one of our jaunts. 'You left this at *our* house,' she'd said to me. 'Last week.' And I remember thinking at the time – even commenting to Max – how encouraging it was to hear her say that. That they really felt they could call his place home. Theirs but not mine. I hadn't thought *that* far. I wonder if it would have made any difference if I'd moved in early on, as had been discussed briefly at the time. I wonder, not for the first time but now perhaps for the last, at our blind faith that I would move in once we were married and that everything would carry on as before. I wonder if there is even a scintilla of hope left for us. I wonder if, deep down, I even want there to be. I wonder then, suddenly, whether Max wants his ring back. Is the fact that he hasn't asked for it a reason to hope?

I open the drawer under the worktop, and place Max's keys glumly inside.

CHAPTER 22

And now it's Thursday. The day on which I have finally agreed to meet Will. As if it were a much rearranged dental appointment. As if 'agreeing to meet Will' was a calendar commitment I have failed to find a window to accommodate thus far. Which is preferable to thinking about it as seeing Will for the first time since we were naked in my bed. I feel so lost without Max. He would know what to do here – which is the most ludicrous thing to think.

In some peculiar synchronicity of thought that I feel reluctant to dwell on, Will and I have arranged that we will meet at the outer corner of the west side of the cemetery that bisects two of Cardiff's main arteries. I said, 'The cemetery,' and he said, 'Good God! I was just about to say the same thing!' Spooky. Though not completely outlandish. It is – or would be, had I the least interest in classifying it, which I don't – what most people would class as a beautiful day. Post tulip, pre-bedding. A pre-dominance of green growth. A Caribbean blue sky punctuated by pretty Pavlova cloud forms. Enough breeze in the air to stir scents and lift spirits. Enough radiation warmth for bare arms and legs – though not mine because I'm sure there's a proto col somewhere that states I'm not allowed to divest myself of hosiery while in the company of Local Education Authority Persons of Importance, which is what I have been this morning. I've been to a meeting. 'Elements of Integration at the Fact/Perception Interface'. Which I don't doubt would have proved a stimulating diversion, except that too many bits of my brain were occupied by something – some*one* – else.

On the Monday evening Will, who is coming here today from some meeting of his own (dress code: 'who gives a f***?'), had phoned me mere minutes after I had lain down on my bed with my wine to consider the massive gap in my own fact/perception interface. The gap in which swirled all the grey areas. Was there going to be no Max in my life any more? I had almost called Max then, because suddenly the consideration of my life pre-Max, and potentially post-Max, made the Max bit reconfigure before my eyes, so it was no longer a making-the-best-of-it time (about which I'd spent stupid chunks of time trying to repudiate or validate), but now the only *good* bit since Emily died. How dare Will Meadows come along and try to brainwash me into thinking it hadn't been so good after all? How *dare* he? But I didn't phone Max, because what was the point? What would I say to him that I hadn't said already?

373

And then I heard my mobile, and I knew it might be Will. And it was, and I answered, and he told me he'd finished working on the children's film now, and that he had it on DVD for me. Then he paused, took a breath and said ok*ay*, he *had* kind of got the message that things were going to be difficult right now, but could we talk? Some time soon? He'd bring the DVD with him, he said hopefully, as if it was some kind of passport. Which made me feel humbled and guilty and – *hell* – tearful again. We fixed a date and I swore I could hear his little pointy stick tapping out the time on his Palm Pilot. Sometimes, being a woman, you find yourself brought up short by how much you can hurt a man. Two men, in fact.

So, let me see. That was on Monday evening. I drank three glasses of wine in the end and was very ranty at school on Tuesday. I even told JP to get the hell out of my face when he attempted to whine at me about the playground-duty rota. I told him he was doing it when *I* said he was doing it and if he didn't like it he knew what he could do. Go to hell, ideally, but I didn't add that. Now it's Thursday lunchtime and I'm communing with the real dead among the daisies and the dandelions, the roses and the wreaths. I decide there's an interesting outdoor component to my dealings with Will. One that might be worthy of further consideration during the long dark days when I'm wondering how the rest of my life is going to shape up. Max and I have never been out and about enough, I've decided. I should have insisted we honeymoon backpacking in New Zealand (my daydream) rather than at the St Cypriano in Venice (his). At the very least we should have compromised. Why hadn't I been honest? Why this tendency to mould my desires to fit his all the time? I seem to be stock-piling all these little bits of reflective hindsight right now. I don't know what I intend to do with them. Use them as a checklist for Dateline some time? To provide solace whenever I regret how I've made things pan out?

I hear the Morgan before I see it. I've already parked and made my way across to the bench I sometimes sit on. I am thinking about how it might have been if Emily was buried here. I could visit her often, then. We could chat about stuff. Would that have been good and useful or harm-ful and painful? I can't decide. As it is, it's just Mum and Dad, two in a bed. Third up, five along from where I'm sitting. I decide not to turn and scan the entrance for Will.

Which means he comes up behind me and because he has woven his way here across the grass (same as everyone) I haven't heard him arrive. I've got a loose idea of the time frame since his car engine cut, but even so, I still start when he speaks. He says, 'Did your mother die after Emily or the other way round?'

He comes round the bench and sits down beside me. I tell him I don't remember telling him about my mum dying. He reminds me that

I did. On Monday, in fact. That I told him my parents were buried here, remember? He already knew about my dad, he says. Did he? I don't remember that either, I tell him. But he does, so I guess it must be so. I tell him my mother died about six months before Emily.

'That must have been hard,' he says. 'I don't see much of my mother, for sure, but it's been a Godsend to have her around these past few years. You must have missed having your mum there for you.'

'No,' I say, because I have thought about this. 'It was the other way round. I mean, given that she'd been ill a while, anyway. It was a comfort, strange though it may seem. Knowing that Mum died with me happy and there being no reason to suppose that would change. I think me losing Emily would have broken her heart. I'm glad she was spared that.'

We lapse into silence and suddenly I realize that we are discussing Emily again. Discussing *me*. I look at him.

'Where are your wife's ashes sprinkled?' I ask him. Not because I particularly want to know, but because some part of me wants to challenge him.

'Roath Park. In the rose gardens.'

'How often do you go there?'

There's a little tic in his jaw now. 'Two or three times a month.'

'With Harry?'

'Of course.'

'Don't you sometimes find you want to be alone with her? So you can, well, not have to keep your brave face in place?' If he understands what I'm saying he's hiding it well. 'When I first lost Ems,' I go on, 'sometimes I didn't want Colin there. It was almost a selfish thing. I could never accept that his grief was as real and raw and painful as mine. Isn't that terrible? Because, of course, it *was*. He was just good at hiding his. I got that way too in the end.'

Another, longer silence.

'No,' says Will, finally. 'I don't go on my own.' And the tic in his jaw is going tic-tic-tic, and he's looking straight ahead and I can see he doesn't want to talk about it any more.

I study him now. He's clutching a clear Perspex folder with a popper on the front. He's got a shirt on today. Something soft. A pale khaki. The chain. The ubiquitous jeans. Different boots. I am wearing perhaps the most well cut of my well-cut suits, and although I have taken off the jacket, I feel like an old lady, sitting here in my tights and clicky heels. Some clothes and a hairclip and a pair of sensible shoes and I feel horribly like somebody's granny. I know he's almost exactly the same age as me, yet I feel I'm in the presence of someone more youthful and hopeful than I am. And I'm the teacher. The sage. The one with all the wisdom. It should make it easier, but it doesn't.

'The children can't wait to see it,' I say, injecting my voice with lightness and nodding at the folder.

It's either that or join in with him looking at me looking at him and trying to decipher what my eyes are trying to say.

'Are we going to talk about us at all?' he says.

Us, us, us. The us of that storyboard. Every frenzied frame of which is embossed on my mind. Still capable – even *now*, on this bench, in this cemetery – of igniting my body with its terrible heat. Of course we're going to talk about us, I tell him. Things need to be explained. So that's what I try to do. I tell him that my head is still in a terrible mess, that I can't sleep for worrying about it all. I tell him that although I know I can't undo what I've done, I wish – I *really* wish – it hadn't happened. I try to explain that I have looked deep inside myself and I now know that there are all sorts of difficult emotions about my daughter's death that I haven't come to terms with. That he was right. That I probably *had* been making the best of it. That I had shut a lot of my hopes and dreams in a box because wishing and hoping were too painful. And that until I'd met Harry, met *him*, my strategy had been working just fine. I told him that coming across Harry was a big thing for me. New job, new school, new people, new worries. Different reasons, of course, but we were both floundering a bit. And that he was also the first child I'd come across since Emily died who had put me back in touch with myself. Understandable – him having lost a mother, me having lost a child – and therapeutic for us both. Of *course* it made me feel good that I could provide him with some support, of *course* it was good that he had someone at school who could empathize with him, find the time to let him talk. Release his emotions. And then I'd met *him* as well and perhaps, looking back, it had been bound to happen – almost an extension of the same process: here was someone else who was manifestly not coping, who was grieving as well, who was lonely and forlorn. Which might have been all there was to it – probably would have been – but for the attraction. How could I deny that? It was there. It was real.

But sometimes, I now hear myself suggesting to him, you don't realize you've got yourself in deeper than you should have done until it's too late. I tell him I've thought and thought and thought yet there is really nothing to think about. I was engaged when I met him. I was settled. This was pure madness. And, similarly, he was in emotional turmoil as well. In no fit state to contemplate the complexity of a relationship with me. I tell him I am under no illusions about where I stood in the scheme of things. Our relationship was born of all the wrong ingredients. That he has answered a need in me – to matter, to *be* needed – that I hadn't up to now acknowledged. Just as I have answered a need in him.

When I stop talking – and, to his credit, he's let me witter on for ages – he turns a little on the bench and slides a hand through his curls.

Then he shakes his head. 'Is that what you think?' he says incredulously. 'Is that *all* you think this is? Why do you have to analyse everything so much? Why can't it just be that you have feelings for me?'

'Because I love my fiancé, Will.' I hold his gaze as I say it. I don't think he much cares for me any more, but fiancé or ex-fiancé, saying I love Max has become like a talisman. A beacon I can wave, as I float down the Styx, to ward off all the predatory monsters. Yet, for a moment, I waver. Is it me who loves Max, or just a version of me? The one that's too frightened to contemplate being alone?

'No, you don't,' he persists. Because that's obviously what *he* thinks. 'If you loved him you wouldn't have made love to me.'

I hate him using that language, although it's true. I *did* make love to him. I peeled off a layer of my armour for him. It wasn't about not loving Max, but he has a point. 'That's naïve, Will,' I lie in the gentlest of tones. 'What happened just happened. It happens all the time.'

'But not to you. You told me that.'

'Well, I was clearly in denial.'

'You're in denial now.'

'No, I'm *not*, Will.'

'That's rubbish. It didn't "just" happen, Holly. It started to happen way back. The minute we set eyes on each other. Why do you have such difficulty accepting that? Why d'you have to rewrite history?

Holly, can't you see? The opposite is true. It had every opportunity *not* to happen. You *made* it happen. Not me. *You* did.'

This is so, so hard. 'Will, I'm not trying to rewrite history, and I'm not trying to make excuses. Christ, I'm just trying to explain how things are *now*.'

'You shouldn't be saying words like that. We're in a holy place. We'll be struck down by a thunderbolt.'

I think I probably will anyway. As if I care. He's only trying to inject a little lightness, I know, but I'd like it better if we did away with lightness, if the weather took a turn for the worse. The sun is too jaunty and the clouds are too fluffy and there's all these little motes of something – some kind of wind-dispersed tree seed is my guess – wafting about and making it look like snow in summer, like the blizzards of blossom in that film with Tom Cruise. *Legend*. That was it. With the pixies and unicorns. I remember what my mum always told me about unicorns, and for half a second I think Will would appreciate knowing. But not now. No. What we really need is rain. The sort that comes flat packed in sheets. That makes everything grey and cold and wet.

'Will, look,' I say, frowning because the seeds in the air provide such a cruelly pretty backdrop to such a painful situation, 'you've lost your wife. She was ill for a long time and then she died. All I'm saying is that whatever you feel for me

381

needs to be taken in context. I'm not saying you're consciously looking to fill a void. I'm not saying there isn't a real attraction between us. I just don't accept that what you feel about me isn't bound up with your loss. It's been a long time. You're lonely. And there's the sex thing—'

'The *sex thing*?'

'Like I said, it's probably been a long time.'

If he could do an indignant face, this would clearly be his attempt to deploy it. But he can't. It just looks like I slapped him. 'How the *hell* would you know?' he chokes.

'Well, hasn't it?'

'All right, *yes*. As it happens, it has. But what the hell difference does that make, Holly? This isn't *about* sex.' Now he is astounded. 'Christ. Are you really trying to say what I think you're trying to say?'

'I'm just trying to point out that it needn't have been me. That it might have been like this with *anyone*. Will, we're going round in circles. I'm sorry, but I can't see you any more, okay? I don't know what's happening with my wedding. With Max. I don't know what I want. I just know we both need to sort out our feelings and accept that what happened happened for all the wrong reasons, okay?'

He looks more astounded still. 'What is all this "sorting out feelings" nonsense? They're not your bloody knicker drawer! Look, Holly. Forget the sex, okay? Just forget it. Let's do the feelings. It's not difficult. And, hey, you're a teacher so you should find it simpler than most. You *feel* things. You don't choose them in Marks and bloody Spencer. You have no choice in the matter. You just *feel* things. And if it makes you feel good and it isn't dangerous or illegal or immoral, you go with it. You get what I'm saying? On the other hand if it makes you feel bad, you don't.' He drew in both a breath and a midge. I slapped his back while he spluttered. He didn't say thank you. I took my hand away. He frowned.

'Do I make you feel bad?' he said. 'Do I? Do I *really*? Okay, yes. Of *course* you feel bad about your fiancé. There's not a lot I can do about that. But that aside, *do* I? Come on. You and me. Do you feel bad when you're with me? I really want to know.'

'No, Will. You know I don't. But in some ways that makes it even worse. Look, I understand myself. I know I have this terrible need to look after people. Harry . . . you . . . but it's not the point anyway.'

'Why not?'

'Because what's at issue here isn't my feelings. It's yours.'

'And your take on me is that I only slept with you because I needed a shag. Great.' He must have seen me recoil at this because he shook his head and started again. 'Okay, *subconsciously* that I just needed a shag. On a conscious level, you think I *think* I have feelings for you, but that I can't trust them because they're all wrapped up in the whole Florence Nightingale, wife-substitute, grieving thing I've still got going on. Right?' I'm nodding. I can almost feel her presence as he says it. 'Hey,' he goes on, 'tell you what. I think I've got the hang of this. I could retrain as a bereavement counsellor maybe.'

'*Will*—'

'I'm right, though, aren't I? Isn't that about the size of it? But it's a load of crap, Holly. It's not *true*. I'm sorry, but I don't accept that you're going to skip off and marry this guy. Not now.'

'I'm not. Not yet, at any rate. I've postponed the wedding.'

'There! You see? I *am* right. So where's the problem? Christ, you just cancelled your wedding because of me—'

'Postponed it.'

'Same thing.'

'But not because of you, Will. That's my whole point! *Because* of you in that since I met you I've come to see that perhaps I'm not as clear about a lot of things as I thought I was. But that's not the same thing as it being because of *you*. You're a part of it, Will, but you're not all of it. And there's this whole thing with Harry—'

'*What* thing with Harry?'

'I told you. I don't want to complicate his life either. He's been through enough.'

'And I don't know that, of course.'

It was a statement, not a question, this time.

We'd been here before. He fell silent. For an age. He shook his head again. Slowly, this time. Then he stood up. Drew both sets of fingers through his hair. Tipped his head back and looked at the sky. Said '*God*,' with some emphasis. Then again. '*GOD!*' Then he sat down again. He didn't look astounded any more. Not a jot. 'It's not true, is it?' he said finally. Flatly. 'It's not, is it, Holly? You're trying to convince me you're not sure of *my* feelings, but it's not even true. It's not mine. It's yours. You can't stop doing it, can you? I've got it. You really *can't* help it, can you? You're just saying all that stuff to try to spare my feelings.'

'Will, I—'

The timbre of his voice changed. 'No, no,' he said. '*Please*. Don't bother. Forget your half-baked theorizing. Forget the counselling. Forget trying to make me feel better. You're only giving me this crap because it makes you feel better about *yourself*. About the fact that you got in over your head. Got a bit carried away by the *frisson*, the attention, the excitement, the idea of this *sad* guy who needed a shoulder to cry on – yours are just *so broad*, right? Because you've been there yourself. But now you've gone too far and you've come to your senses. Well, fine. *Fine*. If that's the case, *fine*. But spare me your damage-limitation speech. *Please*. Shit, I am *so bloody* clueless!'

I could see him ball his fist, and for one awful moment I though he was going to spring up again and slam it into one of the headstones. But he didn't. He just touched it to his forehead. 'Why, oh, why didn't I see this coming?' He unballed his fist and drew his hand through his hair again. Then he slapped his hands against his thighs and formed something approaching a smile. 'Fine,' he said, jumping up from the bench. 'I shan't keep you.' His eyes bored into mine, and he raised a finger towards me. 'You know, I *really* don't need you to feel sorry for me, Holly. Don't need and don't want your bloody pity. So you can get right on back and make it up to your fiancé. Get back to your safe, uncluttered, organized, neat and tidy existence. Just forget me. Have a nice life and all that.'

He started walking then, diagonally across the grass, his long legs straddling the corners of sundry graves as he did so. Then suddenly he stopped and turned again. Pointed. 'But whatever you've decided about *my* feelings, Holly, you're wrong, okay? Got that? You are *wrong*.'

I sit for a long time. Fifteen minutes or more. And it's only when I gather my bits up to go that I notice there's something else in the folder he brought as well as the DVD. It's an invitation to a première for one of his ads. A square card, from an ad agency whose name is vaguely familiar. Not Flipstein and Mangelwurzel, but something similar. The same lengthy huddle of tongue-twisting names. At the cinema in the bay. 'Champagne and Sushi. 6 for 6.30'. A film ad for a well-known brand of trendy men's deodorant. How curious a concept an ad première is. Can it last more than a minute? And what d'you do after that? More champagne and sushi? Go home?

But it's all academic because I won't be there. As I slip it back inside the folder I hear the unmistakable throb of the Morgan engine across the street. I'm jolted by the noise. I thought he would be gone by now. I want to jump up and follow him and tell him I'm sorry. But I don't think I can bear to see his face.

CHAPTER 23

Cefn Melin Primary stops for no one at the best of times. The days roll along, the weeks gather pace. Ours is a dynamic equilibrium, constantly in motion, even for people who'd quite like to get off.

But here is something with which to temper the sharp squeal of the treadmill's revolutions. Just imagining the look on Dafydd Rhys-Woodruff's face is enough to be going on with, and I'm grateful.

I'm passing the junior boys' toilets just after the end of first play and become aware of some snickering within. So I knock, announce, 'Mrs Connors coming in!' and enter this most fetid of fetid places in a school.

Owen Rhys-Woodruff and his acolytes, of whom there are two, are in a state of suspended animation. As well as that, Owen himself *is* suspended. Though certainly not because he's in the process of using the facilities, balanced, as he is, over the partition between two cubicles. I gesture for the other two to come out of the first. Nod at Owen to lower himself. Then I knock at the door of the closed one, which eventually emits a traumatized-looking boy, who has obviously been the butt of some low-life high jinks.

I hold out my hand. Owen places something in it. It's a mobile phone, one that even my Luddite's eyes can see is an all-singing all-dancing video model, just the type of mobile a moneyed pillock like Dafydd Rhys-Woodruff would bestow on his thoroughly spoiled eleven-year-old son. And Owen Rhys-Woodruff is just the sort of boy who would sneak his crown-jewels mobile phone into school, despite what I know would be a no-no by his mother, because ownership of such possessions is the passport to having friends. Plus he can amuse himself and pals at playtime by taking video footage of other children on the loo. What a thoroughly likeable young chap. I send the unwitting movie star back to class and tell him we'll have a proper chat shortly, then send Owen's hapless acolytes to stand outside my office. Then I round on Owen.

Rule 632 – see health and safety issues, chapter eleven – is quite clear in the matter of toilets. Children must not be expected, in any way, shape or form, to have anything to do with their husbandry and maintenance. Just as no litter picks may be instituted on the field, no cleansing of their own foul detritus and grunge may be wholly or in part delegated to a child.

'And you can get some paper towels' I snap – b***ocks to bloody rules – 'and clean all the mud off that toilet.'

Once the repercussions have all been properly repercussed and documented, I try to ring Dafydd Rhys-Woodruff to tell him I have had to confiscate Owen's mobile phone but, sadly, that small pleasure is denied me. He is at a trade fair somewhere in the Midlands. Bidets. Which makes me think of my own: a white elephant. Of elephants. Of counting out the seconds. Of waiting for them to coalesce into weeks, months and years. Just as I did eight years ago.

But a small ray of sunshine is at least headed my way. I get through to Just Penny and to Penny herself, whose first words, once I've told her it's me on the phone, are a somewhat distressed, 'Ooh, so you've heard?'

'Heard what?'

'Oh dear. I don't know *what* we're going to do. I've rung the council and it's possible he won't get a place here at all! He might have to go to that dreadful, dreadful school out at Aberpandy estate. I was going to call you. Is there anything you can do, Mrs Connors? *Anything?*'

Owen, it seems, hasn't got his oh-so-sure place at the public school to which Dafydd, in all confidence, applied. And as the local (and perfectly splendid) comprehensive is already over-subscribed (and as they've already turned down a place there, of course) he might have to go to another. One with 'crackheads and headlice and car thieves' and so on that no person in their right mind would send their kids to. Except the right-minded people who live round there, of course, whose perfectly nice kids are taught by some of my friends. Suddenly not everything on the landscape is bleak. There's hope that young Owen Rhys-Woodruff will become something approaching human after all.

God, but it's taking so *long*. It's been days and days and days and yet I can't seem to reboot my wiring. I'd stick my finger in a socket if I thought it would help. It would kill me, for sure, but this is *killing* me. I've never been in such an inhospitable place.

Max. Gone. As if he'd never existed. I so want to talk to him. I so want to make everything the way it used to be. Yet every time I reach for the receiver or my mobile, something stops me. I'm not sure what it is, but I can't seem to face even trying for a dialogue. Every time I think it, Will's expression at the cemetery is back to reproach me.

Will. Gone. As if he'd never existed. I have called him. Left a message on his voicemail about the film. The children have made him some beautiful cards. I kept thinking I'd go round and drop them off at his house but I didn't because he never returned my call, and I could almost taste how much I'd hurt him and I knew I wouldn't be able to see him without wanting to hug him. I gave them to Harry to give him in the end.

Toni. Gone. As if she'd never existed. Lumbered off into the night in those infernal maternity jeans she finds so necessary but uncomfortable. But less uncomfortable than having anything to do with me. I ring and ring but she hates me as well.

But joy, of a sort. Trallee, trallay! John is away for two days. He's gone up to Leicester for another interview and it seems he has some chance of getting the job. There's only one other candidate and I know who he is. And what he is, too, which is basically useless. He's been applying for headships for the best part of three years. Even John can't cock this one up, can he?

John. Gone. As if he'd never existed. It'll have to do to be going on with.

What won't do, frankly, is not having Glenda. Difficult though our relationship is sometimes (which I have decided, as Mrs Grace suggests, and in the interests of saving some small wisp of self-esteem, to put down to the impending march of hormonal anarchy rather than her just not liking me any more), I need her if the school is to run with anything like its usual efficiency. But her message, left on the school answerphone a whole hour after she would have switched the thing off had she arrived here as per normal this morning, advises me, in her usual chop-chop tones, that she has unexpectedly found herself minus her newest filling plus a toothache, and is off for an emergency appointment at the dentist. She doesn't know, she adds, what time she'll be in. Elevenish? As soon as she can.

Which is ironic. Because a little after eleven, and even less after I have put the phone down on the man who deals with the roller-towel allocation and who is very cross with me for not being Glenda and therefore not knowing whether the delivery scheduled for last Friday did or did not arrive, given that I clearly have nothing more important to think about, a car pulls into the car park out front and disgorges a tall bearded man. I don't recognize him and, with no Glenda on hand to tell me who he is or what he's here for, I reach automatically for my diary to see if I've missed anything. If I have it's being coy, because I find today blank.

By the time I am out of my office and at the front door, he is yanking ineffectually on the handle. I make the usual gestures towards the door-release button and point to the sign, but he seems un-interested in reading it. My hand dithers by the entry button, until he lowers his arm and makes a show of waiting patiently for me to let him in.

Mrs Cairns, apparently, is big in local amateur dramatics. Many's the lunch break these past weeks when we've been entertained with her florid tales of on- and offstage shenanigans at the Cefn Melin Centenary Players' rehearsals for *A Village Affair* (by a playwright of this parish) in which Mrs Cairns is playing a loose kind of lady called Elsie, whose main function is to run around deflowering unsuspecting young men (one of whom is played by the vicar, which was brave of him), while her poor beleaguered husband, a naïve chap, misses every clue that is so painstakingly spelt out before him, and spends much of the play bursting onstage demanding, 'Where are you hiding my wife?' with the obligatory Hilarious Consequences.

I don't know why, but I make a connection. I remember Mrs Cairns talking to me about him. I recall her mentioning how hard they're rehearsing. I think it's in my head that they sometimes meet up for lunch. So when this man with the beard thunders, 'Where are you hiding my wife?' I think it must be a joke.

So, on the basis of some facial hair and what looks like hammy acting, I effect a jovial, if bemused manner, and smile at him. How dozy is that?

Luckily, this malfunction of cognition is but a short one. In about the same length of time it takes a ladder to travel up a stocking leg, I realize that the person in my reception area is most probably not Mr Cruickshank from the Cefn Melin Centenary Players. It also comes to me with equal rapidity that when he boomed, 'Where are you hiding my wife?' he meant it. It was not a rhetorical line being delivered on the occasion of picking Mrs Cairns up for lunch. No, this man, who is glaring at me with some aggression, means business. He has a wife and he clearly thinks I have hidden her somewhere. Whoever she is.

I lose the smile and look enquiringly at him. 'I beg your pardon?' I say. 'Should I know who you are?'

He's looking past me down the junior corridor. He doesn't seem to be listening. His eyes are all darty and bloodshot and angry and have probably leached all the corpuscles from his brain. 'Well?' he says, obviously deaf as well as hirsute. 'Is she here or isn't she?'

'*Who?*'

Now he turns back and makes a face that seems to indicate he's heard me. '*Glenda!*'

'*Glenda?*'

'*Glenda.* Is she *here?*'

So would this be Glenda's husband? 'Would you be Glenda's husband?'

'*Who,*' he roars, and it's now I get the first gust of alcohol, '*the bloody fuck else would I be?*'

If there is a rule regarding best practice for dealing with a drunken man loose in your reception area and using the F-word (and I don't doubt there is) it is of little use to me now, as I fail to recall it. Nevertheless, some dim recess of my brain computes that as here is one angry, potentially violent man, my best course of action is not to provoke him further but to make every attempt to calm him down. All the other bits of my brain are in agreement. Break over, everyone's back in their classrooms. One class does have PE, it occurs to me, but as it's dry, they'll be out on the field. With no Glenda – oh, irony! – I'm all on my own here. Barry could be anywhere, and chances are he is. So I shall have to deal with Gunga Din myself.

I try to remember if I've ever met Glenda's husband, and conclude that the answer must be no. 'She's not here, Mr Heaven,' I say, as calmly as I can. 'She's gone to the dentist to have a filling replaced.'

At this point, another fact pops into my brain: earlier on this morning someone answered the phone in the office and called me to ask where Glenda was. My response 'at the dentist', when relayed to the caller, did not go down very well. I remember hearing Naomi – yes, Naomi – telling the caller sorry, but that was what she had been told.

'The fuck she has,' he says. Had he said that to Naomi? 'Where is she? *Is* she hiding? Or hasn't she slunk back here yet? Eh?'

I'm amazed that someone like Glenda could be married to a man who says 'fuck' every other sentence. It's surreal. I can't take my eyes off him. He's something else. 'That's all I know, Mr Heaven. She left a message this morning. Look, is there anything *I* can do? You seem rather upset. Can I help?'

He doesn't seem to want to take me up on that one. Instead he marches past me and into Glenda's office. I cast about, consider bellowing, 'BARRY!', but don't, then go after him and we collide in the doorway. It's not a terribly big place to search, after all. Another blast of fumes goes up my nose.

'Mr Heaven, she's not in school. If she was I would tell you. If and when she gets here I will ask her to call you. In the meantime, I'd be grateful if—'

He rounds on me. 'Right,' he says. 'Where's *he*, then? Come on!'

Curiouser and curiouser and curiouser. 'Where's *who*?' I blink away the molecular assault on my face.

He breathes in, then lines up the cross-hairs in his nostrils. And here it comes again. 'Fucking Patterson! Who else?'

So much of an actor's craft is in the timing. I don't know if Clemency dabbles in am-dram, but hers couldn't have been better if she'd been RADA's star thesp. Because my back's to the hall entrance and Reception is carpeted, it's the swivel of Happy Boy's eyes that alert me, closely followed by her query: 'Is everything all right, Mrs Connors?'

I turn my back on him to gurn at her and breathe some fresh air. I am flabbergasted by what I've just been told. 'Fine,' I say, eyebrows a go-go. *John Patterson?* 'Just fine. This is Mr Heaven.' Clemency's own eyebrows move fractionally. 'He's after Mrs Heaven. I've told him that as soon as she gets here we'll let her know he's looking for her. So, Mr Heaven,' I add, turning back to him, 'I really must get on. I'd be most grateful if you'd leave now, please.'

'I'm not going anywhere,' he replies. 'Not till you tell me. Where's Patterson? At the dentist's as well?'

'He's not here,' Clemency says, before I do. 'He's at an interview.'

'In Leicester,' I add. 'So he won't be back today.'

Mr Heaven's face clears itself of what has clearly been confusion. 'Bastard,' he says roundly. 'I fucking knew it. Bastard.'

'Mr Heaven,' I say, 'I must insist that you leave the school premises.'

I might as well have been talking to a plate of cannelloni. He stomps past me and sits down on a chair. One of two for visitors – and children holding sick bowls.

'I'm staying,' he says, 'till she gets here.'

'Mr Heaven,' I say again. '*Will you please leave?*'

He fixes me with a glassy-eyed glare. 'I'll kill her,' he says. 'I'll fucking kill her.'

At which worrisome – not to mention perplexing – revelation, Clemency and I, of one mind, leave Mr Heaven to consider his options. (Mrs Heaven, in Reception, with the Candlestick? Thank God we took down the display of the children's hand-painted ceramic tiles. And the ceremonial African spears, come to that.) We consider ours from the relative safety of my office. It's a little before eleven thirty. The children are safe where they are with their teachers. Clemency's own class has a student with them, so they're not on their own either. We've half an hour till lunchtime, so there's no need to panic. We have time on our side.

'Barry,' I say, picking up the internal phone. 'We need Barry. I'll feel a lot happier if he's around. And then I'm going to call the police.'

'The police?'

I nod. 'I don't doubt Barry would make short

work of removing him from the premises, but I'm not taking any chances. Besides, supposing Glenda shows up? That's one drunken man out there. Anything could happen.' I pass the internal phone to Clemency, to keep trying, and pick up the outside extension.

'Jesus,' I say, sliding my finger down my list of important phone numbers. 'I can't think straight. *Glenda? John?* What on earth is this *about*?'

Clemency, phone clasped against her dainty ear, gapes. 'Blimey,' she says. 'You didn't *know*?'

I know nothing, me. I have been so wrapped up in my own problems that I have misrouted most of my emotional intelligence and squandered almost every last drop. I know nothing, me. About anyone or anything. Least of all myself.

'You didn't know about Glenda and John?' she asks again.

'*Glenda* and John?' I reply. 'But I thought you—'

'Thought I what?'

'Nothing. Never mind.' I shall save it, as one of those things we'll look back on and laugh about. Or perhaps not. I expect it'll take more than that.

'You're right,' she says, sighing. Which confuses me even further. 'I should have stayed well out of things. It hasn't helped any, has it? Hasn't changed anything either.' As I'm none the wiser, I shrug to be going on with. It'll doubtless all come out in the wash. 'But she's my friend,' she goes on. 'How can I just stand by and do nothing?'

'What? Glenda is?'

'No. *Sarah*.'

'Sarah?'

'John's wife. I can't believe he could do this to her. And the poor children. It's— Ah! Barry! We need you here. Now!'

Clemency gives him a brief resumé of events, while I do likewise for the police. They're a tad stretched, because there's a demonstration about speed cushions going on in town this morning ('Probably only fifteen sales reps and a man in a van,' the constable quips chattily, 'but you never know with unpopular traffic-management initiatives.' Blood has been spilt, apparently), but they'll get someone along as soon as they can. In the meantime, if he does leave, perhaps I could ring them back. By the time my call's ended, I can see Barry in the distance, going round the back way, as Clemency suggested.

'He knows too, I take it?' I ask her.

'Of course.'

Once Barry's with us I lead the posse into Reception, where Mr Heaven has abandoned the chair in favour of standing with his hands placed jauntily against his hips while scowling out at the car park. He also seems to be swaying. In some sort of trance. A red mist, I presume. God help us.

'Mr Heaven,' I say. He doesn't turn. 'I'm going to have to ask you again. I would be grateful if you'd please leave the premises. I understand that you are anxious to speak to your wife, but it's a private matter and this is not the place to do it. This is a school, and there are children around. I have called the police, and they are on their way. I'm sure you'd far rather leave of your own volition than have to be escorted by—'

'Oh, bugger,' blurts Barry, behind me. 'Oh, *bugger*.'

Glenda's car is pulling into the car park.

The time will no doubt come for the staff of Cefn Melin Primary when the incident that now begins to unfold will pass into the realm of folklore. It will be retold in the staff room as near-legend. There will be oohing and aahing and the odd astonished comment that you'd never think that sort of thing happened around here. But that time is not yet. And will not be for some time. Right now the most pressing matter at hand is how to stop the one from connecting with the other and heading off a bloody murder on the asphalt.

It occurs to all of us at roughly the same time that Glenda, blithely unaware of her husband's car, which is only three spaces down from where she is currently engaged in a parking manoeuvre, does not know what's about to hit her. And although I don't know Mr Heaven well enough to be sure whether his aggression is verbal rather than physical, it's clear that Barry does. He lays an arm across Mr Heaven just as the latter is reaching for the entry/exit button. But the gesture is deflected and the door is now unlocked.

And open. Mr Heaven clearly intends to waste no time letting Barry restrain him from getting at his wife. As one, we shout, '*Hey!* and '*Mr Heaven!*'

and '*Stop!*', none of which has the slightest effect on him. Clemency and I then shout, '*GLENDA!*' very loudly, while Barry hot-foots it across the forecourt in pursuit.

At which point Glenda notices – and she'd have had to be blind not to – that her husband is approaching her car at speed. She hops back in and sensibly locks the doors. Which puts paid to any lingering hopes I might have harboured that he doesn't want to punch her, just to sit down and calmly talk everything through. As does the sight of his fist, which connects with her bonnet at the same moment as the car kangaroos out of its space.

Mr Heaven, surprisingly nimble for a lush, wastes no time in swearing but now veers off to his own car. He's looking for his keys as Barry draws level with him, and obviously intends to pursue her.

'You can't drive, man!' Barry is saying. 'You're in no fit state!'

Which obviously hadn't stopped him driving here in the first place, and seems unlikely to stop him driving away.

'*Fuck off!*' is the next thing we hear. Loud enough for Mr Tinkler to put pen to paper. Which, if he's in his garden now, I don't doubt he will.

Mr Heaven, who I'm sure couldn't give a flying one, is busy getting into his car, despite Barry's best efforts to stop him. Any time now this could turn into a fight. 'Barry, just let him go!' I bellow.

But evidently Barry feels it's his duty to keep hold of Mr Heaven. At the very least till the police fetch up. He's holding the car door open. Closer now, I can hear him trying to reason. 'Come on, man! Calm down! Driving after her now is only going to make things worse!'

But Mr Heaven, wrestling for control of his door, obviously doesn't see it like that. And Barry, strong though he is, is not alcohol-assisted. And he obviously doesn't see it either.

CHAPTER 24

'"Please note,"' I read, from the cheery LED message, '"due to very high demand at present, average waiting time is three hours." Oh, dear. How's it feeling? Is it agony?'

'I'll live,' Barry says.

'I'm sure if you made a bit of noise they'd be quicker.'

Barry looks at me as if I'd suggested he dump his overalls and start choosing flowery frocks as his workgear of choice. 'I'll live,' he says again, although he looks ashen.

He also looks as though he has two broken fingers. We can't say for sure, of course, but given that they look like small zeppelins, and spent several seconds sandwiched between Mr Heaven's car door and its frame, it's probably an accurate diagnosis.

I sit down beside him. I've just been outside to try his wife again. Lunch break will soon be over and I need to get back to school.

'She'll be here in about an hour,' I tell him, slipping my mobile back into my bag. My own fingers have finally stopped shaking. Nothing like a bit of live action violence to make a girl realize she's glad she's not a boy.

Although it was all over remarkably quickly. Directly after the car door slammed on Barry's hand, in fact. Upon which Mr Heaven, who had already fired his engine (and who, to his minuscule amount of credit, did not attempt to drive off with a screaming school caretaker hanging off his window), opened the car door again, released the yelping Barry, then shot off.

By the time we had got Barry inside and made an assessment of his injuries, it was getting on for twelve and the midday supervisors were trickling in, anxious for a rundown of the morning's dramas while they slipped into their pinnies and began to set up. As with Harry all those months earlier, it made sense for me to run Barry down to A and E. So here I was again. It was getting to be a habit.

'This is getting to be a habit,' I tell Barry now. 'I hope this isn't one of those things that come in threes.'

'You been down lately, then?' he says.

For a moment I think he's referring to my mood. It would fit, for sure. But he's not. He can't be. 'Back in January, remember?' I say. 'With Harry Meadows.' It feels like such a long time ago. A time when Harry was Harry Meadows and Will was Will Meadows, and Holly Connors was only months away from becoming Holly Stapleforth and everything and everyone was straightforward and unstressful. Even John was a predictable, and therefore manageable, force.

'Of course,' he says. And of course that's what he'd meant. 'I'd forgotten about that. He was a bit of a tinker for a while, that one, wasn't he?'

'He's through the worst of it, though,' I say firmly. 'I don't think he's been in any sort of trouble for ages.'

Barry pulls a don't-count-your-chickens face at me, then smiles. 'I've always had a bit of a soft spot for that one,' he says. 'Tough life he's had, all told.'

'I guess you've known him since he was little,' I remark, imagining the mini-version. Imagining a younger Will. A Will and Caitlin together. A happy family.

Barry nods. 'He used to follow me around like a lost puppy. "What you doin', Mr Huckley?" "Can I help you, Mr Huckley?" I think he missed his dad a lot.'

Whoa, Neddy. Missed him? Missed him when? Will's allusions to Harry's lost childhood return to me. 'Missed him?' I ask Barry.

'He was away a lot, by all accounts, with work, of course. And then, what with the separation as well . . .'

Barry isn't a donkey so I mustn't prod him. 'Bless him,' he continues obligingly. 'Used to be forever telling me how he was off filming here or he was off filming there.' He's been resting his injured fingers in the palm of the other hand and now he lifts them and pulls a face.

'I didn't know,' I say, stunned. 'Was it for long?'

He nods. 'For a bit. A few months. Barbara – Mrs Grace – was quite friendly with the gran. She used to help in school too. Bad business, apparently.' He tuts to himself. 'But there's nothing remarkable about that these days, is there?'

My brain is whirring now. 'Sadly not,' I agree.

'It's funny how things work out sometimes, isn't it? With her getting cancer and that. God moves in mysterious ways, and that's a fact.'

As is the fact that it's now a quarter to one and the eight billion questions I suddenly want to ask him will have to wait. Damn. 'I'm going to have to get back to school, Barry. Can I get you anything from the vending machine before I go?'

'A quarter bottle of malt whisky wouldn't go amiss. Go on. Get off. I'll see you later on.'

'You most certainly won't. You'll go straight home and rest that hand.'

'Is that an order?'

'It's absolutely an order.' He doffs an imaginary cap and winks at me. 'And, Barry . . .'

'Yes, sweetheart?'

'Thanks for today. And everything. I can't tell you how much of a difference your support has made these last few months.'

He flaps his good hand, embarrassed. 'Go on with you.'

'No, I mean it. I don't know how the school would function without you. Definitely don't know how *I* would. So don't you go retiring on me any time soon, will you?'

He shakes his head. 'On the contrary. I was thinking you might be gone before me.'

'Me?'

'Well, you've hardly had an easy ride, have you?'

'But today changes lots.'

'And am I glad of that! I know glum when I see it. And there's only so much of that a soul can stomach every day.'

'You mean Glenda?'

He rolls his eyes heavenward. 'I mean *you*.'

I remember watching a TV documentary about the Houses of Parliament once. A history programme, explaining the building process. And the fact that much of it was made from sandstone, which is a sedimentary rock and has created problems about which we can now do little. Ignorant of geology as those builders and engineers had been, they hadn't understood that sedimentary rock is composed of layers of sediment, which means that any given lump of sandstone has enormous strength along one plane, but great weakness along another. So if it's laid in a supporting position with its layers vertical, it has a tendency to flake away, layer by layer, at the edges. Lay it with the layers horizontal and it forms a foundation as strong as any igneous rock. But some of the pillars on some of the buildings had been laid with their layers standing up.

I have never studied geology, but as I drive back to work, it's clear to me that we base all sorts of things on a foundation of assumed facts. We trust our houses not to fall down so we sleep soundly in them. We presume other drivers know the rules of the road, so we don't expect them to drive on the wrong side, or to cross junctions without stopping and looking. We know water's wet and that it will make us wet too. We base action and feeling on assumed foundations of knowledge. And now Barry's told me something that has altered my foundations, just as happened with the engineers who inspected the Houses of Parliament, and rewrote their assumptions about how long they might stand. I haven't yet had time to translate thought into theory, but suddenly everything's changed.

When I get back to school the police have been and gone and Glenda is installed in the staff room. I'm quite shocked to find her there, but Mrs Grace, who has stepped naturally into the role of comforter and confessor, explains that Glenda phoned the school only a quarter of an hour or so after we left, having been parked in a cul-de-sac nearby. She came back, it seemed, because it made perfect sense. It was the one place she was sure he wouldn't be.

Glenda is puffy-eyed but stoic and apologetic and all for getting on with her work. Yes, her husband is an alcoholic brute, yes, she should have left him years ago, no, she won't be going home tonight – she'll be going to John's – and no, she really, *really* doesn't want any fuss.

Which means Clemency, who is helping me with the incident report, has to fill me in on the details. 'It's been going on since before I came here,' she tells me. 'It was through John, in fact, that I heard there was a post here in the first place. Sarah and I did our teacher training together.'

'I can't believe I never twigged,' I say.

'Why would you? They're hardly a likely couple, are they? I mean she's almost a decade older than him, for starters.' She lowers her voice. 'I don't know what *planet* he's on, frankly. I mean, to up and leave his wife and kids like that.'

'So John's not even living with his wife any more?'

'God, no. Not since before Christmas. He's got some grotty flat down in Canton. Mind you, she'd have thrown him out if he hadn't left. I mean, wouldn't you?'

Never having dwelt upon the scenario of John Patterson as errant husband, I have no objective opinion. But based on the scenario of John Patterson as childish and malevolent deputy head teacher, I readily concede that I probably would. But so much about him now falls into place. No wonder he has always been so negative, unfocused and generally dishevelled. He has been living a pretty negative, unfocused and generally dishevelled life. No wonder, it occurs to me, he didn't get my job.

Clemency sighs extravagantly and looks out of

my office window. 'It's all so *sad*, isn't it? Right up until today I could have given you all sorts of adjectives to describe what I thought of Glenda, but "compassionate" wouldn't have been among them. I suppose it never occurred to me that Glenda might have her problems too. I met him, you know, at the last Christmas dinner. You wouldn't have known. He was perfectly charming.'

'And probably drunk.'

'Oh, yes, he got plastered. But, hell, it was a party. It was Christmas. You just don't *think* sometimes, do you?'

Perhaps life would feel better if we all stopped thinking. Took everyone and everything at face value. I'm thinking so much that my neurones are all gridlocked. 'So what exactly *was* she up to this morning?'

'John had a puncture, apparently, on his way up to Leicester. And his AA membership had lapsed – as these things do in his situation, I suppose – so he called Glenda and she drove up the motorway to rescue him. It was about seven this morning. She drove him to his interview, turned round and came back. You've got to admire her work ethic, I guess.'

And God's playful approach to bad karma. Puncture as watershed. The idea appeals. 'So how did her husband find out?'

'I don't know. I presume he must have picked up on the phone call. I get the impression all this has been brewing for some time.' She squints at something she's written, then crosses it out. 'Anyway, I guess that's it for Sarah and him. I think she'd been harbouring the hope that it might just be a mid-life crisis – a fling – but it doesn't look that way, does it?'

I shake my head.

'Perhaps he just wants a mother figure. He's quite an immature man, isn't he?'

'A disappointed one, certainly.'

'People, eh?'

'People.'

She puts the cap back on the expensive fountain pen the management-consultant people gave her when she left. She must have made a pretty big leap of faith in coming here. But I think she's made it. And I'm glad. Glad, too, that we can put all the rubbish behind us. It'll take a while to get back to normal with Glenda, but now that all the cards are on the table I know we can.

Clemency's staring out of the window. 'Relationships are endlessly damaging, aren't they?' she says. 'People's capacity for hurting other people. I look at all these little ones in school sometimes and wish they could stay children for ever. Stay innocent. Stay happy. Not many of us manage that, do we?'

No, I think. But we shouldn't stop trying.

Keiran is a happy person. I don't see a great deal of him, but every time I do he is jolly, always full of whistling-to-himself gaiety, back-slapping bonhomie and lashings of 'My shout!' good cheer. Keiran always seems largely unconcerned about most of the things that stress most people most of the time, and apart from the stress that has been their eight-year campaign to make babies – and even in this, he has maintained his composure – Keiran is generally at peace with the world. So it is with a burgeoning sense of unease that I listen to Mrs Grace telling me that he has been on the phone twice while I have been talking to Glenda, and that he sounded a little upset. He'd be grateful, she tells me, if I would call back ASAP.

Things, as I thought, come in threes.

Keiran sounds as though he is sitting in a washing-machine drum, but he is on a train, heading north. He aims to leave it at the next station, but that will still put him in Derby, where he will need to establish how soon he can get another train, heading south. He was supposed to be going to give a lecture.

'But she's been taken to hospital,' he tells me. 'She's bleeding. One of the girls from her office has gone with her, but I'll be hours getting back and I thought she might need you.' He makes no reference to the fact that the last time I saw her I was the one person she didn't want to see.

'I'll go straight there,' I reassure him. 'Don't worry.'

'Thanks so much, Holly. God, isn't this typical timing? I hope there's a train.'

'There'll be one. Don't worry.'

'I got hold of Max too. He's going to go down when he can.'

'Good.'

'She did tell me, you know, about you and Max. I'm really sorry.'

'Well,' I say briskly, '*c'est la vie*, eh? We'll see. Anyway, I'm on my way as soon as I can get away from here, okay? And don't *worry*.'

'Huh!' he says. 'Chance would be a fine thing.'

'I know,' I say. And then I ponder his last words. In what sense would chance ever be a fine thing? Isn't chance the thing that sneaks up and ambushes you just when you thought you had everything under control?

Two things happen then. Both by chance. The conjunction of a lorry shedding its load on the Gabalfa flyover, and making me late, and Toni going off for a scan.

Toni wouldn't see me. I went in and asked where I could find her. I was told, I went to find her, I approached the bed, where she was lying on her side with her back to me, I said, 'Toni, it's me,' and she said, 'Go away.' Just like she was in a movie or something. 'Go away.'

I walked round to the other side of the bed. She told me to go away again. I entreated, movie-style: 'Toni, this is ridiculous. Keiran called me. Are you okay? How are you doing? What's happening?' and so on.

She said, 'No, really. I don't want to talk to anyone right now, okay? Particularly you, to be honest.'

Ouch. And then a nurse with a wheelchair fetched up (which was timely), and she went for her scan, and by the time she returned, Max had arrived, which complicated matters. It might have been a scene in the sort of daytime soap that counts itself lucky if its ratings hit four figures. 'Oh,' he said, as we configured in the corridor. 'Hello.'

'Poor Toni,' I offered up, as conversation. 'Poor thing.'

He moved his head. Might have been a nod. Accompanied it with a throat-clearing. Sat down on one of the two chairs placed just along from the door. Why were they there, I wondered. Perhaps for visitors to sit on while their relatives had bed-baths. Or 'procedures'. In any event, they were jammed up close together. I didn't sit on the other.

'How are you?' I said.

'Okay,' he replied. He didn't follow it up with any of the things *I* might have added in his shoes. 'Fair to middling'; 'Bearing up'; 'So so'; 'Muddling through'. Max has never done un-necessary embellishments. Lawyer's training, I suppose. Every word counts. Every extra word effects changes in nuance or meaning. Only speak if

415

you have something concrete and unambiguous to say.

'Oh, Max,' came a wavering voice from behind me. Toni's. She was being wheeled back to the ward. Max stood up.

'Toni—' I began.

'Thanks for coming to see me, anyway,' she said politely to me, once she was level. I was being dismissed. Max followed her in.

It upset me, seeing Max. Seeing how readily his dignified frame had become welded with all our happy memories. Upset me to see how readily I could see us slotting back into couple formation. Upset me most of all because it showed me how much I would lose, in losing Max. And all so I could properly engage with losing Emily – find myself. Was it worth it? Was I?

But seeing him was a chance at least to make sense of it. So, because I had nowhere pressing to go, to be, to *anything*, really, I stayed a while. I got myself a cup of tea-white-no-sugar from the vending machine I'd remembered seeing in an alcove further along the corridor, and then I went back and sat on one of the two chairs. I had no idea how long Max would be in there, but not long, I judged.

I was right. Fifteen minutes later he was back. I stood up.

'You know, I really wouldn't bother right now,' he said to me, after he'd performed the almost un-noticeable but to me very obvious manoeuvre of frowning a little when he saw me. Confrontation, again. He hated it. Perhaps if he didn't avoid it so much, things would have worked out differently.

No. Don't go there. 'I wish she wouldn't be like this,' I said instead. 'I want to be there for her.'

'Yes,' he said. 'Well. You can't always be everywhere for everyone, can you?' Then he walked past me and on up the corridor. Ten strides on he turned. Forced a smile. 'She will come round, you know,' he said. 'Just give it time.'

Which was so sweet a footnote it brought a lump to my throat. I took a few steps towards him. 'Max, can't we please just talk?'

He considered me for a moment, then walked the remaining few steps that separated us. He knitted his brows and exhaled. 'Holly, what is there to talk *about*?'

'Everything, Max. *Us*. We can't leave things like this.'

He studied my face as if he might find a spot on it that would explain why I was so stupid. Then he sighed. 'What else are we to *do*? You already know my feelings on the matter, and I yours.' He frowned. 'Holly, I'm all done with talking. I know what I want and, more importantly, I know what I *don't* want. I don't want any more children. I am finding it difficult enough to measure up as a father to the ones I already have. What you see is what you get with me. As has always been the case. The same can no longer be said for you. Holly, there's no point in "us" if we don't want the same things, and this is not something we can compromise on. I have been through one wretched divorce and I don't want to risk another. Do *you*? I don't know why this sea change has happened with you, but it has, so we should both be grateful it's happened now. Before it's too late.'

'God, Max, you make it sound like a case you're prosecuting.'

His features shifted. As did his shoulders. It was only when he lowered them that I noticed how stiffly he'd been standing to attention. 'I don't mean to,' he said. 'But if you're waiting for me to recant and beg a reconciliation, you'll be waiting a long time. It isn't going to happen, Holly.'

I reached out a hand to him. It was an instinctive gesture and, every bit as instinctively, he drew his away. I lowered my arm. 'Max, I don't want things to end like this.'

He looked exasperated. 'How else would you have them end, Holly? This isn't a musical. There's no closing number. No finale. Please.' He glanced down at the floor and back. 'Allow me a little dignity, will you?'

'I'm so sorry.'

'So am I,' he said quietly. Then he walked away.

Rather less than lyrically, I was standing by a bin – one of those bins you see all over hospitals that consist of a metal lid and ring, attached to the wall, below which is suspended a strong plastic bag; they say things like 'no sharps' and 'non-clinical waste only'. This one was embossed with the word 'sterile'. And I conceded it had a point. Perhaps there was some poetry in this after all. Blank verse.

CHAPTER 25

'I got my photos back,' Harry says to me, the following Monday morning. He's on register duty with Lauren Ogden and I've watched them all the way from their classroom to Glenda's office, deep in conversation, heads close as they walk. Perhaps she doesn't suck any more. 'Shall I bring them to show you at playtime?'

'Yes,' I say. 'That would be nice.'

I'm going to emulate the strategy of the great Ranulph Fiennes. Though some might argue that his doggedness of spirit is a double-edged sword, what with him having lost digits and bits of face along the way, there is something appealing about his unstinting one-foot-in-front-of-the-other-until-a-Pole-fetches-up mindset. It has got him out of his tent on many a bleak expedition morning when most of us, faced with similarly hostile conditions, would have remained in our sleeping-bags and told the world to go away until such time as it was prepared to be a bit nicer to us. But that sort of thinking's for wuzzers and wimps. I am head teacher of a school. I have My Career to think about. I have to get up and get on. Who cares about digits and bits of face anyway? It's what's on the inside that counts.

At playtime Harry finds me in the playground and pulls a slim sheaf of photos out of the envelope he's holding. Then he goes through them, one by one, carefully supplying explanatory detail. Here's Gran with her budgie, here's my cousin on his skateboard, here's us at the Sea Life Centre in Brighton. I stroked a manta ray. It was *so* lush. Here's me on my quad bike. Do I look cool or what?

'And who's this?'

'Oh, that's Matt.'

'Who's Matt?'

'He's my uncle. It was Matt who took us quad-biking. He lives near Gran and Grandad. He's well cool at quad-biking. Oh, and guess what, Miss?'

'What?'

'I'm going jet-skiing again, maybe. Well, probably, actually.'

'How exciting! Is this for your summer holiday?'

'No. That's Africa.'

'Africa?'

'South Africa, I think. I'm not sure. We're going there after. For three weeks! How cool is that? Well, I think we are. I'm not sure. It's something about work, but it's going to be a holiday too. But we're going to France first. For Dad's prize thing.'

'Prize thing?'

'He's won a prize and we have to go to France to get it. And it's by a beach and everything.

Near where we went last time. So he said if we've got time we can go jet-skiing again. Isn't that beast?'

'It's beast,' I agree. 'What's the prize for?'

'I dunno. Some adverts he's done. Film stuff. Nanny M and Pop are coming too.'

'How lovely.'

'It's wicked.'

'And to Africa as well?'

'They're not coming on that bit. Too many lions.'

'Of course,' I agree. 'Lions. And hyenas. And cheetahs.'

My pulse thumps. Elephants too.

Mrs Grace and I meet, like a pair of vectors, mid-playground, as if drawn there by the sheer force of my subconscious will. I have such a powerful desire to know what she knows that I have even considered dragging her by the hair to my office, and trying her up with bunting until I know every last thing. 'He's a little love, that one,' she says, watching Harry go.

'Hmm,' I say. Prize, I think. What sort of prize?

'Like father like son, eh?' she adds. She's got a half-finished Cup-a-soup in her hand. Beef-scented tendrils of steam assault my nose.

Naomi's out now with the bell in her hand, so we start moving tangentially back to the staff room. 'Break a few hearts, I don't doubt,' she adds, as we walk. I make another encouraging noise. A different one this time. 'Mind you,' she says, just as we turn the corner to the main corridor, 'good looks don't guarantee happiness, do they?'

'No, they certainly don't,' I say, with emphasis.

'I mean, when you look at his father . . .' She pauses, I assume, to consider the goodness of his looks. I wish she wouldn't: it's contagious. 'It's been good seeing him around school again,' she adds.

I am now all ears, although I don't wish to be so. It's not really Mrs Grace. I look at his father all the time in my head anyway – I wish I didn't but I do. He's just there all the time. My tragic widower made more tragic by me. I stop and face her. 'Barry was saying as much the other day,' I say.

Mrs Grace folds her arms under her bosom. 'It all passes through your hands in this job, doesn't it?' I nod. 'Whole childhoods. Not that I know all the ins and outs of it. When do you ever?'

'When indeed?' I offer.

'I doubt we'll ever know now,' she says. 'Much difference it makes anyway. Sad to think it takes something like cancer to bring things into perspective, isn't it? Certainly seemed to knock a bit of sense into her, God rest her. And her mother. I remember that. Lots of comings and goings. I don't think there was much love lost. Still, Dad was a trouper. It must have been hard for him. In all sorts of ways. A real trouper he was, bless him.'

'Blessing him wasn't the consensus round here, from what I've gathered.'

'No?' She drains her soup. Her expression suggests

that, were she two decades younger, we'd be of one mind where Will is concerned. Her soft spot, my hurt place, it's all much the same. 'Still. No surprise, really,' she says disapprovingly. 'And what would most of this lot know about it? Really? They're not in his shoes, after all.'

Boots, more correctly. Converse basketball boots. He has two pairs that I know of. One red, the other black. Plus some trainers. I wonder if he has any proper shoes. I find myself thinking he probably doesn't. What need would he have for them with the life he leads? It's so different from mine, with its protocols and dress codes and politics and hierarchies. And suits. John is wearing one today.

I don't think I have seen JP in a suit since we were all told to 'make an effort' back in '93 or '94 when some politician-on-a-mission came to visit the school. Perhaps it's the Glenda effect, perhaps it's the job, but whatever forces have been at work on his psyche and his wardrobe, he looks much more like the person I used to know. The one who didn't hate me. I almost wish I'd known about John's situation from the outset. Perhaps I could have helped him. But then again, perhaps not everyone on the planet needs Helpful Holly Connors messing in their lives.

But I should help to oil some wheels here and there, and to this end I have been out and bought four bottles of M and S *cava* and some cakes, which everyone lights upon with such enthusiasm and vigour that I almost think I work not in Cefn Melin but in Chad.

It's the Tuesday after half-term, and before we embark on our impromptu celebratory party, we show the film the children made to the school. Clemency couldn't be more puffed up with pleasure, and the children laugh heartily to see me speeded up to seventy-eight r.p.m., rattling around school, dispensing orders and homilies in a Pinky and Perky squeak, while a boy from year five in a pith helmet and shorts does spot on David Attenborough commentary. No wonder I didn't think I'd been filmed much. I didn't *know*. It's an inspired piece of work, the stuff of cherished memories, and sitting at the back of the hall, among this little group of adults-with-their-various-problems, I realize that my team is a family of sorts. And that if I were in any other life I'd be happy. I'm there now. I'm settled. I feel like I belong here. It's just a shame that I don't feel I belong anywhere else.

I look out over the sea of taupe and blonde, mouse, oak and chocolate in front of me. The familiar splashes of ginger and auburn. All those little heads. All those little people, and still I can pick out Harry's exuberant curls in seconds. In a matter of weeks he'll have left here for ever. Moving on, like they all do, while we begin the next circuit. It's not a treadmill: it never was. The cast changes yearly. But I can't help feeling as if I'm on one. Counting out my life on an academic calendar. Dividing up each block of it into terms. But when I'm washing my hands before getting the cakes out, the face looking back at me in the mirror is unfamiliar. Not at all like the person with whom I've been debating all this.

Nor does the inside *feel* like me any more. It is as if layer upon layer of my life since Emily died has been quietly dissolving. I think about Max. His bald statement of fact about 'us'. Will's assertion that I've simply been making the best of it. He's right. I have. Isn't that what we all do? Isn't that the thing *to* do? I recall what I've heard about his own marriage. Perhaps I'm not the only one guilty as charged. Perhaps we're all too damaged by difficult relationships for 'making the best of it' to be anything other than the sensible thing to do.

But there's good news, finally, when I arrive home. A ray of hope, scrawled on the back of a postcard. 'Helen Keller ward,' it says. 'I'm the hippo on the left. In your own time.'

'I decided to be sensible,' Toni tells me when I get there. 'I figured that if I'm going to be beached here like a seacow for weeks, I'd better say I'm sorry. I'm going to get pretty damn bored if I don't get any visitors.'

Things are going to be okay. Everyone's agreed about it. She has a fibroid, that's all. It's not safe to operate now, so they won't. She has to rest to give the baby the best chance. But if she had it tomorrow it would be okay. Everyone's agreed on that. And you can see it in her face. 'I'm sure you

426

have plenty of visitors,' I tell her. I wonder if Max has spoken to her. 'Quite apart from anything else, to do all the fetching and carrying for you. Is that a laptop I see poking out from under there?'

'Well, how else am I supposed to communicate? The mobile's banned, isn't it? And you can't get near the trolley-phone for all the women ringing their husbands to ask them to bring in Pringles and copies of *Heat* magazine. Some of us need to earn a living, you know.'

I shunt a pile of paperwork from the chair to the table. 'How on earth are you going to cope with taking six months off? Actually, don't answer that. You'll be fine. Because, believe me, you won't know what's hit you.'

'You're telling me I won't. One of the mums in here has three kids already. Just half an hour of them visiting gave me palpitations.' She pats the swell of her stomach. 'Though I've certainly not been idle. I've got the whale-music thing going, Keiran's on aromatherapy-massage fatigues, and I'm reading aloud Keats and John Donne. So if my baby does not emerge with a Zen-like stillness about her I for one shall want to know why. Failing that, have you heard of a preparation called Phenergan? I had the mother write it down for me. Sounds like good stuff.'

'You're unbelievable, you are.'

'Well, frankly, honeybunch, so are *you*.' She grabs my hand. 'Are you okay? Seen Max? Are you coping?'

I wonder again. 'I'm okay,' I tell her. 'A little shell-shocked, but okay.'

'I'm so, so sorry,' she says, fervently. 'I keep going over and over it in my head. I was so horrible to you. I don't know what got into me. I was just so . . . well . . . God, *horrified* about it all, Holly. I know I'm tanked up on hormones but it's all so bloody *sad*. I mean, you were supposed to become my sister-in-law, marry Max, and become part of the family. It was all so sorted. I was so happy for you, and now . . . oh, I know it's just sentimentality, I know it *is* just the hormones, but I was dreadful to you, wasn't I? Sulking and selfish and completely out of order. God, was I self-obsessed or what? I was so mad at you for messing everything up. Like, it wasn't allowed because *I* was pregnant and *I* was centre stage and everyone was supposed to be worrying about *me*. Forgiven?'

She stops to draw breath and I nod. How could I not? 'Forgiven.'

She reaches out to hug me. Childlike and mother-figure at the same time. 'Hey, enough already, huh?' she says. 'He came to see me last week, you know. We even had,' she lifts her fingers to form quote marks, 'a Proper Chat. Max isn't about to change, is he? He knows what he's about. So I guess it *was* the right thing, wasn't it?'

The tree outside the window is a blaze of emerald. Spring has become summer and I hadn't even noticed. 'I don't know,' I say. 'I honestly don't, Toni. All I know is that I can't be the sort

428

of wife he needs. Not any more. I thought I could. I thought I could do that whole grown-up step-mum thing with the girls. They've been through so much, and it's no less than they deserve. But it seems I can't. I need something more than that.'

'Your own kids.'

'I'm not sure, Toni. It's really not as focused as that. I just know I'm nearly forty, and I can't bear the thought of it never being an option. It being so for ever. Just as strongly as Max feels the opposite, I guess.'

'You used not to feel like that.'

'I know. That's the worst of it. I really don't know why I do now. I've led him to believe I'm one thing and now I'm something else. At least, that's what I think. I don't know.'

She squeezes my forearm. 'He'll get over it, you know. And, anyway, I don't think he's ready to get married again. Sure, he loved you, but I also think he fell in love with you for all the wrong reasons. Because you were the opposite of Catherine. You never make any demands on anyone. On *him*. Which is not a good basis for a relationship, is it? A relationship should be based on mutual support. Mutual need. Mutual *dreams*.' She jiggles my hand now. 'And you have a perfect right to yours.'

I'm not sure I want to think about dreams. I have so many suddenly and they all seem adolescent, dumb and unrealistic. 'Hey,' I say, 'it's been a boon on the work front, at least. You never did see such a well-run place. My school development plan should be exhibited in the British Museum.'

'Hey, don't you go shagging yourself out. I'm going to be relying on wall-to-wall godmotherly support soon. Oh, and speaking of which, were your ears burning earlier? I was thinking about you. What happened with the ad you had Will Meadows in doing?'

I start. Then I swallow. 'It went fine,' I tell her levelly. 'It's all done. I don't know when it'll be going out. Or where, even. But, yes, it was fun. The children enjoyed doing it. I'm not sure I did, but what does that matter, eh? Anyway, why should my ears have been burning?'

'Actually, not yours, strictly speaking. Will's. I had a memo that he's doing a new campaign for one of our accounts in the autumn and it got me thinking about you and the trouble you had with that son of his. It was a son, wasn't it?'

I still need a second to assemble what I hope is a vaguely disinterested face. 'Harry. Yes. Much better.' I'm nodding at her like a nodding dog now. 'He's doing fine.'

'Thanks in no small part to you, I don't doubt.' She gives me a pat on the arm and the sort of indulgent and maternal look that only heavily pregnant women can pull off. I'm happy to accept it because I'm so happy to be here. 'Not me,' I say. 'Not really.'

'So Will didn't turn out to be feckless, then?'

I can't get used to Toni calling him Will when

she speaks to me. Now I know him so much more intimately than she does, it feels odd. Childish, I know, but I can't help it. I'm almost jealous of their relationship. Of their continuing relationship. Of their autumn campaign. 'He's won some prize or other,' I say. 'Did you know?'

'Will's son has?'

'No,' I say. '*Will* has.'

'Has he now?' says Toni. 'What sort of prize? Most Annoying Parent? That was about the size of it, wasn't it? Or was it just a PTA raffle?'

'Nothing to do with school. Something to do with his work, apparently. Harry was telling me. They're going to some awards thing in the South of France as far as I can make out.'

'*France?* When?'

'End of July, straight after school breaks up.'

'Wow,' says Toni. 'Holly, that is not "some prize". If he's going to France to pick up an award at the end of July that means the Cannes Lions. Which is serious beer, I can tell you. *Big*-time. Wow.'

'Ah,' I say, remembering. 'I think he told me about them.'

'What's it for? D'you know?'

'Haven't a clue.'

'Well, it's nothing to do with us, more's the pity, or I'd know. And it can't be for a single ad because the judging for that takes place *at* the festival. Must be an aggregate award for a body of work. Otherwise he wouldn't know about it now. Well done, Will. I always knew he'd hit the big-time.

It's a wonder he's not made the move into films yet. But I guess with his wife's illness . . .'

I guess too. Seems I can't not.

When I get back from the hospital, I find Dorothy slipping a note under my door.

She's off to her Dolls' House Club meeting shortly, but as she hadn't seen me for several days, she thought she'd stop by and see if I fancied coming up for a glass of something with her later. I shall miss our dress sessions.

'And here you are!' she says, folding and pocketing the note. 'Actually,' she adds, 'as you're here, could you do me a little favour? Hester's on her way, and I've some things to bring down. You couldn't give me a hand with them, could you?'

I follow her up. Tell her I'd love to see her later. Suddenly I seem to have zero social life, with Toni stuck in hospital, Max gone. It occurs to me that, having started again two years back, I now have to start *again*. It's a bit lonely, being a school head. Perhaps I should arrange to visit my brother in the holidays. I haven't seen him since Christmas, after all. But even as I think that, I know it won't happen. We've never been close. Perhaps I'll get myself a cat. No, a dog. They're more friendly. And it could mess up my flat.

'And how are you?' Dorothy asks me, as she lets us both in. I tell her I'm fine. She tuts, pulls a face. 'No, you're not.'

But I don't want to visit the 'not' bit. Old habits die hard. 'Absolutely fine' works for me. So I tell her about John and Glenda instead. How that's one bit of good news. How much I'm looking forward to next term.

'And Max?' she asks. 'Have you seen him? How are things there? Are you absolutely over?'

Yes, we're absolutely over and I'm absolutely fine. That works for me too. Scans well. Yep, I'm reverting to type without any trouble at all.

'You know, I almost think I'm beginning to understand myself, Dorothy,' I tell her, to accompany my nod. 'This has all been about me. It's about having all this love inside and nothing much to do with it. I mean, I know Max loved me, and I know I thought I loved him, and I did, but it wasn't enough. He didn't need me – *it* – enough. And the girls didn't either and . . .' I find a little sigh has made a bid for escape from my lips '. . . and, well, that's why it hasn't worked out. Because I clearly still need to address this dreadful fixation I have with looking after people.'

I say all this in such a jolly and unemotional tone that I could have been reading from the script of a Radio Four play, an afternoon one, with lots of dodgy sound effects, Maggie Smith, Celia Imrie, and that man who reads the *Just William* books – Martin Jarvis. Perhaps Jean Brodie should become my role model. Who would it hurt if she did?

Dorothy gives me a pitying look. 'There's nothing wrong with wanting to look after people,' she says sternly, 'but has it ever occurred to you that it works both ways? That there might be someone out there who would like to look after *you*?'

Chance would be a fine thing, I think but don't say. And, anyway, that's not the way relationships work. Not the way *I* want to enter into one, at any rate. And then I think, Why can't it work both ways? I've never thought like that before. Not since Emily died and I became so adept at looking after myself. Brave faces, forcefields, lumps of concrete, they're all the same. Get behind them and there's only yourself to fall back on. And I sure didn't let myself down.

'By the way,' Dorothy says, as if it were entirely unrelated, and nudging aside my little revelation, 'I've been doing some thinking myself. All this time we've been talking about how your feelings for that Will of yours were just about the fact that he struck a chord with you . . .'

That Will of mine. *Will.* She's back with Will. I blink at her. 'And?'

'He's struck so many chords with you that he's all but performed a whole symphony in your head. Which got me thinking . . .'

'What?'

'That perhaps you've – we've – been coming at the situation all wrong. Perhaps it's not that he's struck all these chords with you.' A car horn sounds in the street below. 'There's Hester. I'd better get my skates on. Do you think you could carry the furniture down for me?'

I pick up the cardboard box she's indicated. It's

full of tiny chesterfields and grand pianos, sideboards, standard lamps and rococo-legged chests of drawers. All the elements required for the sort of gracious living enjoyed by the pocket-size family about town. All elegance and sumptuousness and rich fabrics and warm colours. You never see dolls' houses furnished like my flat. All naturals and minimalism and artfully placed vases. Perhaps that's because families don't live like that.

'And?' I say, as we leave her flat and trundle down the two flights of stairs.

'Hmm?' she replies, negotiating the double doors with her backside. The idea of the symphony resonates in my brain.

'Coming at *what* all wrong?' I say. 'What do you mean?'

'What I mean,' she says, passing through the second door and out into the summer evening, 'is that it might be the *other way round.*'

I don't understand her, but she's off to do her dolls' houses and I'm left standing in the street, puzzled, while the gnats try to nibble at my neck.

After I had watched Dorothy and Hester drive off, I ran back upstairs and got my handbag. Then I went back downstairs and out to my car. I drove all the way to the big hypermarket on the other side of Cardiff Bay and found myself a postcard with a picture of a lion cub on it, which made me feel ridiculously pleased. I wrote on it, 'Dear Will, I heard from Harry that you've won a prize at the

Lions Festival, and I just wanted to let you know how pleased I am for you. He's very proud, as you can imagine. And so am I. Very well done. Enjoy every moment. With love and best wishes, Holly x'

I thought it would feel cathartic, doing that. Form a sort of Maginot Line between us. But as soon as I had finished writing I saw that it was the dullest, most dreary postcard anyone could ever have written and I so didn't want my signing off to be that. It was a postcard you might send to a next-door-but-one-neighbour. Not to a man who'd held you like he couldn't bear to let you go. Not to a man who'd traced a line of kisses from your temple to your toes. Not to a man who'd made love to you. But it was done now. I could hardly go back and get another one. I'd feel too stupid. Plus I'd used up the last stamp in my book, and would have to go and queue at the tobacco kiosk, with its doggedly hopeful conga line of last-minute lottery fans.

So I walked over and posted it in the big double letterbox up the road from the old post office. I didn't even dither about which slot I should use. Then I walked back to the car under a starless navy sky. Just a tiny slice of moon to light my way.

CHAPTER 26

I wasn't actively thinking that anything would happen as a result of my sending Will Meadows a few lines of bland congratulation on a postcard. I had sent my good wishes, he had doubtless received them. He would, perhaps, have slapped it among all the other bits of paper that were pinned up in his kitchen. I had little doubt that he would have said, 'Huh.' Or 'Yeah, right.' Or even 'Yeah. Great. Cheers.'

Or 'Never mind', 'Chin up', 'Move on', perhaps. It is only when I happen upon Harry in the corridor three days later that I concede I have been mulling over Will's oh-so-spot-on distillation of my life-plan *ad nauseam*. Not actively. Not consciously. But it's been in my head.

Harry is looking for a book about magic. He's seen Derren Brown doing stuff on TV and wants to learn how to do tricks. I help him look, even though I'm sure we don't have one. 'Not long to go now,' I say, on my knees with him. 'Less than a week till your trip. Are you excited?'

He shrugs. He's eleven. He's no longer permitted to do excited. 'Yeah, kind of,' he tells me.

'I'll bet Nanny and Pop are,' I say.

He's scrutinizing spines. 'They're not coming now.'

'Oh dear. Why's that?'

'Nanny M's got an ulcer on her leg or something. Not like one in your mouth. It's, like, *big*. She can't walk much till they fix it. And Pop can't come either because he's got to look after her.'

'That's a shame. I expect they were looking forward to the trip, what with Dad getting a prize and everything. He must be a bit disappointed too.'

Harry shrugs again. 'Nat's coming instead, to look after me. And he's too busy being in a mood. He's got to do a speech and he doesn't want to.'

Ah, so there's more going on here. 'Why ever not?'

'Because he's shy, of course.' Harry tells me this so matter-of-factly that I wonder that I had never considered it. He never seemed shy with *me*. Not at all. This shy person's someone I don't know. 'He got your card, by the way,' Harry adds.

I keep looking ahead. 'Oh. Good.'

'I told him he should ask you to help him.'

I pull out a book. But it's mainly about optical illusions. I turn to show it to Harry anyway. 'Help him?'

'With his speech,' he says, taking it. 'I told him you were good at doing speeches. Talking and that. Like you do at school.'

'And what did he say to that?'

'He said he'd make sure he sent it in for your approval. But I think he was being sarcastic.'

His vocabulary's growing daily, I think. And

soon he'll be in high school. It barely seems possible that almost half a year has passed. 'You think?'

He nods and glances down at the diagrams. 'He's pretty grouchy at the moment.'

'Oh dear.'

'And Nat's boyfriend scratched his car with his bike handlebars this morning. So he's going to be a mega-*mega*-grouchy tonight.'

'A big scratch?'

'Nah. But it's, like, his *precious car*, isn't it?' He gives me back the book and flaps his hands in mock horror. 'He's always Mr Microscope Man about that.'

'I'm sure he won't be too upset. It's only a car.'

'Huh,' Harry grunts. 'You don't know my dad.' He hoicks up his trousers and scratches his head, oblivious to the cruel irony of his words. 'Actually, I think we need to get another cat,' he says gravely.

'Really?'

'To cheer him up.'

That night I have my losing-Emily dream again, but for the first time ever I find her. Which is such a strange, difficult business. Horrible, initially, because for the first time in years I clamber back to consciousness thinking I have my daughter back with me. It's so crushing to discover it was only a dream, and the sadness washes over me in such powerful waves that I can do nothing but lie there and let it subsume me for a while. But once I wake properly I think something else: perhaps finding Ems in my dream might be about having accepted that I really *have* lost her. Perhaps she's come back to me for that reason. To say goodbye. To tell me it's time to be brave and re-engage with the world. And now that I've removed the sticking plaster and let the air get to the wound, perhaps I will. Perhaps I *can* do it.

Of course, I get up, I shower, I eat my Frosties, I get my suit on, and once I'm fully functioning, I feel silly and sentimental. Dreams are only the work of busy neurones, after all, reconstituting our consciousness as we sleep. Appealing though it is to have my dead daughter visit, it was just a dream. It doesn't *change* anything, does it?

The thought comes back to me as I sit in on a lesson. We have a work-experience student with us this week. She's called Katie and she's in the lower sixth at the high school. She used to be a pupil here. I even remember her. She certainly remembers me teaching her class country dancing. Goddesses, she tells me. An intricately choreographed dance for groups of eight. She remembers how all the boys refused to hold hands. I was young then. Nowadays I would have made them.

The topic for the class I'm sitting in with today is St Lucia. Year three are learning about its population, geography, main cash crops and economy. The room is garlanded with crêpe-paper streamers, sunshine yellow, emerald green, rich red, happy orange, while facts and figures, charts and pictures adorn all the walls.

There's a huge map on one, with a big yellow arrow. It points to St Lucia. My eyes move across and find the giant continent of Africa. I wonder where in Africa Will and Harry are going. I wonder what they'll be doing there. I think how nice it is that Harry can travel with his father now. And Barry's words about his childhood and his dad so often not being there. Happier times, then. They're having some at last.

By extension, I find I'm still puzzling over Dorothy's words of the night before. What did she mean about the other way round? Did she mean that it was me who'd struck a chord with Will? But why would that make a difference? I know there's something more – I could see it in her eyes – but I can't tease it out. I think about her earlier comment about geography. Circumstance and geography. Those two independent but oh-so-important variables. My gaze moves up from Africa to France, tiny in comparison to the continent, but closer. Then I find Wales, barely visible on this map at this distance. The bit of geography that connects all of us in here. Plus Harry, down the corridor. Plus Will, wherever he is. On a shoot? On an edit? On a dub? I wonder what or who he's thinking about right now, and how lovely it would be if some biology existed to let us know when we're in someone else's thoughts. I wonder about the validity of my belief that someone else has been very much in his since I've known him. So wrong, he had said. I was so wrong about him. And then I think about Emily coming back to say goodbye, and I decide the idea isn't foolish after all.

The bell goes. The class clears. My sixth-form dancer comes to chat to me. She wants to be a teacher. We talk all the way back to the staff room about what a satisfying career teaching is. How even though the terms, the years, the whole career structure is mapped out, it's so challenging, so interesting, so rewarding. Every day is different from its predecessor, I tell her. That's why I love it. Every day new. You never know what's going to happen.

I don't realize quite how much I mean it until I hear myself say it, but once I do, and she's gone, I go straight to my office. My heart is pounding in my chest. My brain is bursting in my skull. I waste no time in picking up the phone.

It rings five times. 'Dorothy?'

'Hello, dear,' she says. 'This is an unexpected pleasure. Is everything okay?'

I tell her everything is fine, and I can hear it in my voice as I say it. 'But you know when you go to visit Sebastian in France?' I ask her. 'You fly into Nice usually, don't you?'

'I do,' she says. 'Yes.'

'And which airline do you usually go with? Who has the best late deals, flight-wise?'

'Well, it varies. My travel agent usually shops

around for me. But, Holly dear, why do you want to know?'

There's a small mirror in my office. On the wall next to my desk. And this time, I recognize the face smiling back. I've not seen her in years, and it's a happy reacquaintance. 'Because,' I tell Dorothy, 'I'm going on a trip. This weekend. So I need to get a ticket.'

CHAPTER 27

Considering it was Dorothy who said 'God save us from "safe", dear,' I know from the tone of her voice down the phone that her face is a picture.

'Just like that?' she says, once I have explained that I don't yet know anything about it, other than what I have gleaned from the Internet. Which is basically the locations of the various lectures, symposiums, meetings and the dates. Nothing more. 'Just like that?' she says again. 'You're just going to turn up there? Shouldn't you at least call him?'

'No,' I tell her. 'Absolutely not. The whole point of it is to surprise him. The whole point is that his parents can't be there, but I can be instead.'

Rubbish. The whole point is no such thing. Well, the surprising him bit is, I suppose. But the real point is that I must stop thinking and start *doing*. If I think, I will think myself out of the doing bit. If I call him I will not be able to bring myself to ask him. How could anyone? 'Excuse me, but can I come too?' He might say no. It doesn't bear thinking about. And in any case, unless I do it I'm never going to know for sure, am I? I can hear the clink of a teacup being placed in a saucer. 'But supposing you can't get an invitation?' she says.

'I will be able to get an invitation. I'm sure of it. He was supposed to be taking both of his parents, wasn't he? But now he's just taking his au pair, which means there's at least one ticket going begging, doesn't it?'

'Supposing he's already given it to someone else?'

Yes. Supposing. I tell myself very sternly that I mustn't suppose. 'I'll just have to take the risk, won't I?' I say firmly. 'Besides, it's not exactly the Oscars, is it? I'll get in somehow. Anyway, if he's winning this big prize they'll have to let me in, won't they? If he says so, they will. And if he doesn't say so, then so be it. I'll just have to look on it as a shopping spree.'

'Well,' says Dorothy, 'I'm not entirely convinced about the "so be it" aspect, but you've certainly thought it through. What about a hotel? You might have trouble with that if it's as big an event as it sounds.'

'I'll get one outside town. There'll be something, I'm sure. And if not, I'll sleep in the hire car.'

'Sleep in a car? Are you mad?'

'No, Dorothy. Not mad. Just reacquainted, that's all.'

She makes a little 'tut' noise. 'Reacquainted with whom?'

'With *me*. Can I borrow a frock?'

★   ★   ★

Because it was such a late booking, I have had to pay a king's ransom to fly business class, which means I have a glass of Buck's Fizz in my hand, a proper napkin on my lap, a man sitting next to me who is apparently something to do with the Paris–Dakar rally and who is visiting a famous racing driver who lives in Monte Carlo, plus the feeling that my mum is sitting on my shoulder alternately dispensing homilies about throwing good money after bad and going, 'ooh, now, there's posh!' I am also, it has to be said, wondering what the hell I am doing here, which is the kind of feeling that never does anyone the kindness of turning up *before* they get on the plane. Dorothy does have a point: this is probably the most ill-advised, ill-thought-out, impetuous, mad thing I have done since the day Emily died. The *only* one. I haven't been familiar with the cocktail of anti-cipation, excitement and anxiety that is net-working with the bubbly in my stomach for years. You don't get to feel like that when you plan your life minutely. You don't get the stress, but you don't get the rush. I nibble pretzels and try to quell the butterflies in my stomach, until, second glass in, the sensation changes. It's quite nice to have some in residence again.

And I haven't been *laissez-faire* about this. I have booked a hotel room. Plus Will's mate, Mitch, has turned out to be a mine of information and a soul of discretion, so I know the when, where and how of Will's award thing: a dinner in a grand hotel, so at least Dorothy's gown and I know where to gatecrash.

I have a car organized. I have a newly purchased road map. Every worst-case scenario I can come up with – and I do – cannot be that bad in the great scheme of things, can it? Because one of the worst things that can happen to anyone, *ever*, has already happened to me. Except all of a sudden my batty theorizing has faltered. I realize I have need as a bedfellow in my life again. And that colours everything. The glare hurts my eyes.

This is the plan, then. Drive from Nice airport to Cannes. Check. Find the hotel as per my new map. Check. Check in. Check. Check the time. Check. Get my phone out and do it. Check. Come on. That's all I have to do. Check. Just press the right places on the keypad and do it. Come on. *Check.* What could be simpler than that?

I went on a seminar once, during the latter part of my deputy headship. It was all about how best to facilitate learning. Lots of complex psychology about cognitive arousal and how the brain's information-processing processes worked. It didn't say anything about what sort of processing malfunction would have one not being able to press the buttons in the right order and ending up not pressing the ME . . . that finds Meadows, but the ME . . . that finds the Merry Balti in Splott.

Perhaps it would have made for an interesting research avenue, because this is precisely what I do. By the time I have assured Mr Chopra (who has one of those sophisticated telecommunications systems that stores all his regular clients' phone numbers) that, as I am in a hotel room in the South of France, I won't be needing a Tikka Bhuna Special, I am in such a sweat of anticipation that I am forced to open my window and fan my face with the 'No thanks! Don't wash my towels!' card.

When I finally get the right number on the screen, Will doesn't answer his phone. The voice at the other end is female. My heart attempts a controlled explosion in my ribcage. Until the Slavic tones jerk me back from the brink.

'Hell-oo?' she says. 'Can I help you with some-things?'

'Is that Natali?'

'Is me.'

'I was after Mr Meadows . . . er, Will,' I tell her, feeling juvenile and bashful.

'Oh,' she replies. 'Ah. Yes, okay. My English is not so good so I give you Harry to speak, then, yes?'

Harry, like almost all children in the world, sounds three years younger at the end of a phone. All huggy and high-pitched and unbearably sweet. I feel more comfortably older again.

'It's me,' I tell him. 'Mrs Connors, Harry. From school.'

'I know,' he says. 'It said your name in the phone. Did you want my dad?'

'Well, yes, actually, Harry, I did. Is he there?'

I can hear outdoorsy, seaside sounds in the background.

'No, he's not,' he says. 'We've just got his phone because Nat's doesn't work here. He's doing some work stuff in the hotel for a while so we've got his phone so he can ring us when he's finished. We're going to the beach after. He's going to come and meet us. Shall I ring him and tell him to ring you?'

Shall he do that? Shall he? Hmm. No, I think. *No.* 'Don't worry,' I tell him. 'You just tell me which hotel it is and I'll go there myself.'

'*Go* there? Er, did you, like, know we're in France, Miss?'

'Yes, Harry,' I say brightly. 'I did. So am I.'

Much as I enjoy a good walk, the Luxotel Cannes Nord (a charmless pile of grey Gallic concrete and green neon) may well be – okay, *is* – very convenient for the motorway but is not remotely convenient for anything perambulatory unless you are a llama or a goat. I could drive to the centre, of course, but I won't. I will most probably, as Dorothy has already warned me, have to park the car in Antibes. Thus I continue the good work of my new devil-may-care, business-class approach to life, and get them to order me a taxi into Cannes. To almost (but not quite) the Hôtel du Festival, which is on the Croisette and looks very festive indeed.

I'm debating with myself about which entrance

is the entrance when a slim figure that I would recognize blind-folded in a blizzard from a satellite appears at the top of the far run of steps. He's got his portfolio case with him and he's just greeted someone. They shake hands, remove sunglasses, make hand-signal reference to the weather. I skip behind a palm and several beats.

Just seeing him in the flesh through new eyes, with new meaning, has knocked my whole world off kilter. So completely and surely that any remaining wisps of doubt that this might still be mainly about finding Harry, or losing Emily, or me wanting more children, or him being a gentleman pirate I've had a silly crush on, or a tragic hero I have developed an infatuation with, or a metaphor for my escape from the sterility of my life, or a counterpoint to my making-the-best-of-it for so long, or just a catalyst to remind me to know-what-I'm-like, or that he's anyone I could ever feel nothing but sorry for . . . are *gone*. All gone. With the wind or whatever else. It's not even the season for the *mistral*, but they're gone.

I can't believe it's taken me so long to work it out. That I've been so stupid for so long. It's the original article. As natural as breathing. The result of an alchemy that's as real and headily mysterious as life itself. Finally, *finally*, Dorothy's words make perfect sense. All those chords did strike home. Were all valid, are all real. But my feelings for Will didn't develop *because* of them. They matter only because, well, doesn't *everything* about a person matter when your heart gets as comprehensively hijacked as mine has been? As it did from the outset, deny it as I might have. Of *course*, I think, almost faint with relief. Dorothy was right. This happened *first*. It was the *other way round*.

The two men part eventually, and now Will is now on the move. Tigger-bounding down the steps to the street, three at a time, while the other guy, who's now taken the portfolio case, heads on into the hotel. I toy fleetingly with the idea of leaping up behind him – bursting from one of the ubiquitous XXL palms that currently serve as my shield. But the idea leaves my head almost as soon as it arrived there. He's off to find Harry now and I presume they'll be waiting. I don't want to hold him up by accosting him. Neither do I wish to be whisked off to where they are. I am flustered enough without a bemused audience to deal with. I can let Harry tell him. Plus leave a message here at the hotel. I follow the man with Will's case through the double doors into the foyer, composing the words in my head.

For my late lunch *sur la plage*, I have a glass of dry rosé, a *salade de chèvre chaude, du pain rustique*, and a slice of tarte au citron. By the time I have finished eating, finished reading-but-not-reading the same chapter of the paperback I was reading-but-not-reading on the plane, finished requesting the bill, then receiving it and paying it, it is almost

451

three and people are dribbling out of the restaurant and back onto the beach. My mobile phone rings just as I'm about to do likewise, and Will says, 'Bloody hell, Holly! I'm absolutely gobsmacked! Where are you? Where are you staying? Did you really just up and get a plane here? How did you know I was here in the first place? Who told you? Bloody hell, Holly, I can't believe it!' I tell him I'm about half a mile away in a beachside café called La Petite Brioche, and he tells me I mustn't move so much as an inch.

The thing about false dawns where chemicals are concerned is that, like teenagers, once produced, they have nowhere to go. So rather than hang around at intersections, scowling at passing molecules and making lewd gestures at them, they go off and have parties in bits of you that don't matter, which means that when pressed into service, they're all hyped up and unmanageable and don't behave as you've been led to expect.

Mine don't, anyway. Thus, in the ten minutes or so between my pressing the end-call button and Will darkening the doorway of the restaurant with his lean and heroic silhouette, I have got myself into one hell of a state. I gulp down the remains of a glass of iced water to cool myself, but even a hydroelectric power station would have been hard pressed to cope. Which, I suppose, is fair enough. I have travelled a thousand miles on nothing more substantial than the questionable premise that my long-incubated and life-changing romantic epiphany makes turning up here the only thing to do. Yet as I hear him tell the waiter that he's come in here to join me (in, oh-oh! Such fluent French! Perhaps he speaks Spanish after all! So much I don't know about him! So much to find out!), it occurs to me that I could so easily have done something else. I could have stayed where I was in Cardiff, telephoned him on his mobile, reconveyed my congratulations about the prize and then tentatively – self-consciously – oh, bloody hell, *so* self-consciously, because now I know what I'm feeling I'm suddenly so tongue-tied, suggested that if he wasn't doing anything after his trips perhaps we could meet up for a drink some time or something. And just take it from there. See what happened next. That is the sort of thing normal people do. But it was never going to be the sort of thing that *I* could do. Not now. Because they might be going straight to South Africa after this, mightn't they? For three more whole weeks. Three more whole weeks! And, God, though I know how ridiculous it is, it feels too long. It *is* too long. I simply cannot sit on this for another minute. If I do, I might crack into a million hopeless pieces. So here I am, behaving like some mad, stalking harpy. *Not* sitting on it. Playing it so terribly earnest and uncool and cards all-a-flutter on the table that I can feel the flames licking at my earlobes.

CHAPTER 28

'I haven't felt so embarrassed since I last felt so embarrassed,' is not what I intend saying, but do nevertheless.

'Which was when you were sitting in my office at home, crying,' he says. And he doesn't look embarrassed in the least. He looks happy. 'Which wasn't *that* long after the last time you felt embarrassed before that, because the feeling was horribly familiar, right?'

'Blimey,' I say, with feeling. 'Did you take notes?'

He taps his temple. 'I didn't need to. I keep it all in here.' He pulls out the chair opposite and starts to sit down, but springs up again. 'Hang on. Stand up a minute, will you?'

So I do and he comes round the table and throws his arms round me and says, 'Wow, Holly. *Wow!* This is just too bloody wonderful for words!'

Which is, it must be said, precisely what I was hoping he might say, but even so, I am unprepared for quite how much of an effect it has on me that he's done it. My God, my God, I am drenched in emotion. The like of which I don't think I've experienced in years. I want to kiss him

454

and have him sit by me so I can press my nose into his hair and sniff it, smooth my fingers into the crevices between his own and feel his breath against the side of my neck. I want to take his palm and cup my cheek in it, let his lips trace a fairy line of kisses on my eyelids, just touch him in every tiny way that I can touch him. Discharge the pulsing of the wanting that has infused my every nerve ending. Let the lightning inside me find its earth. But I don't. We have to sit down and have our tea – we've ordered tea – and have a proper conversation, because the one thing that sits squarely between making the best of it and any glorious future has got to be dealt with first.

'Why didn't you tell me?' I say to him. 'Why?'

'Why didn't I tell you what?' he says back. He looks genuinely puzzled and I realize I haven't seen or spoken to him for an age and that he doesn't have the first clue that I know what I know. Which isn't a great deal, but is everything, really. Without knowing it I doubt I'd be here.

'About you,' I say. 'You told me I was wrong about you. That was the last thing you said to me. It's about your marriage, isn't it? About you and Caitlin.'

Now his expression changes. He draws his brows together a little, as if the word 'Caitlin' has triggered this involuntary response. The response I have seen so many times, but that was obviously not what I had taken it to be.

'You didn't love her, did you? When she died.

I mean, you cared for her, but you didn't love her.' My hands are all trembly again. I wrap them round my cup. 'I thought you did, you see. All that time I thought you were in such terrible pain. I thought—'

He lifts a hand. 'Wrong,' he says. 'You thought wrong, Holly. I *told* you.'

'So tell me again. Tell me properly. Explain to me. I'm here and I'm ready to listen.' And he is ready to tell me.

He puts his cup down and rests both elbows on the table. Then he raises his forearms and spreads his fingers in front of me. I take my own from my cup and intertwine them between his. He touches them together. Stops them shaking by sheer force of them being with his. They are being looked after. It feels wonderful.

'There's not a great deal to tell,' he says.

'Tell it anyway. What happened?'

'Our marriage went wrong for all the usual reasons. I was away all the time filming. She wasn't. It all happened way back. Long before her diagnosis. I guess she was bored. Unhappy. Jealous, even. And why wouldn't she be? We had Harry by this time, and although she carried on working, it was hard. She had to take a bit of a side-step career wise. Whereas if I'd had some other career, it might have been different.' He stops as if ordering his thoughts. I get the powerful impression he hasn't articulated this stuff before now. 'Anyhow, it got so she was spending all her time with her parents.

Why wouldn't she? Her mother helped out with the childcare. And then eventually, this guy—'

'Would this be Matt, by any chance?'

His eyes widen. 'How the hell d'you know that?'

'Harry mentioned him. Said he was his uncle. Which at first I accepted at face value. But then I got to thinking . . .'

'And you thought right. He was – is – the son of Caitlin's parents' best friends. They spent a lot of time together as teenagers.' He smiles wryly at me. 'I guess he was the guy they wished she'd married. No. I know so. Not the long-haired hippie guy she met at college. The one without-a-proper-job.'

'And then you separated.'

'For a time, yes. She took Harry and went back to live with her parents. Crazy, really. *I* was the one who was away all the time. But that was what she did. She wouldn't have it any other way. So we talked. Argued. Reconciled. Argued again. And eventually decided to divorce. We were literally an appointment away from setting things in motion when her cancer was diagnosed. *That* close.' He loosened one of his hands from mine and pinched together finger and thumb. 'And then, wham! That was it. A T4 tumour, they called it. Shorthand for absolutely bloody terminal. It's not, but it might as well have been. I'm sure you can imagine what a bombshell it was.' I nodded. Laced my fingers back in his.

'And?'

457

'We talked some more and we made a decision. She and Harry came home. End of story.'

'But what about Matt?'

'Ah.' He shrugged again. 'He was around, let's say, till she got really poorly. I'm not implying that he ran out on her or anything. Just that, well, she was dying. Towards the end she'd distanced herself so far from the living that it didn't matter any more. It was only Harry who mattered. As it would be.' I nod. 'And Matt's an okay guy. I don't blame him for anything. He was a symptom. Not a cause.'

I find I'm squeezing my fingertips against the backs of his hands. 'It must have been horrible to have to live through. For all of you.'

He nods. 'But it was the right thing. The only thing.' He looks beyond me then. At what? At an image of her face? In response to a hairs-at-the-back-of-the-neck prickle? A lingering sensation of her presence? It's a look I've seen so many times before, and misunderstood. An unwelcome resurgence of memory, for sure, but not of loss. Just of an intensely sad time. 'Probably the most difficult thing I've ever had to face in my life,' he says, coming back to me. 'But we soldiered on. We pulled together, we managed to bury all the bad stuff. Grew up a bit, I guess. We made like everything was fine, and Harry and I nursed her until she died. And the reason I don't talk about it – will *never* talk about it – is that Harry will gain nothing from knowing, and stands to lose a great deal. Not least all the happy memories he has of the short time they had before she died. Of us as a *family*. He must never lose that.'

He unlaces our fingers and takes my left hand between both of his. 'But they're *his* happy memories, Holly, not mine. You're not evicting any ghosts. You never were. Yes, I've been through it. Yes, I've been exhausted. Yes, I've been a bit of an emotional wreck. But just because I wasn't in love with her any more doesn't mean I didn't care. And in some ways it was worse. So many times since her death I've got to thinking about where we'd be now if she hadn't got cancer. If she'd lived. Imagine thinking those things. I'd be one of those part-time fathers who trail around zoos on a Sunday. Missing so much of him. Having the agony, maybe, of him calling someone else "Dad". I'd start thinking those things and it used to do my head in. The *guilt*. The horrible thought that her death was also my salvation as a father. It's not a comfortable thing to find yourself thinking, believe me. Horrible to have to maintain this terrible façade when your principal feeling is of release. But I have to maintain it. For Harry. It's important.'

How many times must he have found himself thinking those horrible guilty thoughts? Too often. I shake my head. 'You have nothing to reproach yourself for, Will. *Nothing*. God, not many men would have done what you did.'

'I did what needed to be done. There were no

459

heroics involved, so don't you go deciding there were. I'm no hero. Like you, I'm just someone who lived through something bad.' He smiles then, lets his gaze travel over me. 'Christ,' he says, even though Our Lady looks down on us from the café wall, 'you're the best thing I could ever imagine happening in my life.'

I kiss the tips of his fingers. 'Besides your car,' I point out.

He nods. 'Well, of *course*. That's a given.'

We leave the restaurant and he kisses me in the sunshine on the front and we have a new plan of sorts on the go. Before I do my alpaca bit up the hillside and start getting ready for this evening, we have to find Harry and Nat on the beach. My mobile is deployed again, and minutes later we're with them, which Harry seems to find much less bizarre and irregular than I do. He doesn't seem fazed in the least.

'Are you coming to Dad's prize thing after all, then?' he asks me.

What? After all, then? I move my gaze along to Will. But it's Harry who clarifies first. 'I kept telling him you would,' he says casually, grinning at his father. And I'm so happy to hear that statement and its simple implication that I almost revert to recent type and burst into a bout of hysterical crying. He'd *wanted* to ask me. He'd *wanted* me with him. God, the whole *business* of wanting – me him and him *me* – is turning my legs to zabaglione beneath me. But the head teacher in me kicks in – there's another child besides me here – and I nod and tell him, 'Yes.'

Harry's face has a new thought on it. 'And are you going to come jet-skiing as well?'

'I just might,' I say, grateful for the supplementary question.

'Come on, then,' says Will, whose eyes are alight with something – conjunctivitis? Embarrassment? Photophobia? I can't tell. My own are too misted by speed-boat diesel fumes and happiness. 'Here's the room key,' he adds, to Natali. 'Get up there and run a bath, okay? Pronto.'

'Okay, keep your hair on,' Harry says. 'See you later, Miss.'

'Harry?'

'Yes, Miss?'

'Something I meant to say earlier. Now you've finished school, you don't have to call me "Miss" any more. Or "Mrs Connors".'

'Oh,' he says, obviously bemused by this new social landscape. 'What shall I call you instead, then?'

'Holly will be fine.'

'Is that what your name is? It doesn't sound like a name. We all thought it was made up.'

'Well, it's real, I can assure you. Like a holly tree?'

'Oh, yeah. Course. Why'd your mum and dad do that?'

'Because I was born close to Christmas,' I tell him. He pauses to consider this intelligence. Then he shrugs. 'Okay,' he says. 'Safe.'

'I like being safe,' I tell Will, as we linger beneath

461

the setting sun and make no particular move to get a taxi organized. 'It's a pretty hard thing to be when you're in my line of work.'

Traffic noses along the Croisette, glinting amber here and there, like his eyes do. 'And fit with it,' he assures me. 'I told you.' I blush, and realize that this man and I will probably make love again tonight. I tingle all over at the thought. Like a dead arm you've slept on. All its nerves re-awakening. All over. Like a rebirth of feeling. It's such a tizz, this, I think. Such a fizz and a tizz. No wonder I've been avoiding the feeling for so long. But Will's arm round my shoulders is re-assuring, and a new thought, thankfully, comes into my head.

'Caitlin's mother,' I say. 'What happened there? Why are things so bad between you?'

He looks sad. 'Caitlin's mother has never accepted that Harry's place is with me. When Caitlin became ill she wanted her and Harry to move back in with them. Which was reasonable, given the circum-stances. It must have been hell for her. *Hell*. And then, after Caitlin died, she wanted to look after Harry. She didn't approve of my "slipshod arrange-ments", and she couldn't see why she couldn't look after him herself. I think she was frightened that with everything that had happened I might cut her off. As if! She's his grandma, for God's sake! What did she take me for? Anyway, we tried things for a while, but it didn't work out. There's only so much disapproval a man can take in a week. I do appreciate her importance in Harry's life, but he's my son. My *life*. And my responsibility, not hers.' He grins at me. 'Long-haired hippie or otherwise.'

His hair's not so long. Just the right length, in fact. Just long enough to meet up with his shoulders and smile. I smile too. 'Maniac long-haired hippie that goes on impulsive flits to the South of France in the middle of the night with a ten-year-old, you mean.'

Will smiles. 'It did the trick. She got the message.'

I'll bet, I think. We amble a little further past all the fat palm trees and regimented swellings of laurier-rose. It's so pretty. 'Do you come here every year?' I ask him.

'Almost. I guess that's why I headed here with Harry. It's a particularly well-appointed refuge, isn't it? And I guess I connect it with a feeling of escape. Anyway, how did you find out about this one? That I'd be here and everything?'

'Toni.'

'Toni?'

'You know. Mango Salad and Dandelion, or whatever it is her firm's called. Toni Weston. My ex-soon-to-be-sister-in-law.'

He stops. 'Oh, is that right?'

I explain about Toni and Max. And in the recounting, it comes to me starkly how I never had this with Max. This effervescence every time our eyes meet, our limbs touch. I didn't know it was missing because I didn't expect to feel it. I thought I was done with all that. 'But she isn't

463

ex-everything,' I tell him. 'She's also the soon-to-be mother of my goddaughter.'

He takes my hand again and we walk on. 'Then that's one lucky goddaughter,' he says, and falls silent. I feel uncomfortable, then, at the turn my thoughts have taken. At the surge of excitement that accompanies the knowing that anything is possible again. I can't articulate it, even as a thought, but it clamours excitedly, like a toddler with an ice lolly almost in his grasp. But then I feel the pressure of Will's hand squeezing my own and that's all he needs to do for me to know, without a doubt, that the same thoughts are in his head. That the 'Is that it?' has now gone from our lives.

For the moment at least. The potential's so scary that I need to change the subject. Save it up for another day and just be glad to have this.

'You know,' I say, 'when Harry first told me about you winning a prize I wondered if it might be for the unicorn ad. I thought it would be rather fitting. It was almost the first thing I ever knew about you. That day I had to take him to A and E and you were shooting a film with a unicorn in it.'

'Er, don't you mean a commercial for a brand of panty-liners?'

I shake my head. 'I much prefer my version, don't you? You'll always be that to me. A tamer of unicorns. But was it a real unicorn? It would so ruin the image if it was just a horse with a stuck-on plastic horn.'

Will tries out a new pretend-affronted expression, which I like much better than the real thing. I'm so pleased to have this chance to make him happy.

'Of course it was a real one,' he says. 'I'm not just any old director, you know. I have contacts.'

'Then I'll tell you something important about unicorns, shall I? Something my mum told me when I was small. A little pearl of wisdom I could take through life with me.'

'Which is what?'

'If one asks you to play leapfrog, say no.'

We'd walked a hundred yards in one direction and another hundred in the other, and we closed on the hotel again just as the prom lights came on and tossed an extra million spangles on the surface of the sea. A line from a poem came to me suddenly. 'She walks in beauty, like the night, of cloudless climes and starry skies.' That was how it felt. That I was walking in beauty.

Ten minutes, the concierge told us, for the taxi. I didn't care if we stood there all night. Not a jot. Not an atom. I had all I wanted. Which brought me up short. 'You should have told me before, Will,' I said, as we waited. 'This – here – *now* – could so nearly not have happened. I could so easily not have heard what I heard. I could so easily have left things exactly where they were. Could so easily have never set eyes on you again.'

'I almost did tell you,' he said, 'several times. It's

465

one hell of a lie to be carrying around with you. But that day I met you at the cemetery was, like, *such* a wake-up call. I was so sure I'd got things wrong with you. I felt such an idiot. So humiliated. So emasculated. It's a very difficult thing to swallow, to think someone's slept with you out of pity. Hey, I'm a man. These things *matter*. Hell, I could even see it in your eyes.'

'My eyes were in denial, Will. You'd messed up my head.'

I'd messed up my own head. I'd been head over heels and refused to believe it because I thought I was already that with Max. All that self-delusion, all that batty introspection, all that fretting that I was adopting a family to make up for no longer having one of my own. But the way we'd made love must have told him the truth. No wonder he'd been confused.

He didn't look confused now. He looked cross. 'Messed up or otherwise, it was a kick in the teeth. I wasn't going to stick around to have my pride rammed down my throat as well, was I? Let alone tell you all that.'

But only pretend-cross. The way lovers can be. 'But I called you, Will. Afterwards. You know I did.' I poked him. 'And *you* didn't call me back.'

His smile became a snort. 'For someone so intelligent you don't know much about pride, do you?'

'Oh, *Will*—'

He laughed. 'I'll give you "oh, Will".' He lifted

my hand to his lips and kissed it. 'It's history now. And what difference would it have made if I *had* told you? Would it have altered the way you felt about me?'

I turned to face him. Against the livid red diamonds on the surface of the water he looked so beautiful, so much the only man I could *ever* be with, that it took my breath away to think how long it had taken me to realize it. But perhaps, after all, that was the best thing about it. The way it had crept up on me so cleverly, so stealthily. If I'd seen it coming I might have fended it off.

'No,' I said. 'It wouldn't. But you know what? Right up until today I would have said yes to that. Because everything felt so bound up in how you felt – or how I *perceived* you felt – about me. It *all* felt so complicated. With Harry and everything to consider. With feeling something *so* powerful and unexpected and, yes, you're right, trying to rationalize it away as being partly down to pity, and not trusting my feelings and feeling so lost and insecure. Until . . .' I made a big show of consulting my watch '. . . let me see . . . about three and a half hours ago.'

He raised his brows. 'What happened three and a half hours ago?'

'I was here at the hotel. Right here.' I pointed. 'Standing by that palm. And you were over there with some guy. You gave him your portfolio case. You were chatting about something. Looking very businesslike. And the minute I saw you, I knew I'd done the right thing. That nothing would have made the slightest difference to how I feel about you.

'I can't tell you what a relief it was, Will. I stood there and I thought, Wow. *Wow*. This *is* it, you big ditz. This is exactly what it feels like. This is how it should be. It really wouldn't have mattered where I met you, or when I met you, or whose dad you were, or whom you'd loved and lost. It would have felt exactly the same wherever, whenever, however I'd met you. The same butter-flies in my stomach, the same racing pulse, the same anxiety, the same nausea, the same bloody palpitations . . .'

He frowned. 'You want to watch that. You could have picked up a bug.'

'It's called being in love, Will. That's all that had happened to me. I fell *in love* with you. At the outset. That's what it *feel* like.'

'I don't know. Ever the teacher, eh? You really think you're telling me something I don't know?'

'So you're familiar with the chemistry?'

'I'm familiar with the chemistry, believe me.' He took my hand. Placed it against his chest. His heart was beating, sure and steady, and, yes, a little fast, beneath my palm.

'Feel that?'

'I feel it.'

'You know what does that to me?'

'Adrenaline. Maybe. It could just be noradrena-line. Depends what your resting pulse rate usually is.'

'*Way* slower than this, believe me, Mrs C. And

I can see you have a great deal to learn about direction. Listen. We've still got five minutes to kill, so here's the storyboard I've got in mind for it, okay? You tip your head back, just a little. That's it. That's the angle. Then you part your lips. That's it. Perfect. Right. Now I do my little bit of dialogue, before the clinch.'

'Which is?'

'Which is "You know what does that to me?", and then you shake your head, and then I say my next line, which is, "Looking at *you* is what does that to me, Holly. Has done it every time since the first day I saw you", and then I guess I should really add, "I love you," before I kiss you, because I've been wanting to tell you that for such a long time. *Aching* to tell you. But you know what? Call me over-sensitive if you like, but I'd kind of like you to say it first.'

'I love you, Will,' I told him. 'I love you. I *so love you*. But, hey, wasn't it you who said actions speak louder than words? Come on, *kiss* me. Kiss me properly. I don't care who's looking.'

'No one can see us. We're standing behind a palm tree.'

'Go on, then. I can't bear it. And I haven't got all night.'

'I'd say we've got for ever if it didn't sound so naff.'

'It doesn't sound naff,' I breathed up at him. 'It sounds perfect.' And it did, and it was, and I knew now that it would be. Harry sploshing in the bath. Emily smiling down from Heaven. Now that *did* sound naff. Perhaps we'd have to tweak the script.

'Sssh . . .' he said. 'Take one. And . . . action.'